TEMPLAR

Also by Michael Bentine

The Long Banana Skin
Madame's Girls
The Door Marked Summer
Smith & Son Removers
The Best of Bentine
Doors of the Mind
The Shy Person's Guide to Life
The Potty Encyclopedia
Lords of the Levels
The Condor and The Cross

Michael Bentine

TEMPLAR

BANTAM PRESS

LONDON · NEW YORK · TORONTO · SYDNEY · AUCKLAND

TRANSWORLD PUBLISHERS LTD
61–63 Uxbridge Road, London W5 5SA

TRANSWORLD PUBLISHERS (AUSTRALIA) PTY LTD
15–23 Helles Avenue, Moorebank NSW 2170

TRANSWORLD PUBLISHERS (NZ) LTD
Cnr Moselle and Waipareira Aves,
Henderson, Auckland

Published 1988 by Bantam Press,
a division of Transworld Publishers Ltd
Copyright © Michael Bentine 1988

British Library Cataloguing in Publication Data
Bentine, Michael, *1922*–
Templar.
I. Title
823'.914[F]
ISBN 0-593-01339-5

Typeset by Goodfellow & Egan Ltd, Cambridge
Printed and bound in Great Britain by
Biddles Ltd, Guildford and King's Lynn

Genealogical table after Lane Poole's
Saladin and the Fall of the Kingdom of Jerusalem,
reprinted with kind permission of Darf Publishers, London

For my Lady Clementina
with love

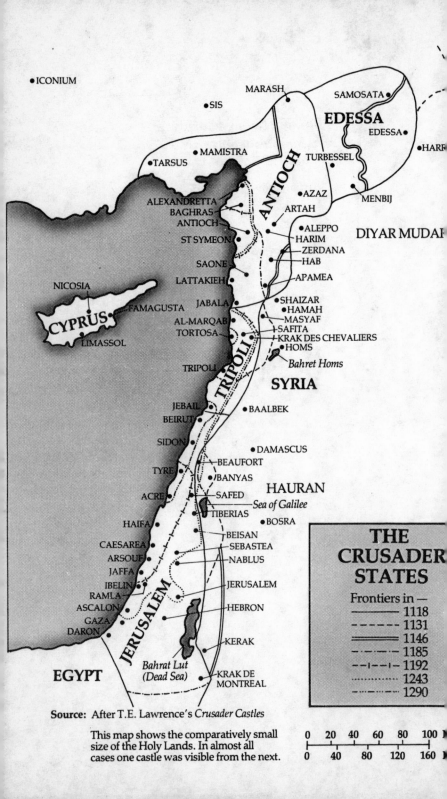

THE
CRUSADER
STATES

Frontiers in —

——————— 1118
— — — — — 1131
═══════════ 1146
—·—·—·— 1185
—·—ı—·—ı— 1192
·············· 1243
—··—··—·· 1290

Source: After T.E. Lawrence's *Crusader Castles*

This map shows the comparatively small
size of the Holy Lands. In almost all
cases one castle was visible from the next.

ICONIUM

MARASH   SAMOSATA
SIS   EDESSA
                              EDESSA
                              HARR
TARSUS   MAMISTRA   TURBESSEL
                                   MENBIJ
ALEXANDRETTA   AZAZ
BAGHRAS   ARTAH   DIYAR MUDAI
ANTIOCH   ALEPPO
ST SYMEON   HARIM
                              ZERDANA
SAONE   HAB
LATTAKIEH   APAMEA
NICOSIA   JABALA   SHAIZAR
                              HAMAH
FAMAGUSTA   MASYAF
CYPRUS   AL-MARQAB   SAFITA
                TORTOSA   KRAK DES CHEVALIERS
LIMASSOL   HOMS
                              Bahret Homs
TRIPOLI
                              SYRIA
JEBAIL   BAALBEK
BEIRUT
SIDON   DAMASCUS
                BEAUFORT
TYRE   BANYAS   HAURAN
ACRE   SAFED
                SAFED   *Sea of Galilee*
HAIFA   TIBERIAS
                              BOSRA
CAESAREA   BEISAN
ARSOUF   SEBASTEA
JAFFA   NABLUS
IBELIN
RAMLA   JERUSALEM
ASCALON
GAZA   HEBRON
DARON
                KERAK
                JERUSALEM
EGYPT   *Bahrat Lut*
         (Dead Sea)   KRAK DE
                         MONTREAL

0   20   40   60   80   100
0   40   80   120   160

Kings of Jerusalem,

Princes of Antioch,

and

Counts of Tripolis

'*Officers plan battles but it is non-commissioned officers and soldiers who win wars.*'

Anonymous Sergeant-Major

CONTENTS

PROLOGUE

Autumn crept gently over Normandy in the year of Our Lord 1180. The forests of Northern France leisurely shed their crisping leaves, before the November gales swept their branches bare. The woods were tangled with dried bracken, the ground mantled by a covering of loam. Smoke from the charcoal burners' fires hung motionless at man-height, bringing magic to the scene and cover for the game.

A distant hunting horn sounded. The pounding of hooves, snapping twigs and trampled bracken, heralded the approach of the chase. Leading the pack by a mile rode an eager youngster, astride a chestnut war-horse. The youth's new doeskin jacket and fine hunting-boots marked him as a member of a feudal family; so did the splendid horse.

His handsome face was alive with excitement; his leather-clad thighs gripped the charger's barrel of a body as though welded to the high-pommelled saddle. The young Norman's brown curly hair exactly matched the chestnut coat of his horse and his peacock-blue eyes were afire with the chase. It would be hard to guess which of these two magnificent young animals most enjoyed the hunt. Both were immersed in the ecstasy of effort.

Simon de Creçy was precisely seventeen years old that crisp October morning. The deerskin hunting-costume was a birthday present from his uncle, Sir Raoul de

11

Creçy. The destrier, Pegase, had been his uncle's gift the year before. Horse and rider were an inseparable team, a potentially deadly weapon in mediaeval warfare, where armoured horsemen were the spearhead of attack.

On entering the clearing Simon reined in Pegase. At that moment an old king stag with damaged antlers broke cover at the opposite end of the glade. Simon silently unslung his Welsh longbow, an unusual weapon for a Norman squire. He 'knocked' a cloth-yard shaft to the string. The big animal paused, sniffing the smoky air. The creature's hesitation was its final mistake. The stag's ears caught the hum of the bow-string as the heavy hunting-shaft flashed across the glade. It thudded home, up to its goosewing fletching, in the animal's heart.

For an agonized moment the old creature reared up, instinctively turning to flee; but the weight of the broken antlers brought it crashing to the ground, its brown eyes already clouding in death. Simon de Creçy crossed himself and cantered through the clearing, his hunting knife ready for the mercy stroke. It was not needed. The king stag was dead. The youngster dismounted and fell to his knees beside his prey, surprisingly intoning a prayer for its departed spirit. He had culled the ageing creature because he knew that a far worse fate awaited the stag, now that its long life had slowed its reactions.

'Better a quick death from a broadhead arrow, than a lingering end in the jaws of Uncle Raoul's hounds,' he muttered. Simon raised his hunting-horn to blow a moot, summoning the rest of the pack to the kill, when another sound reached his ears.

The youngster instantly recognized it as the clash of arms, confirmed by a faint cry of: '*A moi! A moi!*' The distant shout came from the direction of a dell at the edge of the forest. Simon sprang into the saddle, urging his destrier into a gallop that carried them through the bracken like a surfboat through breakers. At the same time he sounded an urgent call to the hunters behind him.

Simon broke out of the undergrowth and took in the dramatic scene before him. A tall, thick-set horseman, muffled in a pilgrim's hooded cloak, was fighting off a group of robbers. They assailed him on all sides as he curvetted his big horse to meet their attacks.

The intended victim was armed with a heavy sword, wielded with practised ease, while his attackers desperately tried to unhorse him. Most of the robbers were armed with daggers or short swords. One giant assailant brandished a nail-studded club. Two more lurked on the outskirts of the mêlée, seeking a clear shot from their crossbows. Two robbers lay gasping out their life's blood from wounds slashed by the skilled swordsman. A third knelt in agony, clasping his bowels which protruded from his open stomach.

Simon drew back a cloth-yard shaft. At the same instant one of the crossbowmen fired, hitting the pilgrim in the shoulder. When the wounded man fell so did his plunging destrier, screaming from a blow which had ham-strung it. The horse crashed down on top of the rider, pinning him to the ground.

With a yell, the rest closed in. Their leader, a grossly fat man, raised his falchion to finish off their victim. Suddenly his eyes bulged as Simon's arrow thudded into his belly. Even before he fell, shrieking, a second shaft from Simon's yew-bow split the jubilant crossbowman's skull, sticking out a hand's breadth beyond his head. The surviving robbers fled. A third arrow sliced into the shoulder of the retreating giant. With a howl of pain he turned and, berserk with rage, lumbered towards Simon, swinging his club high.

Before the young Norman could shoot, two arrows whistled out of the undergrowth, spitting the giant robber through the neck and chest. Still he stood, roaring defiance.

Out of the forest galloped a tall white-haired knight, spurring his charger straight at the Goliath. With one stroke of his sword, Sir Raoul de Creçy severed the shaggy head, sending it rolling across the dell.

Like a tree before the forester's axe, the decapitated giant's trunk crashed to the ground. The tall horseman reined in his charger and slid from the saddle to kneel beside the wounded pilgrim. Simon dismounted to help him. The rest of the yeomen in the hunting-party streamed off after the fleeing robbers to give them swift death at the sword's point. In twelfth-century France justice was quick and terrible. The feudal system administered the High Justice, the Middle and the Low. The sword, the axe and the hempen rope were the sole arbiters of the law.

Simon released the ham-strung horse from its agony then, with the help of two foresters, he eased its great weight off the pinned rider. Meanwhile, Raoul de Creçy gently cut off the shaft of the crossbow-quarrel. He drew the rest of the bolt out from the back of the wounded man's shoulder. The half-stunned pilgrim, a well-built sixty-year-old, opened his eyes and winced with pain; but no sound escaped his lips.

As his eyes focused on the face of the elder de Creçy, a smile crossed his scarred, sun-tanned features. 'Raoul!' he croaked. 'At last!'

The Norman knight nodded his white-maned head. 'Bernard de Roubaix,' he said gently. 'You make an unlikely pilgrim.'

Simon's eyes opened wide in wonder when his uncle cut away the pilgrim's robe, revealing a long white surcoat beneath. It was heavily stained with blood, matching the crimson of the broad cross sewn upon its front. Beneath the tunic gleamed a suit of chain-mail. This had protected its wearer from the worst of his assailants' blows. Only the crossbow bolt had pierced the coat of mail. 'You are a Templar, sir!' gasped Simon.

Beneath the grey complexion of shock, the wounded knight's face flushed with pride. 'This is the boy?' he whispered. 'He favours his father!'

Raoul de Creçy nodded as he bound up the Templar's shoulder. 'Simon saved your life, Bernard. By the time I arrived, it was all over. The lad did well!'

The wounded knight's face, seamed and puckered with old battle-scars, relaxed in wonder. 'It is Destiny, Raoul,' he murmured. '*Inshallah!*' Then he fainted.

1

THE CALL TO ARMS

For five days and nights, Raoul de Creçy and his nephew fought for the Templar's life. The rusty crossbow bolt had set up a savage infection that sent his temperature soaring. For hours he lay raving in delirium.

On the fifth day, the fever broke. Bernard de Roubaix lay in his sick-bed, weak as a new-born lion cub. He slept the deep healing sleep of those who return from the dark corridor of death. Brother Ambrose's potions and poultices, made of herbs culled from the nearby abbey garden, had been miraculously effective. But without the de Creçys' devoted nursing, the wounded knight would not have survived.

Simon was fascinated by their mysterious guest, but his uncle gave him only the barest details about the Templar.

'Bernard de Roubaix is an old war-comrade, from the days of my service in the Second Crusade. We have not seen each other for over sixteen years. I did not know that he had returned from the Holy Land.'

'Did my father know him?' asked Simon, ever curious to hear about his long-dead parents, neither of whom he remembered.

'Indeed, your father knew him well. No man could have asked for a more loyal friend than Bernard de Roubaix.'

'Was he with my father when he died?' The youngster was eager to know more.

'No!' said the elder de Creçy. 'He was not!' The Norman knight's manner was dismissive. 'Enough of this, Simon. When de Roubaix is better, he will have much to tell you. Until then you must be patient.'

'But I know so little about my parents, ' protested his nephew.

The old knight's face was stern.

'I've told you, Simon, that when the time comes you will know more about these matters. Till then you must wait. The Templar knights have had the ordering of your upbringing. No doubt it surprises you that the great wealth of the Templars has paid for everything at de Creçy Manor, from the upkeep of the whole estate to the feeding and housing of the retainers. When Bernard de Roubaix is ready, he will explain it all to you. That is why he has come.'

His nephew looked startled. Raoul smiled fondly at him.

'Bernard was on his way here when you saved his life. Now he intends to take you back with him, to Templar headquarters, at Gisors.'

Simon gasped, his mind whirling with the impact of his uncle's words.

The young Norman squire's life, from childhood to the present, had been confined to de Creçy Manor and its estates. Everything there had been governed by the orderly progress of the seasons.

In spring, the crops were sown and the lambs were born. Summer brought forth the abundance of wheat, barley and oats which, with the livestock and vegetables, made up the staple diet of the feudal family and its large body of vassals and retainers.

The manor was too far north to produce enough grapes for wine, but the estate boasted fine apple orchards which provided the old knight's household and the people of the surrounding countryside with excellent cider. Milk was plentiful and the rich cream of Normandy produced a fine assortment of aromatic cheeses.

Simon's schooling had been intensive, as though his uncle wished to cram the boy's head with as much knowledge as possible.

Therefore, from an early age he had taken an active part in the hard work of farming and now helped to run each department of the estate, from cattle and sheep husbandry to the breeding of the great war-horses for which Normandy was famous.

Simon was a credit to Raoul de Creçy and a fine example of young Norman feudal manhood. His life was fully occupied from early rising at dawn to falling asleep soon after sunset, beside the roaring fire in the manor's great-hall.

During his orderly young life nothing as sudden and dramatic as the arrival of the wounded Templar had ever happened. Now, abruptly, his whole future had been thrown into the melting-pot of Destiny.

Simon suspected that the circumstances of his birth had been deliberately shrouded in mystery. Naturally, he was consumed by curiosity to find out the truth. However, the news that the famous Military Order of the Templar Knights had been responsible for his strict and unusual upbringing at de Creçy Manor, had come as a shock.

The youngster always thought of his Uncle Raoul as his surrogate father. He loved the old knight with a fierce loyalty, and accepted whatever the elder de Creçy said as the truth.

His guardian returned Simon's devotion and had dedicated his life since the boy's birth to his upbringing, education and welfare, treating him as though he were his own son.

Due to severe wounds suffered during the Second Crusade, Raoul de Creçy could not sire a child. The Norman knight still limped from the Saracen spear-thrust which had unhorsed him in battle and robbed him of his manhood.

For years, he had been haunted by the prospect of having to tell his ward the truth about his birth. Now the moment was near.

With the ample Templar funds, de Creçy had been able to raise Simon to the threshold of manhood, affording him every opportunity to learn the arts of war and peace and teaching him the chivalrous responsibilities of knighthood.

From the time that the boy was strong enough to bear arms, the old Crusader had passed on to him the skills that he had learned from fighting in the Holy Land. Raoul knew that soon he must lose him, for his military training by the Templars, and the knowledge of it bit deeply into his heart.

On the tenth day, Bernard de Roubaix was strong enough to get up from his sick-bed and take a bath. A great oaken tub, made from half a cider cask, was rolled into his bedchamber. Soon it was filled with steaming hot water plentifully laced with Brother Ambrose's herbs, including his favourite remedy, an extract of *Aquae Hamamelis*, distilled from witch-hazel, the old Roman cure for stiff limbs and sore battle-wounds.

The elderly Templar's body bore many marks of his past battles, mainly from savage encounters with the Saracens. His sinewy, brown trunk and long limbs were covered with scars. Though the ageing knight had lost weight during the crisis of his fever, his powerful frame still exuded an aura of great strength.

At the age of sixty, Bernard de Roubaix was as fit as any man twenty years his junior. His whole life, from his adolescence onwards, had been dedicated to waging war in the name of Christ, both as a crusading French, or Frankish, knight and, later, as one of the Templars, or, to give them their full title: 'The Poor Knights of Christ of the Temple at Jerusalem.'

During his ritual bathing only Raoul and his ward were permitted to attend de Roubaix. Both of them sensed that, as the wounded knight relaxed in the hot bath, the time had come for their guest to tell them the purpose of the mission that had brought him from the Holy Land.

Simon gazed at the old Templar in awe. From his thick mat of grey, curly hair to his flowing white beard, Bernard de Roubaix looked every inch a battle-hardened warrior of the strictest Military Order in the Crusades, the 'Holy Wars' which had been waged in the Holy Land for over a hundred years. His broken nose and seamed face were tanned by countless days under the

18

Palestinian sun, yet his bright, hazel eyes held humour, mercy and kindness in their depths.

Here, thought Simon, was a warrior-monk with the goodness and compassion of true chivalry, the code of honour of the fighting chevalier. He sensed that Bernard de Roubaix was a born leader, a paladin whom any man would be proud to follow.

Simon was perceptive beyond his years and, due to the devoted instruction of his guardian and tutor Brother Ambrose, he was also literate. This was a rare thing in those times. In fact, Simon was able to write and converse in Latin, French, Arabic, and even English, the latter tongue having been taught him by Owen the Welshman, an old Crusading archer, who also had trained him to use the deadly Welsh longbow.

In the low-ceilinged bedchamber warmed by a blazing log fire during the long Norman winter, Simon stood silently beside the steaming cider-cask bath, constantly replenishing it with hot water. Realizing that at last the veils of mystery surrounding his birth were to be stripped aside, he was trembling with excitement.

He was never to forget that night in the flickering shadows of the wounded Templar's fire-lit sick-room, while de Roubaix soaked his battered body in the hot, healing waters, and the Norman knight skilfully massaged his old war-comrade's big shoulders.

'Ah, Raoul!' the Templar said, with a contented smile. 'You always did have the gift of healing. You should have become a Hospitaller. Those hands of yours have eased many an aching limb and soothed countless bruised bodies.'

De Creçy paused in mid-massage and smiled, a broad grin oddly unmarred by the livid scar across his mouth from a razor-sharp Saracen scimitar.

'When I was a prisoner in Damascus, I learnt to massage from the master-healers there. *Massa* is an Arabic word, Simon. It not only means to touch, but also to heal. The Saracens know far more about this great art than we do.'

At this, Bernard de Roubaix nodded his head in agreement.

'Saladin's own personal physician came from Cordoba, in Spain,' continued de Creçy. 'There he was called Maimonedes. He is a Jew, a true master of the art of healing. The Saracens call him "Abu-Imram-Musa-ibn-Maymun". He has Saladin's full confidence in his remarkable healing ability, and is revered and respected throughout all Islam.'

'But surely, that is witchcraft?' Simon burst out, aghast at these words.

The old Templar gave a deep, rumbling laugh.

'Believe me, young Simon, you still have a lot to learn. Now mark me well. The Jews are an ancient people, the inheritors of a vast store of knowledge that was nearly lost to the world for ever when the great library at Alexandria was burned down.

'Since then, successive Hebrew scholars have dedicated many lifetimes to preserving all the knowledge that had been contained there before that unforgivable act of arson. Maimonedes told me he was convinced that the conquerors of Egypt had deliberately destroyed what they considered to be dangerous knowledge, much too valuable to be entrusted to the profane.

'We Christians owe the Jews a heavy debt for their foresight in preserving the Gnosis, as it is called. Through their act of courage in saving the forbidden knowledge contained in the Alexandrian library, all mankind has benefitted. Without their extraordinary effort, the Gnosis would have been lost.'

This was a viewpoint on the Jews that Simon had never heard before. In feudal France there was much persecution directed against the people of Israel and the young Norman had heard little spoken in their favour. These flattering remarks, coming from such a knowledgeable source as Bernard de Roubaix, came as a surprise. Simon resolved, forthwith, to revise his own attitude towards these remarkable people.

'Never forget,' continued the Templar, his hazel eyes glowing with a mystical light, 'that Our Blessed Lady, the Virgin Mary, was Herself Jewish and so, of course, was Joseph, her husband. Yet the Archangel came to tell Her that She alone of all womankind had been chosen to bear the Christ child. She was the Immaculate Conception.'

The silence in the dancing shadows of the fire-lit bed-chamber was absolute, until the Templar continued: 'The Christ-Spirit entered the Infant Jesus at His virgin birth, and a Jewish rabbi performed the sacred rite of circumcision on the holy babe.

'I have never been one to join in the unjust persecution of such an ancient and remarkable people, for they have taught me much. Maimonedes became my close friend and instructor, and from him and his Saracen mentor, the great Osama of Isphahan, I learned many of the wonders of the Gnosis.'

The old Templar gazed deeply into Simon's eyes.

'Never underestimate the wisdom and compassion of the Jews,' he said.

Raoul de Creçy broke the subsequent silence.

'This power of healing, which is still taught among the Jews in the Holy Land, was passed to me by a very remarkable woman, Miriam of Manasseh,' he said. 'If it is witchcraft, it is indeed a strange way for the Prince of Darkness to manifest his evil.

'Maimonedes is famous throughout the Holy Land for the comfort and healing he has brought to those in pain and suffering, irrespective of whether they were Jews, Gentiles, Christians or Muslims. They all know such a great healer is on the side of the angelic forces, and could never be one to serve the dark legions of Hell.'

De Roubaix nodded his agreement. 'Raoul, you have taught the boy much, but he still has a lot to learn of the ancient ways.'

He turned to Simon.

'Come, boy, and place your hands between mine. I have much to tell you, but first I want you to give me your solemn oath of silence.'

'As you wish, sir knight,' said Simon.

The Templar's voice became sombre and the shadows in the bedchamber seemed to lengthen.

'Swear by the Blessed Virgin,' he intoned, 'and by all that you hold sacred, that whatever I shall reveal to you

21

will, for all time, be your secret as well as mine. Swear that you will remain silent regarding its content, for ever.'

The old knight continued grimly, 'Should you ever break this oath of silence, you must understand that your tongue will be cut out and buried in the sand of the seashore, where the water rises to the height of the tide. Simon de Creçy, do you still wish to take the oath?'

'I do,' said Simon hoarsely, shocked by the severity of the penalty.

'Then swear it on the hilt of my Templar sword which, when held upright, becomes the symbol of the Cross, on which Our Lord Jesus Christ was crucified.'

De Creçy, who had been witnessing the oath-taking ritual in silence, handed the Templar's heavy, cross-hilted sword to Simon. The young Norman solemnly repeated the oath and kissed the bronze hilt. When he had done so, both old knights visibly relaxed.

'Simon,' said the Templar, 'everything I tell you is the truth. First, your name is not de Creçy, and Raoul is not your uncle.'

Simon cast a stricken look towards his surrogate father.

'That does not mean that the love you bear each other is any the less real,' de Roubaix continued. 'Raoul has been all things to you. Had he been given a son, he could not have loved him more.'

'I know,' whispered Simon, his voice choking.

'Secondly,' the Templar said, 'your father is dead.'

'But surely that happened a long time ago?' The young Norman's shocked objection was framed as a question.

'No,' replied de Roubaix. 'It is barely a year since his death occurred, in Damascus. That is why I have come to this manor.'

Suddenly, the Templar's voice was stern.

'Simon, by the power invested in me as a humble knight of the Order of the Temple at Jerusalem, I order you to accompany me to our commanderie at Gisors, there to train as a cadet in the Corps of Templar Sergents.*

*The French title 'sergent', meaning 'one who serves', is used throughout to distinguish it from the more recent military title 'sergeant'.

'When you have completed the training, if you are thought worthy to be enrolled as a full sergent in our Order, you will be taken to the Holy Land: there to do the bidding of our present Grand Master, Arnold de Toroga.'

Simon's senses were reeling from the force of these revelations.

'Then you want me to become a Templar knight, like yourself, sir?'

'That is for Destiny to decide, Simon.' As he spoke, de Roubaix was smiling. 'Except in rare cases, a knight must be so dubbed before joining our Order. Both Raoul and myself were Frankish knights. I became a Templar and your guardian became a *Donat*, giving his land and all his possessions to our Order without actually becoming a Templar knight. This was because he felt that, by the nature of his wound, he could not undertake the Oath of Celibacy in its full meaning of total self-deprivation of physical love with a woman, by the act of Will.'

The Norman knight nodded his agreement as the Templar continued.

'Simon, you will become a sergent cadet in the corps, as your father would have wished. Your guardian and I are both sure that, eventually, you will win the golden spurs of knighthood and thereby become eligible to join our Order. As soon as I am fit, we will leave for our commanderie.

'However, I must remind you once again that should you ever speak of these matters, your tongue would indeed be cut out, even if your guardian or myself were the instruments by which that deed should be done.'

The Templar's face was granite. He obviously meant every word he had spoken.

'And my father, sir knight? Who was he? Having taken the oath of silence, surely I am entitled to know?'

Bernard de Roubaix, who was drying himself before the fire, smiled broadly.

'Of course you are, Simon.'

The old knight paused for a long moment.

23

'Your father was one of the bravest chevaliers in all Christendom. He was our closest friend. His name was Odo de Saint Amand, late Grand Master of the Order of the Temple!'

2

THE CORPS OF SERGENTS

For the rest of that night Simon slept uneasily, his sleep coloured by vivid dreams. Ever since childhood, the young Norman had experienced these visions, some ecstatic, others nightmarish glimpses of horror from which he would wake screaming, to the comfort of Raoul de Creçy's soothing reassurance.

His dream that night was one of flying like a bird, leaving his earthly body asleep in the manor, while his 'subtle-body', the exact double of his physical one, soared high above a distant landscape. It was an experience he had known many times before.

By the rolling hills and rocky escarpments, deserts and lush oases passing far below him, Simon knew that this was a vision of the Holy Land.

In essence the dream was always the same. Simon was lost and desperately searching for his father. Suddenly his dream turned into a nightmare. The skies through which he flew were sundered by jagged flashes of lightning, forcing Simon to fly lower over the strange landscape.

Beneath him a heavy mist swirled and seethed, as though imbued with a life of its own. Within its repellent grey shroud Simon caught horrifying glimpses of demonic creatures, their faces those of the long-dead. One of them bore the likeness of the decapitated giant whom Raoul de Creçy had so recently sent to Hell.

The headless corpse, worm-eaten and swollen to twice

its giant size, held its shrieking head high in the air, the gnashing jaws seeking to tear Simon's flying form to pieces.

The youngster gave a loud shout of terror and immediately woke up, bathed in sweat. His bedroom door opened and his guardian stood irresolutely on its threshold.

Simon cried out: 'Uncle Raoul!' Terrified, he instinctively held out his arms to his surrogate father.

It only needed that simple gesture to bring them together. The white-maned Norman knight hugged Simon close to him, while he soothed away the horrors of the night, just as he had done when Simon was a child.

'A fine Templar sergent I'll make,' said the youngster, ashamed. 'Here I am, seventeen years old and crying like a baby!'

His guardian smiled fondly, hugging his ward close to him.

'There is no shame in tears, Simon. You are only saying goodbye to your childhood. From now on you are a man; one with a great destiny. Go with my blessing, for I know that a wonderful future awaits you in the Holy Land. You must follow your star, Simon. It will lead you to fame and fortune.'

For the last time, the young squire and his ageing guardian slept side by side, closely embraced like father and son.

Simon's whole life had changed dramatically. For seventeen years he had known only the company of men, each one of them a teacher and a friend. Among these were his guardian, whom he loved like a father; his teacher, the learned Brother Ambrose, from the nearby Cistercian abbey; Owen the Welsh archer, who had served with Raoul de Creçy in the Holy Land, and all the retinue of foresters and yeomen farmers and servants, who made up the old Norman knight's household.

Strangely it was a house without women, other than the middle-aged female servants who always left the manor before nightfall. Yet it had been a happy home for Simon, whose young life seemed to have been the hub around which the de Creçy household revolved.

Now all this devoted effort was to come to an end with Simon's imminent departure. Such was the strange way of the Templars.

Simon's case was, of course, exceptional in one respect. His birth, as the natural son of a Grand Master of an order sworn to celibacy, had made his upbringing a matter of strict secrecy.

As Bernard de Roubaix explained to him: 'Our Order came into existence some sixty years ago. It was formed by a small nucleus of knights, led by Hugues de Payen and Godefroi de Saint Omer, as Grand Master and Marshal respectively.

'Other knights involved were Hugues de Champagne, Payen de Montdidier, and Archambaud de Saint Amand, while the remainder, Andre de Montbard, Gondemar, Rosal, Godefroy and Geoffrey Bisol, soon joined them to form the first chapter of the "Poor Knights of Christ of the Temple at Jerusalem".

'These extraordinary men banded together to protect the helpless pilgrims who had suffered such grievous losses on the road from Jaffa to Jerusalem, an old Roman road some sixty miles long. Many of the victims, young and old, had perished at the hands of robbers and despoilers, and this situation had become intolerable. For that reason our Order was formed, with the primary role of halting this slaughter of the innocents.

'The Templars, as we became known, swore an oath of poverty and chastity, choosing the difficult path of celibacy in a land where there is much free love.

'We adopted, as our seal, the insignia of two knights riding a single horse to denote our vow of poverty and, originally, Templar knights wore only the cast-off clothing and equipment donated to them by others.

'Nowadays, our equipment and our horses are provided by the Order. Our banner, the Gonfardon, we call the Beauseant. It is a black and white flag on which the black section is in proportion to the white part of the banner, in accordance with the tenets of the mystical

Golden Section, an axiom of the ancient Sacred Geometry.

'Saint Bernard de Clairvaux, the great Cistercian, laid down the *règles*, or rules, by which the Order of the Templars is governed. These disciplinary regulations are inflexible, allowing no laxity; hence your clandestine upbringing as the natural son of one of the Order's most famous Grand Masters.

'This secret could have done irreparable harm to the Order, but it is kept safe in the hands of a few trustworthy men, of whom you, Simon, are now one. That was the reason I asked you to swear the Sacred Oath.'

Simon had all the normal desires of any healthy young man, but his womanless surroundings had been a deliberate attempt by Raoul de Creçy to preserve his ward's chastity. However, there was nothing perverted in this unusual behaviour on his guardian's part.

Simon's lineage was a noble one. Odo de Saint Amand had been no ordinary man, but a chevalier whose deeds were legendary. Bastardy was no stigma in these times and many knights bore the charge of the *bar-sinistre* on their shields, to denote that they were the natural sons, born out of wedlock, of those particular feudal families.

Often, these illegitimate sons were from the European nobility and in the Holy Land, among Saracen families, the same sensible attitude to bastardy had been adopted.

Only the fact that Odo de Saint Amand was the Grand Master of the Templars, sworn to celibacy, had prevented him from joyfully acknowledging Simon as his natural son.

Bernard de Roubaix was impatient to take his new cadet to Gisors, the Templar fortress that dominated that part of Normandy, and the intensive training which awaited him there. As soon as his wound was healed, the old knight was ready to leave.

The day he chose was Christmas Eve 1180, for de Roubaix wanted no protracted farewells over the great Christian holiday. He well knew how reluctant his old friend, Raoul de Creçy, was to lose his adopted nephew, and he reasoned that the sooner this pain was over the better.

Simon's leave-taking from his childhood home was tearful and heart-wrenching. His guardian and each of his teachers and friends wept many tears. These were grim and violent times, when human life was cheap, but a display of emotion was not considered to be a shameful thing and strong men wept openly.

Simon and de Roubaix set forth laden with gifts, among which was Raoul de Creçy's own Crusader sword, a superb example of the Damascene weapon-maker's art.

'I know that you will bear it with honour,' said the old knight, his bright eyes awash with tears. 'This blade has never taken a human life without good reason.'

For the last time they embraced and wept, both their hearts close to breaking.

The elderly Cistercian, who had given Simon fluency and literacy in three languages, had brought his pupil an ivory breviary, the result of many months of painstaking carving, with failing eyesight.

'Carry this with you, my son,' he quavered, his voice choking with emotion. 'It will comfort you in travail. Pray for us, Simon, as we pray for you.'

Owen, the Welsh archer, whose skill with the long yew-bow had given his young pupil such a deadly edge in survival, hugged him with true Gallic fervour.

'Go with God, Simon *bach*,' he croaked hoarsely. 'Owen will never forget you!'

His parting gift was a new leather quiver, filled with three dozen of the finest cloth-yard, goosewing-feathered shafts that the skilled bowyer and fletcher could make.

Amid hugs and loving tears, the young Norman squire set out on the long journey that would take him to many lands and bring him many adventures. Simon was about to fulfil a strange destiny.

The road south to Gisors led through the same forest where only weeks before Bernard de Roubaix had nearly lost his life. Winter had set in and the two riders, leading their spare pack-horses, slowly made their way over the crisp layer of newly fallen snow.

Long before noon they had left the woods, which marked the southern boundary of the de Créçy estate, and soon found themselves hard put to it to follow the snow-covered track leading to the Templar commanderie.

Although Gisors was an easy day's ride under normal conditions, the weather further hampered their progress with a sharp blizzard. It was not until the storm had cleared that the great keep of the Templar fortress hove mistily into view, glowing salmon-pink in the westering sun.

Gisors was just one stronghold in the great system of Templar commanderies that stretched right across France, Spain and Portugal, with outposts as far apart as England and the Holy Land.

In their homeland of France, the Templars had established a complex interlocking system of abbayes, manoirs, granges and fermes, the latter being fortified farms, built for defence and supplying most of the victualling for the Order's widespread activities. From forage for their horses, to food, clothing, arms and equipment for their knights, sergents, and the rest of the huge corps of lay-brethren, farriers, armourers, clerks and stonemasons, carpenters and shipwrights, the Templar Order was completely self-sufficient.

Moreover, their fleet, now numbering in excess of sixty vessels, both transports and war-galleys, roamed the seas, bringing trade and riches in gold, silver, silks and rare spices from many distant lands.

Such a powerful organization as the Templars was widely respected and, had not Bernard de Roubaix been disguised as a pilgrim on his journey to de Créçy Manor the ill-fated band of robbers would never have dared to attack him. The penalty for doing so was death. On this cold winter's day, both the old knight and his squire felt secure in the knowledge that, with the Templar bearing the distinctive cross of the Order on his white robes, they were quite safe to journey where they pleased.

On the way to Gisors, the Crusader had been enlightening Simon on a number of Templar activities. One of these was the Order's invention of what later became called 'merchant banking'.

The young Norman was amazed at the system's extent and power. He had no idea of how widespread the Templars' financial network was, throughout the western world.

In de Roubaix's words: 'Templar funds are behind many ventures throughout Europe and the Mediterranean. Rumour even has it that our fleet trades with strange, hitherto unknown lands, across the great Western Ocean.'

The old Crusader chuckled, a deep rumbling growl. 'Few people realize the way we operate our finances over long distances. Instead of transporting heavy loads of bullion, in gold and silver, which is a perilous business at best, we Templars simply carry a single document, which we call a "Letter of Credit". By presenting it to the marshal at its destination, another Templar commanderie in whichever country it happens to be, I can exchange the properly attested document for precious metal up to the amount stated in the letter.'

The Templar laughed at his young squire's bewilderment.

'More than that, Simon. If I gave such a letter, approved by the Grand Chapter of our Order, to a merchant adventurer, he would be able to use it to equip himself with a ship and a crew, supplies, arms and sufficient funds for the voyage.

'The merchant only has to bring back a valuable cargo, and we Templars charge him a modest percentage of its worth in return for financing the venture.'

'But the vow of poverty, sir knight, surely that cannot still obtain with such great wealth pouring into the Templar coffers?' Simon protested.

'The vow of poverty only applies to the monkish knights of the Order, no matter what our rank may be, *not* to the Order itself. We Templar brethren own nothing except our horses, our armour, robes and arms. On our deaths, we are buried in our uniform and our armour, sword in hand. We own nothing more.

'As you can see, Simon, I carry no money, only letters of credit for a modest sum, should I need to pay for a night's lodging or require a new horse. On presenting one of these documents to any Templar commanderie, the person to whom I owe money will be reimbursed with the sum that I have written into the letter. He merely exchanges the document for gold or silver, as required.'

Simon shook his head in wonder. He had no idea of the ramifications of the Order. Bernard de Roubaix continued: 'The Temple even advances the huge amounts required for the building of many of the great Gothic cathedrals which are slowly rising all over Christendom.'

'What of these strange rumours about the Templar fleet trading with unknown lands?' asked Simon eagerly, his romantic soul deeply stirred by the visions this conjured up.

Once again, de Roubaix gave his growl of a laugh.

'The Arabs and the Jews aren't the only ones to practise the secret art of navigation. Both Our Blessed Lady and Her servants, the stars, guide our ships to many wondrous lands, way beyond the western horizon, to places so far undiscovered by others.'

With de Roubaix's fascinating commentary to pass the time on the ride to Gisors, the day flew past.

Abruptly, the Templar halted, pointing towards the great stone keep, shimmering in the last rays of the sunset.

'There is our headquarters in Normandy. As you can see, Simon, the tower-keep commands the town, the valleys and the forests surrounding it. Our Templar strategy is based on the manning of such commanderies along the routes of the pilgrimage to the Holy Land.

'The Romans once held the same position here. They had a fine eye for the high-ground, in both attack and defence. Had the Romans not been pagans, they would have made good Templars.'

The big knight laughed and set spurs to his new steed. He broke into a canter and then a gallop, to try out the mettle of the fine grey war-horse that Raoul de Creçy had presented him with to replace his dead destrier, killed by the robbers. Simon, even mounted on Pegase, had a hard time keeping up with the old Templar.

The rough snow-covered trail winding up the steep hill led to the gates of the castle, set in the stout stone walls that encircled the central artificial mound on which the tower-keep was built.

Due for rebuilding and even stronger reinforcement, the already massive outer walls contained the large inner courtyard and extensive grounds, providing quarters for the Corps of Sergents, and stabling for the horses.

These latter buildings were constructed in the form of low-roofed barracks, hugging the inner perimeter of the battlements.

De Roubaix broke a long silence, which had fallen between them. 'This is where you are going to spend the next few months, Simon.'

The young Norman gazed at the Templar fortress, over-awed by its air of impregnability. Seeing the look of wonder on his protégé's face, the old knight grinned.

'Gisors is not as strong as it looks. We have plans in hand for rebuilding it. Wait till you see all the great castles in the Holy Land. For example, Krak des Chevaliers has walls twice as thick as this. I tell you, Simon, the whole of Gisors would fit into one corner of Krak and not be noticed.'

'When did the Templars build this Krak des Chevaliers, sir knight?'

'We didn't! It was largely the work of our colleagues in the Holy Land, the Order of the Hospital of Saint John of Jerusalem.

'Only a few of the many castles in Palestine were built by Templars. Some we adapted from the original fortifi-cations constructed by the Turks and Saracens. The Hospitallers, whom some call our rivals, are mighty builders, and we even garrison some of their biggest castles, as they have insufficient brethren to man all their fortresses and still carry out the merciful work of their hospitals.'

'How many castles are there in Palestine?' Simon was a

fascinated disciple, whenever the old Templar imparted some of his hard-won wisdom.

De Roubaix grunted his obvious displeasure at the thought.

'Too many by half! Since the First Crusade, which was fought with the sole purpose of winning back the Holy Land, and especially Jerusalem, for Christians to visit on pilgrimage, there have been many adventurers who have joined in our Second Crusade with profit and riches as their only goal.

'These so-called "nobles", for many of them have doubtful ancestry, took the title of the town or port that they conquered, and now rule the area adjacent to the strong-points they garrison.

'There are so many castles in Palestine, that they lie within line-of-sight of each other. Therein lies the weakness of our campaign. You see, Simon, the Crusade is a mobile war and sitting safely in great castles is not the answer to meeting our greatest threat . . . Saladin!'

The name issued from de Roubaix's chapped lips in a mist of chilled breath.

'When that mighty Saracen warrior finishes his present campaign in Egypt and moves his Ayyubid forces north to the Holy Land, we are to going to face our greatest challenge, for Sultan Saladin is the finest cavalry commander since Charlemagne, the first Holy Roman Emperor.

'There is a peace treaty in force at the moment, but some imbecile among the greedy Frankish knights is certain to break it, by raiding one of Saladin's rich caravans on its way to Mecca.'

De Roubaix growled and spat his disgust into the snow.

'Then we will see which battle-plan works the best. Shutting ourselves inside these great bastions of stone, besieged by the Saracens, or going out to fight Saladin's Ayyubids, lance to lance. That is our only chance, Simon!

'You will be a part of that struggle, and this is where you start your new life, and your great quest, as your father would have wished.'

De Roubaix crossed himself and cantered forward, closely followed by Simon.

34

At the entrance to the castle they were challenged by the guard, but this was merely a formality. Although he was riding an unfamiliar horse, the Templar was instantly recognized and the sergent of the guard gave the order to raise the portcullis and let them ride into the inner courtyard.

When the heavy inner doors finally swung open, a stocky, grey-bearded man-at-arms, wearing the black tunic of the Corps of Sergents, marched briskly forward and saluted de Roubaix.

'Good to see you back, sir knight,' he said, in a voice like distant thunder. 'I see you have brought our new recruit.'

The veteran soldier indicated Simon.

'Yes, Belami,' replied de Roubaix. 'This young squire is all yours, to train and teach, bully and cajole, as you see fit. Above all,' the old knight paused significantly, 'you will protect him with your life!'

'Then, sir knight, it will be my duty and my pleasure to carry out your orders.'

Simon warmed instantly to the broad grin on the rugged good-humoured face of the veteran sergent who, he had noticed, had only his right arm, his left one ending above the wrist in a leather-sheathed hook.

Bernard de Roubaix caught Simon's surprised expression and smiled grimly.

'Belami can handle lance, battle-axe, sword, mace or dagger with his one arm better than most knights can do with both.'

The veteran winked at Simon, his bright blue eyes gleaming in the walnut-brown of his craggy features. He gave another wide grin, revealing a generous mouthful of worn, even teeth.

'I do my best, cadet,' he growled. 'I see you carry the Welsh longbow, and your quiver is filled with cloth-yard shafts. Can you shoot as well as a Welshman?'

Before Simon could reply, de Roubaix did it for him.

'Three would-be murderers lie dead in the woods near de Creçy Manor because of Simon's shooting. Some misguided villains tried to kill me, Belami, and nearly succeeded. I was closer to my Maker than I have been for a score of years; in fact, since the day you severed the head from that Saracen who had me spitted on his lance!'

Belami looked concerned.

'I trust you came to no scathe, sir knight?'

The Templar smiled grimly.

'A scratch! I took a bolt in the left shoulder. *Rien!* But I lost Eclair, a good horse. I mourn him still. What think you of my new horse, Belami? It is a gift from Raoul de Creçy.'

The stocky sergent walked slowly round the large grey stallion, nodding his grizzled head as he mentally ticked off each point, for and against.

'Not as fast as Eclair, I would say, but a fine animal for all that. Raoul de Creçy is a good judge of horseflesh. What name does your destrier bear, sir knight?'

'Boanerges. He is named after one of the "Sons of Thunder",' de Roubaix laughed. 'The good Lord knows, he farts loud enough.'

The two old soldiers chuckled, savouring the coarse jest. Simon looked surprised at this raw joke, coming so unexpectedly from de Roubaix. Seeing this, the Templar smiled.

'Simon, we Knights of the Temple are expected to ponder on holy matters, and of course we do. Saint Bernard of Clairvaux rightly directed us to eschew worldly thoughts, light banter and other follies of the flesh, and encouraged us to hold weighty and sober discourse with our brother Templars. But it would be a sad day if two old war-comrades, like Belami and me, could not enjoy a camp-fire jest.'

The young squire's face relaxed and his boyish laughter rang out to join theirs. The Templar knight slapped the hindquarters of his squire's horse.

'Off with you, Simon. I leave you in the skilled hands of the finest sergent of our corps. Listen to every word he says. Seriously or in jest, whatever Belami tells you is worth remembering. Twenty years' fighting in the Holy Land has taught him much. I owe my life to Belami many times over. So listen and learn. One day, Simon, you will be grateful for his wise words.'

So saying, Bernard de Roubaix turned his grey war-horse and trotted off to the Knights Templars' quarters in the tower-keep, while Belami led Simon over to the humbler barracks which housed the cadets of the Corps of Sergents.

The veteran already knew a lot about his new pupil, for de Roubaix had sent dispatches back to Gisors. Furthermore, his shrewd eyes had already assessed Simon, and the old soldier liked what he saw.

'Did you know my father?' Simon blurted out incautiously, half-guessing the truth.

Belami turned to him, his seamed face expressionless. His tone was forbidding.

'I also took a solemn oath, many years ago,' he said.

'But I now know who my father was.' Simon whispered the words. 'Bernard de Roubaix told me.'

Belami took a long look at the young Norman's eager face, and his expression softened.

'Then I don't have to tell you what a fine man he was.' The veteran lowered his voice. 'But the less we speak of him, here, the better. There are sharp ears in Gisors. Keep your counsel, *mon ami*, and I will keep mine. Here is my one good hand to seal the bargain.'

The old sergent extended his powerful right arm and his iron-hard palm enveloped Simon's right hand. In that moment, his pupil knew that he had found a friend for life.

The sergents' barracks were clean and orderly, being washed out every day by the duty cadets. At this time there were only seven of these youngsters, left over from the previous course which had recently moved on south to Marseilles, where they would take ship for the Holy Land.

These remaining cadets, due to sickness or injuries sustained during their training, were considered to be temporarily unfit and, therefore, would have to wait impatiently for several months for the next available ship to Outremer.

They were a representative cross-section of the corps'

young cadets. Their homes were as far away as Flanders and Brittany. With the exception of the Breton, the others came from Normandy, its fiefs, and Flanders, Picardy and the Loire. All of them were alike in one way. Each was bitterly disappointed at having missed the ship to Palestine.

They were also eager to impress the newcomer with their newly acquired knowledge and experience. This amused Belami who had just finished their preliminary training, and still considered them to be raw recruits.

'This is Simon de Creçy, our latest cadet,' he announced to the group of semi-fit youngsters, some of whom were hobbling on crutches, while others had arms immobilized by heavy bandaging or were still recovering from fever. One cadet even had his face bound up by a soft leather strap round his head and chin, having broken his jaw. Temporarily, he was unable to speak.

They crowded round the new arrival, bombarding Simon with questions.

'Where are you from, boy?'

'Which part of France is happy to be rid of you?'

'Did your family kick your arse out, or were you mad enough to volunteer?'

The usual adolescent, barrack-room banter of young soldiers greeted the newcomer.

Simon grinned good-naturedly, taking the rough quizzing in his stride. His tall, broad-shouldered frame and determined young face had already assured him of the physical respect of his brother cadets. They were now trying out his wits, to see how quick they were and whether Simon would make a good addition to their ranks.

'I'm from Forges-les-Eaux, where we make iron men,' he quipped. 'I was "volunteered" by my Uncle Raoul.'

Simon still used his guardian's old title.

'When you are all fit and well again, I'll be happy to show you what drinking the iron-rich waters of our village of Forges-les-Eaux does for a man.'

'You must be rusty!' cried a grinning cadet from Lille.

The rest guffawed, and the slight nervous tension that

newcomers tend to feel in such circumstances immediately eased.

However, Simon wasn't to be let off so lightly. The other cadets grabbed him, and, mindful of their injuries, Simon didn't resist.

'Come on, Rusty,' they cried, instantly giving Simon a nickname. 'Let's see what you're really made of!'

The shouting cadets seized a horse-blanket and made ready to toss their new companion in it. It was the usual imbecilic initiation ceremony that most young soldiers believe they have invented. It wasn't easy for the temporarily handicapped bunch of cadets to toss Simon a half-a-dozen times, but somehow they managed it.

The young squire only fell out twice and, apart from a few bruises, survived the ordeal with his customary good temper unruffled.

'All right, Rusty, you'll do,' laughed the thick-set youth from Brittany. 'My name is Yves.'

Immediately a flood of personal information burst out of the young cadets.

'My name's Gaston.'

'I'm Phillipe.'

'They call me Gervais.'

'That's Pierre, with the broken jaw.'

'I answer to Etienne.'

Shouting and laughing the seven cadets crowded round their new comrade-in-arms, relieved that such an easy-going companion had joined their corps.

Belami, who up till then had been an amused witness to the initiation, now interrupted them.

'*Alors, mes braves,*' he growled. 'You've all been unlucky, careless, or just plain stupid, but it means that you've got to wait for the next available transport from Marseilles. At the least it's going to take three months. Bernard de Roubaix just told me.'

This news was greeted by groans and cat-calls. Belami held up his hand for silence.

'So, for Simon de Creçy's benefit, we are all going to go through basic training once more.'

More cries of protest met this statement.

The master sergent continued, unmoved: 'You may think that you know it all. I assure you, *mes camarades*, that you don't. Otherwise, you wouldn't be here today.'

Belami clapped Simon on the shoulder.

'Bernard de Roubaix tells me that this young squire rides well, shoots well, and can handle sword and lance. I have never known him to overstate matters, so I accept what my knight says as Gospel.'

The veteran smiled wryly.

'Apparently, Simon de Creçy can also read and write and speak several languages, among which he will find Arabic the most useful. He even speaks English!'

A loud guffaw broke out from the cadets at this piece of information.

'I agree with you, *mes amis*, that it is a barbarous tongue. Even the English nobility prefer to speak French. The point I am making is that we have here a reasonably bright cadet who wants to get out to the Holy Land as much as you do. So the more we help him to complete his basic training, the quicker we are all going to get on to that long road south to Marseilles. *Comprenez?*'

That did the trick and the young cadets set to work with a will to speed up Simon's training. The usual rivalry and horse-play was forgotten and an enjoyable time was had by all.

Most of them were soon fully recovered from their various injuries or sickness, and all of them were so busy that none became bored by their repeated training programme, which was exactly what Belami had intended.

Every day, long early-morning runs over the rolling wooded countryside preceded horse-drill, lance-drill, and sword-drill. Endlessly, they practised tactical riding in formation, charging and wheeling round to charge again, curvetting, gambading, cabrioleing, and every other trick and manoeuvre in the cavalry manual. By the end of their training, they rode together like one horseman.

They worked hard, ate well and slept like the dead.

News finally arrived from the south that the next Templar transport ship had left the Holy Land, to pick them up from Marseilles in a few weeks' time. This information was greeted with loud cries of joy, and even Belami had to admit that his eight cadets were as fit and ready as he could make them.

In fact they were so well-trained they saved the veteran's life. It happened this way.

As part of their instruction in the art of warfare, Belami had taken his small force down to the Seine for an exercise in river-crossing. At the part of the river-bank that the veteran had chosen for the demonstration, the Seine flowed rapidly between high, rocky cliffs.

The clifftop was heavily wooded with good-sized trees, so there was ample timber to construct a raft. All that the cadets had to do was to cut the trees down and drop them over the cliff on to the narrow foreshore below.

The recent March rains had loosened the structure of the cliffs and an unexpected late frost had further attacked the crumbling rock-face.

In an hour, a stout raft had been lashed together by the cadets and was ready for testing. As usual, the veteran sergent went aboard the wooden structure to inspect the handiwork and try it out.

The raft was floating close offshore, secured by a rope to the roots of a fallen tree jutting out from the bank. For some reason the knots didn't satisfy Belami, who was engrossed in retying them more securely.

At that moment, a heavy landslide took place as a large part of the frost-damaged cliff collapsed, sending a huge section of rock crashing into the Seine. The resulting massive displacement of water caused a tidal wave to bear down upon the raft. Before the startled veteran could jump for the shore, the roaring body of water had upended the raft, breaking loose one of the logs. This struck the sergent on the head, stunning him and hurling him into the raging Seine.

Belami was wearing full armour and, unconscious, disappeared without a struggle into deep water.

Some of the horrified cadets could swim, but none as well as Simon. Fortunately, he had stripped off his chain-mail to tackle the tree-cutting, and had so far not replaced it. Throwing off his boots, the youngster dived into the foaming water and swam straight down, directly over the spot where he had seen Belami disappear.

Simon could just make out the indistinct form of the unconscious sergent, tangled in thick waterweeds. His eyes were shut and his mouth was open, spilling a stream of bubbles upwards.

Realizing that there was no time to waste, Simon grabbed Belami's dagger from the sheath at his belt and chopped away the entangling weeds.

With a few powerful kicks, the cadet forced the two of them to the surface. As they broke free from the river's hold, a loud cheer of relief greeted their reappearance. A rope was thrown and caught by Simon. In a few moments, rescuer and rescued were pulled ashore.

The cadets' relief was short-lived. Their veteran instructor looked horribly dead. Once again, Simon had reason to bless Owen, the old Welsh archer, and the lessons he had taught him. The tough bowman had been brought up among the coracle-fishing community on the banks of the River Severn in South Wales.

He had shown Simon how to swim like one of his native Welsh otters and, mercifully, he had also taught him how to deal with a victim of drowning.

'Quick! Help me to get Belami face down over that tree-trunk,' Simon cried. The cadets, relieved to be doing something positive to help, carried the unconscious veteran over to the fallen tree and laid him across it, as instructed by Simon.

Simon realized that there was no time to strip off the sergent's armour, and straight away got on with his attempt to save the drowned man's life. The young Norman knelt astride Belami's back and bore down hard on the old soldier's broad rib-cage.

By alternately bearing down and releasing the pressure, Simon managed to expel most of the muddy water from Belami's system.

'Turn him over!' he ordered, and the other cadets promptly obeyed him.

Taking a deep breath, he now applied his mouth tightly to the unconscious man's lips, at the same time pinching the veteran's nostrils as he forcefully exhaled into him, breathing directly into Belami's lungs.

This Simon did several times, while he got another cadet to press down on the veteran's chest as he previously had done.

To his watching companions, it all looked like sorcery. Several of the cadets hurriedly crossed themselves.

Suddenly Belami started to choke, vomiting up more water. His eyes flickered blearily open.

'Sit him upright!' Simon shouted, in his excitement.

As the others did so, their fears of sorcery were strengthened when the veteran vomited up the rest of the water. Despite their superstitious fears, they cheered lustily.

'A miracle!' cried Pierre de Montjoie, whose jaw had now mended.

'Witchcraft!' breathed Phillipe de Mauray, shivering with terror.

'Neither!' said Simon, grinning with relief that his efforts had succeeded. 'It's an old trick, taught me by Owen the Welshman. He told me that the Romans had used this method long before they came to Britain. Blessed be Our Lady that it worked. Apparently it does not always do so; it is effective only if you can use it on the victim as soon as possible after they have drowned or been asphyxiated.

'Owen also told me that local wizards and warlocks used the same trick, to "bring back the dead", and in the case of someone like Belami, whom they can get to soon enough, their efforts have often worked. You can imagine what a reputation this apparent miracle could make for a sorcerer!'

Sorcerer's trick or not, it had saved Belami's life.

Incredibly, only twenty minutes after the veteran had been dragged from the Seine, he was able to rise groggily to his feet.

The first thing he did was to kneel and give thanks to the Blessed Virgin. Then he hugged Simon, amid the relieved laughter of his cadets. Finally, he bawled them all out for not building the raft correctly.

'Whoever lashed that loose knot should be horse-whipped!' he said, and meant every word.

The veteran, first and foremost, was a master sergent. To him, correct procedure was everything.

Belami of the Templar Corps of Sergents was back on the job.

3

THE LONG ROAD SOUTH

By April 1181 Simon's initial training at Gisors was completed. Along with the remaining seven cadets he was ready to take the long road south.

Belami had excelled himself. Simon was now proficient in the use of every weapon, including the more unchivalrous arts of warfare, such as kicking, eye-gouging and garrotting. The battle-wise veteran had taught the young Norman everything he knew about killing or disabling an opponent.

Simon had earned Belami's praise and the respect of his fellow cadets, who welcomed this formidable addition to their ranks. During the months of intensive activity, the young squire had caught only an occasional glimpse of Bernard de Roubaix, as the Templar rode out on special missions or returned some days later. The old knight was a busy man and deliberately refrained from interfering in Simon's training, so that there should be no hint of favouritism, which might antagonize the other cadets.

Nevertheless, he had kept a close watch on Simon's progress and Belami had reported regularly on the youngster. The Templar was delighted with the veteran's assessment of his protégé.

'The boy has a natural warmth which endears him to his friends. Yet I have never seen him misuse this quality to get himself out of trouble. If there is a problem, he faces it. He will make a fine war-comrade. His handling of weapons is exceptional, especially when using his longbow. With that weapon, Simon is a sorcerer.'

The Templar chuckled.

'Have you anything else to tell me, Sergent?'

Belami hesitated.

'There is one thing that bothers me, sir knight. Simon was brought up in a womanless home. He has been taught to treat a woman as a lady, with chivalry and courtesy, which is as it should be. But, at the same time, he has been encouraged to think of womankind in general, and especially young women, as a trap for the innocent and a snare for the unwary.

'I know that Raoul de Creçy only intended to keep Simon chaste, for as long as possible, in view of the hopes you both entertain for the lad's future as a Templar knight. This, after all, was the dream of his father, Odo de Saint Amand.'

Belami paused uncomfortably.

'But this attitude has made Simon, who is a fit, normal youngster, extremely shy with women.'

Again the veteran hesitated.

'That could lead to future problems, in the Templar world of men.'

Bernard de Roubaix knew that Belami was making a valid point. Deviation from normal love was not unknown in the ranks of both the Templars and the Hospitallers, though it was only covertly referred to, in whispers.

'I'll consider the matter, carefully,' he said. 'As Simon is not yet a dubbed Templar knight, I see no reason why the company of ladies should be forbidden him.'

The old knight hesitated, embarrassed by the situation.

'This doesn't mean that I approve of licentious behaviour. Curse it, Belami! Use your own judgement. You are no saint in these matters, yet I never heard of any woman complaining that you had done her scathe. But, you old scoundrel, don't let the lad have too much licence. Remember, you are there to protect him from all perils, and that includes the wiles of unscrupulous women.'

After Belami's latest report, the Templar knight sent

for Simon. He was delighted by what he saw. The young cadet was the picture of health, his handsome face leaner from the hard training, and his tall powerful body in perfect condition. Bernard de Roubaix fully approved.

'Belami has told me good things about you, Simon. My congratulations on your quick thinking. You undoubtedly saved Belami's life, just as you once saved mine. That strange trick of resuscitation is worth passing on to your comrades.' The old knight's eyes twinkled. 'Though few men drown in the deserts of the Holy Land.'

Simon grinned.

'We leave for Paris tomorrow, sir knight. I am glad to have this opportunity to thank you for all your kindness. Belami has told me of your interest in my progress. I am most grateful. I am sorry that I have not been given the time to visit my uncle . . . I mean, Sir Raoul. But I hope when next you see him, you will give him my deepest homage and respects.'

'And your love, Simon. It is not a sign of weakness to use that word. I know what you two mean to each other. Of course I shall tell him how much you love and miss him, and how proud Belami and I are of you and your excellent progress.'

Simon blushed and stammered his thanks.

The old Templar Marshal felt the same affection for the natural son of his late Grand Master as did his closest friend, Raoul de Creçy.

'I must leave you soon, Simon. Our Grand Master has ordered me to deliver you to Paris and then return to semi-retirement with Raoul, at de Creçy Manor. I will enjoy that, for he is my oldest friend.

'My time will also be taken up with conducting a routine tour of inspection of the Templar properties in this part of Northern France. I shall also audit the farms' accounts, and supervise the routine supply of victuals and forage for all the Templar commanderies in the area.

'It will be a busy, useful life still, but my heart – nay, both Raoul's and my heart – will be with you in the Holy Land.'

De Roubaix's words reminded the youngster that the

last link with his old life in Normandy would soon be severed. He choked back a sob.

'Come now, my dear boy.' The Templar himself was close to tears. 'Your guardian and I will hunt and fish and swap stories of the Holy Land. Old men are best left together with their memories of the past. You, young Simon, are our future!'

Bernard de Roubaix sighed. At least he was going to enjoy his last few days with Simon.

'I want you to accompany me on a visit to Chartres. The other cadets will go along with Belami to our headquarters in Paris, but I want to show you over your father's favourite church: the cathedral of Notre Dame de Chartres. Be ready in one hour.'

Simon saluted and ran to tell Belami and his comrades that he would see them later on, in the capital. He then rejoined the old marshal, and together they set out for Chartres.

This city lay to the south-west of Gisors, approximately three days' ride away. En route, they stopped at a farm at Mantes, kept by a retired Templar sergent. He had served with both de Roubaix and Belami, before leaving his left leg in the Holy Land and retiring to Normandy with a Templar pension.

This wizened old fellow greeted de Roubaix warmly and produced some excellent cider for Simon. To the Templar, he offered unfermented apple juice.

Their next stop was at a grange owned by a Frankish knight, Robert d'Andelys, who had also fought beside de Roubaix in the Holy Land. The two old Crusaders talked long into the night, while Simon listened enthralled to their exciting reminiscences.

Finally, just after sunset on the third day, the travellers rode into the courtyard of the Templar commanderie at Chartres.

It had been a fascinating journey for Simon, for during the long ride the old Templar had once more opened his heart to his squire. The young Norman was fascinated by de Roubaix's tales of Outremer, for many of the old knight's battles had been fought alongside Simon's father, when he was Grand Master. Moreover, it was obvious that de Roubaix held Odo de Saint Amand in high esteem and spoke of him with great affection.

Their mutual enjoyment of the journey was like that shared by father and son. Not that Bernard de Roubaix had supplanted Raoul de Creçy in Simon's love, for no one could do that, but there was now a strong bond of affection between them, and the Templar felt the same heart-tugging sadness that Raoul had experienced, at the thought of Simon leaving to fulfil his destiny in the Holy Land.

Their progress was through rolling countryside, heavily wooded and graced by eye-catching displays of early spring wild-flowers. Primroses and bluebells richly carpeted the floors of the forests, while chestnut, apple, and cherry blossom covered the trees in the many orchards.

At Chartres, their first task on rising at dawn was to visit the cathedral. This fine monument to man's love of God had been built and decorated during the past fifty years. It occupied the site of the previous church, built by Fulbert, the great Benedictine. This had been burnt down a half-century before.

Fulbert's church had, in turn, been raised by the Benedictines, following the destruction, also by fire, of the first Christian church to stand there.

In all, three churches had been built on the same site, which had previously been dedicated by the Druids to the worship of the pagan god, Lug.

This use of a pagan sacred-place on which to build Christian churches puzzled Simon and he mentioned this to the Templar Marshal. De Roubaix explained this apparent anomaly.

'It is because the site itself is sacred, whether to pagan worshippers, or to the Christians who succeeded them. The ground is full of the *Wouivre*, the "dragon-power" which carries the telluric currents of the life-force through the earth. These subtle energies, which flow like the blood in our veins, follow the course of the "waters-under-the-earth". This sacred site, where the cathedral now stands, is located over a meeting point of these underground streams. The waters come swirling up to the surface, in the form of a natural well, or *puits* as we call it. That is where you find the *Wouivre* – if you look for it!'

Simon was enchanted by the cathedral. To the young squire it seemed that the lovely building had always graced that sacred spot and would remain to do so for ever. There was such a sense of permanence about the cathedral that neither he nor the Templar sensed that Destiny would ever decide otherwise.

They admired the imposing front of the cathedral, with its impressively carved portico and the fine windows set high above the pointed ogive of the arched doorway. This was one of the first cathedrals to be built in the revolutionary new Gothic style, characterized by the lofty vault of the nave and, throughout the building, the noble sweep of the sharply pointed arches.

'All this was built without plans!' announced the Templar, to Simon's surprise. He went on to explain how this extraordinary feat had been accomplished.

'The master-masons used a wide plaster-floor on which they scribed out everything, from the sweeping curves of the Gothic arches to the rounded and cantonned forms of the supporting pillars.

'These ingenious craftsmen possessed the skills of the great temple-builders of the Holy Land. They were mathematicians who understood the principles and axioms of the Sacred Geometry of Euclid and Pythagoras, and here, at Chartres, we can see the practical results of those beautiful truths.'

Simon was fascinated.

'Do you mean to say, sir knight, that all these marvels were created by the use of geometry alone?'

The old Templar smiled.

'Not entirely, Simon, for the craftsman's eye sees a hidden beauty that the geometer, unaided, cannot release from the stone. So it was with the master-masons who built this masterpiece with their perfectly cut stone ashlars.

'They achieved these results by using Nature's way of

forming those shapely curves. To explain it simply, the masons employed withes, long flexible reeds or thin laths of bendable wood, which, when held against a series of small weights laid out on the plaster-floor, helped to guide the scribing-compasses along their flowing lines.

'Nature's forms cannot be bettered by mere men, no matter how skilled they are in the craft of drafting. Such shapes are given to us mortals by the Great Architect of the Universe. We cannot improve upon the work of the Almighty. It is perfect.'

As they walked round the exterior of the great cathedral the wise old knight pointed out the simple decoration, which reverently enriched the building without vulgar ostentation.

'The statue of Saint George, the subjugator of the Dragon, which, of course, is the symbol of the raw pagan power of the sacred site, and the figure of Saint Theodore, the guardian angel of this holy place, both stand above the south door, or "Knight's Entrance", as it is called.

'Note that these figures are lifesize. They are wearing the chain-mail of the warrior-monk, and their feet are carved "*en equerre*" "squared" correctly, as befits the Sacred Geometers they represent.

'I was taught the wonderful art of geometry as part of the Great Work, when I was a prisoner in Damascus and Isphahan. The Saracens treated me well, even though I was a Templar, for one or two of our Grand Masters had maltreated the heathen savagely.

'Be that as it may, I was shown great civility, yet my captors knew that I possessed no ransom. I even met the great Arabian philosopher, Osama. This wise old teacher completed my training in the Sacred Geometry, the rudiments of which I had learnt from another fine scholar, called Abraham, a Jewish sage whom I met in Tiberias.'

A natural teacher himself, de Roubaix explained to Simon, in simple terms, many of the outstanding features of the cathedral.

'First, let us consider the sacred site itself. This was chosen by the Ancient Druids for its power. Centuries ago, a great stone dolmen was placed here, by methods that we still do not fully comprehend.

'Somehow, it was transported from many miles away, where it had originally formed part of one of the ancient stone-circles found in this part of the country.

'When the cathedral was built, it took a heavy wheeled platform of massive construction, pulled by a team of draught-horses, to move the dolmen the few yards to its present resting-place, in what is now the crypt of the cathedral. How did the Druids manage to move such a huge stone from their magic circle to the new site of their pagan temple?'

The Templar growled with laughter at Simon's obvious bewilderment.

'Don't worry your young head over the problem, Simon. Many great scholars are as puzzled as you are. Perhaps the answer lies in the Druids' knowledge of the Ancient Magick.

'Whatever their magical methods were, their motive was the same as ours: the worship of the Light and the veneration of Our Blessed Earth-Mother, as typified by and embodied in the great stone dolmen beneath our feet.'

Simon looked surprised.

'But, surely, the pagans and ourselves worship entirely different gods, or rather, in their case, a pantheon of gods, goddesses and Nature spirits.'

The Templar smiled knowingly.

'Actually, Simon, Our Blessed Lady of Chartres is worshipped by many names. The Ancient Egyptians called Her Isis, the Greeks named Her Gaia. We call Her Our Blessed Virgin Mary. She is the Mother of Our Lord, and She is the Heavenly Mother of us all. That is what we Templars believe. This is Her sacred place. That is the "Mystery of the Site"!'

By now they had passed under the portico arch and entered the cathedral. Their voices unconsciously lowered as they walked through the portals, from the bright spring sunshine outside into the cool shade of the vaulted nave.

Simon immediately noticed a shimmering pattern of light dappling the broad flagstones of the cathedral floor.

He was fascinated by the dance of sunlight on the stone pavement, and de Roubaix noticed his squire's interest in its colourful display.

'That is the second Mystery, that of the Light! See, Simon, how the three tall windows, set in the front façade, cast these beautiful patterns. This is because the craftsmen have recently installed an intricate network of small lead frames, called "cames", which hold together many differently shaped pieces of coloured glass inside the stone mullions of the window arches. These pieces of stained-glass, as they are known in the craft, are first painted and then fired in a kiln, before being fitted into the lead "cames", forming a picture of an event in the life of Our Blessed Lady of Chartres.

'You can see some of these craftsmen working on the windows, up there on the scaffolding, high above our heads.'

'From whence come these master-masons who can build such a wonderful work of art?' asked Simon, awe-struck by the echoing vault of the lofty nave.

'Many of them come from around the area of Lake Como, in Italy. We call them the Comocini. They are indeed master-masons. Every one of them is a free man, for the work of constructing and decorating these great sacred buildings is not for vassals, serfs and slaves.

'Each free-mason is a brother of one of the famous Craftsmen's Guilds, or companies. They are known as "The Children of Master Jacques", "The Children of Father Soubise", and' – here the old Templar covertly made a curious sign with his right hand – '"The Children of Solomon the King".

'We Templars understand the strange ways of these Guilds, for, from the shape and form of the Temple of King Solomon, the Master Magician of Jerusalem, came the Divine Proportion of the Sacred Geometry. This has been used exclusively throughout the construction of this beautiful cathedral.'

Simon was lost in contemplation of the stone master-piece that surrounded them, enveloping them in its sense of peace and serenity.

Bernard de Roubaix continued, in a hushed voice: 'Saint Bernard of Clairvaux, the renowned Cistercian scholar, gave us the *règles*, the rules by which we discipline our lives as Knights of the Temple. They bind us to the form and shape of our duties and regulate the way that we live, in much the same way that the Sacred Geometry determines the shape and form of the finished stone ashlars, with which the Temple of Solomon and this cathedral were built.

'You see, Simon, only by strictly observing the rules of Cosmos, given to us by the Great Architect of the Universe, can we construct such a work of art – which is, of course, what our own lives should be. We are God's creatures, made in His own image, and our lives should conform to the perfection of His rules.'

A blinding light seemed to illuminate Simon's mind. His voice was hushed.

'I can see that now. This cathedral is a sermon in stone, teaching each of us how to live. It is all set out, here, in the perfect proportions of the ashlars.'

'Precisely!' cried the Templar. 'You have grasped the great lesson that this place teaches us! Your father used to call this cathedral: "An instrument for communicating with God".

At that precise moment the sun came out from behind a cloud, filling the vaulted nave with dust-moted beams of light. Simon gasped at its beauty, and they both instinctively fell to their knees and said the Pater Noster and the Ave Maria. It was a magical moment.

'That was a perfect example of the "Mystery of the Light",' remarked the old knight, rising to his feet. 'Now for the delightful "Mystery of the Sound".'

Bernard de Roubaix drew his dagger for he had the right, as a Templar knight, to enter the cathedral armed.

Reversing the blade, he lightly tapped its pommel against the side of the nearest column. A clear note sounded, rising to the vault of the nave. De Roubaix smiled and struck a second cantonned pillar. A different note sounded. The Templar moved rapidly down the long colonnade, tapping each highly stressed pillar, till the whole nave of the cathedral rang with the sound of the magical music of the stone columns, like a choir of angels.

Simon nearly clapped his hands with delight, but wisely refrained.

As the beautiful sound died away, a cowled figure, in the white mantle of the Order, appeared and advanced, smiling, to greet de Roubaix.

'Bernard, I knew it was you, my friend. How you love to make our cathedral sing.'

The cowled Templar uncovered his head to reveal a gaunt, white-bearded face, filled with gentle strength.

This was Robert de Guise, a famous Crusader, who had given up his dukedom to join the Order.

'Well met, Robert,' said de Roubaix, embracing his old comrade-in-arms. 'This is Simon de Creçy, my squire.'

'You must be related to Raoul de Creçy,' said de Guise. 'He is an old war-comrade and a dear friend of mine whom I have not seen for years. I trust he is well?'

'He is in excellent health, sir knight.'

To save Simon from becoming involved in a lie, explaining his relationship with Raoul de Creçy, Bernard de Roubaix interjected.

'Simon is off to the Crusade, Robert. I brought him to the cathedral as a reward for doing so well in his training at Gisors.'

De Guise smiled.

'Did Belami give you a hard time, my son?'

'No, sir knight,' replied Simon, with a grin. 'Sergent Belami gave me a wonderful three months of his valuable time. Thanks to him, and the things he taught me, I may, with Our Blessed Lady's help, serve the Order without disgracing myself in the Holy Land.'

'Well said, my boy.'

De Guise gazed in admiration at the handsome cadet's powerful frame.

'By Our Lady, they grow them tall and strong in Normandy!'

'Forgive us, Robert,' said de Roubaix. 'There are still some things I must show my squire, and we have little time.'

The ex-duke nodded his understanding.

'Of course, Bernard. Please feel free to wander where you will. The cathedral is full of marvels. Enjoy them, my son, while you have the chance.'

The eminent Templar gave Simon his blessing and left them to their exploration of the rest of the building.

'Did he know my father, sir knight?' Simon asked eagerly, as soon as Robert de Guise was out of earshot.

'Not as your father,' replied the Templar quietly. 'But as Grand Master, of course. Be cautious, Simon. We must not talk of these matters, especially in the cathedral where every word carries, no matter how softly we speak.'

'Forgive me, sir knight.'

The young squire blushed with shame at his lapse of discretion.

'It's natural enough to wish to know more about your father,' de Roubaix said in a whisper. 'Just be more careful, my boy.

'Let us return to the last Mystery of the cathedral. This is the "Mystery of the Shape and Form of the Building". These secret proportions are the basis of the Sacred Geometry. We call it the Golden Mean.

'Stated simply, the essence of the Divine Proportion, or Golden Section, as the Ancient Egyptians thought of it, is Unity in ratio to the root of five, plus one, divided by two.'[*]

To illustrate his meaning, the Templar traced the figures out in the dust on the floor, using a withy that he had taken from a bunch of reeds stacked by the masons against the wall.

'Thus, $1 : \dfrac{\sqrt{5+1}}{2}$

'This gives us the proportion of Unity to 1.618, in round figures. *Id est*: the Golden Section is 1.618.'

Again, he drew out the figures in the dust which had settled on the flagstones from the work proceeding high above their heads.

'Each stone ashlar was marked up by the master-

---

[*]To simplify matters, the modern numerical notation is used.

masons using this proportion, in pattern first, and then, after the stone had been roughly quarried and brought here, it was carefully finished and placed in its exact position, as required by the tenets of the Sacred Geometry. This means that all the final cutting and assembly was carried out on the floor of the nave, the transept, and the whole of the rest of the cathedral.'

Simon was entranced.

'And the Maze, sir knight?' he asked, indicating the large, labyrinthine pattern inlaid on the flagstones of the nave.

The old Templar paused, smiling thoughtfully, while he stroked his beard.

'One day, Simon, you will no doubt solemnly perambulate the Great Maze of Chartres, in accordance with the Sacred Dance of Life and Death . . . but, until then, I cannot explain to you the "Mystery of the Maze".'

At this point, a terrible scream rang through the cathedral, shattering its peace and tranquillity.

Startled, they looked up, to catch a horrified glimpse of a spread-eagled figure, with whirling limbs, hurtling from the high scaffolding.

Still shrieking, the terrified craftsman plunged down, to crash on to the flagstones. The poor wretch was killed instantly.

Simon, aghast, instinctively started forward, but de Roubaix's command rang out: 'Do not touch the victim of the *Wouivre*! We are both armed, so neither of us is in a State of Grace. Here comes someone better suited to administer the Last Rites. Let us pray for his departed soul.'

They both clashed down to their knees and intoned the Pater Noster.

When they had finished, to Simon's surprise, the Templar continued praying in a half-heard, unknown tongue, making certain curious signs which he carefully concealed from watching eyes, save those of his squire. At the end, he rose to his feet.

'Come, Simon,' he said softly. 'It is time for us to go. The *Wouivre* is present.'

Without another word they left the cathedral, which suddenly had become icy cold and now seemed filled with shadows. Simon was trembling with shock.

Outside, in the midday sunlight, he felt better. The Templar turned to his young squire.

'Simon, what you have just seen was no accident. That was a sacrifice demanded by the *Wouivre*.'

'Do you mean it was witchcraft?' asked Simon hoarsely, still aghast at the craftsman's dreadful death.

'Perhaps,' replied the Templar. 'But more likely it was due to the expiation of some mortal sin, committed by the unfortunate mason and not absolved in the Confessional. Under no circumstances should a craftsman undertake work on a sacred task, within the confines of such a holy place, unshriven. The *Wouivre* came to collect the penalty for such blasphemy. It is death!'

The next day, they continued their journey to Paris. After the free-mason's sudden death, silence had fallen between them, but, by the following morning, the warm spring sunshine had dispelled their depression. Bernard de Roubaix continued his dissertation on Templar matters, without again referring to the tragedy.

Simon was so engrossed in his mentor's flow of information that he soon relegated the previous morning's accident to the back of his mind; yet the horrific picture of that shrieking figure, hurtling to its death, kept reappearing in disturbing flashes of memory. The Norman squire was still very young and, though he had killed both animals and men, sudden death affected him more than was usual in those violent times.

It took them three days to cover the distance to Paris and they stayed each night at different Templar fermes. These fortified farm-buildings were constructed around a central courtyard, into which the animals could be driven in case of attack; hence the name 'ferme', derived from '*fermé*', meaning 'closed'.

Knight and squire approached Paris from the south-west, on the lower, left, bank of the River Seine. They had covered over one hundred miles since leaving Chartres.

The capital city of twelfth-century France had grown at a feverish pace over the past twenty years. At the time, more than 100,000 people lived within the perimeter of its fortifications, or clustered round the *environs* of Paris, just outside its walls. This made it one of the largest cities in the Western world.

It had been developed by the Romans, as a nostalgic reminder of their own capital city, for Paris, like Rome also rested on low hills. The garrison-settlement, which acted as the headquarters of Roman legions stationed in Gaul, had soon become an important centre of trade.

This was because of the River Seine, which was fully navigable at all seasons of the year, bringing an abundance of supplies from the northern French coast and the rich farmlands and vineyards of the west. This strategically important river, winding its way through the Roman garrison-town, had also reminded the successive legions stationed there of their native Tiber, meandering through Rome.

Simon was enthralled by the bustling scene that seethed around them as he and de Roubaix slowly paced their horses through the mean streets. These were little more than muddy lanes, for the *environs* of the south bank of the river did not enjoy the same facilities as those of the northern part of the capital. The city on the right bank of the Seine was inter-cut by wide, cobble-stone *rues*, inherited from the *vias* that once had been the arteries of the Roman garrison-town. The left bank *environs* were slums by comparison.

The filthy, winding lanes were lined on either side by crudely built houses, hostelries, wine-shops, brothels, stalls and hovels. Perpetually shaded by the rickety, overhanging second stories of the bigger buildings, these narrow cart-tracks stank of urine and excreta, animal and human.

The noise was deafening: an ear-splitting mixture of creaking carts, clattering utensils, squawking fowls and other loudly protesting animals on their way to market. Added to this cacophony were the loud cries and raucous shouts of abuse, shrieked curses and ribald laughter, which accompanied the frenzied activity in the overcrowded alleys.

Simon had been intrigued by Gisors, overawed by Chartres, and excited by the thought of seeing Paris for the first time, but now that he had actually arrived there, he found it overpoweringly unpleasant.

Bernard de Roubaix hated it, as always, and could hardly wait to get back to the peace and quiet of his beloved native Normandy.

As they forced their war-horses through the jostling crowds of stinking humanity, Simon had no time to notice the many admiring glances directed towards him by women, young and old alike. The tall, handsome, black-tuniced young cadet rode beside the elderly, white-surcoated Templar, their chain-mail glinting in the few beams of sunlight that reached the shadowy lanes.

At last, they broke out of the maze of mean backstreets and emerged on to the sunlit riverbank *quais*, to catch their first glimpse of the cathedral, Notre Dame de Paris.

Built on the Île de la Cité, and started only seventeen years before, this huge building was the same age as Simon. But it had grown at such an astounding rate that the impressive height of the great edifice now dominated the city.

Undoubtedly, it was the most ambitious project of this era of Gothic cathedral architecture, and Simon could hardly wait to see inside it.

Approaching Notre Dame, they rode slowly along the *quais* which lined the left bank, enjoying the fresh air the river breezes brought into the fetor of the slums. These wharves were packed with cargo vessels of all kinds, and were the key to the growing wealth of the rapidly expanding capital.

Paris, at that time, enjoyed an extensive trade in exotic foreign goods, as well as being the central market for farm and other domestic produce, arriving daily at the quay-sides of the left and right river banks.

Normandy, Picardy, Brittany and the Lowlands, as well as most parts of France under the domain of the French king and the Burgundian duke, sent Paris their best cattle, sheep, pigs, fish, cheese, vegetables, fruit and wine to grace the tables of those who could afford to pay.

From further afield, England sent wool, and various Mediterranean countries shipped rugs, silk and cloth, silverware and glass, ceramics and fine weaponry, armour and leather goods – in fact, all the rich profusion of expensive luxuries that foreign craftsmen could devise and make.

The new University of Paris attracted a different sort of wealth, the riches of knowledge, which came pouring in from many lands. But at the same time this great centre of learning brought in large sums of money from the foreign students sent by wealthy parents, eager to give their sons some of the finest education in Europe.

Nobles and commoners, rich and poor, greedy and selfless, all flocked to the busy capital, for as many different reasons as there were visitors to Paris.

Because of the need for so many kinds of services generated by this heavy influx of demanding visitors, Paris became a haven for the poor, so long as they were fit enough to slave away at whatever menial tasks there were available. There was never any shortage of such hard work, much of which was connected with the unloading of cargo, its storage and distribution.

All this was carried out by the *Jacquerie*, the mass of French peasant labour who lived in the hovels and the shacks of the slums on the left bank.

The *quais* of the Seine made up a noisy and noisome scene, but fortunately the fresh river breezes and the smell of Oriental perfumes and spices from the exotic foreign cargoes did much to alleviate the stench of the *environs*, as far as the riverside was concerned.

When de Roubaix and his squire crossed over the south bridge to the Île de la Cité, the contrasting peace and tranquillity surrounding the huge cathedral, which was still under construction, came as a welcome relief.

Oddly enough, now that Simon was close to Notre Dame de Paris, he did not feel the same sense of awe that he had experienced when he had first seen the smaller cathedral at Chartres.

Though far from completion, already there was an ostentatious opulence about this great cathedral which was missing from the simpler, more reverential, architecture of the first building.

Just as Simon had felt that Chartres was a sermon in stone, so he now saw the cathedral of Notre Dame de Paris as a blatantly flamboyant display of the vast wealth of the Roman Church. That was sufficient to affect the religious sensitivity of the devout young Norman.

Moreover, the same sense of alienation assailed him when, after leaving their horses with an ostler, the Templar and his squire entered the cathedral.

Although, as before, their voices unconsciously lowered on passing through the portals of the sacred building, Simon felt none of that sense of spirituality and inner peace which he had previously enjoyed so ecstatically at Chartres. For him, Notre Dame was a disappointment.

Bernard de Roubaix immediately sensed his squire's sudden change of mood. He, too, held the same views about Notre Dame de Paris.

'It is the absence of the *Wouivre*, Simon,' he said. 'Here, in this cathedral, it is sleeping. At Chartres, the Dragon is awake. But, sadly, in this great building, even though the outer fabric is nearly complete and, by rights, we should feel the presence of the Guardian of Our Blessed Lady, instead we are aware of his absence.

'This is because the pride and arrogance of the builders has grown commensurately with the amount of wealth being poured into its construction.

'The *Wouivre* prefers a simpler, more devout dedication to the real purpose of the building, as a perfect instrument for communication with God. Notre Dame de Paris is not being built with that sole purpose in the minds of its arrogant constructors.

'Therefore the *Wouivre* dragon sleeps. But it will awaken for the celebration of the ancient rites of the seasons. Come here after it has been completed, when the rituals of the equinoxes or the solstices are being performed with all due reverence, and you will find the *Wouivre* awake.

'However, now that we are here, Simon, pray with me for the success of your mission to the Holy Land.'

Side by side, knight and squire clashed down to their knees and poured out their souls to Our Blessed Lady of Paris.

On their account, for a short space of time, they felt the sleeping Dragon stir in his long slumber and they both sensed that the Virgin Mother had heard their devout pleas.

De Roubaix had little more to say about Notre Dame de Paris and they soon left, to cross over on to the right bank and make their way to Templar headquarters.

If anything symbolized the power of the Order, it was this centre for the Grand Chapter in Paris. Yet their massively-built Temple, like the commanderie at Gisors, was already marked out for rebuilding into an even stronger fortress.

Simon was suitably impressed by the high walls, with their numerous *mâchicoulis*. These were jutting abutments, like small boxes, distributed along the battlements. If attacked, they would each hold an archer in a cramped fighting-compartment, to shoot down on besiegers attempting to scale the walls.

The towers at the ends of the walls were topped by conical spires, and the large inner courtyard was backed by the great keep which contained the Chapter House, forming the heart of the stronghold. This was the prime focus of the Order's temporal power in the West, and its formidable presence dominated the capital city of France.

Simon felt oppressed by the sheer size and weight of the outer walls. He was relieved to pass under the grim portcullis and emerge into the sunlit inner courtyard. Bernard de Roubaix had visited the Temple many times in the course of his duties, but he always felt the same sense of oppressive confinement which was troubling his squire.

Like Simon, the old Templar was essentially a man of action who loved to be in God's open air, a countryman born and bred in Normandy. Though a large part of his life had been spent inside the walls of many fortresses, he had never felt comfortable in any of them, particularly inside the Templar headquarters at Paris.

Bernard de Roubaix was well known to the guards, and the visitors quickly passed through the required formalities. Their horses were led away by the duty-farrier for reshoeing, and they were welcomed immediately by Belami and his small company of eager young sergent-cadets. Surrounded by such warmth and friendship, Simon soon lost his sense of oppression, which quickly dissolved amid the laughter and cheerful banter.

Even the disapproving glances from Templar knights, on their way to partake of their none-meat, failed to dampen the cadets' high spirits. Moreover, the avuncular presence of the famous old knight tacitly sanctioned their conduct.

'So, Simon, now that you've seen the wonders of Chartres, how say you?' asked Belami, giving him a bear-hug.

'It's a miracle. I don't think I have ever felt such a presence of peace and beauty anywhere before.'

'And what of your feelings towards Notre Dame de Paris?'

'Not the same at all.' Simon paused. 'Beautiful? Yes. Awe-inspiring? Of course, it is far from being finished but, somehow, it's just not like Chartres.'

'I know.' Belami nodded his agreement. 'I feel exactly the same. The *Wouivre* seems to be sleeping at Notre Dame de Paris. At Chartres, the Dragon is always present, guarding Our Blessed Lady.'

In contrast to these deep thoughts, Simon was soon immersed in the usual imbecilic banter with his fellow cadets which all youngsters seem to share in a military environment. It is a timeless experience and is the essence of the comradeship that pervades any young *corps d'élite*.

In Paris, there was no time for sight-seeing, which was a disappointment to Simon who wanted to see the new University. But, since their arrival, every one of the cadets had been busy, preparing for the long road south to Marseilles.

The few days' delay had been occasioned by the gathering together of a large party of pilgrims, merchants, and mercenaries, whom the sergent-cadets were escorting to Provence, from where most of them would continue on to the Holy Land.

The services of a Templar escort could be procured by paying the Order a reasonable sum, but the travellers first had to produce adequate evidence of a bona-fide reason for their journey. This escort service was popular with those pilgrims who could afford it, and was looked upon as an assurance of safe passage by merchants and others unskilled in the use of arms to defend themselves.

However, some of the travellers were mercenaries, young adventurers headed for Outremer, there to join up with whatever Frankish fighting-force had the price of their swords. They also were glad of the opportunity to share the journey with the escort of eight young cadets, led by the grizzled old veteran.

They considered that the presence of a Templar unit, no matter how small, gave them the right to seek shelter in the commanderies along the way. For them, also, it was money well spent. Certainly the escort looked well-trained.

Roving bands of outlaws and other landless renegades, sometimes led by feudal outcasts, were still a menace on the long, lonely roads to the Provençal coast. But the young Templar lances would keep all save the boldest from attacking the convoy of wagons.

Most of the pilgrims were middle-aged, some with wives and daughters, but there were others, besides the mercenaries, whose journey to the Holy Land was not motivated by a devout desire for Grace, or spiritual fulfilment. These were merchants, and the risk inherent in their journey was a considered part of their trade.

But to the more vulnerable among the pilgrims, the young sergent-cadets looked like guardian angels, and the younger women favoured the eight good-looking youngsters with many covertly admiring glances.

One lovely Italian girl, the daughter of a Milanese silver-smith, was entranced by the tall, chestnut-haired Norman with the peacock-blue eyes.

Maria de Nofrenoy was only sixteen years old when she fell deeply in love with Simon, literally within minutes of her first setting eyes upon him. All the passion of her ripe young body rose, nearly choking her with its intensity.

Her heart-shaped face, graced with fine skin and a warm, generous mouth, revealing perfect teeth, was further jewelled by the hint of passion in her dark-brown eyes. Her every glance towards the unsuspecting Simon promised him delight.

'There has got to be something wrong with the lad,' Belami muttered to himself in despair. 'He must be blind, not to notice that blossoming flower.'

The veteran quickly had to dismiss such thoughts as he concentrated on rounding up the straggling pilgrims and their cumbersome possessions, which were piled insecurely on an unsuitable assortment of rickety carts.

'Jesus knows I am a patient man,' he grumbled to Simon. 'But why must we shepherd half the worldly possessions of Northern France all the way to Provence? I tell you, Simon, most of this rubbish will get no further than Dijon, never mind Marseilles!'

Cursing fluently in Arabic, which is a marvellous language for that purpose, Belami spurred his horse over to Bernard de Roubaix, to complain about such typical civilian stupidity.

The old Templar, who had heard it all before, especially the Arab curses, nodded sagely.

'*Inshallah*, Belami. When the wheels come off, leave the trash behind.'

'Holy Mother of God,' swore the veteran, raising his eyes to heaven. 'One old duck has brought her rocking-chair! That has got to go, now!'

'Nay, Belami,' laughed de Roubaix. 'Her wagon will fall to pieces long before you get to Dijon. Better that she blames it on the Devil than pours her curses on the meddling Templar sergent who threw away her favourite rocking-chair in Paris. She will find another in Marseilles.'

It had been two exasperating days for Belami and his

cadets, before the caravan finally wound its way through the south gate of the city's perimeter wall.

Simon, Bernard de Roubaix and the veteran sergent embraced with full hearts and welling eyes. They knew it was to be for the last time. The Templar knight watched his friends wind their way out of sight; then, blowing his nose violently, he wiped away his tears and cantered back through the gates, to make his solitary way back to Gisors. There, following his orders and the dictates of his heart, he would spend the rest of his days at de Creçy Manor with his old friend Raoul. At least the two veteran Crusaders could share their sadness at the absence of their ward in the Holy Land, waiting eagerly for the letters which they knew he would write.

These would help to ease the pain of their parting from the most important person in their lives. Both of them knew that Simon was to enjoy a great destiny, and that, in his own way, he would seek the Holy Grail of Knowledge, the Gnosis of the Magi.

This was the Age of Chivalry and the legend of King Arthur and the Knights of the Round Table was heavily influenced, if not inspired, by the deeds of the great Military Order of the Templars. There was even another Avalon in Burgundy, near Beaune, and, after all, Lancelot du Lac came from France.

Many believed implicitly in the authenticity of this great circle of chivalrous knighthood. Both de Roubaix and de Creçy saw Simon as another Sir Percival, the peerless knight of the Arthurian court about whom the Troubadours, roving poet-magicians, sang their ballads, bringing the legends to archetypal life in the minds of those who listened to their magical songs.

The two knights also believed in the reality of King Arthur and his magical circle of True Chevaliers. They accepted their validity in exactly the same way they believed in the authenticity of the True Cross on which Jesus had died, and which, encased in silver, had led them throughout their Crusade in the Holy Land.

From Paris, the Templar-escorted pilgrims' route lay south-east to Dijon, some 230 miles, following the course of the Seine as they proceeded towards its tributaries. Though de Roubaix and Simon had covered thirty miles a day on their journey to Chartres and Paris, the pilgrims and their rickety transport so hampered the Templar caravan that, even over these straight Roman roads, they made scarcely twenty miles between dawn and sunset. In all, it took them eleven days to reach Dijon, leaving a pitiful trail of broken carts and possessions along the way.

This small city was a thriving centre for the sale of the region's farm-produce and had become a focus for the wine trade, started centuries before by the Romans and later developed by followers of Charlemagne, the first Holy Roman Emperor of Christendom.

Surrounding it were the estates of rich nobles, and the country homes of feudal families and well-to-do merchants, as well as the manors, granges and fermes of the locally based Templars. These contrasted starkly with the hovels of the poor.

Dijon, the Dibio of Roman times, was now the home of the Duke of Burgundy. It was perched athwart the River Bourgogne, which in turn flowed into the Saône, and here, for a long exasperating day, Belami and the cadets wrestled with the repair of the rapidly disintegrating transport. It was enough to drive a man to drink.

As this was some of the finest wine-producing country in Europe, Belami decided that his cadets had earned some recreation, so, when they had finished the emergency repairs, and while the farrier was reshoeing some of the horses, the veteran introduced his small troop to the pleasures of Burgundian wines.

Although Templar knights had sworn an oath of abstinence, there was no such binding requirement upon the ranks of the Order's sergents, and, though Belami would not countenance the indiscipline of drunkenness, he saw no reason why his cadets should remain parched in the midst of plenty.

He joined in, modestly partaking of a flagon or two, as an example of restrained drinking. Belami chuckled to himself as he suddenly visualized his old comrades-in-arms, twenty years before in the Holy Land. They would hardly recognize me now, he thought. Certainly not by his present abstemious drinking habits, in contrast to his former image of a wine-swilling hell-raiser.

'This wine is excellent.' The veteran smacked his lips appreciatively. 'At my age, *mes braves*, I take my time to savour such a vintage. In the old days, when I was your age, I gulped it down by the barrel. It could just as well have been pig-swill.'

The cadets laughed loudly, their tongues loosened by the Burgundian wine.

'How did you fight, *mon cher sergent*, if you were drunk?' queried Pierre, the handsome, dark-eyed, self-confident youngster who evidently came from a noble French house, but who, so far, had not been forthcoming about his background. His quick wit and courage, however, had already won him the prize of Simon's close friendship.

Belami chuckled.

'As always, *mon garcon*, with one hand and the strength of a bear!'

'Didn't the wine affect you at all?' asked Phillipe, the tall, quiet lad who also had found himself drawn to Simon's warm companionship.

'Yes!' admitted Belami. 'After a dozen flagons, I thought I was fighting twice the number of heathens!' The cadets enjoyed that sally, uproariously.

'Its a bad habit,' growled the veteran. 'Don't cultivate it! I nearly got slung out of the Corps for my hell-raising. Only the intercession of my commanding officer, the late Grand Master and the finest man I ever served under, saved me from getting a boot in the backside.

'But for Odo de Saint Amand, I wouldn't be with you today, enjoying this fine wine. Drink up, *mes braves*, for we must be on our way by dawn.'

During the long journey south, Maria de Nofrenoy could hardly keep her eyes off Simon. Her heart pounded every time he came near her, which was as often as she could think up excuses to gain his attention, ostensibly for help with her father's troublesome transport.

She longed for the touch of the handsome Norman's strong hands on her voluptuous body, which virtually ached to be taken by her intended lover.

Simon's fine features and startling blue eyes filled her dreams, sleeping and waking, but especially when, at night, she tossed restlessly in the back of her father's wagon, racked with desire.

Maria was still a virgin, but her fiery Milanese nature gave her a physical maturity beyond her years. Until this journey to Marseilles, her experience of young love had been confined to a few stolen kisses and some unskilled fondling with her father's apprentice in Paris. The youngster had been caught in the act before much had happened. He had been soundly beaten and dismissed, despite Maria's protestations that it had been her fault. Now she had fallen deeply in love with Simon and longed for him to take her virginity. All the other cadets would have been delighted to become her lover, but Maria only had eyes, and sighs, for Simon.

To Belami's relief, his favourite cadet was at last beginning to take notice of his adoring admirer. The veteran was now certain that Simon was neither abnormal nor physically handicapped.

It was all his years of chaste conditioning in Raoul de Creçy's womanless household that had delayed the young Norman's normal development. Simon was acutely shy with women, and young women in particular. But even his acute self-consciousness with the opposite sex could hardly stop him responding to Maria's bountiful charms, and the evident eagerness with which she silently offered them for his approval.

Twice, when helping her to deal with faults in the de Nofrenoy wagon, Simon had found himself close to Maria, their bodies touching. Each time the thrill of contact had set them trembling, the girl's natural perfume filling Simon's nostrils like the scent of wild-flowers. The earth was waking to the lustiness of May; calling to its young to heed the urgent music of the Great God Pan. Simon and Maria were responding to the magical tones of the Syrinx, and the blood throbbed in their veins.

One moonlit night, encamped by the roadside, Simon was on guard when a light footstep spun him round, his sword drawn. Before he had time to challenge the prowler, Maria's soft fingers brushed his lips, silencing them. Her trembling body pressed against his. In the silver light, Simon could see the long, brush-burnished hair framing Maria's eager face. With a soft hiss of steel on leather, he resheathed his sword. The lusty youngster swept the trembling girl off her dainty feet, holding her tight in his mail-clad arms.

Their mouths met and melted together. Maria's questing tongue slipped between Simon's moist lips. Enraptured, he responded, his senses reeling with desire, all Brother Ambrose's dire warnings flying from his mind like newly freed wild birds.

Simon felt his manhood rising in Maria's tender grasp, while beneath his rasping chain-mail breeches, her thighs eagerly opened to his throbbing erection.

The rest would have been the natural conclusion to such passion. But, at that moment, the flickering light of a flambeau shone on their shocked young faces.

They both gasped at the moment of discovery, Simon wilting in shame and Maria instinctively covering her flushed face with her hooded mantle.

To Simon's relief, a soft chuckle told him that Belami held the torch. It was extinguished immediately as the veteran thrust its burning end into the dew-damp grass. His finger to his lips, he gently chided them: 'Not now, *mes enfants*, and not here! Back to Papa, Signorina. Don't fret, Simon, your secret is safe with me. But I would have words with you, *mon ami* . . . alone!'

The softest kiss from a giggling Maria told the young Norman that all was not lost and, as the beautiful girl slipped away into the darkness, Belami put his powerful right arm around his young friend's shaking shoulders.

'Simon,' he said, 'what has happened, has happened. No great sin has been committed. You have kissed a beautiful and willing girl. That is all. And had nature taken her natural course, that would not have been a sin either.

'I have never been in agreement with your over-strict upbringing. Much as I respect and honour both your knightly guardians, I think they have wrongly interpreted your father's wishes.

'Remember, Simon, you would not be here if your father himself had not responded to Our Blessed Mother's call to love.

'You are not yet a Templar knight, foresworn to eschew all earthly love with the Oath of Celibacy. So, for the love of Our Blessed Lady – and believe me, Simon, I mean no blasphemy – you should know something of the beauty of true love, before you renounce it for ever.'

As a father embraces a favourite son, Belami hugged Simon to him.

'Jesu knows I am no saint, for I have loved many women, but the maid, or matron, was always willing and none of them, to my knowledge, took any scathe from our mating.

'You are only doing what every lusty young animal does at this season of the year. There is no sin in that, for we would have no future without natural love. Believe me, Simon, the great god Pan is not dead!'

Then and there, the shaken youngster poured out his soul to his worldy wise friend, telling Belami of his past doubts and fears. The smiling veteran listened patiently while Simon told him of the lonely struggle, when happy boyhood turned to the uncertainty of his lusty youth.

'I've had dreams that brought me wondrous ecstasy, but with the dawn came the guilt of hell-fire, searing my soul with terror. Is that not truly the work of the Devil?'

'No, Simon, it is not!' Belami chuckled. 'It is, rather, the work of Our Blessed Earth-Mother. Believe me, *mon ami*, you will have plenty of time to avoid mortal sin *after* you have taken your knightly vows as a Templar. . . .' The veteran paused. 'If that is what you really want to do!'

He grinned broadly. 'Enough of this solemn talk. We'll down a goblet of hot spiced wine, for the Burgundian air strikes chill at this hour – which is why you are trembling, is it not, *mon brave*?'

72

Belami knew well why Simon was shivering, but gave the youngster a valid excuse for his embarrassment.

'Belami, what would I do without you?'

'For one thing, you would be having a wondrous time with Maria!' laughed the veteran as they walked towards the circle of wagons to enjoy their mulled wine and an hour or two of sleep, pillowed on their saddle and wrapped in blankets beside the dying camp-fire.

4

ALARUMS AND EXCURSIONS

The pilgrim caravan slowly wound its way alongside the reeded waters of the Saône, until it joined the fast-flowing river Rhône at Lyons.

This was another great Roman key-point, guarding the head-waters of the long river valley that stretched south to the delta of the marshy Camargue. It was a thriving port for the wine trade, and an important Templar stronghold. Here Belami left two of the young cadets, Gervais de Lattre and Yves de St Brieuc, the tall lad from Lille and the sturdy Breton. Both were bitterly disappointed at not being able to continue, but a recurrence of their fevers forced Belami to his decision to leave them, to reinforce the Templar garrison at Lyons.

'Better to do a good job here than to become a liability to a garrison in the fever-ridden lands of Outremer.' They were wise lads and saw Belami's point. He cheered them up. 'When your ills have been fully cured, you can join us later in the Holy Land. Till then, *mes braves*, good hunting – and not too much drinking to drown your disappointment!'

Lyons was the hub of the Burgundian wine trade, and heavily laden barges set off from its *quais* to rush down the fast-flowing Rhône and deliver their cargoes of wine and fine hides to Provence, where many ships awaited them.

The specially built, flat-bottomed river barges were

manned by powerful oarsmen and equipped with wide sails. Their pilotage was a skilled operation, guiding them between the shifting sand-bars that the fierce current constantly piled up and dispersed. When empty, these same wherries had to be laboriously towed back up the long river. They were either drawn close inshore where the current was weaker by teams of draught-horses, or they were dragged up-river by parties of wretched prisoners. All in the name of the great god Bacchus.

Because of the cost of skilled river pilots and lack of space due to the cargoes of wine barrels aboard, few pilgrims could afford the luxury of that swift, roaring downstream passage. Nevertheless, several of the merchants and the wealthier pilgrims chose to pay for this rapid voyage down the Rhône. The rest of the caravan, less the two sick sergent-cadets, continued by the long valley route. While they did so, the relationship between Maria and Simon blossomed into an intense love affair.

It was all innocent enough; snatched moments of delight when her father was safely asleep in the back of the wagon. These trysts were quite frequent, due to the silver-smith's fondness for Burgundian wine, but sadly the interludes had to be short, because Simon and the five other sergents now had to take over the guard duties of the two missing cadets. The youngsters' time together, though delightful, was still too short to achieve a satisfying conclusion. Usually their brief rendezvous climaxed with sheer youthful desire, before much else could be achieved.

Always Belami, unseen and unheard, kept watch to ensure that they had a few undisturbed moments of peace. The veteran was no voyeur, but his keen ears could hardly not hear their passion. He grinned to himself in the darkness and quietly hummed old Provençal love songs.

This idyll was interrupted with dramatic suddenness.

Their route southwards had been so uneventful, apart from one elderly pilgrim dying and being buried beside a wayside shrine, that their former vigilance had lost its keen edge. It only needed that momentary lapse of watchfulness at an inopportune moment to bring near-disaster. It came a few miles north of the city of Orange, opposite the Gorge de l' Ardèche. Just before dawn, Belami woke abruptly with all his senses alert. For him, a faint cry and the sound of a sword hissing from its sheath had raised the alarm. The dawn mist hung low over their encampment on the river bank, and the wet grass had muffled the hoof beats of approaching horses. The veteran needed no sentry's challenge to identify the intruders as hostile. At Lyons, he had been warned about a band of renegades led by a dishonoured knight, Etienne de Malfoy. Honest men did not approach an encampment at that hour by stealth. With a mighty shout: 'Alarm! Alarm! *Aux armes, mes braves*,' Belami bounded upright, his two-headed battle-axe in his powerful right hand. He was already armoured in his suit of chain-mail. The veteran always slept en route wearing his harness, and, by regularly changing his *jupon* or undershirt, he absorbed his sweat and prevented the onset of fever and ague.

The camp guard sprang to arms, but the robbers were already among them. The intruders struck indiscriminately, killing men and women in their frantic search for plunder. Two of Belami's cadets were already dead, their chain-mail harness lying uselessly beside their hacked bodies, a dreadful lesson in the necessity of preparedness.

The three surviving cadets, Simon, Pierre de Montjoie and Phillipe de Mauray, were standing back to back, forming a deadly triangle, fighting for their lives. There was no sign of Etienne Colmar, the young cadet from Flanders.

Belami burst into the desperate mêlée like the Angel of Death, his murderous battle-axe a scyth of destruction. One robber rolled in agony, clutching the stump of his upper arm and fountaining blood, until he slumped forward, unconscious. Another's carcass crashed to the ground, decapitated by a single blow. A third would-be murderer met his end as Belami sank his battle-axe up to the socket in the screaming man's mailed chest.

Simon seemed to be everywhere, his darting blade

slipping below his opponent's guard, to rip into stomach or throat. He had found no time to string his bow before the renegades struck out of the mist.

The surprise attack had succeeded against the unarmed and the defenceless. But faced by determined young warriors and the veteran sergent, whose battle-axe sheered through chain-mail and steel helmets, the robbers fled in disorder. Their leader, a black-bearded, swarthy hulk of a man, surcoated in red and fully armoured, swore loudly as his demoralized gang of cursing cut-throats stumbled past. Their panic communicated itself to his black charger and, before he could curb it, the war-horse had turned and galloped off into the mist, its rider impotently tugging at its reins.

The renegades left seven of their dead or dying behind them. Simon and his companions leant on their reeking swords, their breath coming in smoky gasps as they drew in the chilly early morning air. Belami turned over the dead until he found one body in which life still flickered. The man was badly wounded, his left side ripped wide open by Simon's searching blade.

'*Aidez-moi, camarade*,' he croaked through pain-gritted teeth.

'To hell, certes!' muttered Belami. 'But first, your leader? Who is the whore's son?' His poniard was at the renegade's throat.

'Etienne de Malfoy! *Merci, camarade*!' The robber's eyes were wide with terror.

Belami seized the cross-tipped staff of a murdered pilgrim, lying contorted beside them. He held it to the agonized man's lips. '*Te absolvo!*' breathed the veteran, and drove his dagger up to the hilt in the renegade's chest.

A gout of blood shot out of the dying man's mouth and his spirit fled. Belami looked up at the white faces of his cadets. They were shocked by his deed. The veteran's features were granite hard. 'A wounded man, with half his guts outside his body, can live in torment for an hour or so. My dagger was merciful. One day, *mes camarades*, you may have to do the same for me.' He paused significantly. 'Or I may have to do it for you.'

Simon had dispatched wounded deer for the same reason. The *coup de grâce* was well named. Sudden realization struck home. He clapped a hand to his sweating brow. 'Maria! *Mon dieu*! I had forgotten her.'

Belami laughed, breaking the tension. 'She is all right, Simon. I saw that pretty minx stick a stiletto in the carcass of one misbegotten son of a she-goat, as he tried to rob her father. The old man was having the truth throttled out of him as to where he had hidden his silver. Don't cross that dainty child, Simon. She can be a hell-cat!' Belami searched the corpses of the renegades for the spoils of war, but found little of value upon them. Then the cadets rolled the bodies into the fast-flowing Rhône.

Simon sought out Maria, who was tending her trembling father. They embraced passionately, their desires aroused even more by the battle-fever which still had not left them. When Simon returned, Belami told him: 'We haven't heard the last of this renegade de Malfoy. I was told of his murderous deeds at Lyons. It seems that he holes up in the Gorge de l'Ardèche. He's a local legend of sorts, born in this region. He knows this valley well, which makes it difficult for punitive forces to winkle him out. There is no substitute for local knowledge.'

Belami paused thoughtfully. 'When we get to the commanderie outside Orange, I will ask the Marshal to give me some men from his garrison. I have a strong feeling that it would be better to take some local men-at-arms and go in after that black-bearded whore's son, than to let him recover his murderous gang's morale and wipe out the next pilgrim caravan with another of his dawn ambushes.'

While Belami was telling Simon his plan for dealing with de Malfoy, the cadets were counting up their losses.

'It's not good,' growled the veteran at length. 'Two of our comrades are gone, Gaston and Gerard. Both hacked to pieces without a blow being struck on their side. See how they were unarmoured, *mes braves*. Learn by that!' The old soldier spat. 'Baby-killers!' he swore in disgust. 'They were only children.'

Ten pilgrims, mainly old and defenceless, were dead;

four women, two young and two elderly, had been raped and then savagely disembowelled. Phillipe vomited when he saw their gaping abdomens. The others averted their eyes as they covered up the ravaged dead.

'How can men behave like this? No beast is so savage. This is naked evil,' said Pierre.

'You're right there, *mon brave*,' said Belami grimly. 'These renegades are steeped in witchcraft. They are in league with the Devil.' He crossed himself as the others shuddered, for they felt the Dark Lord nearby, drawn to them by the stench of death! 'These curs are possessed. Their foul deeds speak for themselves,' said Belami.

'How could it all have happened in such a short time?' gasped Simon.

'The fight lasted longer than you think,' replied Belami, wiping his battle-axe. 'We were at swordplay with them a good five minutes. That's time enough for rape and robbery. The women were probably awake and going to fetch water and replenish the camp-fires. The robbers dealt with them first, to stop them raising the alarm. Those devils must have seized them beside the spring.'

'But the guard? How did they approach our sentry undetected?' asked Simon.

'That's my fault,' said Phillipe guiltily. 'Oh, I was alert enough, but I thought I saw one of the women approaching my post to bring me water. But it was a robber wearing a woman's hooded cloak. He must have taken it from one of his defiled victims. I turned to thank "her", and the next thing I knew I was lying on the ground, with my head ringing from the robber's blow. Pierre was just running him through. I drew my sword and joined in as the other murderers attacked us.'

'It was a cry and your sword being drawn that finally woke me,' said Belami. 'The blow to your head and Pierre's swordplay must have roused me a moment before, but I clearly remember the sound of a sword leaving its sheath. Well done, lads, you have acquitted yourselves like true Templar sergents.'

They knelt for a short prayer on behalf of their murdered comrades. All of them were mystified by the disappearance of the only other cadet, Etienne Colmar, the young man from Flanders.

The mystery was solved when they found him dead, impaled to a tree by a lance. He had also been unarmoured. Obviously the deed had been done by the mounted renegade knight. The other murderers had been armed only with swords and daggers.

The three dead cadets were buried side by side, with crosses of roughly bound branches set above their murdered bodies.

Simon saluted them with his sword, his face taut with grief. 'You're right, Belami, we should go in and avenge them. That rat's nest must be smoked out, and those vermin exterminated.' The others nodded their agreement.

'Now,' ordered the veteran, 'we must get to the commanderie outside Orange as quickly as possible. I want de Montdidier, the Marshal there, to let me have half his men right away. We must hit de Malfoy while his cut-throats are still groggy.'

A few hours later, Belami was raging with impatience, facing the second-in-command at this Templar outpost. Eugene de Montdidier, the middle-aged Commanding-Marshal, had been laid low by a savage attack of arnaldia, one of the most hazardous fevers of the Holy Land. The veteran Crusader would have acceded to Belami's request without hesitation but, by the Devil's bad luck, he was raving in delirium when the pilgrim caravan arrived.

His deputy, Louis de Carlo, another old Crusader, was adamant. He flatly refused to weaken the garrison while his commander was *hors de combat*. Nothing that Belami could say or do seemed to shift his stance, or change his attitude. He offered the pilgrims a safe haven in the commanderie's courtyard, and aid and nostrums for the sick and wounded, but he regretfully denied Belami the reinforcement of a single man-at-arms.

The Templar commanderie guarded the eastern end of a tall bridge, originally built by the Romans, spanning the Rhône and carrying the western route of pilgrimage across the river to the city of Orange.

It was a vital link in the strategic chain of Templar fortresses and the old Crusader had a valid argument in maintaining its full strength. However, Belami's powers of persuasion were those of a veteran Crusader who had experienced even more service than had the second-in-command. Reluctantly, the incumbent temporary Marshal finally yielded a miserly nine men-at-arms, leaving the garrison to be defended by the thirty-one Templar auxiliaries who remained.

Unfortunately, Robert de Burgh and Homfroi de Saint Simeon, the garrison's most experienced Templar knights, were absent in Orange.

'They have gone to the city for a meeting of the Templar Chapter at the Abbey. Were they here, Belami, I could safely entrust my duties to them. They have local knowledge of the region and would be invaluable. Can't you wait until they return? Of course, I see your argument, that de Malfoy is vulnerable at present because of his losses and the failure of his attack. But nine men-at-arms is all I can spare you. God be with you, Belami.'

'That makes thirteen of us,' replied the veteran sergeant. 'The good Lord had that number at the last supper. We'll hit the renegades at the same time as they hit us, just before dawn.'

'Be cautious, Belami,' the old crusader warned him. 'The Gorge de l'Ardèche is a perilous place. High rocky cliffs and the winding river make the perfect spot for an ambush.'

Irked by the second-in-command's continual carping, the veteran, for once, let his impatience to get even with de Malfoy override his better judgement. Sergeant Louis de Carlo, the fat old temporary commander, was long past fighting himself, but he had been a tough soldier in his day and knew what burned in Belami's heart. At midnight he watched him ride out with the three cadets and nine mounted men-at-arms, and deep inside himself he longed to join them.

Belami had two foresters among his small force. Their local knowledge gave him an edge. It was past two o'clock in the morning when they reached the entrance to the Gorge. The moon had risen late and gave them enough light to push into the gloomy depths of the precipitous valley, winding along either side of the Ardèche River.

So far, they had progressed a mile into the canyon without discovery. Their horses' hooves were muffled with sacking and they moved silently. Still Belami was uneasy.

'There is no guard,' he muttered to Simon.

'That is strange for an experienced knight like de Malfoy,' Simon whispered back. 'There was a barrel of wine missing from the de Nofrenoy wagon. The renegades may be sleeping off their drinking.'

Belami nodded. 'You could be right, Simon. Beaten men drown the memory of defeat in wine. Let us hope they sleep soundly.'

Guided by the two foresters, they wound their silent way up the Gorge. Suddenly the leading forester stopped as the moon rode out from behind a cloud. His finger rose to his lips. Belami advanced quietly to join him and motioned to the rest of them to move up beside him. Not a word was spoken.

Before them, a group of blanketed men lay sprawled around a dying camp-fire. The Templar crossbowmen slid behind cover and took aim. Simon quietly unslung his yew-bow. Belami nodded his head and the archers fired simultaneously. The five crossbow bolts thudded into the blanketed shapes on the ground and Simon's first arrow transfixed the huddled form of the seated watchman. Belami immediately knew that they had been duped. Their targets were blanket-wrapped dummies. Suddenly a shower of arrows, fired from the rocks above, thudded down around them. Two sank home into Belami's men, reducing him to a command of ten.

The rest of them had fallen flat behind such cover as they could find. This move was greeted with jeers and catcalls from the unseen renegades. Over-confident, they now made a fatal mistake. Thinking their opponents had suffered far more casualties than they actually had, the jubilant robbers left their cover and ran down the steep slope to finish the job.

The Templar force played dead until only a few yards separated them from their assailants. Then they rose and fired, Simon loosing shaft after shaft in rapid succession. Every crossbow bolt found its shrieking mark and the Norman's arrows mowed the outlaws down, one by one. Their charge wilted, and shrieking with terror, they turned to flight. Remounting their horses, the Templars thundered after them, cutting down their demoralized opponents as they ran.

Belami brought one tall robber to the ground with a stunning blow; leapt from the saddle and had his poniard at the man's throat before he recovered consciousness. 'Where is de Malfoy?' grated the veteran, his dagger blade shaking with fury. There was no mercy in his eyes.

The terrified robber replied groggily, 'Gone to attack the commanderie. He's planned it for a long time. De Malfoy left the valley by a secret route, through the caves near the entrance. Our ambush was to hold you, while he hit the Templar stronghold!'

'He must be mad. The garrison can easily hold him off.' Belami was puzzled by the outlawed knight's apparent folly. 'If there's more to tell, say it now, or I'll cut off your ears.' There was nothing melodramatic in Belami's words. He meant exactly what he said.

The robber continued hurriedly: 'They're disguised as pilgrims. The western route of pilgrimage crosses the bridge. The guards will suspect nothing.'

'Hell-fire!' cried Belami. 'Back, *mes braves*, or it will be too late.'

'Mercy!' shrieked the robber.

'God's mercy is not so easily earned. You betrayed your comrades. Die!' The veteran's dagger, plunged into the man's heart, silencing his babbling pleas. The Templars leapt back into their saddles and, as the dawn light filtered into the gloomy depths of the valley, they rode out of it like men possessed.

It had taken two hours to make their silent approach. They came thundering out of the Gorge in minutes and covered the distance to the bridge in half an hour of hard riding. As they rounded the last bend before the bridge, they saw an oily cloud of black smoke rising from the commanderie. Reining in their foaming horses, they cursed or prayed as their fear dictated. Approaching the bridge from the other side the triumphant de Malfoy was leading his outlaws, every man heavily laden with loot. This was to be their undoing. Reluctant to drop their rich booty, they hesitated for a few fatal moments. The eleven avengers, white-hot with fury, swept down the road and hit them like an avalanche.

Belami's men were armed with lances. The deadly steel-tipped ash spears cleaved the robbers through like spitted meat. From then on it was out swords and a mêlée of slashing blades, glinting in the dawn light.

Although outnumbered four to one, Belami's berserker force cut their way through the bulk of de Malfoy's men.

The fact that the robbers had been caught halfway across the bridge was another factor in their second resounding defeat. Totally demoralized, they fled. '*Sauve qui peut*!' was the despairing cry as they jostled past de Malfoy. He cursed and cut down his own men as they swept around him.

Simon's arrows accounted for three more, as he fired from the saddle. Belami's battle-axe lopped the limbs off another four screaming robbers. The Templar force hacked down twenty of the renegades and the cross-bowmen picked off the others. It was a massacre.

De Malfoy was left alone on his curvetting black charger, his sword running red from the blood of his own men. One other outlaw remained with him; a slim, fair-haired youth who now tried to make his escape by riding, lance couched, at Simon who was nearest.

De Malfoy raised his sword and threw it into the river below. '*Je me rends*!' he shouted hoarsely. 'I am a dubbed knight and can pay a heavy ransom.'

Simon ignored the charging horseman and bent his warbow. 'Here is your ransom!' he cried and the heavy bowstring twanged. The shaft whirred across the bridge and sank up to its fletching in de Malfoy's red-surcoated chest.

With a loud groan, he leaned out of his high saddle and

crashed down onto the stone parapet. In his death agony he twisted round, sliding over the edge of the tall bridge. De Malfoy was already dead as he splashed down into the foaming Rhône and disappeared in the welter of white water.

'Look out!' Belami's warning came too late, as the charging renegade's lance tore into Simon's right side. The young Norman just had time to half-turn in his saddle, dropping his bow and reaching for his sword. Then the lance hit him, a glancing blow but slicing a deep gash in his chain-mail and the flesh beneath. Simon reeled in the saddle as the escaping renegade charged past.

Belami spurred his horse forward to intercept him. Phillipe and Pierre closed in on either side of Simon, preventing him from falling from Pegase.

The fair-haired robber dropped his lance and drew his sword to parry Belami's blow. The battle-axe sheared clean through the steel blade and smashed into the terrified young renegade's effeminate face, bloodily splitting it in two. He died instantly.

Bent back across the cruppers of his galloping horse, the dead outlaw was carried off up the valley.

Belami cantered over to Simon and inspected his wound. 'It's deep,' he said, 'but he'll live.'

The mêlée had lasted barely three minutes from start to finish.

'Maria!' gasped Simon, in an agonized whisper. 'See to Maria, Belami.'

'Don't fret, boy. Phillipe, Pierre . . . get him tended to immediately. I'll find the girl.'

Belami galloped over the bridge and clattered through the open gates of the Templar stronghold. The fact that these heavy double doors were standing agape indicated the complete surprise engendered by de Malfoy's ruse.

The courtyard was littered with pathetic bundles of blood-stained cloth that once had been the pilgrims. Their looted wagons were still burning, causing the thick smoke that the returning Templars had seen.

Whilst Simon was helped by his comrades, Belami

dismounted, picking his way through the dead bodies of the slaughtered garrison and heading for the keep.

Most of the murdered Templars still had their weapons sheathed. They had died without returning a blow. But one or two others had sold their lives at the price of a dead murderer.

The second-in-command, old Sergent de Carlo, was one of the few who had struck back. Two robbers, one with a gaping throat and the other with his skull split in half, lay in a contorted heap in front of the veteran sergent's body. He was pinned to the door of the keep by a lance. 'At least Louis died a soldier's death,' muttered Belami, easing out the lance and deftly catching de Carlo's heavy body as it slumped to the ground.

The Templar entered the keep, knowing full well what he would find. De Malfoy had chosen the chapel to carry out the worst of his appalling crimes. The sick Marshal de Montdidier had been hacked to pieces as he lay raving in delirium. His monkish cell was like an abattoir.

In the Templar chapel, the renegades had urinated and defecated on the altar, smashing every religious symbol that they could find. Their Devil's work was foully evident in the number of raped and disembowelled women lying spreadeagled over the altar steps.

Belami crossed himself at the revolting sight, even his hardened stomach turning at the reeking stench that hung in the mephitic air. The sense of evil was over-powering.

A whimpering sound led the disgusted veteran over to the small vestry. Sword drawn, he kicked open the door.

Maria lay bound with a cut bell-rope to a table, on which a blood-stained altar cloth had been laid.

She alone of all the ravished women, young and old, had not been disembowelled. Her body was covered in bruises and spattered with filth. Her once lovely face was dreadfully swollen from a bad beating and her mouth hung open in shocked horror. A dreadful whimpering sound came from her. When Belami released her bonds, she shrank from him in piteous terror.

The Templar sergeant tenderly picked her up in his powerful right arm, and supported her limp body with the stump of his left waist.

He held her close to his chest, like a father carrying a frightened child. Gently he bore her out of that dreadful place, into the sunlight.

As they emerged from the charnel-house, Simon, supported by Phillipe and Pierre, saw who Belami was carrying. The youngster, pale as death from loss of blood, croaked out: 'Maria!'

'She lives,' said Belami simply. Simon gave a groan and slumped unconscious in his comrades' arms.

Belami looked up as a party of Templars rode into the smoke-filled courtyard. It was led by the two absent knights, returning from the Chapter-house's meeting at the Abbey of Orange.

Even these experienced Crusaders blenched at the scene of wholesale slaughter that greeted them. The men-at-arms had uncovered another dreadful sight. The old Italian silver-smith, de Nofrenoy, had been impaled on a sharpened stake. Evidently, he had been reluctant to divulge where he had hidden his silver. His wagon had been literally taken apart before de Malfoy had found the secret cache, cleverly concealed in a false-bottomed water-barrel.

Belami handed over the ravaged girl to the care of the Templars and crisply reported the whole story of his mistaken attempt to wipe out de Malfoy.

The veteran sergeant spared himself nothing in the telling. 'It was all my fault, sir knight,' he told de Burgh.

'On the contrary, Sergeant Belami.' The experienced Crusader knew the veteran's reputation of old. 'De Malfoy must have planned this attack when he found out that we had left for the Chapter meeting at the Abbey. Your counter-attack made his plans misfire. He had to leave some of his men behind to contain your force. That Devil's spawn had spies everywhere. My men tell me your cadets did well. I congratulate you, Belami, *not* censure you!'

Despite de Burgh's wise assessment of the situation, the

old soldier blamed himself. 'Never let anger govern your decisions,' he told his remaining cadets, as he saw Simon comfortably placed in a Templar wagon for the journey to the hospital at Orange. 'I'll visit you as soon as I've finished my full report,' he told the wounded boy.

A messenger had been sent to the city and some nuns, Sisters of Mercy from Saint Lazarus, came to the commanderie to take charge of Maria. 'Poor child!' said Belami. 'Her mind has gone. I'll bet my good right hand that black-livered swine de Malfoy made her watch her father's impalement.'

'How can men do such bestial deeds?' Phillipe was aghast.

'They are possessed by the denizens of the nether-pit,' said de Burgh. 'They allow their carnal desires to control their minds and bodies, until they have sunk below the level of the beast. Then, under the spiritual law of "like-attracts-like", their souls are taken over by demons, who enter their debased bodies and use them like puppets.'

Belami and the rest of the men-at-arms cleaned out the desecrated chapel and the Abbot, who had returned with the Templars, reconsecrated the altar.

'This is the work of the blackest witchcraft. De Malfoy must have been a powerful sorcerer to have wreaked such vengeance against the house of Our Lady. The chapel still reeks of evil. Only time, great piety, prayer and love will restore its air of sanctity. Holy ritual by itself is not enough to drive out the awful feeling of sin from this ravaged church.'

The Abbot had been a Crusader. Though he had seen many terrible sights, there was something so diabolic about de Malfoy's systematic foulness that he felt his spirit shrink within him.

When he had heard Belami's confession, he agreed with de Burgh. 'You cannot blame yourself, my son. Because of what you did, that spawn of Satan is dead at last. God alone, he knows what other dreadful harm he would have wrought. That fair-haired young fiend, whom they tell me you killed, was his devil's acolyte, de Malfoy's perverted altar-boy. You have rid this part of the land of great evil. *Te absolvo* Belami, my son. Go with God!'

Poor Maria stared mindlessly into space while the good Sisters healed her body. When Belami went to see the Mother Superior, she told him: 'The child will never let another man touch her. In time we may reach her mind. We will look after her. Like a number of our blessed saints, the poor child has been cruelly martyred. Our Blessed Lady is loving and compassionate, especially to those so dreadfully abused by the bestiality of men.'

The gentle Mother Superior shuddered, then reassured him: 'Maria is an orphan. We will receive her into our Order. It is the Will of God, and Our Blessed Virgin.'

Belami knew this was the best thing for the girl, but he doubted if her ravaged mind would ever recover. When he went to visit Simon, he told him several patent untruths to reassure his favourite pupil. 'Maria's coming along well and sends her love,' he said, without blinking his shrewd, bright eyes. 'She's going to stay with the good Sisters until she can be collected by her Italian relatives,' he continued, with total conviction.

Simon, despite the Hospitaller's soporific herbs, was still in considerable pain and his drugged mind detected no falsehood in Belami's report. He felt only a great sense of relief that Maria was being cared for so well. With a heavy sigh, the young Norman let go his tenuous hold on consciousness and lapsed into a deep, healing sleep.

5

CORSAIRS

Both Phillipe and Pierre had received only minor wounds during the mêlée on the bridge, but with Simon's more serious gash in his right side it was two weeks before he could put foot to floor.

All during the crisis of Simon's suffering, Belami and his two comrades had kept a ceaseless watch, bathing the jagged wound with compresses soaked in witch-hazel, and applying dressings of clean linen dipped in boiled wine-vinegar. The Hospitaller, an elderly Brabanter, approved of these measures and bustled around with a Greek sea-sponge, bathing Simon's fever-racked body with cool spring water liberally laced with hyssop.

Between them they kept the flies away from the youngster's open wound, till his body fluids had closed the gap, temporarily held together with clean thorns. The Hospitallers had learnt much about the healing arts from their Saracen opponents in the Holy Land.

For four days the crisis raged in Simon's torn body. By the fifth dawn his fever had abated, like a summer gale, and his skin was cool to the touch.

When he opened his eyes, he saw Belami's grinning face. Mistily, he focused on the veteran's beaming smile. 'Belami!' he croaked, his lips painfully cracked by the fever. The old soldier's eyes were moist as he held a wet sponge to Simon's lips. Its oil and witch-hazel dressing soothed the cracked skin and the youngster was able to drink some cool spring-water through a reed. All the while Phillipe and Pierre, who had been sleeping outside Simon's small bedchamber, held their comrade comfortably propped up between them.

Their venture had brought all four of them very close. It is the only virtue of combat, that those who share its hardships and dangers and fight side by side find a comradeship stronger than brotherly love. The memory of the horror, the pain and the fear is thus sublimated by the shared experience of battle and, mercifully, that intense feeling of unity remains. Only death itself ends this hold on each comrade-in-arms. It is the sole worthwhile experience in war.

During Simon's delirium, his subtle-body had left his tortured physical form, as it lay twisting and turning on the wooden slatted bed.

The Simon who flew high above a misty landscape felt no pain, from the moment of release from his material body until he returned to it, as the height of his fever passed.

He skimmed across the alien plains, rivers, hills and craggy cliffs of the same landscape that had always been the setting for his strange flying dreams. Now he knew for whom he was searching: his father, Odo de Saint Amand.

Below him the mist would sometimes swirl into a writhing sea of shroud-grey clouds, seething over the ground.

Once again, nightmare forms would rise like the drowned dead to the turbulent surface, reaching up with skeletal hands to snatch at his flying form, their leering mouths agape with a terrible hatred. One of them was the arrow-pierced, rotting form of Etienne de Malfoy, his eyeless sockets glowing with virulent green fire and the foul stench of death issuing from his lipless mouth. Then the dawn would come and with it Simon's subtle counterpart was drawn swiftly back into his pain-racked body. It was the fifth morning when his suffering became bearable and the young Norman woke to the caring comradeship of his three close friends.

'*Inshallah*!' said Belami, and hugged Simon's emaciated body. The fever had burned off any excess body fat that the young man had on his sinewy frame. He looked like a young Jesus. 'Some Provençal beef and good red wine is what you need, *mon brave*. You'll be fighting fit in no time.'

The experienced Hospitaller, André Devois, started Simon off with bread soaked in goat's milk, and quickly weaned him on to more substantial fare. Within three days, the young Norman was making rapid progress. But with his returning health, Simon's guilt surfaced and nagged unceasingly, disturbing his much-needed sleep.

Belami took a firm stance on this. 'You have no reason to blame yourself, *mon ami*,' he insisted. 'I know your monkish upbringing has loaded you with a sense of sin. Your love for Maria is *not* a sinful thing. The girl is doing well and she is lucky not to have fared as badly as the others. The Good Lord and Our Blessed Mother protected her.'

Belami crossed himself, as much for his glib lies as for the mention of the Virgin's name. Though a religious man in the sense of his unswerving fidelity to Christianity, the old soldier's compassion had a special quality that had come from his long experience of the Holy Land. It was truly ecumenical. This sensitivity might seem incompatible with such an effective killing-machine, but Belami was far more than that.

Simon had this same innate sense of compassion, though he was nearly eighteen years old and had already killed seven or eight men; but these had all been criminals bent on killing him or his comrades. He felt no guilt about this, yet his dalliance with Maria had raised many doubts in his young mind. These were now torturing his conscience.

Belami set about dispersing them as quickly as he could. 'You have broken no vows and I swear you had no time to take the girl's virginity. You are both as innocent as new-born babes, so forget it. Take my rede on it, Simon. It is better so.'

The healing process and the youngster's rapidly return-ing strength soon brought Simon out of the darkness of guilt and into the light of a new resolve. He was more determined than ever to justify his dead father's faith in his destiny, and to reach the Holy Land as soon as possible. However, this presented a problem. Due to the delay caused by Simon's wound, the four comrades found that on arrival in Marseilles, they had missed the Templar ship which they had intended to be their transport.

This dismayed the three sergent-cadets, but Belami was more resourceful and approached the nearest ship loading supplies and reinforcements for the Holy Land. This vessel, a broad-beamed, Venetian-built transport, had cramped accommodation within its ninety-foot length for thirty horses and one hundred men. Its deep draught and high, curved sides of stout timbers, copper-nailed to heavy wooden scantlings and massive ribs, gave just sufficient room for its passengers, human and animal, cargo and crew. The usual Venetian rig of lateen-sails had been replaced, on both the fore-mast and the main-mast, by square rigs. This was more in accordance with North-ern European custom than Mediterranean practice. There was a slight disadvantage in less ease of handling, but this was offset by the sturdiness of the structure. Furthermore it allowed the fitting of small fighting-tops to each mast-head. These served as lookout crow's-nests, or contained bowmen as well as handy rocks and amphorae of oil to drop on other ships' crews attempting to board. The lofty positions were reached by climbing 'rat-lines', rope-ladders attached to the rigging.

The bulky vessel was owned by the Order of Hospital-lers. This contemporary Order of monkish knights was a rival military organization, and often clashed at its highest levels with the Templars. But that rivalry did not extend beyond good-natured banter between their competitive ranks of sergents.

Belami made friendly overtures to a Hospitaller ser-gent, Jean Condamine, as grizzled a warrior as the veteran himself. Condamine had the additional burden of being medical orderly to the Knights Hospitallers, in their dedicated work of healing.

Members of this alternative corps of sergents were also

not expected to observe total abstinence and a few flagons of Provençal wine proved to be the right lubricant to set the wheels in motion. Belami soon persuaded his opposite number in the Corps of Sergent Hospitallers to provide passage for the four Templars and their horses. The latter would have been the more difficult proposition, but it so happened that on this voyage, only twenty Hospitaller horses were being transported on the *Saint Lazarus*.

The bulk of the passengers were crossbowmen and sergents, as well as some mercenaries who had joined the crew as extra protection. This was a very real need, as Barbary Coast pirates, corsairs from the North African coast, had recently been active and had succeeded in securing several valuable prizes.

For this reason, the Hospitaller ship was also armed with two mangonels, one in the bows and the other sited on the aft poop-deck, both weapons being capable of slinging heavy rocks over a hundred yards.

This was another reason Belami had chosen the vessel out of the fifty or so cogs, lateen-sailed merchantmen and other large trading and fishing vessels which lined the *quais* at Marseilles.

They still had several days to wait before embarking, so Belami set out to show his comrades how to pass the time in this most important port on the western Mediterranean coast. With an instinct born of long experience, Belami had nosed out a small wine shop that had decent accommodation attached to it. With this lodging went good food and excellent local wine. There was also a genial landlord, who had once been a mercenary himself, and a buxom wife and three daughters to complete the household of hardworking, hospitable Provençals.

'This is far better than bothering the local Templar garrison with four temporary guests,' said Belami, with a sly grin. 'I have reported to the local Marshal and said that we are staying with old friends. He is an easygoing knight, for a Templar, and had heard about our contretemps at the commanderie. He voiced no objections to the present situation. In fact, he congratulated us on removing de Malfoy.'

'Didn't he want to know more about the slaughter of the pilgrims?' asked Phillipe tactlessly.

'Not in detail,' replied Belami curtly. 'Such losses happen from time to time, and de Malfoy had previously wiped out other small groups in a similar fashion. Our removal of that foul stain on knightly chivalry has made us *persona grata* with the local Templars and the Hospitaller garrison. Otherwise, they and our comrades at Orange would have been forced to smoke out that nest of vipers themselves.

'So' – he beamed expansively – 'go and enjoy yourselves. There's plenty to see and do in Marseilles. Take my advice and get to know more about the Order of Hospitallers and their work. Our Grand Masters may not always agree, but we unknighted sergents need to work in close liaison with each other, if we are to survive in the Holy Land.'

The others took Belami at his word and, through the veteran's ship-board contact, were soon made welcome among the group of Hospitaller sergents and men-at-arms with whom they would journey to the Crusade.

Whether the shock of his wound had affected Simon's memory of recent events, or because Belami's well-intentioned evasions had done their work, amid all the excitement of embarkation and the busy scene at Marseilles, he lost most of his guilt and only thought occasionally of Maria. As usual, Belami had been right.

The three Templar sergents learnt a lot from their contemporaries among the Hospitallers. As the lovely Italian girl's face faded from Simon's memory, his mind became filled with new and exciting information about the Holy Land. Apparently, many of the massive strongholds which had sprung up to guard the hard-won gains made by the Crusaders, had been built or enlarged by the Hospitallers. They were great constructors of both hospitals and castles, often reinforcing strongholds originally built by the Saracens and other Muslim nations throughout Palestine, Syria and the Lebanon.

The formidable Krak des Chevaliers, a great stone pile

of intricate fortifications, dominating the surrounding countryside with its massive keep and multiple towers, was largely constructed by the Hospitallers, though from time to time it was also garrisoned by Templars.

The three excited lads wandered around the busy port, accompanied by the same number of Hospitaller sergents. These other youngsters had been in Marseilles for two months, preparing supplies for the voyage, so they were well versed in local knowledge. They pointed out the Greek, Roman and Venetian influences on the growth of the bustling port, and took Simon, Phillipe and Pierre on a guided tour of the merchants and markets that jostled for priority in provisioning the many foreign vessels berthed alongside the *quais*.

There were also barges carrying wine from Dijon and Lyons, and wherries filled with fruit and vegetables from the countryside near Orange and other towns of the lower Rhône. Wagon-loads of meat and dairy-produce came in daily from the surrounding region, and the general excitement of the arrival and departure of the many kinds of shipping made a constant panorama of interest, for both visitors and locals.

Like the *quais* of Paris, the scents of spices and fruit kept the more hideous smells of the port at bay; even the aromas coming from the fish-market were swept clean by the constant sea-breezes. It all fascinated the sergent-cadets, and both Templars and Hospitallers enjoyed their comradeship, modestly enhanced by good Provençal red wine.

It was during this idyll of bustling peace that the three remaining cadets had the opportunity to be young again. Too much violence and heavy responsibility had temporarily dulled their enjoyment of life, but now their youthful high spirits reasserted themselves.

Pierre was a great asset in the rebuilding of his companions' morale, which in Simon's case had also been affected by his wound, and his unjustified guilt over the fate of Maria.

'I like this place. Marseilles has got an atmosphere that beats Paris,' Phillipe remarked ruminatively, as he sipped his wine from an olive-wood goblet. 'It's like the calm before the tempest.'

'It's the fish-market, *mon garçon*,' grinned Pierre. 'The stink coming from the rotting *fruits de mer* has a soporific effect, like opium. Give me the stench of stale wine at the Quai de Berçy, and the rich aroma of the sewage coming from the Seine, any time! Now that is what I call an atmosphere. There is nothing like Parisian shit to get you going, first thing in the morning.'

The young Templars and Hospitallers laughed uproariously, as much from the effect of the noon-day sun and the good red wine as at Pierre's raw joke.

But Phillipe, their quiet companion, now seemed to have fallen into a reverie, looking far out to sea as though he could see some vision beyond the horizon.

Simon noticed it first.

'What ails you, *mon gar*? You were miles away, just now.'

Phillipe gave a start, as though waking from a day-dream.

'It's just a feeling I've had. Last night I dreamt I was in the Holy Land, outside the gates of Acre, and nobody would let me in.'

'I should think not!' Pierre's cheerful voice joined in. 'After three weeks at sea, without a hot bath, it would be a miracle if they let any of us in!'

That morning, however, even Pierre's ebullience was not enough to dispel Phillipe's sense of foreboding.

'It's not healthy,' remarked Belami, when Simon told him. 'All this waste of time, hanging about Marseilles, gives the boy too much time to think. Phillipe is a serious lad, keen to get on to the Holy Land. That's all! Get him out into the countryside and keep his mind busy.' The veteran sergent paused, with a wry grin on his nut-brown face.

'And lay off the red wine at midday. It has a depressing effect, unless you sleep it off in the afternoon, or work it off in the arms of a good woman.'

Most of all, it was the local people who helped to restore Phillipe's youthful morale.

The Marseillais themselves were a colourful mixture of Gallic, Roman, Venetian, Iberian, Genoese and other sea-faring folk, who had settled in the environs of the port and around the delta of the Rhône, the Camargue. Simon and the others rode out to see this strange marshy land which, over the centuries, had risen from the mud and sand of the multiple channels of the wide river estuary.

The Romans had developed important centres at Arles and Aix-en-Provence, building hippodromes and amphitheatres for their chariot-racing and gladiatorial games, according to the whim of the ruling classes. As in the whole Roman Empire, this had been done by the slaves and when Rome fell many of these freed bondsmen had settled in the area. The amphitheatres were now used for storage or markets and the hippodromes made excellent stabling for the extensive trade in the wild horses which freely roamed the Camargue.

During these trips, Simon and his friends also learned about the structure of their rival military Order.

'The ranks are much the same,' said Marc Lamotte, a red-headed, efficient Hospitaller sergeant, three years older than Simon. 'We also have a Grand Master, who spends too much of his time fighting the Saracens and other heathens when he should be building more hospitals. We desperately need more accommodation for the homeless and the sick. I feel it is my bounden duty to concentrate on healing the sick and feeding the needy, rather than on killing healthy heathens.'

Simon smiled. 'It's not your fault, Marc. Leave the fighting to *our* military Order. We'll keep the routes of pilgrimage open for you, and you can get on with building your hospitals and refuges.'

'I wish it was that easy.' The Hospitaller shook his head ruefully. 'There are many wise and clever men among the heathen. They know a lot more than we do about the art of healing. My uncle was a Hospitaller who was once a prisoner in Isphahan, and he told me about the Arabs and their use of *massa*, the art of healing by the laying-on of hands.'

'It's the second time I've heard about that,' said Simon.

'Uncle Raoul and Bernard de Roubaix told me of such healing methods, back in Normandy.'

Simon's thoughts flew momentarily to de Creçy Manor, which now seemed a thousand leagues away. He sighed nostalgically, but his attention was soon recaptured by the Hospitaller's dissertation on his Order.

'We also have seneschals and marshals to administer our castles and hospitals, and a gonfanonier, who is entrusted with our sacred banners and who keeps our heraldic rolls and maintains points of order in our discipline. Then come the Knights Hospitaller themselves, good fighting men with the additional skills required to comfort the sick and dying; and finally, as you know, we sergents who are the "plaster" that holds the whole structure together.'

Their laughter rang with the good-humour of youth and shared experience. It felt good.

Simon's wound had healed well and the warm sea-water made bathing practical, thereby accelerating the whole process. Belami gave him a short work-out at swordplay and the Norman cadet stood up well to all the veteran's sly tricks.

'You let me win that round,' he laughed, as he knelt with one knee on his mentor's chest.

'I'm glad you think so,' growled the old soldier, whom Simon had neatly tripped. 'You're much better than you think you are, Simon.'

On their fifth night in Marseilles, they boarded the *Saint Lazarus* and, as dawn broke, she slipped her moorings and raised sail to catch the early morning breeze.

The current of the Rhône was not as strong as it had been in its long race for the sea. It gently eased them out into the fairway and the two square-rigged sails quickly bellied with the off-shore wind. They needed no harbour pilots to guide them to the open sea and soon they had passed the outer markers and were headed out into the breezy reaches of the Gulf of Lyons.

Simon, Belami, Phillipe and Pierre gazed over the stern-rail at the slowly receding shore. Each of them silently wondered what lay ahead.

The *Saint Lazarus* was a fine sea-boat, well designed and constructed for her work as a trans-Mediterranean transport. Slow and stately, she comfortably covered her average of some sixty sea miles a day.

Only Phillipe suffered from *mal de mer*, the exhausting price that the sea extracts from landsmen. Pierre had spent his boyhood in small boats and Belami had made many sea voyages in Templar vessels. Simon also had enjoyed many happy hours rowing on the lake on his uncle's estate, or swimming and boating on the long stretch of the River Andelle, close to the de Créçy domain. Their stomachs managed well enough and Phillipe soon recovered, so the whole crew and its eighty passengers 'shook down' well within a few hours of meeting the short swells of the great land-girt sea. Sunshine and blue skies soon produced a feeling of languorous pleasure that their light duties did little to dispel.

At dawn on their fifth day at sea, some 300 miles from Marseilles, this idyll was shattered. Until then the winds had held steady and the apple-bowed transport had ambled along at a steady three knots. Then the wind veered and faltered. This was an opportunity that was quickly seized by corsairs who had been following them at a discreet distance.

There were two pirate galleys – fast, handy vessels favoured by the corsairs of the Barbary Coast. Their tactics had been skilful; following the lights of the transport vessel guided by a lookout, precariously perched at their lateen-sailed mast-head. This meant that the unlit pirate vessels were nearly invisible, hull down near the horizon. In contrast, the Hospitaller ship had unwisely used a poop-lantern, safe enough for navigation in ordinary conditions but perilous in pirate-infested waters.

As the wind failed the corsairs struck, increasing the beat of their galley's oars until they rapidly came within range of the mangonels which both galleys carried. They were spotted immediately they appeared over the horizon, and the transport's drummer sounded the alarm.

The Hospitaller knight, Gervais de Redon, was more

experienced in dealing with the sick than in commanding a sea-battle, but his veteran Sergent Condamine was well-versed in this kind of warfare. He immediately enlisted Belami's aid and gave him command of the mercenaries. With the Templar sergents, this gave Belami thirty men. He quickly mustered them and told them to keep out of sight until the corsairs attempted to board them. They were to be his strategic reserve.

Jean Condamine sent twenty of his crossbowmen to join them, holding back the other thirty, ready to engage the enemy at long range.

At 200 yards' distance, the corsairs opened fire with their more powerful mangonels. At first the large smooth rocks that these hurled splashed into the sea nearby, but, on closing the range, they whirred over the transport's mast-head or holed her sails.

As soon as the pirate galleys came within range of the transport, Jean Condamine advised de Redon to open fire and, by a lucky chance, the third shot from the aft-mangonel planted a goodly sized rock on the second galley, approaching their port-side. It swept two corsairs off the fore-deck, and their mangled corpses fell into the galley's wake.

The pirates gained two more hits, their rocks killing a crossbowman instantly with a chest-crushing blow, and maiming a horse in its padded stall below. As soon as they started to register hits on the transport, the corsair captains switched from catapulting rocks to hurling Greek-fire. These weapons were hefty sealed earthenware pots, filled with an inflammable mixture of pitch, oil and naphtha. When the pitchers broke, the mixture spontaneously burst into flames and water was ineffective in dousing it. Vinegar was the recommended liquid used to combat Greek-fire. For this reason the sides of the transport had hides well soaked in a vinegar mixture draped over the gunwales, and other hides wetted with the same preparation were kept ready in buckets beside the two masts.

As soon as the Greek-fire came inboard, the men-at-arms and the crew tackled the flames with these extinguishers. The lack of wind, which had played them into the corsairs' hands, now failed to fan the chemical fires and they were soon extinguished.

Meanwhile, the crossbowmen had been keeping up a steady fire on both galleys, which were now rapidly closing in on either side. Several Hospitaller crossbow bolts had found their mark, cutting down a dozen pirates. Still the corsairs were undeterred and swept in for the kill.

Grappling lines attached to four-pronged hooks were swung across the rapidly narrowing gaps. Several of these grapnels took hold of various parts of the transport's bulwarks, one pinning a shrieking sailor to the port-side rail.

Neither pirate galley suspected Belami's stratagem of the hidden men-at-arms. The triumphant yells when the Moorish crew ranged alongside were loudly overconfident.

Several of the galleys' oars had splintered as the pirate vessels closed in for boarding, badly injuring the rowers behind them as their heavy hafts jerked back viciously onto the chained slaves. Swarms of corsairs stood by their ship's inboard rail, ready to climb up the pronounced 'tumblehome' of the high-sided transport vessel.

All the time, the Hospitaller crossbowmen poured down a deadly shower of whirring bolts. Many pirates screamed their last battle-cry as these short shafts thudded home into their lightly-armoured, brown bodies. Even so, hordes of corsairs climbed hand over hand up the grappling ropes, or swung down onto the Hospitaller ship from their galley's rigging.

In line with Barbary Coast tactics, the attack was synchronized from both sides; each galley simultaneously sending a large boarding-party across the narrow gaps separating them from their victim.

Simon had been posted on the aft-castle of the high quarter-deck. From there, he now poured a deadly fire from his Welsh longbow into the boarding corsairs. Shaft after shaft feathered home into screaming Moors, some arrows actually nailing them to the transport's wooden sides. Then Belami was upon them, his two-headed Danish battle-axe crunching through steel helmets, chain-mail and reinforced round shields like parchment.

Beside him, Phillipe and Pierre wielded their heavy Crusader blades with all the skill Belami had drilled into them. From their concealed positions, the rest of the Templar's command suddenly emerged to face the surprised corsairs. The Hospitaller sergents first used their lances, then, as each spear-point pierced a screaming victim, they drew their swords and hacked a gory path to the ship's rails.

'Keep close together!' yelled Belami. 'Force them back to the rails!'

Old Condamine, the wily Hospitaller veteran, rushed down with Simon from the aft-castle and together they hewed their way towards Belami. In a moment, the tables were turned. Where triumphant Moors had swarmed aboard, piles of corsair corpses now littered the transport's deck. Despite the sea-breeze the whole ship reeked of disembowelment and death. Stones crashed down from the transport's fighting-tops and small barrels of flaming oil and pitch were hurled into the waists of both pirate-galleys. All the while, the withering shower of Hospitaller crossbow bolts rained down on the pirate crews.

With yells of despair, some of the trapped corsairs tried to leap back onto their galleys, many of them falling with a death-shriek between the grinding sides of the three vessels.

'They're breaking!' shouted Belami. 'One last charge and we've won!' The sergent's small force responded with renewed fury; even the crossbowmen dropped their weapons and waded in with their reeking swords.

Suddenly, it was a slaughter; a massacre of Moors, demoralized beyond rallying. Hospitaller blades quickly severed the grappling-ropes and the stricken galleys slowly drifted apart, on either side. One was uncontrollably ablaze, as her own store of inflammable missiles exploded in the flames. The other galley, badly mauled and under-oared, struggled to pull slowly away from its intended victim, which had so quickly turned into a deadly avenger.

Simon and the surviving crossbowmen still kept up a brisk fire, mowing down any corsair trying to deal with the flames on either galley.

'The wind!' shouted Condamine. 'See! The sails are filling.'

With a hoarse cheer, the Hospitallers and their allies lent a hand to make sail and the cumbersome transport slowly forged ahead, soon leaving the ravaged galleys far behind. One of them was sinking. The other was hopelessly crippled.

Breathless with their efforts, their blood-spattered mailed chests heaving as they gulped in the fresh sea breeze, the victorious Crusaders paused to bear-hug their comrades and count the cost of the corsairs' defeat.

Twenty of the Hospitallers, crossbowmen and men-at-arms, lay dead. A dozen more were wounded, some seriously. To Simon's horror, Phillipe was one of these, a Moorish arrow between his ribs. He lay supported by a weeping Pierre de Montjoie while Condamine and Belami tended to his deep wound. As Simon bent over his dying friend, Phillipe's eyes fluttered open, a question in their failing depths.

'We won!' said Belami. 'We sent them back to Hell, Comrade!'

'God be praised!' whispered Phillipe, and smiled. His faint grin turned into the rictus of death as the Dark Angel enshrouded him. Tears flowing freely, Pierre and Simon hugged their dead friend.

The Hospitaller sergent took Belami aside. 'We will bury them at sea. It is our custom.'

'Not Phillipe de Mauray, you won't! I promised him the Holy Land and there we'll bury the boy.'

'So shall it be, Belami,' growled the Hospitaller. 'There's an empty water-barrel to spare. We'll pickle the brave lad in brine.'

And so they did, heavily salting the vinegared water and gently lowering Philippe's body into the preserving mixture. The iron hoops were hammered down over the lid and the water-cask became a coffin for a brave young Templar.

The cost had been high, but the sea-battle had ended in a resounding defeat for the much feared Barbary Coast corsairs.

'When my turns comes,' Pierre de Montjoie said to Simon, 'bury me in the Holy Land. If possible, wherever we bury Phillipe.'

As the youngster burst into hot tears, Simon held him close.

The elderly Hospitaller commander, de Redon, had acquitted himself well in the general mêlée, spitting one corsair on his sword and smashing another's skull with his mace. Now, he skilfully attended to the wounded, staunching their bleeding and dressing their wounds, with his store of clean linen, ointments and herbal extracts.

Gervais de Redon had no head for battle-command, but he was a superb physician and healer.

The *Saint Lazarus* made landfall in Sicily, and refilled her water-barrels, replenishing her stores with fresh meat and fruit which the Hospitallers considered to be a prophylactic against fever, and a necessary laxative where shipboard life restricted normal exercise.

From Syracuse the transport set off on the longest leg of the journey to the Holy Land, the one-thousand-mile voyage to Acre. Their ship would avoid landing in Cyprus, which was under a hostile dictatorship, and there was to be no call this voyage at Malta.

Cyprus was still smarting from the rapine and slaughter visited on that beautiful island by the Frankish Crusader Reynald de Châtillon, who had taken it over after a vicious campaign. It was now under a stable autocracy headed by Ducas Isaac Comnenus, who had set himself up as Emperor, and the islanders charged visiting Hospitaller and Templar ships very high prices for revictualling. In that climate of hatred, it was safer and more economical to head straight for Acre, the main Crusader port in the Holy Land.

6
ACRE, THE GATE TO OUTREMER

The Hospitaller transport was greeted by the cheering crowds which lined the long battlemented walls of Acre. Coloured banners, pennants and guidons belonging to Frankish knights were set alongside the sombre gonfalons of the Hospitaller and Templar garrisons, all of them waving jauntily in the strong sea breeze.

The eight-pointed silver Cross of Malta, starkly defined by its black field, fluttered from the mainmast of the *Saint Lazarus* as she rounded the headland and sailed majestically past the fortified island known as the Tower of Flies. Another twenty minutes and she had dropped anchor under the grim walls of Acre.

Because of her deep draught the ship was moored alongside the jutting mole. It was a tricky task transferring the valuable war-horses from their cramped quarters in the ship's hold across the swaying gangplank. All the animals were terrified and unsteady on their legs from lack of exercise. The only way the heavy destriers could be coaxed on to the thick planks of the landing ramp was to blindfold them and lead them across with their rider and a familiar ostler on each side, soothing and encouraging them.

However, once they set hoof on dry land the big chargers recovered quickly, soon cantering away their unwelcome ship-board lassitude.

Pegase nuzzled Simon's hand, as they transferred from

ship to shore, and when his young rider remounted at the end of the mole, the great Norman war-horse pranced and curvetted ecstatically.

Calaban, Belami's horse, was second across and also rapidly regained his accustomed élan, happy once again to feel the veteran's sturdy thighs astride his broad back.

Acre's sea-gate stood open to welcome the long-awaited and much-needed cargo of vital supplies. The reinforcements of heavy cavalry and well-trained person-nel were especially appreciated, and the arrival of the skilled Hospitallers gave new hope to the wounded and the sick, at present in the care of the city's woefully undermanned Hospital staff, some of whom were them-selves down with fever.

The feeling of heartfelt relief was apparent. The whole city was en fête.

Those of the new arrivals who were strangers to the Holy Land were agog with excitement, and all of them were delighted by the warmth of the welcome they received. The Hospitaller ship's commander thanked his Templar guests for their gallant help, expressed his regrets at Phillipe's death and offered them the hospitality of his Order in Acre. But as there was a small garrison of Templars in the city, Belami was obliged to report there first. Jean Condamine embraced them warmly. 'Com-rades in battle, friends for ever,' he said simply.

Phillipe's body was carried ashore with due reverence and, as agreed between the three Templars, he was buried, still embalmed in the water barrel, directly outside the walls. This was the spot where, had he lived, he would have first set foot in the Holy Land. Belami had a natural sense of what was fitting.

'That's where I would like to be buried,' Pierre de Montjoie reminded Simon of his promise.

'Let's hope it doesn't come to that,' replied the young Norman.

'I can think of a lot worse places for a grave,' remarked Belami. 'With the stone walls of Acre behind your head and the warm waters of the landlocked sea at your feet, it makes a fitting resting-place for a Crusader.'

They silently prayed for the repose of Phillipe's soul, their hands resting on the pommels of their drawn swords, points down in the ground, Crusader-fashion. Then they remounted and cantered through the city's massive gates, making their way through the narrow, crowded streets of the main Crusader fort.

Inside the walls, the sights and smells were new and bizarre; no less obtrusive than those of the European cities, but more exotic and intriguing. Every Arabian-style house seemed to have a stall outside its sun-baked brick walls. The more opulent homes were covered with carved plaster. The poorer houses were clad with dried mud. The roofs, which were either domed or fancifully tiled, as in the case of the homes of rich merchants, contrasted starkly with the dried palm-thatching laid across the bamboo roof-poles of the hovels of the very poor.

The clamour of the streets was just as deafening as in Paris, Lyons and Marseilles, but the background chorus of speech was startlingly different. The air rang with the glottal flow of Arabic, the lisping cadence of Armenian, and the musical sounds of Latin. To these languages were added French, Spanish, Italian and Greek, while a small Teutonic contingent gave a guttural counterpoint to the general cacophony.

Oriental spices – cardamom, cumin, coriander, peppers, cinnamon, nutmeg and ginger – competed with the perfumes of Arabia, attar of roses, frankincense and sweet-scented orange-blossom, to drown out the stench of horse dung and cow manure that liberally bespattered the narrow alleyways.

To Belami the familiar scene evoked many memories of his years of crusading in the Holy Land. For Simon and Pierre it was a revelation. They could see into many of the craftsmen's open shops, as they slowly forced their horses through the babbling turmoil. What they saw astonished them. Bernard de Roubaix had been right when he told Simon that the Middle East was not an uncivilized backwater of ignorance. These hard-working craftsmen were converted Moors, Arabs, Turks, Armenians, Syrians and Persians. Others came from even further afield. Moreover, the intricate instruments, fine weaponry and ornate artefacts they were fashioning, were well in advance of anything similar that Europe could produce. One Arabian metalworker, white-bearded and gaunt as a desert-hawk, was putting the finishing touches to an astrolabe, a fine example of the instrument-maker's craft.

Another broad-shouldered Arab, with the sinewy hands of a blacksmith, was forging a glowing Damascus blade from an amalgam of red-hot iron and steel bars. 'A sword fit for a prince!' breathed Pierre.

Everywhere, artists and craftsmen, carpet-weavers, tailors, armourers, bowyers, fletchers and leather-workers worked side by side in a panorama of skill and knowledge. It awed the young sergents as they ambled along, wide-eyed.

'We Christians are the ignorant ones,' said Simon, with commendable honesty.

Pierre de Montjoie grunted his assent. He could scarcely credit or appreciate the wide gap between the two cultures of Christianity and Islam, presently locked in their bitter struggle for supremacy. He felt a surge of frustration that the very people he had come to convert to the faith of Christ obviously knew more about the arts, crafts, and sciences than did his own kind. It came as an unpleasant surprise, unsettling Pierre for days.

Belami had once experienced similar reactions to eastern abilities, but since his first campaign in the Holy Land he had absorbed much of the wisdom of the Middle East.

For Simon de Creçy, it was all magic. As a scholar, whose quick mind could absorb knowledge like a sponge, he revelled in each new enlightenment.

That comes from his mother, thought Belami. His father was ever the man of action. He learnt much of his philosophy from the lady, who gave him the son he never dared to acknowledge.

Simon still did not know who his mother was, but in his veins flowed the blood of an exceptional woman.

The Templar headquarters in Acre was more in the nature of an official presence than a strong garrison. The burly Commanding Marshal, Robert de Barres, greeted them with little warmth. 'I was expecting a reinforcement of seven more cadets besides yourself, Sergent Belami. Bernard de Roubaix wrote to me in those terms,' he said sternly, his perspiring face flushed with annoyance.

Belami stepped forward, saluted, and gave a concise report of the events in France and at sea. He did not spare himself in any way, but mentioned that his actions in the de Malfoy affair had been approved by the acting Templar commander at Orange. The veteran stressed the courage and devotion to duty of all his cadets, both living and dead. It was a concise model of military reporting. When he had finished, he saluted and stepped back into line with Simon and Pierre.

De Barres reluctantly was impressed. However, he noted with pleasure Simon's handsome features and fine physique. The florid Templar Marshal enjoyed male beauty.

As the commander of the present force of Templars in Acre, Robert de Barres felt that the larger Hospitaller garrison reduced his own standing and authority. He tried to make up for this by imposing excessive disciplinary pressures on his men. This had not enhanced his popularity with the Templar garrison under his command.

Belami sensed this underlying antagonism and set out to establish his own position and that of his young sergents. Only one of the Templar garrison had previously served with the veteran. This was Gilbert d'Arlan, a shrewd old soldier from the Ardennes. The balding Crusader greeted Belami with a bear-hug, obviously overjoyed to share his responsibilities with such a stout-hearted and wily comrade-in-arms.

'It's all changed since our days together, Belami,' he chuckled wryly. 'It's become politics now. Little real fighting and much manoeuvring for power. There's even rumours that the German contingent is here to form its own Teutonic Order; but, knowing the hard-headed Huns, that's going to take a long time. They're good soldiers, but heavy-going, Belami. Still, there are quite a few of them about and more on the way, so they say.'

'Strong-in-the-arm and thick-in-the-head,' Belami quoted, with a bellowing laugh. 'They're good men to have on your side. I wouldn't like to fight against the Huns. What's the garrison position, old friend?'

Like Belami, Sergent d'Arlan gave a concise report of the military situation in Acre.

'The city walls are as strong as ever and a few more towers have been added. The command is under the seignory of the constable, Almaric de Lusignan. He musters ten of his own Frankish knights. They help him run things. Then there's Balian of Jaffa, a good chevalier, as well as Pagan of Haifa and Raymond of Scandelion, both brave men, with a further twenty-one knights under their joint command.

'In addition Count Joscelyn, Jordan de Terremonde and Gilles de Calavadri, all experienced Crusaders, can each put a dozen or so more knights into the field. So, with a few lesser dignitaries and their following, we can make up a roll-call of about eighty Frankish knights.'

Belami whistled his surprise. 'That's not much of an army to greet the Saracens with, when they come.'

Sergent d'Arlan grinned. 'There's still the Templar and Hospitaller garrisons to be reckoned with. All told, we can muster 150 brethren, mainly Hospitallers, and that includes their sergents as well. As usual that means that the Corps of Sergents will bear the brunt of the action; plus the auxiliaries, of course.'

'What about them?' asked Belami.

'They are turcopoles, as always,' replied d'Arlan. 'Three hundred good lances, if somewhat lightly armed.'

Belami nodded, turning to Simon and Pierre to explain. 'The turcopoles are auxiliaries. They are good fighting men. Fine horsemen and bowmen, and reliable in battle. I've commanded them many times before. I will recommend that de Barres gives you each command of a troop of twenty turcopoles, and I will command a double troop.

That means' – he paused and smiled – 'you are going to become full sergents.'

Simon and Pierre gave a whoop of joy. Belami interrupted their exuberance. 'You're not confirmed in your rank yet. That's up to the Marshal, but I don't think you need worry. Eh, Gilbert?'

The other old soldier nodded his assent. 'And don't think you know it all,' he warned them. 'Belami has got a lot more to teach you. But your best teacher, and a hard one at that, is the Holy Land itself. The desert can kill you quickly, if you give it half a chance. The wadis, and the narrow passes through the mountains, are ideal places for ambush. And remember, *mes amis*, the heathen knows every inch of his own land. So learn it as quickly as possible yourselves. A good commander must have a keen eye for the terrain. Only then can he choose the right place for the killing-ground.'

Sergeant d'Arlan didn't mince words. That was why he was such a good soldier.

When de Barres formally confirmed the new sergents in their rank of Troop Commanders, he embraced each one of them. Belami noticed that the Marshal lingered over his contact with Simon's slim, powerful body longer than the occasion called for. The veteran Templar sergent didn't like that. The last thing Simon needed was a problem with his new Commanding Officer.

The youngsters were overjoyed to find themselves promoted officially and set out to celebrate with Belami, d'Arlan and other young sergents of the Templar garrison.

'All right,' said their mentor, 'we'll sink some good red wine at your expense, *mes braves*, but from tomorrow, it's double-drill, till you two can handle your troops as well as you handle your swords.'

The streets of Acre were bustling with activity after the long afternoon's sleep. The sudden darkness had not yet fallen and, as it was mid-summer, there was a constant parade of the citizenry of this wealthy city, strolling back and forth in the cool of the evening.

112

Belami pointed out the different shields bearing the charges of various Frankish, Spanish, Italian and German knights. These bucklers hung outside the lodgings of their owners, denoting the knight's presence within. 'De Beaumont, Colin and David de Blois, Honfroi de Beau-lieu, Cartier de Manville, Robert d'Avesnes. . . . I recognize many of them. Ah! There's an unfamiliar one. A black gryphon, restant on an azure field; overall, a Teutonic Cross. That's a German charge; one of the new Teutonic knights for sure. *Ola!*' Belami abruptly changed the subject. 'Now there's a pair of beauties for you!'

The veteran pointed to a rich litter, carried on the broad shoulders of four massively built Nubians, probably eunuchs. The litter curtains were open as it was still a warm evening, even with the sea-breezes funnelling up the narrow streets. Inside the litter were two young women, one a delicious brunette, the other a pouting red-head of generous proportions. Both were richly dressed and giggling like young girls. As they passed the group of young sergents, both young women cast admiring glances at Simon's tall figure and classical features. They were still looking approvingly at him when the flow of the bustling crowd swept them round the corner.

'One thing hasn't changed,' grinned Belami. 'The whores are still good-looking in Acre.'

It was a startlingly different perspective on the Holy Land to the ones Simon and Pierre had been taught. Old Brother Ambrose had certainly never mentioned it.

Later, as they were leaving the small wineshop where they had been modestly celebrating, the youngsters saw yet another aspect of life in Outremer. This time it was a matter of life or death.

Their Commanding Officer, Robert de Barres, was the central figure involved. He was strolling down the Street of the Armourers, accompanied by two of his most trustworthy turcopoles. Belami, Simon and Pierre had just bade their new friends good night when, like a flash of summer lightning, it happened. One moment de Barres was leaning into a swordsmith's shop, admiring a splendid Damascus blade to which a final polish was being applied. The next instant a tall Arab, dressed in a striped *gallabieh* and wearing a hooded kaftan, drew a hidden dagger and plunged it down on de Barres' back.

'Assassin!' yelled Belami, a fraction too late. In a blur of action, the veteran drew his own dagger, hefted it for a fraction of a second, and hurled it.

The assassin had failed to pierce the Templar Marshal's coat of chain-mail. He raised his dagger to strike again as the knight was turning to meet the second blow.

Belami's dagger flashed across the narrow street and buried itself up to its hilt in the assassin's throat. With a gurgling cry, he collapsed at his intended victim's feet. Before he had gasped his last breath, de Barres had drawn his sword and passed it through the dying man's heart.

Simon had started forward to help the Marshal, but Belami had stopped him.

'Stay out of this, *mon brave*,' he said curtly.

The old soldier crossed the street and saluted de Barres.

'I trust you are unwounded, sir knight. These assassins use poisoned daggers. Would it not be wise to call a Hospitaller to tend you, sir?'

De Barres grimaced in pain. The blow had bruised him cruelly.

'Thank you for my life, Sergent Belami,' he said grudgingly. 'That was quick thinking. Templar marshals have long been a prime target, since our late Grand Master, Odo de Saint Amand, tried to wipe out the Assassins. Fortunately the skin is not broken. I have my chain-mail to thank for that. You certainly live up to your reputation, Sergent.' His attitude abruptly changed. 'Well done! Thanks to Our Blessed Lady and yourself, I am unwounded.'

Once he had recovered from the shock of his near-assassination, the stern disciplinarian was genuinely grateful. Later, back at the Templar barracks, Simon asked Belami: 'Why did you stop me joining in? And what had my father to do with these Assassins?' Belami looked grave.

'First, neither you nor Pierre knew that Assassins usually work in pairs. That put you both at risk. Second,

114

your father was a dedicated opponent of the Cult of Assassins. Had he not died in Damascus, in 1179, as a prisoner of the Saracens, the Assassins would have murdered him for sure. These devils never give up once they mark a man or woman for death.'

The veteran explained more fully: 'The Cult of the Assassins is a branch of the Shi'ite Moslems. They are an extreme fanatical cult, completely out of line with Muslim compassion. We call them Isma'lites. They were founded in the last century by a crazy Persian. His name was Hassan-as-Sabah. He set up his headquarters at Alamut, which means "Eagle's Nest". This was in the Daylam Mountains, far away to the north. The Muslims call the Assassins the *Hashashiyun*, because they believe that this murderous sect uses the magical herb, hashish, both before and after a cult-killing. Outwardly, they are a political group dedicated to murder. But the real basis behind their religious façade is black magic. In other words, *mon ami*, these Assassins are powerful sorcerers.'

'You mean, they have magical powers?' asked Simon.

'So they say, and certainly they seem to exert a terrifying influence on the people of the whole Middle East. Even Saladin himself, the great Ayyubid leader, is afraid of them, and he is a lion of courage. Apparently, two attempts have already been made on his life by Assassins, the last being nearly successful.'

'I thought they only attacked Christians,' interjected Pierre, who had just joined them.

'Not at all! The cult will make a target of anyone who crosses their chosen path. Saladin, like Odo de Saint Amand, tried to destroy the vermin. In our late Grand Master's case, the Assassins' own Grand Master, Sinan-al-Raschid, or, as we all know him, The Old Man of the Mountain, escaped on an apparently riderless horse.'

'How did he accomplish that miracle?' laughed Simon.

'You can chuckle, my boy, but it happened,' said Belami. 'A riderless horse was seen to escape from the Templar ambush and, a few minutes later, there was the Assassin leader astride it, on the skyline.'

Pierre's eyes bulged with disbelief. 'How could you possibly know that, Belami?'

'I was there, my doubting friend. Our Templar Grand Master was as amazed as I was. Personally' – Belami said seriously – 'I think the black-hearted *djinn* was clinging on to the side of the saddle of the so-called riderless horse, heading into the glare of the sun and concealed by his saddle cloth. It's a trick I have seen Scythian horse-archers use to make their enemies think they have fallen off.'

Everyone believed in witchcraft and sorcery, and magick existed with the same reality as lightning, disease, and death. This was the secret behind the Assassins' successful use of terror as a tactic.

Later, when Belami was once again alone with Simon, he said: 'Sinan-al-Raschid must never find out that you are the son of Odo de Saint Amand. That would be your death-warrant!'

Simon smiled, but his grin faded at the expression on Belami's face. 'You mean this Old Man of the Mountains can have me killed, like treading on an ant?'

'Anywhere, any time,' Belami said grimly. 'His power reaches out, like a long arm, beyond the shores of Outremer . . . even to Europe, and the hyperborean island of England. That is why I have no wish to see you involved.'

'There was a man nearby,' said Simon, 'A tall red-head with a straggly beard; also dressed in a kaftan. I would not have noticed him, Belami, but he had only one eye. The other one was concealed beneath a black patch.' Simon recalled the event vividly.

'That would be the other half of the Assassin's team,' said the veteran. 'I don't think he saw you, Simon, but he undoubtedly saw and remembers me in action. Don't worry, I've got eyes in the back of my head. I always keep an eye out for Assassins.'

Templar duties in Acre were much like those of the rest of the garrison but, as with the Hospitallers, they had their own discipline and could leave the city on patrol whenever they wished. More than anything else, Templar finances kept the Crusades alive. Their extensive trade ventures brought them immense wealth, and their ability to transfer large funds, without having physically to transport the heavy bullion, was of immense importance. Despite the Pope's Tax and the Head Taxes being gathered throughout Europe and England for the Crusade, the Templar treasuries led the way financially. Hence their complete freedom of action.

Simon and Pierre were soon trained in the use of siege-artillery, and de Barres spent a whole day explaining the strategy and tactics of Acre's main defences. 'As you can see, our outer defences are more than sufficient to delay a siege for many months,' he said. 'We can also be kept supplied by sea. When you arrived, you were under the protection of our trebuchets and mangonels. These can cast their rocks and Greek-fire to a distance of 300 yards. Don't look so surprised . . . This great range is given to them because their mountings are sited on the high towers of Acre. If Saladin ever attacks us, he will have to bring his own siege-artillery close in to match our hitting power. We outrange him by over one hundred yards.'

The two sergeants nodded their understanding and de Barres, who since his dramatic rescue from assassination had relaxed some of his iron discipline, laid a friendly hand on Simon's shoulder.

'They tell me you are a fine archer, de Creçy,' he said, with what he intended to be a warm smile. Actually it was a hideous gap-toothed grin, the marshal's front teeth having been smashed in by a Saracen's mace. 'You can employ that talent effectively from these walls. The frequent *mâchicoulis* that adorn the battlements jut out sufficiently to cover scaling ladders and other attempts to storm the city walls; but there is only room for one crossbowman in each of these stone-boxes. You would do better, Sergent de Creçy, behind a wooden mantlet set up on one of the towers.'

While he spoke, de Barres squeezed Simon's biceps in a friendly lingering fashion, an action the sergent disliked intensely, but refrained from shrugging off. Belami also noticed this gesture on the part of the Marshal and was troubled.

'As you will soon learn out on patrol in the desert, one of our most important tactical needs is water,' the Marshal continued. 'Use it sparingly, for the heathen knows every spring and oasis for miles around and can poison them all. Your own water supply, in your goatskin bottle, is literally your life. The sun dries up the skin quickly and soon takes the life fluids from our bodies. Sergent Belami, from experience, knows the vital importance of the careful rationing of water in the desert.'

When de Barres had finished his briefing, he asked his sergents if they had any questions.

Simon asked: 'Sir knight, why are there so many castles and strongpoints on this map? Surely the Templars are only here to patrol the pilgrim routes from Acre through Jaffa to Jerusalem?'

De Barres considered the question. 'That *was* the *original* idea, and one of which I thoroughly approved. However . . .' He hesitated, then launched forth into an unexpected tirade. 'The reason for this fortifying of the Holy Land is greed for power. We Templars help garrison them, of course, but we have only built a small number of castles, and those are sited at important places on the routes of pilgrimage. *Not so the others*!'

Obviously de Barres was mounted on a favourite hobby-horse. 'Greed and lust, those are our real enemies. The Assassins can be bought for gold, and many of their murders are arranged by Christians, against Christians. Nowadays it's all politics in the Holy Land. Things have changed since our day, Sergent Belami. Princes, kings, lords, and counts now vie with each other for control of the Kingdom of Jerusalem. Tragically, young King Baldwin is dying, even as he rules; that means that Guy de Lusignan, Raymond III of Tripoli and Reynald de Châtillon, and others who are equally unscrupulous, have the real control in Jerusalem. King Baldwin IV is stricken with leprosy, which is one reason why the Hospitallers who tend him hold such a powerful position in Jerusalem – more powerful, I sometimes think, than that of our own Order under Arnold of Toroga, the Grand Master.'

There was no stopping de Barres' flow of self-righteous

anger. 'I ask myself, is this a Crusade or a race for temporal power? The answer is obvious! Believe me, brethren, there are now more whores than pilgrims in the Holy Land. Watch out that you do not fall into mortal sin with these spawn of the Evil One.'

He stopped abruptly, seething with rage, and, turning on his heel, left them.

When he had gone, Belami signalled to his junior sergents to follow him out of earshot. He told them: 'Watch out for that one, *mes camarades*. The sun from too many long patrols in the baking desert has done our brave Marshal some mischief. I know his reputation. Physically, he is still fit, and the Templar is a courageous knight in battle.' His voice lowered. 'But the desert sun does strange things to a man. Heed my warning, especially you, Simon. *Don't find yourself alone with him.*'

'But a lot of what he said seems to be right,' commented Pierre. 'Everywhere we see great wealth and many unattached young women. Wherever that condition exists, there is usually trouble.'

'There's no denying that,' muttered Belami.

'He still didn't make the situation any clearer, about the great number of castles in the Holy Land,' said Simon, puzzled.

'That's a question that's hard to answer,' replied the veteran. 'Most of the castles and strongholds are in line-of-sight of each other. This is, of course, for mutual protection. But garrisoning all of them ties down too many knights, sergents and auxiliary lances. The Crusade is really a mobile war, requiring quick movement of cavalry to any trouble-spot. Locking up all these forces inside strong walls only gives the initiative to the Saracens.

'When Saladin moves, which one day soon he must do, we will need every lance and mounted man-at-arms to meet his lightning thrusts. Keeping all our forces in castles and behind city-walls is purely a *defensive* strategy, to guard the nobles' wealth. This is a Crusade, not a cursed rearguard-action to protect greedy potentates' ill-gotten treasures.'

'What did de Barres mean about there being more whores than pilgrims?' asked Simon.

Belami grinned. 'I'd say they were about equal in numbers.'

The two youngsters looked shocked.

'Oh, come now, *mes braves*! Not all whores are bad. De Barres thinks of every woman as the "spawn of the Evil One", but then he is different from us. I've known some good-hearted whores in my time, and one or two golden-hearted ones as well.

'I've also known a Mother Superior who was as evil as Lilith, the female demon, and some bad whores among the nobility disguised as countesses and ladies of the Courts. I treat a whore like a queen, whereas de Barres treats a queen as though she were a whore!'

He laughed his usual, rumbling bellow. 'For your information, Simon, there are some fifty castles and strongholds in the Holy Land, and many whores of both kinds are inside all of them.'

Armed with that useful piece of tactical information, they retired for the night. It was early, but at dawn the next morning they were detailed to carry out their first desert patrol with the turcopole troops, along the route from Acre to Tiberias, on the shores of Lake Galilee.

Politically, the Kingdom of Jerusalem was in a mess. Chaos would have been rampant but for the presence of the Templars and the Hospitallers. The Second Crusade had lost its original impetus, and only the threat from Saladin's Saracens in the south kept the Frankish forces from each others' throats. Lattakieh, Antioch, Jaffa, Tiberias, Tyre, Ascalon, Jerusalem and other fortified cities, while supposedly being part of the Christian kingdom, seethed with rival factions hatching conspiracies, plots and counter-plots.

A precarious treaty existed formally between Saladin and Baldwin IV, but if unscrupulous men like Reynald de Châtillon planned to raid the rich Saracen caravans en route to Mecca, then the treaty would be a fragile thing indeed.

Saladin, though just and merciful, was not a man to be

betrayed. A brilliant strategist, he already knew well how to handle a campaign against such static lines of defence. That was how he had subdued Egypt.

If provoked, he would move north into the Holy Land to protect his Saracen caravans. It was only a matter of time, and the sands were rapidly running out.

7

TIBERIAS, THE GUARDIAN OF GALILEE

Belami was glad to get his small command out on patrol, over the thirty or so miles separating Acre from Tiberias. The fifty turcopoles were under the sub-command of Simon and Pierre, the veteran having divided these lances into three troops; two sections of fifteen light-cavalrymen to each young sergent, with the remaining twenty horsemen making up his own command.

The turcopoles carried stout cane lances with wicked steel tips, and most of them were armed with a light Scythian bow and a quiver containing three dozen arrows. These light-cavalrymen were highly skilled in scouting and patrol duties. They were also expert trackers.

Their body-armour consisted of padded cotton jackets, called *alquôtons*. These were quilted and reached to the knees, being split at the backside and crotch to facilitate riding. Under this protective jacket some of the turcopoles wore chain-mail vests, looted from dead Saracens. Only a few of them could shoot accurately from the saddle, like Saladin's Scythian skirmishers, but, dismounted, the turcopoles shot well over long distances. However, their light arrows did not have the same penetrating power as Simon's heavy cloth-yard shafts.

The turcopoles rode superbly and could stay on patrol from dawn to sunset. They were so expert with their lances, they could even use them to hunt down desert jack-rabbits for the pot. Brave and resolute, under the command of the right kind of sergents, they were a fast-moving and formidable force.

Belami was proud of them. They certainly made an impressive sight as they cantered through the gates of Acre and set their faces east towards Galilee. Dawn was just breaking.

During their routine patrol they passed small groups of pilgrims and merchants, en route to Tiberias or crossing their patrol-line on the longer journey south to Jerusalem. Some of these groups included women, the families of pilgrims, or the wives and daughters of itinerant merchants. Few of them, young or old, failed to notice the handsome Templar sergent mounted on Pegase. Since the tragic interlude with Maria, Simon had once more retreated into his shell of acute shyness with women. Deliberately, or unconsciously, the young Norman ignored these provocative glances. His mind was still whirling with the exotic sights he had seen in Acre. These were so unlike his own strange dreams of the Holy Land, which had been more concerned with flying low over the rolling landscape and avoiding the clutches of nightmare creatures, than with making love to desirable women. All the stories told to Simon by Raoul de Creçy and Brother Ambrose had been concerned with the chivalrous deeds of Templar knights in battle, rather than about their relationships with damosels in distress, or otherwise.

If these stories had ever contained a hint of romance, it had been on the part of Frankish knights; chivalry had always been their impeccable motive and the ladies involved were invariably chaste and virginal. Only at Gisors had Simon heard another side to the legends of King Arthur and the Round Table. The story of Guinevere and Sir Lancelot du Lac had shaken him quite a bit.

Now that Simon had seen some of the damosels and ladies of the Frankish knights, his senses had been shocked even more. Most of the women belonging to Crusaders' families were protected by harem-style security. Nevertheless, many of the bolder women at Acre could be seen unveiled in public, something that no Muslim woman would do.

These Christian ladies, damosels and matrons, had taken notice of Simon on many occasions. One pretty brunette had stopped her litter, to ask the young Norman the whereabouts of a certain goldsmith. Her ruse would have been transparent to any experienced young man, who would have seen it as an open invitation. Not so Simon who, to Belami's despair, took his lovely enquirer's question literally.

'Sadly, my lady,' he had said, courteously averting his gaze from her ripe, half-concealed bosom, 'I know not this particular goldsmith, but this whole street is full of them. Any of them will tell you, I am sure.'

As he saluted and cantered off, Belami groaned. 'I'll have to do some more work on that boy,' he said to a laughing Pierre.

However, this encounter had not left Simon unaffected. As he bent down from his saddle towards the young girl's litter, his senses had been rocked by her heady perfume. This, with her freshly bathed aroma of rose-water, had aroused his manhood, which had stirred uncomfortably inside his chain-mail breeches. Red-faced with embarrassment, he had cantered off in order to regain control of his whirling senses.

Later, Belami had found a note tucked into his junior sergent's chain-mail hood, obviously slipped into its folds as Simon had bent down to answer the damosel's enquiry.

'This is an invitation to dine with the lady, complete with her name and address. She must have been after you for some time, Simon.' Belami threw back his head and roared a great bellow of laughter. 'Wake up, boy, or the most wonderful experience in our earthly life will pass you by. Our Blessed Mother will not be denied!'

Poor Simon was confused and shocked by Belami's remarks, but he was equally disturbed by the memory of the lovely maiden's seductive scent.

'It won't be long now,' Belami told Pierre. 'Simon is beginning to reawaken. That business with Maria de Nofrenoy shook him up badly.'

124

The three sergents rode at the head of their troops, until Belami signalled his junior commanders to join him at the point of the column. 'Do you see that long cloud of dust?' He pointed to the north. 'That's one of the Saracen caravans, moving towards Mecca. It's just the sort of rich haul that Reynald de Châtillon can't keep his thieving hands off. If he's up to his old tricks, our treaty with Saladin will come to an abrupt end. Watch out for trouble, *mes braves*. That's why we're out here on patrol!'

By the length of the dust cloud, Simon and Pierre could see that Belami was right. It had to be a wealthy venture, as well as a *Hadj*, the sacred pilgrimage made by Muslims to Mecca.

'Who exactly is this Reynald de Châtillon?' asked Simon curiously. 'We've heard a lot about his exploits, and little about the man himself.'

Belami snorted. 'The one tells you about the other. He is a Frankish adventurer, somehow dubbed knight, probably for services rendered to some unscrupulous prince. One thing *is* certain. He came to the Holy Land some years back and married the Princess of Antioch, who had been recently widowed. That was back in 1153. Reynald, otherwise known as Reginald, is the younger son of Geoffrey, Count of Giem, so he was penniless.

'Princess Constance had a rich dowry and that set him up nicely. William of Tyre, the famous chronicler who has recently returned to Europe, disliked de Châtillon and wrote outspokenly about his marriage. Some say that the old chronicler, an archbishop, was hounded out of Outremer by Reynald, who never forgives an insult or an injury.

'As Lord of Antioch, he ravaged Cyprus before Isaac Comnemus took it over. His excesses in the Holy Land are well known, and his persecution of the Patriarch is legendary. After all, the Patriarch is supposed to be the highest religious authority in the Holy City. He is the Pope's rival representative, and de Châtillon treats him like an underling. I tell you, Reynald is a rogue, a swindler, a liar and a thief. He was once captured by Saladin. In return for Reynald's treacherous protestations of loyal friendship, the Saracen leader, who never lies himself, let him go. A foolish thing to do!

'Reynald de Châtillon repaid Saladin's generosity by betraying his trust and, rumour has it, he is even now planning to build a fleet by the shores of the Red Sea, to become the first Crusading corsair. *Merde!* De Châtillon is no Crusader. He hasn't got a sincere bone in his whole body. He's after loot in the Red Sea ports, and Saladin's rich caravans, laden with gifts for Mecca, offer enormous wealth in booty.

'I tell you, lads, we're in for big trouble over that one's greed. Any day now, he'll overstep the mark. Then Saladin will be down on him, and us, like the Avenging Angel of Death.'

None of them realized how prophetic Belami's words would soon prove to be.

At that time, they were passing through a desolate area of sand and salt-bush, on the road to Galilee. This stark dust-bowl was waterless and depressing; a flat plain rising towards two rocky hillocks, called The Horns of Hattin, or Hittin as the Arabs had named it. It looked so uninviting that Simon remarked on it. 'What a terrible place! I shouldn't like to be caught there by hostile heathens.'

'You've got a good eye for battle-terrain, Simon. The Horns of Hattin is a bad spot to be ambushed. In the First Crusade, a massacre of Christians took place there and, some say, their lost spirits still inhabit the area.'

The veteran crossed himself and his junior commanders shivered, even though the late afternoon heat was still oppressive. 'I suppose one could make a stand on one of those hillocks, but it would be a forlorn one.' The old sergent shook his head. 'Come one, now. It's only a few miles to Tiberias. I want to be there before nightfall.'

The troops had been dismounted, walking their horses. At Belami's signal, they swung back into their saddles and set off at a canter towards the end of their patrol. None of them fancied a cold night in the desert. Certainly not at that terrible place.

Once the sun had set and darkness swept rapidly over the land, the sand and rocks soon lost their heat of the day, and the harsh desert wind blew in from Galilee. It became bitterly cold at night.

As Belami galloped down the column to speed up the rear-guard, Simon felt a shiver ripple down his spine. Yet the sun had not set. Suddenly he knew why: several of his dreams had been of flying over this same desolate landscape, whilst monstrous shapes tried to seize him. He shrugged off the feeling of intense depression which had suddenly crept over him, and loudly ordered his troops to keep up as he galloped forward.

An hour later the patrol rode up to the gates of Tiberias.

The city's fortifications had been well sited on a bluff overlooking the Sea of Galilee, the southern half of which it was intended to guard. On the waters of the large, inland sea, Jesus had once walked in the middle of a storm. Simon's thoughts turned to this incident as they approached the town. The Saviour's words: 'Peace! Be still!' echoed in his mind, as the young Crusader conjured up the picture of Christ incarnate, stepping from the fishing boat which bore him and walking on these waters, suddenly as supportive as thick ice. 'A miracle indeed!' he muttered, as he first set eyes on the blue Lake of Galilee.

This scene also seemed familiar to him in some strange way. He then realized that during his nocturnal flights, he had skimmed low over its shining surface. Simon knew that he could draw a map of the whole inland sea, even though its northern shores were now hidden under the evening mist.

He gasped, prompting Belami's question: 'Anything the matter, boy?'

'It's all strangely familiar. I feel as though I have been here before,' Simon stammered.

It was Belami's turn to be astonished. 'But you have, Simon,' he said. 'Though how you could remember that, beats me. You were brought here by your father, only days after your birth. He baptised you himself, in the waters of Galilee.'

'How do you know that, Belami?' asked Simon in amazement.

'I was there, lad. I was holding you in my arms. I had *two* hands then. Simon . . . I am your godfather!'

The two men, still mounted, rode flank to flank and embraced warmly, their tears flowing freely. Minutes later, they entered Tiberias leading an impeccable column of mounted men.

Both the town and the castle, with its stout towers and central keep, were contained within extensively fortified walls, battlemented and massively built. This seignory came under the control of Raymond III of Tripoli. His wife, Eschiva, a formidable, good-looking woman in her middle years, was to prove herself to be a gallant seneschal under siege conditions. At the time that Belami and his command arrived, the lady was feeling bored. Very little of interest was happening in Tiberias and her husband was away, on a visit to Antioch.

She and her niece, Lady Elvira, both of the noble house of Bures, welcomed the break in the monotony of their life in this part of Outremer. Belami and his small troop of light-cavalry were surprised to receive an enthusiastic welcome as they entered the city.

Raymond's self-adopted title of 'Lord of Tiberias' indicated the strategic importance of this heavily fortified town, rather than its size, which was not impressive. But the strong fortifications, backed up by a tough garrison and the inevitable siege-artillery of trebuchets, mangonels and stone-throwing ballistae, made up for the town's lack of grandeur.

Its garrison was adequate enough to withstand a siege, but not sufficient to mount large-scale patrols. Whenever it was visited by dignitaries, such as Guy de Lusignan, Count Joscelyn, or Reynald de Châtillon, it set out to impress its guests. Banners and bunting were hung everywhere along its short narrow lanes, and the wine-shops and small eating-places brought out their best for the visitor's retinue. Nevertheless, Tiberias was a social backwater and even the visit of a Templar patrol was something of an occasion. Belami was surprised to be invited, along with his two junior sergents, to dine with Princess Eschiva and her niece, Lady Elvira, together with the officers of the garrison.

When they presented themselves, after a hasty shower under the barracks' pump, they were dressed in their Templar uniforms, but all three wore clean *jupons*, the spare undershirts they carried to keep as a change from their sweat-stained garments. They had scrubbed their chain-mail with sand till it shone, for rust was no problem in such a dry climate. Only around the shores of the salty Dead Sea did a Crusader's armour, or his weapons rust.

The three Templar sergents looked impressive with their helmets held in the crooks of their left arms, chain-mail hoods thrown back and the long black surcoats of the Order bearing the Templar Cross.

'Princess, I bring you greetings from Robert de Barres, Marshal of the Templars at Acre,' said Belami in his growling diapason. 'Please also accept this humble gift of sweetmeats, from Sergent d'Arlan of the Hospitallers.'

The veteran signalled Simon to step forward with the gift. As the Norman presented the straw container of *Rahat Lacoum*, the rose-water and citrus-flavoured sweetmeat of the Turks, known as 'Delight', Lady Elvira gave him an admiring look. The Princess Eschiva, whose boredom was enhanced by her husband's absence, also favoured them all with a seductive smile on her generous lips. She was well-preserved and still attractive, with a full figure matched by a sensual face which once had been very beautiful. Even at the age of forty-five, this remarkable woman could still set a man's pulses racing.

Lady Elvira was taller than her aunt and her classical features were framed in luxuriant hair, burnished by continual brushing to a deep bronze lustre. Her eyes were startling, having gold flecks sparkling in their dark-brown irises. Simon was reminded of a rare stone that old Father Ambrose had once shown him. A 'cat's-eye', he had called it. The same mysterious chatoyance seemed to shine in the Lady Elvira's eyes. Simon felt disturbed by them. As for Pierre, he fell in love with her within an hour of first seeing her.

One glance at Pierre's face told Belami what was happening to his young comrade. The veteran made a mental note to tell him about the follies of falling in love above his station. Pierre was a sergent, Elvira the daughter of a count. There was, however, a surprise to come.

A buxom serving-wench with a ready smile soon caught Belami's attention. The old campaigner knew that he would not sleep alone in Tiberias.

Princess Eschiva was full of questions about Europe, ranging from what the ladies at King Louis' court were wearing, to which new dishes were being served to the Royal Household. The Lady Seneschal had heard that the sergents had recently come from Paris, so presumed that they must know some of the answers.

Neither Belami nor Simon could offer any information on these apparently vital matters, but surprisingly, Pierre de Montjoie could. In fact he was a rich source of knowledge of court etiquette, behaviour, cuisine and intrigue. After two flagons of good French wine, Pierre excelled himself.

Neither Simon nor Belami had been forthcoming about their respective family backgrounds, so up until then, Pierre had been reticent about his own. Now, suddenly, it all came bubbling out of his merry mouth.

'The de Montjoies are the Frankish branch of our family, which comes originally from Santiago, in Spain,' he said. 'The castle near Jerusalem, Château Montjoie, was built recently by an uncle of mine.'

Belami and Simon looked at their comrade in astonishment as he continued: 'I was brought up in the French court, where my father, Count Denis de Montjoie, is an adviser on Spanish affairs. The reason I enlisted as a cadet in the Corps of Sergents at Gisors is a simple one. I quarrelled with my father and he disinherited me.'

The guests at the banquet were fascinated by Pierre's words.

'It all started because my youngest sister, Berenice, was due to be betrothed to a wealthy knight, Albert de Valois. He is nearly sixty years old and a widower twice over. My sister was then only twelve years old.

130

'Poor little Berenice was terrified and she ran away to me, begging me to hide her. I thoroughly disliked de Valois, who is a lecher, and I took Berenice to my childhood friend, Princess Berengaria, herself then only fourteen years old but wise beyond her years. Berengaria of Navarre is a wonderful girl. She instantly knew what to do and asked for help from Queen Eleanor of Aquitaine, the wife of King Henry of England. Berengaria knew that the Queen's first husband had been Louis of France, and that the royal couple had been on the Crusade in Outremer. There, Queen Eleanor had been a close friend of Berengaria's uncle.

'The Queen happens to despise the practice of child-marriage and she took Berenice under her protection. My sister is now thirteen years old, and she is one of the Queen's ladies-in-waiting. Queen Eleanor loves both Berenice and Berengaria. They're quite safe from reprisals from Albert de Valois.

'My father, of course, was furious and disowned me. To get my own back I decided to seek my own fortune as a Templar sergeant.'

The evening was a resounding success. Moreover, the Lady Elvira took an immediate personal interest in this appealing young sergeant who was really of noble blood. She was no fool and knew that family quarrels seldom last for ever. Princess Eschiva approved of Elvira's rapt attention to Pierre's fascinating story. The Lady Seneschal was an intelligent woman and quickly saw the possibilities in this situation. Pierre de Montjoie had achieved eligibility with one short speech.

Belami was fascinated. 'God's wounds, boy, do you expect me to call you "Sir Pierre"?'

'Hardly, my revered senior sergeant,' laughed Pierre.

'So you really are in line for hereditary knighthood?' Simon was delighted.

Belami clarified the situation.

'You'll make it, all right. You'll be dubbed knight, Pierre, for certain. Just remember that until that happy hour you are my junior sergeant, and will remain so 'til they clip on your golden spurs. *Savez*?'

131

'*Oui, je sais!*' grinned Pierre, who was thoroughly enjoying the sensation that he had caused.

'I'll drink to that,' cried Simon, raising his flagon.

'To destiny!' said the veteran, and downed his wine in one draught.

Afterwards, Belami took Simon to one side. 'Come with me for a ride; there's something I want to show you,' he whispered.

They made their excuses to Princess Eschiva, saying that their duty of nightly inspection called, and then withdrew, leaving Pierre surrounded by admirers, all eager to hear the latest scandals at the French court.

The Templars rode out of the gates of Tiberias and taking a path which led down the steep bluffs to the lake shore, they emerged on to a broad strip of sand.

The moonlight shone clearly in the chill air of the Galilean night as they broke into a gallop along the brightly lit shore. When they came to a line of fishing boats, drawn up near some dark huts, they slackened their pace and, dismounting, led Pegase and Calaban over to a spring for a well-deserved drink.

'You never stop learning,' remarked Belami. 'Pierre a nobleman! *Eh bien*! *Tant mieux*!' He grinned broadly in the silver moonlight. 'Your father loved to come here, Simon. It was by this spring that he and your mother used to meet.' Belami's voice was tinged with nostalgia.

'Who was she?' Simon asked eagerly.

Belami's eyes were gentle. 'Sadly I still can't tell you that, Simon. Bernard de Roubaix did not give you her name and by my oath of silence, neither can I.' Seeing the look of disappointment on Simon's face, he continued: 'Suffice it to say your mother was very beautiful; her soul even more so. Your father learned his philosophy from her. When she died, most of your father died with her. Only his sense of duty kept him going. He had a job to do and he did it, but the heart of Odo de Saint Amand went with your mother. Not being able to acknowledge you, his son, must have been his hell on this earth.

· 'He went after the Assassins as a penance. Sinan-al-Raschid became the symbol of his bitter frustration. You know some of the rest.'

Seeing Simon's stricken look, Belami tried to comfort him by changing the subject. 'Your father had some strange thoughts about Galilee. He believed that Jesus was a *ship's* carpenter. That was why Our Lord got on so well with the fishermen. Our late Grand Master believed that Jesus built Peter the Fisherman's boat, along with many others, on the shores of Galilee.'

Simon was fascinated, turning the thought over in his mind. 'Why did my father think that, Belami?'

'Your mother gave him the idea. She told him that it was a local legend. When you think about it, it's quite logical.' Belami warmed to the subject. 'After all, Jesus was about fourteen years old when the Holy Bible loses track of him. Then we don't hear about him until he returns, aged around thirty, from out of the desert, to be baptized by the Holy Saint John, the Baptist.'

'It's an interesting point, Belami. What happened to Our Lord in those missing years?'

'Your father and mother believed that after Jesus had been arguing constantly with the rabbis in the local temple, he was marked out as a trouble-maker. After all, he was only thirteen years old. His father, Joseph, was worried about his clever son's strange behaviour and asked a friend of his, one Joseph of Arimathea, to take the boy with him on his ship. Remember that this Joseph, who appears later in the Holy Bible, was a trader and visited many foreign places on his voyages. What more natural than that this trader, who could always use a good ship's carpenter, should take Jesus with him? After all, the Lord, even as a boy, was apprenticed to his father, the master carpenter of Nazareth.

'Certainly, Jesus knew about boats, and later he became the close friend of fishermen, like Peter. Fisherfolk are not usually eager to give their friendship to those who do not understand their dangerous profession. Yet they listened to his instructions about where to cast their nets. Our Lord must have been an expert on boats and fishing!'

133

'You mean to say that Our Lord spent all those years . . . let's see now, about fifteen years . . . with Joseph of Arimathea, or at Galilee?'

Simon was intrigued, his mind racing with the possibilities.

'Why not?' said Belami. 'English Crusaders have told me that a trader called Joseph of Arimathea visited a holy place in the west of their country, where tin is mined. If I remember correctly, it is called Glastonbury.

'They also told me they believed that Jesus came with him. Monks have built an abbey there and it has a famous thorn tree which, they said, blooms once a year, on Christmas Day. This mysterious tree is supposed to have been grown from Joseph's walking staff.' Belami sighed reflectively. 'Who knows? After all, it is only speculation.'

Suddenly, the young Norman felt a wave of peace sweep over him. He smiled as in the distance he noticed a tall man bending over one of the beached fishing-boats. The figure of the fisherman was quite clear, silhouetted in the moonlight, and Simon could see that he was bearded.

'Things don't change much here,' he remarked casually to Belami.

'What makes you say that, *mon brave*?'

Simon pointed to the distant figure beside the boat. 'That fisherman over there. He could have been Simon, called Peter, or even Jesus himself, inspecting a fishing-boat, all those years ago.'

'In the moonlight? Well after midnight?' Belami chuckled. 'Where is this dedicated person? I don't see him!'

A cold shiver rippled up Simon's spine. He pointed towards the distant boat, drawn up on the shore.

'There!' he cried, but the figure had gone. 'Jesu!' he muttered, without blasphemy. 'He was there. I saw him as clearly as I see you, Belami.'

'A trick of the moonlight, lad. Perhaps a little too much wine as well. There's no-one there, Simon. Put it down to the magic of Galilee!'

But Belami had felt that same icy ripple up his spine. 'It's getting chilly,' he said, shaking himself like an old dog. 'Come on, Simon. I'll race you back.'

In a moment they were mounted and galloping along the moon-lit shore, their horses' hooves kicking up a fine spray from the water's edge.

'Fishermen or ship's carpenter, I swear I saw him in the moonlight,' muttered Simon to himself.

The next morning, they woke early and inspected the defences of the walled town. Later, Belami, who had made his official report to the garrison commander, rejoined his comrades. He chaffed Pierre about his resounding success with the ladies.

'You've scored a triumph there, *mon ami*. I swear the Lady Elvira is under the spell of the de Montjoie magic. So is the Princess Eschiva. She has her eagle-eyes on you, my lad. My guess is, she's already making out the list of wedding guests.'

Pierre laughed. 'Steady there, Belami. You're jumping a few fences ahead of me.'

The veteran grinned broadly. 'Don't you be too sure, my fine young cock. The Princess is a very determined woman. By the look on the Lady Elvira's face last night, so is she. She's a beauty, eh?'

'That she is!' breathed Pierre, rapt in his thoughts of the tall maiden with the mystical, gold-flecked eyes.

His comrades smiled at each other. 'Take my rede on it, Pierre,' chuckled Belami, 'your wedding goose is being prepared.'

He turned to Simon. 'I have met an old friend. One who knew your father well.' His voice had dropped, even though they were now out of earshot of Pierre. 'But he doesn't know that you are the son. I'd like you to meet him. Abraham-ben-Isaac is his name. He's a skilled instrument-maker who taught your father many things.'

'But surely he's a Jew?' Simon was puzzled. 'A convert, perhaps?'

'Not Abraham! He's Jewish and will remain so. A remarkable man. Artist, artisan, and philosopher. Truly a wise man. We're going to see him this afternoon.'

Simon could hardly wait. When he met Abraham,

135

there was no feeling of anti-climax. The tall stooped, elderly scholar was everything that Belami had said.

The grey-bearded savant appraised the young Templar sergent, his shrewd eyes lighting with pleasure as soon as he heard Simon's surname.

'Raoul de Creçy must be a close relative?' he remarked. 'I knew him well. A fine man. Alive and well, I hope?'

'Indeed, sir,' said Simon. 'He lives in Normandy.' He paused for an instant. 'My— Uncle Raoul brought me up at his manor, near Forges-les-Eaux.'

'So!' mused Abraham to himself. 'You certainly remind me of someone, but not Raoul de Creçy.'

Belami quickly interrupted them. 'Young Simon is quite a scholar, Abraham. He's eager to ask you many questions.'

The lean face of the elderly magus radiated wisdom. 'If I can answer them, I will,' he smiled. 'What subjects hold your interest, young man?'

'Brother Ambrose taught me something of astronomy and mathematics. I know little enough, but I can speak and write Latin, French and Arabic. My mind is full of questions to ask you, sir. Forgive my troubling you when you should be sleeping on this hot afternoon.'

Abraham smiled, his heavy lidded eyes opening wide with amusement. 'Gentiles and Saracens sleep after the noon-day heat. We Jews like to work in the shade, when things are quiet. See, my young friend. I have been making a new astrolabe for the "Lord of Tiberias". He is a keen student of the stars.'

'Bernard de Roubaix sends greetings,' broke in Belami.

Abraham chuckled, a rich warm sound. 'There is another old friend. A glutton for knowledge, that one. We used to meet here, whenever your late Grand Master' – the old man's keen eyes suddenly looked shrewdly at Simon – 'Odo de Saint Amand, visited Tiberias. Those were most enjoyable times.'

Belami again deliberately interrupted Abraham's chain of thought. 'Simon's father died in the Crusade. I

136

brought the boy back to Normandy with de Creçy and he and Bernard de Roubaix both earnestly requested me to search you out for that very reason: to teach the boy.'

'I would be honoured, Belami. Will you trust me with him, or will you stay?'

Belami's voice softened. 'Nay, Abraham. I leave you to drill some of your wisdom into his thick Norman head.'

Simon had already fallen under the gentle spell of the old scholar. In the weeks that followed, he came to love Abraham for his wisdom, his compassion and his honesty. The feeling was mutual. From the moment Abraham had seen Simon's classical features and looked into the Norman's startling peacock-blue eyes, Abraham had recognized the young Templar's lineage. But Simon's secret was as safe with the son of Isaac, the magus, as it was with Belami, de Creçy and de Roubaix. Abraham would never betray it.

The weeks flew by as Abraham filled every off-duty hour of Simon's time with a flood of knowledge. The Jewish genius for absorbing facts and figures had kept most of the treasures of the destroyed libraries at Alexandria and Byzantium well preserved in the storehouse of their race-memory. The Jews were the guardians of the Gnosis and only imparted it to certain of their own posterity, or, on rare occasions, to those whom they trusted, such as Simon de Creçy.

Abraham taught him about the Sacred Geometry, the Divine Proportion, the universal importance of shape, weight, form and number; the principles of magick, and the summoning of will-power.

Simon absorbed it all, like a Greek sea-sponge. He was beginning to see why Bernard de Roubaix had taken him to Chartres for that mysterious tour of the cathedral.

'The cathedral's stones are merely a statement,' said Abraham. 'Just as you would inscribe figures with a reed on a wax tablet, draw or carve hieroglyphs on a temple wall, or write characters down on parchment. The *thought* behind it is everything. Otherwise, the whole thing is mere vanity.'

He looked deeply into Simon's rapt face. 'Solomon was

a great magus. An Ipsissimus! A master of masters of the Great Work, the Alchemy of the soul of man. This is the turning of dross into gold and is symbolic of the true path of the Gnosis. The Great Work is the transmutation of the gross materialism of man into the golden Essence of the Spirit of God. Do you understand me, Simon?'

'You mean: to turn yourself into the image of God?'

'No, Simon! That is blasphemy! No man becomes God. We Jews worship no graven image of our God. We are even forbidden to speak His name. Instead we use the word, Adonai, meaning Lord. Our God has many names. Your Jesus, upon the Cross, cried out: "Eloi! Eloi! Lama Sabactani." That is Aramaic, Simon.'

'It means: "Lord, Lord, why has thou forsaken me?" does it not, Abraham?' asked Simon.

'Not entirely, my boy. It was an invocation by Jesus, crucified and in agony, to the *Eloihim*: the great Angelic spirits. Remember how the veil of the temple was rent, when Jesus gave up Christ's Spirit?'

'"Into Thy Hands I commend my Spirit",' breathed Simon reverently.

'The hands of the *Eloihim*, Simon. Had the Hands of God touched Calvary, His power would have been greater than that of a wandering star, crashing to earth. The place would have been devastated for many hundreds of leagues around. The power of God's servants, the *Eloihim*, was even sufficient to rend the veil of the temple.'

Simon never forgot the fascination of those magical sessions with the Jewish philosopher. His lessons were practical as well. Abraham showed him the use of the treadle-lathe, to turn the fine screws and small nuts and bolts used in his instrument-making. He learnt the alloying of brass and tin to make bronze; the fashioning of metal; and, above all, the application of mathematics to the accurate measurement of matter, space and time.

But it was the spiritual exercises that Abraham taught Simon that set his mind alight with new ideas. Truly, Abraham-ben-Isaac was the one who opened Simon's mind to the wonders of the Universe.

His teachers in Normandy, especially Brother Ambrose, had started Simon off on the long journey down the endless road of knowledge; but it was Abraham-ben-Isaac, the Jewish instrument-maker of Tiberias, who widened that narrow path into the broad highway of the Gnosis.

8

SUMMER LIGHTNING

Simon's intellectual idyll at Tiberias came to an abrupt
end with the arrival of Robert de Barres. There were two
reasons for his visit. First, he had a routine call to make on
the town itself; second, he could not get disturbing
thoughts of the handsome young Templar sergent out of
his mind. The arrival of a Templar ship, carrying a large
number of reinforcements, had given de Barres the
opportunity to leave Acre and to see how Belami's desert
patrol of the area around Tiberias was progressing. His
visit ended like a strike of summer lightning.

Belami was not expecting the messenger who brought
him news of de Barres' visit, and shrewdly guessed the
real reason behind it. He cursed loudly and prepared for
trouble. It came only days after de Barres' arrival.

By juggling the duty roster, the veteran had kept his
protégé out of de Barres' way, but eventually the inevitable happened. Simon found himself alone with the big
Templar knight.

Robert de Barres had spent a restless night, his
thoughts filled with Simon's handsome presence. There
are as many degrees of love and lust among those who are
attracted to their own sex as among more conventional
lovers. Robert de Barres' feelings for Simon de Creçy
were the cravings of lust, as animalistic as a lonely bear on
heat. He wanted to possess Simon's body with a brutal
longing.

As soon as they were alone, the burly, sweating Templar made his move. It was more in the nature of a physical attack than a lover's overture. Belami had been right. The baking suns of one thousand days of patrolling the pitiless deserts had inflamed the brave man's brain. De Barres craved for the coolness of Simon's body to quench his raging passion.

The young Norman struggled against the big Templar's overpowering advances, trying hard to restrain his Marshal's uncontrolled mauling as all the frustrated desires inside the obsessed man's mind burst forth.

As they panted and heaved, wrestling wordlessly in a silent, tightly locked, unnatural embrace, de Barres' hot breath smelt strongly of wine. This was another breaking of his Templar oath. As well as being insane with desire, the Templar knight was drunk.

They struggled with all their strength; Simon to protect his manhood from de Barres' powerful, groping hands, and the big knight to break down his resistance. Madness had engulfed de Barres' tottering senses. In fury, he seized a mace which was hanging on the wall of the guestroom, and tried to stun Simon. Luckily, the young sergent was wearing armour, only lacking his helmet which he had removed when the Marshal had sent for him. Even then a half-parried blow nearly knocked him out.

Simon's senses were groggy, but he still resisted de Barres' frenzied attempts to rape him. A large table splintered under a second blow from the mace, just avoided by inches. At that moment, the door burst open.

It was Belami. One glance was enough for him. He saw that de Barres had gone insane. He slammed the door shut behind him and drew his sword. 'Marshal de Barres,' he said, in an even tone, 'you are a sick man. Drop the mace! I will send de Creçy for the resident Hospitaller.'

The crazed Templar gave a loud bellow of fury and again raised the mace, this time to attack Belami. The veteran seized a nearby chair to use as a shield, but as he did so de Barres' face suddenly changed from its sunburned redness to a hideous purple. His eyes bulged and he gave a dreadful choking cry, dropping his mace to the

141

stone floor. His mouth gaped wide, showing his broken teeth. Blood spouted from his throat.

Half turning, hands pawing at the air, the overweight Templar Marshal crashed back against the wall and slid down it, landing in a heap at its foot.

'Jesu!' swore Belami. 'Our Blessed Mother has struck him down!'

The two sergents crossed themselves. They hurriedly knelt beside their Marshal's unconscious form as his heels drummed against the tiles.

Belami loosened de Barres' armour and tried to revive him, while Simon ran for the Hospitaller. Brother Manuel was a Spanish knight of the Order of Saint John of Jerusalem, a skilled healer and physician.

There was nothing he could do. By the time he arrived, Robert de Barres was dead, his eyes staring vacantly in his livid face.

'Tragic. It was a fatal stroke. His heart has burst. Pray for him, brethren,' said the Hospitaller.

As they knelt in prayer, the phsyician closed the dead Marshal's glazed eyes. Simon was still shaking from the ordeal of de Barres' attack. Belami signed to him to remain silent.

When the short prayer for the dead was over, the veteran said: 'My young colleague had been summoned by the Marshal to make his report on the garrison defences. Robert de Barres, God rest his soul' – they crossed themselves – 'was suddenly stricken and, in his death-agony, crashed against the table. He was a heavy man and it splintered under his weight. Sergeant de Créçy tried to control the Marshal's wild convulsions, hence his dishevelment. He was badly bruised in the process. It is indeed a tragic day for the Order, Brother Manuel.'

The Hospitaller shook his head in sad assent. He obviously accepted Belami's story.

'It is the Will of God and our Blessed Saint John,' he said with due reverence. 'I will arrange for his immediate burial.' The Hospitaller's practicality exerted itself as he went on, in lowered tones: 'This summer heat will putrefy the body within hours. Best to bury the Marshal today.'

Belami had done the right thing by protecting the Templar's reputation. Before sunset the big body of Robert de Barres had been placed in a quickly constructed coffin made of local cedarwood, and with due pomp and ritual, in the absence of a Templar brother knight, had been interred by the officiating Hospitaller, Brother Manuel de Ortega.

The Princess Eschiva attended, deeply shocked by the sudden death of an old friend and an honoured guest, and suitably dressed in becoming black, accompanied by the Lady Elvira, swathed dramatically in a black riding cloak. With them were assembled most of the garrison, including the turcopoles. As both the Hospitallers and the Templar sergents wore black as their uniform, the sombre occasion was impressive. For other reasons, Simon and Belami would long remember it.

No sooner had the funeral service finished, than de Barres' body was lowered into the deep grave dug by the three Templar sergents as a last gesture of respect for their dead Marshal. The final shovelful of sand had just been thrown over the new coffin when an exhausted turcopole arrived on a foam-flecked horse. He rushed straight over to Belami and reported, in Arabic: 'Reynald de Châtillon has sent a large patrol to attack a rich Saracen caravan. If you leave now, Sergent Belami, you may be able to head them off. This message comes from Sergent d'Arlan of the Hospitallers.'

Belami's last briefing from de Barres had been a command to keep a Templar presence on the Saracen route to Mecca, in order to prevent this kind of predatory move on de Châtillon's part.

'Saddle up, *mes amis*,' cried Belami. 'I will explain the situation to the Princess. We ride north immediately. With luck the raiders will be moving slowly, conserving their energy for the attack. If we are too late this can only lead to war.'

Templar patrols travel light, all possessions other than field rations and weapons being unimportant to the Order. Pierre barely had time to bid Eschiva farewell, and Simon none at all to say goodbye to Abraham-ben-Isaac.

lami took only a minute to report to the Princess, and
express their gratitude for her kind hospitality.

Within ten minutes of the messenger's dramatic arrival,
the Templar patrol cantered out of the gate of Tiberias
and headed north. The summer storm was about to break.

As Simon rode at the head of his troop, his mind was
throwing off the shock of the dreadful events of the
morning. He suddenly recalled some words of Abraham-
ben-Isaac: 'Coming events are foreshadowed. The creative mind picks up these shadows, as flashes from the
heliograph of a scout's polished shield send a warning
message to a desert patrol. From what you have told me
of your flying dreams, my son, you have this prophetic
gift, or curse, whichever way you look at it.

'I can teach you to control these dreams, in which your
soul rises from your sleeping body like the Horus hawk
from the sleeping Osiris. Up to now, these visions have
been involuntary nocturnal adventures. Now you will be
able to place yourself into a meditative trance and release
your subtle-body at will, to wander through Netsach, the
place of creative thought.'

In the week that followed, the Jewish magus had taught
Simon the technique of relaxation, to induce a trance-like
state of sleep.

'At first, you must *never* do this alone. I taught your
father to do the same thing.' Abraham's gentle smile was
radiant with affection. 'Oh, yes, Simon de Creçy, I
recognized your father's face when I first beheld your
own. Have no fear. Your secret is safe with me. I too have
taken the oath of secrecy of Solomon the King.'

At that they had embraced. Now Simon was about to
fulfil his destiny.

The patrol rode hard into the darkness, led by an
Armenian scout from the garrison at Tiberias who knew
the lie, or ley of the land, even better than Belami. They
stopped for a short rest when the moon had slipped below
the hills on the horizon.

Three hours later, the false dawn saw them awake and
once more en route northwards. They would be only an

hour or so behind de Châtillon's raiders who certainly would have camped for the night, knowing that their prey would have done likewise.

As Simon slept the short, refreshing soldier's slumber, his subtle-body slipped, voluntarily this time, from his blanketed form, lying pillowed on his saddle. Under Abraham's careful instruction, he had finally been able to achieve this magical projection alone. Now he could roam at will through the mystical places of the Sepiroth, concentrating his will to keep his soul within the realm of Netsach, the domain of creative thought.

What he saw alarmed him. Below him, the Saracen caravan lay encamped, only a small number of Scythian and Ayyubid guards keeping watch. They were not suspecting treachery. Simon, from his hovering position above the camp, saw the Frankish raiding party closing in silently upon them. Then he woke. It was just before dawn.

Immediately, he touched Belami's sleeping form on the shoulder. Before he could withdraw his hand, the veteran had seized his arm and thrown him over his blanketed body on to the soft sand beyond. As he recognized Simon's half-stunned features, he said grimly: 'Never do that again, *mon brave*. I could have had a knife in my hand.'

Simon's voice was urgent. 'Alarm!' he cried. 'We must get out of here, now! I've dreamt that de Châtillon's men are about to attack. I'm sure they're not far from here.'

'That's good enough for me. I know from Abraham that your dreams don't lie,' grunted Belami.

He leapt to his feet, shouting to rouse the rest of his command. Within minutes, they were saddled up and heading north, riding fast.

The chrome-orange light of the early morning sun was burnishing the bottom layers of cloud as they galloped north. By not sparing their mounts Belami showed his faith in Simon's prophetic gift, but after twenty minutes of hard riding they were reduced to a canter. At that moment the turcopoles riding 'point' ahead of them, raced back and pulled up in a cloud of dust.

'The Saracens! They're just over the next rise.' The cavalry scouts pointed.

'That does it! Don't spare your horses,' yelled Belami. 'Charge!'

At first grimly silent, and then, as the clash of arms came to their ears, yelling like madmen, the turcopoles thundered over the desert sand. They topped the steep ridge in a flurry of fine dust and hurled themselves down the sandy slope beyond. Already, the Saracen caravan was fighting for its life. It was faring badly.

De Châtillon's men had killed several of the Ayyubid and Scythian guards silently, with the knife. The rest of the caravan's escort huddled in a rough circle, protecting a single black tent with their lives. Obviously some Saracen of importance was inside.

Belami's turcopoles, screaming like banshees, crashed into the unprotected backs of the Frankish horsemen. Simon had unslung his warbow and fired two arrows before their charge hit home. The cloth-yard shafts thudded into two Frankish horsemen, leaving their mounts riderless.

Suddenly, in the shadowed opening of the black tent, a woman appeared, dagger in hand, obviously determined to sell her life dearly.

A close-helmeted Frankish knight, who seemed to appear from nowhere, charged straight at her, raising his own dagger to cleave the woman to the heart. His blow never struck, as Simon's arrow pierced his raised arm. With a loud curse, he turned his charger and rode straight at the Norman archer, keeping low behind his horse's head to forestall a second unerring shaft, while he tried to draw his sword with his left-hand.

Simon, whose Templar code of ethics as a sergent in the Corps forbade him to kill a Christian knight unless attacked first, hesitated. Not so Belami, whose battle-axe whirled round and then flew from his right hand, straight at the charging horseman.

As the yelling rider crashed into Pegase nearly

unseating Simon, Belami's axe thudded into the Frankish knight's chest, cutting straight through his mail-protected surcoat. With a high-pitched shriek, the steel-helmeted horseman was swept from his saddle to fall with a clash of armour at Simon's feet. Belami dismounted just as de Châtillon's men turned away in panic-stricken flight.

The turcopoles rode after them, leaving several of the defeated raiding-party lying wounded or dead on the blood-spattered ground. Belami tore the bucket-shaped helmet off the dead knight.

'As I thought,' he growled. 'This is no chevalier of France. It is an Assassin. He must have joined the raiders, unseen, during the night.'

'You are right, Sergent,' said the feeble voice of a wounded knight nearby. 'I am Roland de Buches, Commander of Reynald de Châtillon's scouting force. My orders were to attack the caravan, not to kill women.'

'Then the lady must be someone very close to Saladin. Why else would an Assassin go to such lengths to kill her?'

'How did you know?' asked Simon, bewildered by Belami's killing of the 'Christian knight'.

The sweating veteran laughed grimly. 'No Frankish knight attacks with a dagger. A battle-mad chevalier might attack a defenceless Saracen woman, but it would be with lance or sword. He was fully armed, yet he dropped his lance and drew his dagger. It had to be one of Sinan-al-Raschid's men. They are sworn to kill Saladin, *or* his family.'

Simon approached the trembling woman, who was still veiled. 'I hope, madam,' he said gently, 'that you are unharmed.'

. He spoke in Arabic. To his astonishment the slim veiled woman replied in French.

'By Allah's mercy, I am untouched.' Her voice was low and melodious. 'Thank you, sir, for saving my life.'

'These are Reynald de Châtillon's cut-throats,' Belami explained. 'As Templars, we were ordered to intervene if these raiders attempted to molest any caravans on the Holy *Hadj* to Mecca. A thousand pardons, Your Highness.'

The veiled woman laughed, a gentle trickle of sound. She

was now quite composed. 'How did you recognize me, Sergent?'

'The black tent gave away your identity, Your Highness. It has none of the usual rich decoration of costly Isphahan rugs. All educated Crusaders know that Sitt-es-Sham is the noble and modest "Lady of Syria", and that her brother is the illustrious commander of the Saracens, Sultan Saladin.'

Again came the light laughter, like a summer breeze.

'Most flattering, Sergent, but not *all* of the truth, I think.'

Belami chuckled. The Lady of Syria was too sharp-witted for him. 'It became obvious who you were, Your Highness, when I realized that an Assassin was attacking you. Only one of Sinan-al-Raschid's murderers would go to those lengths to kill such a target. My humblest apologies for not arriving sooner.'

The lady spoke again, this time in Arabic. 'The young sergent – what is his name? His bowshot was miraculous.'

'Simon de Creçy,' the veteran said. 'My name is Belami, and this is Sergent Pierre de Montjoie.' He indicated his other colleague, who had just dismounted to join them. 'Our swords are at your command, Your Highness.'

The three Templar sergents saluted her, kneeling.

'Please rise, gentlemen,' Sitt-es-Sham continued, in lisping French. 'Can you give me an escort to continue my journey towards Mecca? As a woman, even a Saracen princess, I am not allowed within the sacred place where our holy *Khaaba* rests. But I have many gifts for the needy in Mecca, and hungry mouths cannot wait too long for food.'

Each of them rose and bowed his homage. Then a strange thing happened. As Simon paid his respects, apparently accidentally the Lady of Syria let drop her veil. For a moment, Simon gazed into a face of great gentleness and beauty, graced by magnificent eyes of the deepest violet hue.

'The eyes of an angel,' thought Simon as his heart pounded with excitement. Then the veil was instantly replaced, only the glorious eyes remaining visible. Once

148

again, her enticing laughter sounded faintly behind her *yashmak*.

Assisted by her few Ayyubid guards who were still unwounded, the three sergents saw her safely mounted on her pure white palfrey and, with an escort of twelve turcopoles detailed by Belami, Saladin's beautiful sister rode out of the camp, once again headed for Mecca.

Without glancing back, Sitt-es-Sham rode out of sight into the glare of the rising sun.

'Don't stand there like an expiring carp, Simon, we have much work to do. And by the way, Sergent de Creçy, you have just been paid the highest compliment that any Muslim lady could give you. And from a princess, too. You, my friend, have caught a glimpse of her beauty *unveiled*. Few men have ever seen Sitt-es-Sham as she really is. Khay'am the Persian astronomer-poet, would have treasured such a moment. It was pure romance.'

'It was an accident,' Simon said, blushing. 'The Princess dropped her veil by chance!'

Belami sighed deeply. 'Simon, my dear godson, sometimes I wonder what you use for brains.'

With a bellow of laughter, the Templar Crusader remounted and cantered round the site of the encampment, counting the dead and wounded for his report. One thing was certain, it would not reflect well on Reynald de Châtillon. And when Saladin heard the full story from his sister's own lips, de Châtillon's days would be numbered.

None of them knew that this barbarous attack on a peaceful Saracen caravan would prove to be the end of the hard-won truce. The summer lightning had been the overture to a terrible storm, which was now about to break.

9
THE ROAD TO JERUSALEM

When Belami's patrol returned to Acre, the new Templar Marshal, Roger de Montfort, had just been appointed. The Princess Eschiva had sent word of Robert de Barres' death to the Grand Master of the Temple, Arnold de Toroga, at Jerusalem. From there, a fast-riding messenger had reached Acre in under three days, and the senior Templar knight, who had only recently returned on the latest ship to the Holy Land, was installed as Marshal of the Templar garrison. Belami knew him from the old days and respected de Montfort for his bravery and honesty. He was also a knowledgeable, and therefore a merciful, man. He heard Sergent Belami's report in silence, and congratulated him warmly.

'Well judged, Belami. Your tactics were impeccable. I mourn Robert de Barres' sudden death, but I am not surprised. He had not been a well man for some time. Too long in the Holy Land, eh, Belami?'

'Sadly, sir knight, yes!' replied the old soldier, without enlarging on the matter.

'Sergent,' said de Montfort, 'I am sending you and your command to Jerusalem. Your reputation among Templar Crusaders is enviable. I have written to Arnold de Toroga, suggesting to our Grand Master that he reinforces you with some of his over-manned garrison, and allows you to maintain a free-ranging, mounted patrol, to keep ignoble knights like de

Châtillon out of trouble and to try to preserve the *Pax Saracenica*.'

Belami drew in his breath sharply. De Montfort smiled. 'I know it is not going to be easy, but obviously you have got two excellent junior sergents with you, and you will be given a command of not less than one hundred lances. Of course, that's a flea-bite against Saracen hordes, but it will suffice to keep de Châtillon and others of his ilk in order.'

Belami came straight to the point. 'Sir knight, I thank you for your confidence in me, but I cannot contain de Châtillon's whole force. There are strong rumours that he is building a small fleet to carry out a pirate expedition against the Red Sea ports. I can stop him on land, with God's aid, but without ships I can do nothing against de Châtillon on water.'

De Montfort looked grave. 'Of course not, Belami. I can only expect you to do your best. Your patrol lines will be to protect pilgrims moving south to Jerusalem, and Saracen caravans moving on to Mecca. Do your duty, Sergent, as well as you can. He gripped the veteran's right hand. 'Take care of yourself, old comrade.'

Belami saluted and left to tell the others just how difficult an assignment they had been given.

Two days in Acre sufficed to fill the small gap in their ranks. Belami had only lost five turcopoles in the dawn attack and de Montfort gave him a free hand in selecting his replacements. On the third morning, as dawn broke, they once again rode out, headed this time for Jerusalem.

Their patrol route took them south-east, towards the Holy City, over fertile rolling countryside. In distance it was about ninety miles from Acre, but in ambience Jerusalem was a continent away. Life in Acre was simple and businesslike, as the city's duty demanded. The Crusader port of disembarkation and the sea-gate to Outremer, by its very nature had to concentrate on these aspects of its existence. As Simon and Pierre had seen, and Belami knew of old, there were diversities of pleasure to be had in Acre, but on the whole the busy crusading port was a garrison town, and as such life there was relatively austere. Not so in Jerusalem.

Here was the hub of the Crusades, the central spindle round which the complex structure of the Christian kingdom of Outremer and Outrejourdain revolved.

Their line of march had led Belami's command past Nazareth and Mount Tabor, and along the twisting course of the River Jordan which they followed between ranges of low hills until the Holy City rose into view, shimmering in the midday heat of their fourth morning of hard riding.

Belami had deliberately led them to the north-east side of the city, to give Simon and Pierre their first glimpse of the focus of the Crusades as seen from the Mount of Olives. To do this he had forded the brook Kedron, and led his command up the slopes of the famous Mount just as dawn rose to bathe the Holy City in its chrome-orange light.

The slight detour had been well worth their stumbling efforts in the dark.

Opposite their position on the slope, the eastern battlements of the long walls encircling Jerusalem shone in splendour. There were the unmistakable shapes of the Dome of the Rock, the Royal Palace and the Al-Aqsa mosque, all built within the area where once had stood the great Temple of King Solomon. Facing them were two entrances, the Gate of Jehosaphat and the Golden Gate, the first giving access to the city and the second leading to the temple area.

The sacred city glowed in the growing early morning light. Its tall towers, mosques and domes, minarets and truncated spires of Christian churches, formed an intricate pattern of shapes and forms that captured the imagination and sent it soaring.

Standing four-square on its rocky base, Jerusalem dominated the whole surrounding area. Approximately eleven hundred yards long and nine hundred yards wide, the entire city was formed in the shape of a rough rectangle, packed with seething activity, religious, commercial, political and military; the sacred and the profane.

From Tancred's Tower on its north-western corner, the wall and its western ramparts ran south, pierced only by the Jaffa Gate. It then swung past the massive Tower of David to the Sion gate on its southern flank, where the wall turned north-east, in a series of angled battlements, to the Gate of Silban.

Finally, following the edge of the escarpment, it swept due north along the eastern plateau, facing Belami and his troops on the Mount of Olives until it turned west to form the jagged outline of its northern perimeter defences.

These walls were pierced by the Gate of Flowers, the Gate of the Column of Saint Stephen and finally the zig-zag Postern of Saint Lazarus.

'The Holy City indeed!' breathed Simon, in awe of the sunlit spectacle before him. Belami chuckled at the look of wonder on his junior sergents' rapt faces.

'As I told you, Simon, the proportion of whores to pilgrims is about equal. This is the religious centre of Christendom, and saints and sinners lived here centuries before Our Lord pursued his path of agony, carrying the True Cross on his scourged back.

'The Great Temple of Solomon, the Master Magician, has been destroyed, but within its site Christian churches and Muslim mosques have taken its place. Look your fill on Jerusalem's whited sepulchres, bathed in the brightness of God's sunlight, and remember it like this . . . in all its earthly glory.' His tone altered, sharply. 'It's not such a wonder *inside* the walls. The Holy City it undoubtedly is, but Jerusalem, the centre of our kingdom, is also as full of intrigue as a rotted corpse is crawling with worms.'

Without another word, the tough old soldier remounted and led his command down the long slope, across the brook Kedron, and cantered up to the eastern Gate of Jehosaphat.

To the challenge from the guard, Belami replied: 'Templar business requires no explanation. Sergent Belami and his command demand entry to the Holy City.'

His homely accent and obvious air of authority made a better passport than a score of documents. With a scraping of heavy timbers, the broad cedar bars backing the

153

gate were laboriously withdrawn and the tall doors swung ponderously open. The column of Templar light-cavalry entered Jerusalem.

As soon as the last turcopole had cleared the portals, the heavy doors were closed with a clang and the wide wooden beams shot home. The Regent of Jerusalem was taking no chances with the present edgy situation.

The Templar troops rode into the city and approached their headquarters by a roundabout route. Belami wanted his young comrades to see something of the Holy City which, even at this early hour, was a hive of activity.

Life started early in Jerusalem, before the scorching sun took the edge off the efforts of its industrious citizens. These workers were numerous, though many less-hard-working inhabitants gained a precarious living by begging or by undertaking menial tasks, such as porterage or night and day watchmen's duties, to stop the widespread pilfering. Though the penalties for theft were severe, such as the loss of fingers or even the severance of the robber's hand, there were still plenty of thieves in Jerusalem.

Simon and Pierre were enthralled by the passing scene as they made their way through the busy crowds. Whatever they had already seen in Paris, Lyons, Marseilles, Acre and Tiberias was eclipsed by the richness of the varied crafts and exotic merchandise which were being displayed, made, or repaired in the narrow streets of Jerusalem.

The clamour was even more insistent than it had been in Acre, and the wide variety of languages defied identification. To Latin, Greek, Arabic, French, Spanish, Italian, German, Genoese, Pisan and occasionally even English, were added Armenian, Turkish, Kurdish, Maltese, and Hindustani, Perm and Urdu from the lands of Persia, Afghanistan and India. The speakers of these last languages were traders bringing rare spices and finely made goods along the caravan trail of the Silk Route, which ran from Outremer to Cathay.

To this ear-piercing racket were added numerous church bells, ringing in Matins, and the sounds of military trumpets, the clash of cymbals and the thunder of drums.

As for colour, there was the plethora of merchandise: silks of every hue; carpets and cloth made of wool, cotton and satin, all dyed in every vegetable-extract colouring known to the alchemist.

Like Acre, Jerusalem smelt of rich incense and pungent spices, the musky perfumes of the Orient and the heady distillations of orange-blossoms, roses, violets, lilies, wild orchids and mimosa; but to such a degree that these sensuous aromas cut down the background stench of animal and human waste products to manageable proportions. In time, the visitor hardly noticed these other, unpleasant odours and breathed in their rival exotic scents with languorous pleasure.

That early morning ride round the Holy City made a lasting impression on Simon, if not on Pierre whose earlier life at the French court had somewhat blunted his senses with a variety of luxury. In Jerusalem, the city beggars left the Templar troops alone, knowing that the Order had taken the vow of poverty. The local citizenry respected the Templars for reasons other than wealth, for here were the swords and the lances which kept Jerusalem free of the Saracens.

The native working population knew that if Saladin reconquered Jerusalem, the 'converted' locals would get short shrift. Beheading by a blow from a razor-sharp Saracen scimitar would be the quick way out. Torture of the most excruciating kind would be the more likely fate of any of the 'Faithful' who had backslid into Christianity.

In the year 1181, there were about 1,000 knights and unknighted lances, all told, including sergents, among the two great Military Orders of the Hospitallers and the Templars. The lances were made up mainly of mounted turcopoles and other mercenaries, and acted as light scouting forces, or even joined in the charges of the heavily armoured knights. Their numbers were scattered all over the garrisons of Outremer and Outrejourdain. Another 1,000 or so Frankish, Spanish, Italian, German and other European chevaliers could be counted upon to fight for Christendom, but that was all. The huge discrepancy between the opposing forces was obvious, for facing them

Sultan Saladin could muster at least 15–20,000 cavalry, including the finest horsemen in Arabia.

The Second Crusade had petered out and if a Third Crusade was to be mounted, after this precarious period of truce, many more Christian reinforcements would be required to fight it.

The Frankish forces relied heavily on their auxiliary infantry, made up of crossbowmen and spearmen, to act as a back-up for the knights, and to man the walls of all the Christian strongholds, to resist the Saracen forces when Saladin decided to make his move. The feeling everywhere was 'when', and not 'if'. That happy alternative was now being discounted by most thinking pilgrims, and certainly by the Crusaders themselves.

Belami finally broke off his 'tour of familiarization', as he explained it later to the Templar Marshal, Hugh de Belfort, who had been somewhat impatiently awaiting his report.

'On patrol, you saw no signs of Saracen activity?' asked the incredulous Marshal, who was not as familiar as others with Belami's record or his unconventional methods.

'Only the flash of their heliographs on the horizon, as they passed messages of our progress from hill to hill. We were watched closely all of the way. News of our engagement with de Châtillon's men must have travelled fast across the land.'

'God's wounds!' cried de Belfort. 'The whole situation is as explosive as this new-fangled gonne-powder, of which we hear so much. Damn de Châtillon's soul to hell! This is a difficult enough job, Sergent Belami, keeping peace among the cut-throats in Jerusalem, without that insane upstart de Châtillon causing more trouble. Poor King Baldwin is almost incapable of ruling now, and de Lusignan gains more power every day. When our unfortunate monarch dies from his dreadful disease, let us pray that our Grand Master can influence the Barons to choose Raymond of Tripoli as regent, to advise the new boy-king, who will undoubtedly succeed our present invalid monarch. Raymond is no saint, but he is better than the others, especially de Châtillon.'

This diatribe had been more due to de Belfort's habit of talking to himself, than intended to be an accurate briefing of the political situation for the benefit of the experienced veteran, but it confirmed every suspicion that Belami had.

Such was the veteran sergeant's past reputation that it was only twenty-four hours before Arnold de Toroga, the Grand Master of the Templars, ordered him to attend the Chapter; something that, in normal times, would have been unheard of.

The Templar Chapter-house was octagonal in shape, for reasons of the Sacred Geometry, and contained twelve stone benches, ranged round the walls, with one Templar knight seated on each marble throne. The Grand Master stood in front of his *prie-dieu*, placed in the centre, fronting a small altar on which a cross, made up of two Templar swords laid at right-angles, had been placed. The Grand Chapter was a Templar High Court within a system that was theoretically controlled by the King of Jerusalem. As it contributed a great deal to the kingdom's funds and supplied a large part of its military strength during the Crusades, the Templar court's existence was not only tolerated but the Grand Chapter's political power tacitly acknowledged.

Belami marched in alone and saluted the Grand Master. The veteran recognized many of the Chapter members, with whom he had previously served. A flicker of a smile hung on his lips, as he noted at least three previous commanders. They, in return, allowed themselves a nod of acknowledgement.

The Grand Master spoke: 'Sergeant Belami, I welcome you back to Jerusalem. The Order needs your invaluable experience and knowledge. I understand from Marshal de Montfort that you bring fifty lances with you, and that you also have two young sergents, whom you have personally trained and highly recommend. Your actions over the rescue of Sitt-es-Sham have been duly noted and are approved.

'I am giving you a one hundred more experienced auxiliaries, half of them turcopoles and the rest crossbowmen.'

'Infantry, Worshipful Grand Master?' Belami's tone was disapproving. 'That will hold up my command, for certain. We will need to move swiftly, sir, if we are to prevent de Châtillon's forces from raiding in the Red Sea area.'

'We can spare you no more cavalry,' said the Grand Master sternly. 'I need every lance I can muster to hold the Kingdom of Jerusalem against the Saracens. You will have to use infantry as well.'

'I have carried out such combined manoeuvres before, Worshipful Grand Master. Over short distances, this is only practical during an attack. On patrol it exhausts both men and horses as neither infantry nor cavalry can move at the other's pace.'

'Then divide them into a striking-force and a reserve-force, Sergent Belami. That is the best I can suggest. In fact, Sergent, it is an order. Thank you for coming. Dismiss!'

Belami saluted smartly, spun on his mailed heel and marched out of the Chapter-house. He was furious.

'Knights!' he muttered. 'By-Our-Lady knights! They never listen.'

From reliable sources, such as old comrades and ex-commanders, Belami soon pieced together a true picture of the chaotic forces at work in Jerusalem.

The dying young King Baldwin IV – was almost powerless. The Regent, who was officially Guy de Lusignan, grudgingly shared his power, if not his authority, with Raymond III of Tripoli and Reynald de Châtillon. The old Patriarch, Almaric, the Pope's rival representative in Jerusalem, had been hounded out of the city, just as Archbishop William of Tyre, the famous chronicler, had been forced to leave Outremer by de Châtillon. Greek Orthodoxy had achieved schism with Rome much earlier, leaving a gap between the forms of Christianity. A puppet patriarch, Heraclius, now acted as the all-powerful barons' spokesman on Church matters. This left the Templars and the Hospitallers as the only truly independent forces in Jerusalem.

Belami, who had already dreamt up a possible solution

to the problem of his command's mobility, was busy welding together his new force of combined cavalry and infantry when de Châtillon made the next move. Reynald's small fleet – built, as he fondly imagined, in secret – was now launched into the Red Sea.

Meanwhile in Damascus, Saladin, the supreme commander of the Ayyubid sultanate, and his numerous allies, were listening to his sister's account of the unprovoked attack on her caravan. Sitt-es-Sham and her retinue had returned to Damascus with a strong escort, provided by the guardians of Mecca. Flanked by such a powerful force of fighting men, no Christian raiding-party had dared molest them.

Her story of her unexpected rescue by the Templar sergents left Saladin with mixed feelings. The first was righteous wrath that the infidel traitor, de Châtillon, should have repaid his trust with such barbarous treachery; his second reaction was one of confusion.

Saladin had once sworn to behead any Templar who fell into his hands, after a massacre of his people by an over-zealous Templar force. Now he would have to revise this oath, an action which, for a devout Muslim like Saladin, was a moral somersault.

However, Sitt-es-Sham was adamant. The three Templar sergents, whose names she had obtained, had saved her life and probably her honour as well from an Assassin disguised as a Frankish knight. Therefore, they must be suitably rewarded.

Saladin gave grateful thanks to Allah for his sister's safe return, and made a mental note to spare and honour the three brave Templars, should they ever fall into his hands. He then swore to kill de Châtillon, and immediately gave orders to summon his generals. As far as Saladin was concerned, the truce was ended. From now on, it was no longer the *Pax Saracenica*, but *Jehad* or 'Holy War'!

10

JEHAD

The leader of Islam was a complex man, of great humility and unmatched courage. Unlike the archetype of a Muslim leader, the Ayyubid Supreme Sultan was an intellectual, with little love of the hawking, hunting or feasting which had distracted many of his royal predecessors. His only sport was polo, for he was a marvellous horseman and saw this fast-moving game as a form of chess played with cavalry. His mastery of the great board-game had been given to him by his teachers from Damascus University, along with a love of the Gnosis, especially the arts and sciences of astronomy, mathematics, architecture, music, natural-lore and beauty in all its forms, as the work of Allah, the Only God.

Damascus, which he had wrested back from the Christian infidels, personified for him all that was beautiful in Arabian architecture and city planning. Its many shady groves and numerous gardens, large and small, public and private, were oases of colour, perfume and natural beauty, and the Sultan's greatest pleasure was to enjoy these peaceful havens, alone. In other words, among all the Muslim leaders, Sultan Saladin was unique. This was why his actions and reactions were hard to predict.

Tall, handsome, and in middle-age still surprisingly fit and active, this Prince of Ayyubids was an extraordinary personality, with the gift of immense charm. Though shy and retiring as a boy, by diligent study and application he had grown into a skilled leader who could keep his counsel until it was needed. Only when asked for his opinion would he give it. Saladin was neither a braggart nor a liar. When he spoke, it was to tell the truth.

Add to these qualities his devout belief in the righteousness of the cause of Islam and you had a leader capable of throwing back the crusading hordes who had desecrated and plundered the Middle East.

Back at Tiberias, Abraham-ben-Isaac had described the Saracen leader to Simon thus: 'Salah-ed-Din was born in 1138, one of seven brothers and one sister. His father was Ayyub-ibn-Shadhy, an official in the retinue of Zengi, the Atabeg of Mosil. His mother was Nejm-ed-Din. His father had been a warden of Tekrit, a fortress where Zengi had once taken refuge after a disastrous defeat. When Zengi's fortunes changed, he remembered that he had once owed his life to Ayyub-ibn-Shadhy, and took him into his retinue.

'Although Saladin's father was a Mohommedan, he himself was a Kurd, of the clan Rawadiya. A gallant and war-like people, they had a great sense of honour and hospitality. Saladin inherited all of his father's tribal virtues.

'Saladin's full name is Yusuf Salah-ed-Din, meaning, "honour of the faith". It is a name that he richly deserves.

'In all the Middle East, Simon, you will not find a more honourable, chivalrous or devout man. In addition to those qualities, he has the courage of a desert lion and the stubbornness of a mule. He is indeed a formidable opponent for Christendom to blunt its claws upon.

'Osama, Prince of Sheyzar, a great scholar and philosopher, took the bright young son of Ayyub-ibn-Shahdy under his wing. Osama was a supreme magus, with great insight into the characters of people. In the young Yusuf, then only a boy, the wise magician must have recognized all the qualities of greatness. Saladin was only thirteen when they met, yet Osama sensed the boy's destiny. You, Simon, would be fortunate to meet such a man.'

'I have already,' Simon had replied confidently. 'You, my teacher, Abraham-ben-Isaac, are *my* Osama!'

The old philosopher had been pleased, but had shaken his head. 'I am not on the same plane of development as Osama, Prince of Sheyzar. He is the sort of being that you Christians refer to as a saint.'

During his many conversations with Abraham, Simon had learnt a lot more about Saladin. He knew about the Saracen leader's education, at Baalbeck and Damascus, and his early life at Nur-ed-Din's court. This Atabeg was one of the sons of Zengi who, in 1146, had been assassinated, and Nur-ed-Din had taken on his murdered father's whole retinue to serve him.

Nur-ed-Din, like his father Zengi, had recognized the young Saladin's qualities, even at that early age.

During the First Crusade, with its rapidly changing fortunes of war, Saladin had been too young to take an active part; but, as his father's fortunes had prospered under Nur-ed-Din's regime, so had his own.

His ability to absorb knowledge had soon marked him out at university and, when he was old enough to serve the son of his father's old benefactor, he had come to Nur-ed-Din's notice as a bright young troop-commander. From then on, his promotion to captain and then to commander-of-cavalry had also brought him to the attention of Nur-ed-Din's colleague, Shirkuh, a Saracen general of great dash and ability, distantly related to Saladin. Yusuf Salah-ed-Din's star started to shine, for all to see.

'This was a two-edged blessing,' chuckled Abraham, when he had come to this part of Saladin's life. 'Fame in battle and the young cavalry-commander's obvious intelligence not only made him a valuable asset to the sons of Zengi, it also marked him out as a possible future rival. Saladin was clever enough to realize the situation and played down any pretensions that he might have had to power. He served the brothers faithfully and well, and with complete dedication. The sons of Zengi, who were constantly alert for signs of treachery, acknowledged Saladin's honesty and chivalrous behaviour. They could find no fault in him, so he lived with honour and fortune. It was a tricky time for clever men, especially with the proven ability to command the respect and love of their troops.'

Saladin was, above all, a devout Muslim and a great student of divinity and theology. He loved to hear learned scholars quoting passages from the Koran, and his unswerving orthodoxy protected him like a shield.

'He was no ambitious sheikh, seeking power, fame and wealth,' continued Abraham. 'Saladin was a passionate believer in Islam and, above all, wanted only to be an instrument of the Will of Allah. As a pupil of Ibn-aby-Usrun, the greatest theological scholar of his age, and as a favoured student of Osama, Saladin was already set on the broad highway of the Gnosis. That is why, Simon, Saladin is the true leader of the Saracens – because he is honest, brave, just, and merciful.

'So honour him, my son, for he is your greatest adversary. Christendom has a worthy opponent in Saladin, the "Honour of the Faith".' Abraham paused. 'My voices tell me that one day you two will meet. I know that the outcome will determine your destiny.'

Simon de Creçy never forgot Abraham-ben-Isaac's words. They came to mind as he helped Belami train his new command. In essence, the veteran's tactics were simple, and therefore impeccable.

His 'flying column' was composed of excellent light-cavalry and well-trained infantry, the only difficulty being that the latter slowed down the former. But Belami had soon solved that problem.

Taking a leaf from the Roman legions' book of tactical deployment of such mixed troops, the wily old soldier trained his men to work in unison. When his cavalrymen rode, an infantryman ran alongside each horse, holding on to the horseman's stirrup. This meant that the flying column on patrol could only move as fast as an infantryman or a crossbowman could run; however, when the cavalry dismounted, to walk their horses, the infantry could, after a short rest, easily catch them up.

During an actual attack, the best archers rode pillion on the turcopoles' chargers, slipping off at the last moment to support the final charge with flights of crossbow bolts.

It took a lot of training, much cursing and frayed tempers, but blessedly it worked.

Belami's flying column was nearly as fast on patrol as it had originally been without the infantry. The shrewd veteran had found a viable answer to the problem that the Grand Master had set him; which is precisely what the intelligent old Templar knight had known he would do. Arnold de Toroga was no fool.

When Reynald de Châtillon finally launched his small fleet and set off down the coast of the Red Sea, he was infuriated to find that a Templar flying column was often paralleling his course by land. Target after target became too difficult for him to plunder unnoticed. Only when he split his fleet in two, did the angry de Châtillon succeed in landing and ravaging the Red Sea ports, mainly on the African side.

Belami could not stop the raiders altogether, but he made things as difficult as possible for them. The result was that only a small number of the crusading corsairs' targets were ravaged or besieged, like Aydhab on the African shore. This delaying tactic gave Admiral Lulu, an Egyptian fleet commander, time to deploy his ships and relieve the siege of Eyla. The raiders still had time to attack and sink an Arabian pilgrim-ship bound for Jeddah, leaving no survivors, and they burned shipping at both Al-Hawra and Yambo. The Muslim world was horrified but, had it not been for Belami's presence at many of the other targets, the slaughter would have been much worse. Time and again, the Templar flying column forestalled a Frankish attack and massacre. Naturally, de Châtillon was furious and eventually had to call off his unprovoked raids in the Red Sea area.

The climax came when Admiral Lulu landed his forces, mounted them on Bedouin horses obtained locally, and cut de Châtillon's raiders to pieces in the Gorge of Rabugh. Reynald de Châtillon barely escaped with his life and most of his men were killed. The Lord of Kerak then hastily retreated to his fortress at Kerak de Moab, which was as near impregnable as a castle could be.

It may seem strange that Belami's mission had been to

hamper Frankish forces, but such were the intricate political moves of the time. Belami had not lost a single man, cavalry or infantry, but he had prevented large-scale massacres of innocent people by the Lord of Kerak. That alone had banked the fires of Saladin's revenge more slowly and, vitally, won Arnold de Toroga more time in which to reinforce his garrison at Jerusalem.

The *Pax Saracenica* was in tatters, the *Jehad* was ready to start, and on 29 September 1183, the Saracen commander crossed the River Jordan, ravaged the fertile plain of Ghaur and sacked the town of Beysan, which had been deserted by its Christian defenders.

He then advanced up the valley of Jezreel, and camped beside the Well of Goliath. Saladin had thrown down the gauntlet.

Belami hurried back to Jerusalem and reported to the Grand Master of the Templars.

'But, Belami,' Simon protested, 'whose side are we on?'

'Certainly not de Châtillon's, *mon brave*. That murdering bastard has destroyed the truce and betrayed the Christian cause. He would have slaughtered every man, woman and child in those undefended Red Sea towns. The fortunes of this political war have changed and we now have to face Saladin's wrath. But at least *we* are not child-murderers.'

The veteran was right, and Simon and Pierre knew it. 'These Crusader politics are beyond me,' said Pierre de Montjoie ruefully. 'But it's better to be part of a Crusade, to bring Christianity to the heathen, than to be branded baby-killers by history.'

'Which proves,' growled Belami, with a grin, 'that you aren't the idiot that I sometimes take you for.'

All this toing and froing had occupied many months and though it had seemed a waste of time to the two junior sergents, it had welded Belami's flying column into one of the most effective tactical units in Outremer. Its test in battle was soon to come.

Saladin was to prove a tough opponent. The fact that Zengi, the Atabeg, had been assassinated by his own retinue, kept Saladin constantly alert. Twice, the Assassins of Sinan-al-Rashid's murder cult had struck, both times narrowly missing accomplishing their mission. At the last attempt, only Saladin's chain-mail hood, which protected his head and neck, had stopped the blow. It had been a near thing and since then he had kept a close watch even on his trusted companions, for one of his assailants had been a member of his personal bodyguard.

Now that he had openly declared the *Jehad*, the Saracen leader was doubly vigilant.

His last victory against the Crusaders, before the truce, had been at 'King Baldwin's Folly', the Castle of Sorrows at Jacob's Ford. Saladin had besieged the stronghold for five days. Finally, the stout walls had collapsed, due to the Saracen sappers' mining them and then burning the supporting wooden props inside the mineshafts.

On the fifth day, he had entered the castle, set the Muslim prisoners free and then razed the whole fortification to the ground. Since then an uneasy truce had reigned until the Holy War had been declared.

During another previous battle – a combined Templar, Hospitaller and Frankish attack on Saladin's camp at the Meadow of Springs near Mesafa – Saladin had defeated the Crusaders and captured their leaders. These included Raymond III of Tripoli, Balian of Ibelin, Baldwin of Ramla and Hugh of Tiberias. In addition to these important Frankish knights, he had taken prisoner the masters of both military orders. Odo de Saint Amand had been one of them.

All the knights except Odo were freed, in return for ransom and their solemn word that they would not continue their fight against Saladin. Only de Saint Amand refused to take this sacred oath and offered no ransom whatsoever.

'Templar money is not mine to use to free myself,' he had said defiantly.

Saladin had admired the Grand Master's ferocious fighting and, once more, offered him his freedom *without* ransom if he would take the oath. Odo de Saint

Amand refused once again, and died in prison of fever, in Damascus, a few months later.

Saladin regretted his death and buried him will full honours, as befitted a brave and chivalrous opponent. Subsequently the other knights *all* negated their sworn vows and plotted against Saladin throughout the truce. Their archbishop had absolved them all.

When Belami told Simon the circumstances of his father's death, he had emphasized Saladin's generosity.

'How long had my father been Grand Master?' Simon asked.

'From 1171 to 1179; eight years of dedicated service to the Order. When you were born in 1163 your father was a Templar knight. In the following eight years, by his skill, dash and daring, he had become Grand Master of the Order of the Temple. He died a soldier's death, Simon. Saladin respected and honoured him not only as a soldier, but also as a scholar. The Saracen leader gave your father every opportunity for ransom, or his word of honour, in return for his freedom. Saladin is as chivalrous as the best of our Christian knights, if not more so.'

With Belami's return to Jerusalem, and his full report of de Châtillon's raiding and the destruction of his force at the Gorge of Rabugh, Arnold de Toroga had also received new Templar reinforcements from Acre. His force was now up to full strength and he offered the Order's services to Guy de Lusignan, now the undisputed regent in Jerusalem.

The tortured body of the young King Baldwin IV was near death, his limbs useless and actually decaying. His mind was still active, but his ability to command had nearly gone. De Lusignan saw his chance and summoned the entire forces of the kingdom to his aid. Raymond III of Tripoli, both the Grand Masters of the Temple and the Hospitallers, the Ibelin Brothers, Reynald of Sidon and two powerful visitors, Godfrey, Duke of Brabant and Ralph of Mauleon, all flung their political weight behind him. Even the despicable Reynald de Châtillon came racing up from Kerak de Moab, to add his lances to the rest of the Crusaders'. Politics has a short-lived conscience.

'Judas Iscariot! We know how far we can trust de

Châtillon. But we have no choice. Suddenly that lying swine is our ally. Please God, I don't have to save his worthless hide!' Belami was scathing but, as always, he obeyed orders.

Out from Jerusalem rode the Crusaders, making a brave show of their knightly banners, exotic guidons and brightly painted Frankish shields, in contrast to the sombre black surcoats of the Hospitallers and the Templar Corps of Sergents, and of course the all-white garments of the Templar knights. With them went the turcopole cavalry, and the auxiliary infantry. In all, after leaving a small garrison in Jerusalem, the Crusaders mustered one thousand knights and lances and a further 10,000 infantry. They had no idea that Saladin's forces totalled well over 20,000 troops, cavalry, mounted-archers, skirmishers and infantry, divided into three main forces. These were led by Saladin himself, with Taki-ed-Din, his favourite nephew, and his elder brother, Feruk-Shah, in command of the other two divisions. The Saracens were all seasoned warriors, fast-moving and deadly in battle. They outnumbred the Franks by over two to one.

If Belami's method of combining infantry with cavalry columns had been used, the Crusaders would have had the advantage. Unfortunately, the cavalry columns were slowed to the marching pace of their trudging infantry, giving the Saracens the advantage of greater mobility and speed.

The young Homfroi de Toron, who was hurrying to join the Frankish forces with his stepfather's troops from Outrejourdain, was cut off by the Ayyubids and his troops massacred. He himself, though only seventeen, fought bravely but had to retreat to Kerak, where he sought refuge. As a fighting force his decimated troops were finished.

The first battle between the two armies in Saladin's *Jehad* was to be fought out on the Plain of Jezreel. Belami's flying column went into the attack, with Simon and Pierre leading the one hundred mixed cavalry and infantry, the veteran himself commanding the remaining fifty turcopole lances. Belami's job was to break up the Saracen skirmishers, a thousand Scythian horse-archers, who could all shoot from the saddle.

Every time the skirmishers swept in to release a cloud of arrows, Belami's mixed force was there to intercept them and blunt their attack. Moreover the Scythians were losing many men to Simon and Pierre's crossbowmen, who were rushed into battle, pillioned on the turcopoles' chargers. As they leapt to the ground and discharged their deadly crossbow bolts, dozens of Scythian skirmishers hurtled from their saddles.

The Saracen skirmishing line wheeled round to retreat. Immediately Belami and his sergents charged their ranks, spitting the shrieking Scythian horse-archers on their lances. Before the skirmishers could re-group, the Templar flying column had swept round and regained the cover of their own dismounted crossbowmen. Then they repeated the tactic finally picking up the crossbowmen to ride behind each turcopole and rejoin the Frankish column. It was a perfect copy-book manoeuvre.

Had Guy de Lusignan been a more efficient commander, his whole force could have used the same tactics. Sadly, the Regent of Jerusalem was an excellent politician but a poor general. He dithered and halted the Frankish force at the Pools of Goliath, instead of immediately advancing against Saladin's main force before they had formed up their crescent-shaped line of battle.

The Franks, Templars and Hospitallers relied heavily on outmoded tactics. They had always used their chief tactical weapon, the sheer weight of charging knights in a compact mass, to break through the heathen ranks. De Lusignan was confident he could use the same hoary old manoeuvre yet again.

Belami swore in Arabic, his favourite language for effective cursing.

'Why can't the By-Our-Lady idiot see that Saladin is waiting for the Frankish charge? By the bones of the Prophet, when old "Iron Breeches" finally lumbers forward with his knights, that wily Saracen will open his centre ranks and let the force of the charge expend its

169

weight on thin air! Then Saladin will wheel his crescent of cavalry round and attack de Lusignan's rear, as our knights break up into loose formations beyond. A child could see why Saladin has formed his cavalry in that great crescent formation. God give me strength! Why are we commanded by fools?'

As things turned out, apart from desultory clashes of small cavalry units on both sides, de Lusignan stayed encamped by the Wells of Goliath while his commanders argued hotly.

The real reason for his hesitation was the unexpected size of Saladin's army. Its crescent formation seemed to stretch, from horn to horn, a full mile of cavalry. To attack it, now that it had manoeuvred into its most effective battle-line, seemed like suicide. De Lusignan had failed to hit the Saracens while they were forming up, and now it was too late.

Saladin tried to lure the Franks into a headlong charge, but failed to entice their divided leadership into battle. The whole fiasco disintegrated into small patrol actions and showy, feigned attacks by the Scythian horse-archers. The sky became clouded by long-range showers of their arrows, but few of these light shafts feathered in the armoured Frankish troops, and instead sprouted from the ground like wheat-stalks. In return, the Crusaders' heavier crossbow bolts emptied many Scythian saddles.

After five days' desultory sniping, and a few losses among the Frankish army, de Lusignan withdrew to safety behind Jordan's banks.

Belami was furious. 'Well, Simon,' he said, 'what do you think of our brilliant battle? What a waste of By-Our-Lady time and energy!'

'I'm confused,' replied the young Norman. 'I could easily follow our own actions. Your tactics worked perfectly, Belami. Why didn't our Grand Master exploit the advantage we gave him?'

'Why can't pigs fly?' growled Belami. 'What's your rede on this non-existent battle, Pierre? Come on, boy, as a prospective knight you're supposed to tell *me* what to do, one day. How say you?'

'It's a farce!' swore Pierre disgustedly. 'A By-Our-Lady cock-shot. We did better against de Malfoy.'

Belami and Simon laughed grimly but the veteran was worried. 'If this is how de Lusignan intends to continue, we may as well retire behind strong walls and hope we are relieved before we are starved out.'

The first clash of arms in the Holy *Jehad* had been a futile gesture, bad for morale and a sign of worse to come.

Saladin was puzzled by the unusual Frankish reluctance to fight. They had missed their opportunity when the Saracens were moving up into position, and now they seemed content to retire behind the River Jordan. The astute Saracen leader had also noted the well-drilled actions of a small flying column led by the Templar sergents. Their manoeuvring of combined cavalry and infantry would be a hard tactic to overcome if it was adopted universally among the rest of the Frankish forces. One of his scouting forces, which had been engaged against de Châtillon's raiding columns in the Red Sea area, had reported similar tactics being used there by a Templar column. What was puzzling, was that they appeared to be hindering the Frankish raiders, without actually fighting them. The report had seemed unimportant at the time but, having seen these manoeuvres effective in action against his Scythians, it suddenly made sense to Saladin.

But why had the Templars tried out their new tactics against their own allies? The Saracen's shrewd brain worked on that problem, until he remembered his sister Sitt-es-Sham's report of de Châtillon's attack against her caravan on her way to Mecca. Could *those* three Templar sergents also be responsible for these intriguing new manoeuvres? Undoubtedly, they had saved Sitt-es-Sham from death or worse. Presumably they had been acting under orders from their Grand Master, to try to preserve the *Pax Saracenica*. Why? Perhaps to gain time to obtain more reinforcements?

The Saracen commander decided to send more spies into Jerusalem. He already had a hundred reliable men there. The mystery irritated him. Saladin liked to know the answers to riddles. Chaos upset him. The Sultan was essentially a 'cosmic man'. He liked everything to be in order. For him any new developments in the infidel camp needed to be explained.

He fell asleep, still pondering on the strange tactics. His last thought, before sleep claimed him, was that he would like to meet the men who had thought up that well-executed manoeuvre. He wished they had been Saracens rather than Templars.

Saladin's next move would be against Kerak, his arch-enemy Reynald de Châtillon's stronghold, south-east of the Dead Sea.

During the indecisive battle on the Plain of Jezreel, neither Simon nor Pierre had been engaged in hand-to-hand combat other than with the lance, though Simon had shot four Scythians out of their saddles during the exchange of arrows.

To his surprise, both he and Pierre had been hit by several Saracen shafts, but the light reed arrows had failed to pierce either their own armour, or the heavy quilted cotton bodycloth of their chargers. Belami, too, had found no opportunity to use his battle-axe and he also had been hit by Scythian shafts, without them penetrating his chain-mail.

'I've seen Crusaders looking like porcupines,' he remarked, 'with Saracen shafts sticking out all over their surcoats. Yet only one or two shafts did any real damage; a hit in the throat, face, or unprotected hand being the only danger. The lesson is simple. Keep every part of you well-covered and your head down during those massed arrow-flights that they send over at long-range.'

The whole affair had been an anti-climax. The blazing row that developed back at Jerusalem was over Guy de Lusignan's perilous indecision. Some like de Châtillon and Raymond III of Tripoli, flatly accused him of cowardice. The dying King was shocked and angry.

In his appalling state, the poor wretch had asked de Lusignan to install him in the Regent's city of Tyre, where the sea-breezes would be more beneficial to his leprosy. Inhumanely, de Lusignan had refused to accommodate him. With his remaining strength, King Baldwin IV deposed the Regent and proclaimed his nephew, also called Baldwin, the six-year-old son of Sibylla, his sister, his heir.

De Lusignan was furious and returned to Ascalon, another of his possessions. He then shocked everyone by denying his allegiance to the dying King. Belami was as shaken as the others.

'It just shows how much things have changed since I have been away from the Holy Land. I would have bet my last besant that de Lusignan was a good field commander and a trustworthy knight. I even hoped the High Council would put him in charge, rather than de Châtillon or Raymond III of Tripoli. By Judas Iscariot, I was wrong!'

The tough old sergeant shook his head in bewilderment. 'I've seen Guy de Lusignan in battle, fighting beside Odo de Saint Amand. In those days he fought well. I wonder what woman has weakened his will?'

Simon grinned. 'You sound more like Brother Ambrose than Belami. "Spawn of the Evil One", was his description of women. Anyway, why a woman? Perhaps disease has done the mischief.'

'It's possible,' replied Belami. 'But he looks fit enough. My instincts tell me it's a woman. Perhaps the King's sister, Sibylla? God, he knows, she is ambitious enough, and she is de Lusignan's wife. Yes! That must be the answer! Why else would be Lusignan deny allegiance to the King save at her ambitious prompting? Somehow, I am certain that Sibylla is behind all this sudden uncertainty and indecision. Maybe she has some secret scheme with her husband? Who the hell knows!'

The veteran angrily shrugged his head and spat accurately at a dung-beetle, sending it scurrying for cover.

His outburst surprised his junior sergents, who had never seen Belami put out by politics before. Until then he had kept up with each development in the political field, but had shrugged them off cynically.

Actually, Belami was deeply concerned by the defection of de Lusignan. It had come at the worst possible time, with Saladin on the march, the King in the final stages of leprosy, and the barons divided.

'What a By-Our-Lady mess,' swore Belami. '*Mes amis*,' he turned to his junior commanders, 'you are about to see something that has not happened for many years.' He paused dramatically. 'I, Belami, Senior Sergent of the Corps of the Order of the Temple, am going to get dead drunk!'

Which he did, ending up by smashing a wineshop to pieces and only being subdued by the efforts of ten soldiers of the watch. Nobody got seriously hurt, beyond a few bruises and the loss of some teeth. The publican received compensation from the Templar treasurer. Belami got a severe reprimand from Arnold de Toroga, as did Pierre and Simon for aiding and abetting their senior sergent. Their hang-overs, however, were worse than their punishment. Cheap red wine, in quantity, can be a fiercesome thing the morning after.

Their joint penance was a direct posting to Kerak, to train the garrison there in the new tactics involving cavalry and infantry. Arnold de Toroga, the Grand Master, was a clever man and chose a subtle punishment to fit the crime. Kerak was de Châtillon's castle. Belami groaned with frustration.

'Trust the Worshipful Grand Master to think up something really special!' Then he laughed his great bellow of mirth. 'Damn me for a fool! It serves me right. *Allons, mes amis*.'

He roused his companions, who were both nursing their aching heads. 'We ride to Kerak. I hear there is to be a wedding at the castle. Homfroi de Toron is to marry the Princess Isabella, yet another marriage of convenience for political reasons. He is only seventeen years old and she, poor mite, is barely twelve years of age. Perhaps Pierre can arrange for Queen Eleanor of Aquitaine to kidnap her before the ceremony. Kerak! *Merde de merde*! Now there's a boring place for you!'

The way it happened, that was the last thing Kerak

turned out to be. Unknown to any of them, Saladin was even then mustering his forces to march against Reynald de Châtillon's castle. The Saracen leader had right on his side, might under his command, and murder in his heart.

11
DESPERATE TIMES

The month of November 1183 brought a flood of guests to Kerak for the wedding of two great noble houses, Toron and Comnenus. Reynald de Châtillon and Queen Mary Comnena had little in common, but both of them saw this marriage as an opportunity to bring together two of the kingdom's opposing factions. As a cousin of the dying young King, Isabella might well prove to be an important pawn in the barons' power game.

To ensure the air of gaiety which such a marriage required, entertainers of many kinds: musicians, dancers, jongleurs and singers, had been brought from all corners of the Kingdom of Jerusalem. The fact that Saladin was on the move did not dampen the air of high spirits and festivity that pervaded the heavily fortified castle and town of Kerak de Moab.

The great pile of rock had been constructed to act as a garrison base, from which forays and sorties could be launched to intercept any caravan or large body of troops moving between Syria and Egypt. It was a strategic thorn in Saladin's foot, just as Reynald de Châtillon was a sore that had to be excised from the body of Islam. Both hurt Saladin's cause and therefore were prime targets for the *Jehad*. The Saracen leader determined to kill the lord of Kerak and raze his castle to the ground.

Just as Belami and his flying column came within

sight of Kerak, large dust clouds on the horizon heralded the approach of the Saracen army.

'At least life in Kerak won't be dull, now,' grunted the veteran. 'Get a move on, *mes braves*.'

This was easier said than done, for streams of refugees, farmers and shepherds had appeared from every quarter of the compass, yelling and screaming abuse as they drove their flocks and produce-laden carts towards the fortified town.

Belami lashed his way through them with his whip, acting as a traffic-controller to hurry the panic-stricken country-folk through the main gate.

The garrison had been alerted by the large dust-clouds in the north-west and now manned the castle walls, while a few bolder souls hurried down the streets to help Belami and his troops set up a holding rear-guard action outside the town walls. The garrison could not have cared less about the fate of the peasants, but if there was to be a siege, which now seemed inevitable, every cow, calf, sheep, lamb and goat, even camels and horses, would be a valuable source of food.

Swearing like a camel-driver, Belami had bullied, beaten, pushed and shoved most of the terrified peasants through the main-gate, and then ordered them to the safety of the frowning battlements of Castle Kerak.

As the last shepherd's rump was kicked through the gate, Saladin's skirmishers appeared, galloping over the ridge.

'Get the crossbowmen in position, Simon,' the veteran yelled above the deafening racket coming from men and beasts milling around the inner courtyards.

'Pierre, be ready to counter-attack before the main force arrives. Just one charge will do it. Then wheel round and get back, as fast as you can. I can see the outline of their siege-engines on the ridge. That means the main force will be slowed up by them. Simon, *à moi*!' The young Norman hurried over.

'Up to the castle with you, lad. I want every trebuchet and mangonel ready to fire at Saladin's main force when it comes within range. Like Acre's, Kerak's siege-artillery is mounted on the tallest towers. A few rocks about the Saracens' ears will halt their advance. We'll not hold the lower town for long. Best to soak the houses in lamp-oil and naphtha, and then let the heathen in. After that, we fire flaming arrows into in the town. That'll keep the whoresome *cannaille* busy.'

Immediately, Simon was off, racing up the sloping street to the castle. Belami had no time to see if his orders, or rather urgent suggestions, were being carried out when a whirlwind of Scythian horse-archers came racing out of the setting sun.

'Fire!' yelled Pierre, and a storm of crossbow bolts whirred out from the Templars' hidden position among the rocks outside the town gate.

The westering sun glared hotly into the defenders' eyes, but they shot well, waiting until the skirmishers were close enough to ensure that each bolt found a certain target. Saddles emptied rapidly and screaming horses, with their entrails hanging from belly-wounds, turned and raced back through the Scythian ranks.

Before they could regroup, Belami shouted: 'Charge!'

Pierre's troop immediately thundered out from the lower town and hit the disorganized skirmishers like a wall of death. Down went horses and riders in a shambles under the weight of the turcopole charge.

'Regroup!' shouted Pierre, and expertly wheeled his men round to race back to the covering crossbowmen. These were continuously firing into the thick of the Saracen horse-archers, one man shooting while a second crossbowman reloaded. Belami's fifty archers thus became twenty five men, each firing as fast as five shots a minute. It was a deadly barrage.

A second wave of Saracen skirmishers raced across the sloping plain, to reinforce their scattered advance-guard. As they did so, heavy rocks came whirring through the air, causing havoc among the startled riders. A further flight of smoking earthenware pots smashed into their swirling ranks. Simon's message was being acted upon. Greek-fire was also coming from the trebuchets on the castle walls.

Belami yelled again and led his own troop of turcopoles into the counter-attack. Their lances spitted the skirmishers right and left. The veteran's battle-axe mowed a swathe through the Saracen horse-archers, who were now unable to shoot back for fear of hitting their own men. It quickly became a massacre.

'Fall back!' shouted Belami. 'Through the gate. Pick up our archers on the way.'

As one man, his well-drilled troops wheeled round and raced back to the rocks, swerving to a momentary halt beside each of their crossbowmen. Then, as the foot soldiers mounted pillion, the cavalry galloped through the gate, which clanged shut behind them. Pierre and Belami were the last through the heavy double-doors before they were slammed home and bolted. Belami had only lost four men while dozens of Saracen skirmishers lay dead outside the walls of Kerak. First blood to the Templars!

Simon came racing down the sloping street and pulled up beside them. Pierre grimaced as Belami pulled a light Saracen arrow out of the youngster's thigh. His coat of mail had stopped the others. Several Scythian shafts stuck out from both the sergents' heavy surcoats. Otherwise they were unharmed.

'Now that's what I call a battle!' cried Pierre, his face alight with the excitement.

Belami growled: 'Shut your big mouth, boy and get the Hospitallers to tend to your leg. Simon, what's being done?'

The Norman grinned. 'The Seneschal knows you of old, Belami. His men are busy soaking the lower town in lamp-oil and naphtha.'

Belami looked relieved. 'Get up on the walls and hold them in play with the crossbowmen. No barrage this time; just use careful sniping to keep them at bay. They'll charge for sure. As soon as they do, retreat to the castle. We're going to need every man we can get on the main fortifications.' He looked around. 'Where the hell is de Châtillon?'

'Outside, making a break for the gate. The Lord of Kerak has been out to meet some tardy wedding guests.

They're going to get a hotter wedding reception than they bargained for.'

To Belami's delight, the speaker was d'Arlan, the old Templar sergent from Acre, who had arrived a week earlier with a Templar-escorted wedding party from the coast.

The two old veterans embraced briefly, laughing like truant schoolboys.

'Open the gate. One door only!' shouted Belami. 'Let the great Lord of Kerak enter!' His derisive laughter was lost in the creaking of the wide wooden bars as they were withdrawn to allow the door to open.

As soon as one half of the main town-gate swung back, a party of foam-flecked horsemen galloped in.

'Welcome, my lord,' shouted Belami. 'Close the gate, *mes amis*, or we'll have Saracen company for the wedding.'

The ponderous door swung shut behind the dishevelled party of terrified wedding guests. Without a word of thanks, de Châtillon galloped on up to his castle and disappeared inside the gate. The others followed.

'If we didn't need that pig, I'd have left him outside to Saladin's mercy,' Belami muttered to d'Arlan. His old colleague chuckled wryly.

'You're a By-Our-Lady wonder, you old goat!'

While the Templar crossbowmen held the Saracen light-cavalry at bay, Saladin's main-force slowly approached the town. By the number of large siege-engines they had brought with them, this was to be a lengthy affair. Belami blessed every sheep, lamb, goat and cow that he had driven inside the walls and up to the castle.

A panting Frankish infantryman stumbled up to him and saluted.

'The town is soaked in lamp-oil, *mon Sergent*' he rasped in the Languedoc dialect of Outremer. 'When do we fire it?

'When our Saracen guests arrive, *mon brave*,' said Belami. 'We must be hospitable. The night air strikes chill in these parts. We'll give them a nice roaring fire to warm their heathen bones.'

At that moment the Saracens' main-force sent in a wave of heavy-cavalry, under cover of flights of arrows, which raked the town walls.

'Back to the castle,' yelled the veteran Templar sergent. 'Let the heathens ram the gate.'

The Saracen charge swept up to the walls, covering a party of infantry. They were carrying interlocked shields, in the classic Roman *testudo*, or 'tortoise' formation. Thus protected, they pushed a heavy battering-ram into position in front of them, and proceeded to attack the double gate.

Showers of Scythian arrows swept the town walls, which were now empty. Nobody was hit.

'Retreat!' yelled Belami, and his small force backed up the street, the crossbowmen covering the splintering gate. Belami knew that for his trap to work it must not look contrived. They must appear to be fighting every inch of the way.

As the gates fell to repeated blows from the iron-headed ram, a horde of yelling Saracen infantry burst through it. They were mainly archers.

Immediately, from Belami's second line of concealed crossbowmen, a barrage of bolts whirred down among the attackers. They fell, mown down like ripe corn.

'Back!' shouted Belami, and led his command to their third and last position, above the lower town. The gates stood wide open, hanging in shreds from their great hinges. Through the narrow gap poured Saladin's cavalry, supported by a mass of yelling Fatimid infantry.

Soon, these were milling around in the narrow streets and courtyards of the lower town. Almost immediately they spotted the loot which had been left conspicuously in the oil-soaked houses. The stench left behind by the terrified defecating livestock which Belami had forced through the narrow gates, disguised the smell of oil and naphtha. This was purely accidental, but invaluable.

When he judged that the greatest number of Saracens had entered that could be allowed in without arousing suspicion, Belami gave the signal. It was a single fire-arrow, fired by Simon.

The flaming head of the cloth-yard shaft crashed into the postern guard-house. A moment later, the small building burst into flames. Immediately a shower of fire-arrows flew out from the battlements of the castle and thumped home through the open windows, into the piles of inflammable material within. With a crackle of flames, fanned by a strong evening breeze whistling in through the open gates, the town became a roaring furnace.

Screaming Saracen looters rushed back into the streets, their clothes already burning fiercely. Greek-fire, from a tower-mounted mangonel on the castle walls, added to the inferno.

Without glancing back, the Templars and turcopoles raced for the castle. Belami stayed until last, then, as the bridge over the castle fosse was destroyed, the veteran grabbed a rope, slung to him by d'Arlan from the battlements, swung over the deep ditch and climbed up one-handed to the cheers of the watching garrison.

Below him was a vision from hell. Shrieking Saracens burned like tinder.

'God! I hate doing that to brave men,' muttered Belami, and clashing to his knees, he said a swift prayer for the heathen dead.

The lower town was soon a gutted charnel-house. 'It's going to be a long siege,' said Saladin when he heard the news. 'Those men know what they are doing!'

Queen Maria Comnena and the Lady Stephanie, the respective mothers of the bride and bridegroom, decided to go ahead with the wedding as planned. Isabella and Homfroi had been betrothed for three years.

'How do you feel about this marriage?' Simon asked Pierre. 'Your sister Berenice was only twelve as well.'

'There is a big difference, Simon. My sister's bridegroom-to-be was five times her age. Spring married to autumn can sometimes be a happy arrangement, but January married to December – never! Homfroi is only five years older than his bride-to-be, and besides, Isabella obviously adores him. They probably played together as children, and their marriage won't be much more than play-acting 'til Isabella comes of child-bearing age.'

The main hindrance to the wedding came from Saladin, who immediately started setting up his big siege-engines in the razed part of the lower town. Just before the young couple's wedding day, the Saracen mangonels and trebuchets started hurling large rocks at Castle Kerak. Their working tempo increased when they found the range, and soon great stones thumped and crashed against the tall towers which jutted out from the castle's massive walls.

Inside the fortress, an air of forced gaiety gave way to a genuinely festive spirit as the wine flowed freely. The garrison replied to Saladin's catapults with carefully aimed missiles of their own, and even succeeded in knocking two of his mangonels to pieces.

At the height of the wedding-feast, with its colourful displays of expensive silk dresses and rich satins, stately dances and excellent entertainment by the many professional musicians, jugglers and acrobats, Queen Maria was so carried away by the success of the besieged wedding that she sent some of the marriage-feast dishes out, under a flag of truce, with her compliments to Saladin.

It was the kind of courteous bravura that the Saracen leader appreciated.

He promptly sent a messenger back, under the same white flag, to enquire which tower in the castle contained the marital bedchamber so that his siege-artillery could avoid attacking it, to let the wedding night be enjoyed in peace.

The whole arrangement was civilized and humane, and an indication of the Saracen leader's compassionate nature. However it didn't interfere in any way with his determination to take Kerak, raze the fortifications to the ground and kill Reynald de Châtillon, personally.

The treacherous Lord of Kerak had managed to smuggle out two messengers, under cover of these courtesies, and at night they made their stealthy way through the Saracen lines. They stole two Arab horses after killing the guards, and raced for help.

At the same time three homing-pigeons, bearing identical messages asking for help, were released to make their way to Jerusalem. Even though Baldwin, the leper King, was desperately ill, he summoned the Royal Army, under the command of Raymond III of Tripoli, and the large relieving force raced south to raise the siege.

The great walls of Kerak withstood the barrage from the Saracen mangonels and trebuchets without cracking, and Homfroi de Toron and his child-bride, Isabella, passed a peaceful wedding night in each other's arms.

In the morning, Saladin resumed the full bombardment of Kerak. Desultory sniping by archers on both sides produced a few casualties, but these were mainly Saracen, some of them due to Simon's unerring accuracy with his powerful longbow.

News of Raymond and the Royal Army's approach soon reached Saladin. He decided that the time had not yet come to meet the massed Crusaders in open warfare. With the strong garrison in Kerak on one side of them and the royal army on the other, the Saracens were now at a definite disadvantage.

That night, under cover of darkness, their siege-artillery was moved quietly out of range and, as the sun rose over the eastern ramparts, it became obvious that the Saracen army had silently withdrawn. The short siege was over. By 4 December, Saladin had moved back in the direction of Damascus.

The triumphant King Baldwin, suffering badly from his stoic journey in the royal litter, was carried into Kerak amid wild rejoicing and, after a drunken celebration, the wedding guests left for their various homes. However, there was still discord between the rival factions, wedding or no wedding, and the sensitive little Isabella was upset by it. Her new husband, who genuinely adored her despite their arranged match, did his best to comfort her.

The relieving force also brought exciting news for Pierre de Montjoie. Apparently, his father had died in Paris, unmourned by most of his family, and on his deathbed had decided to reinstate Pierre as his official heir. This meant that Sergent de Montjoie was elevated immediately to the rank of Count, and was automatically handed his Golden Spurs. Pierre was a knight.

Belami laughed like a hoarse schoolboy when he was told and, after embracing Pierre, who was still limping from his arrow-wound, he made mock obeisance to the new knight and count.

Pierre gave the veteran a tight bear-hug and burst into tears.

'Dammit, boy, or rather Sir Pierre, or Count de Montjoie, what the hell are you crying for?' asked Belami.

'I'll have to leave you both and return to Paris. I hate to do that. It's been a wonderful two-and-a-half years with you and I'll never find such comradeship again.'

'There's no chance of your becoming a Templar knight, I suppose?' enquired a grinning Belami.

'Not me, dear friend,' said Pierre, wiping his eyes on his sleeve. 'A sergeant I was and a sergeant I will always remain, in my heart. Who in God's Blessed Name would want to be one of our By-Our-Lady Templar knights? I'm only going because Berenice needs my guidance and love, and my new estates will have to be looked after.'

When he left for Acre, with d'Arlan's returning party of Templar guests, the three comrades wept openly. Belami and Simon would miss their merry companion for his warmth, friendship, humour and loyalty, as much as he missed them.

'We'll all meet up again,' said Belami, his voice gruffer than usual. 'But it will be a few years from now.'

'Keep yourself out of trouble,' said Pierre to Simon, his eyes brimming. 'I want you to be my brother-in-law.'

They waved him out of sight and themselves set about returning to Jerusalem. King Baldwin had heard about Belami's new tactics and his remarkably skilful handling of the initial action at Kerak, during de Châtillon's temporary absence.

'I need men like those Templar sergeants to guard my young heir,' he said.

That was taken as a direct order and Arnold de Toroga had no power to gainsay it. So, back to Jerusalem rode the Templars and their flying column.

When Belami and Simon arrived at the Holy City, there was a surprise visitor waiting for them. Abraham-ben-Isaac had been temporarily released from service in Tiberias by Raymond, and had come to Jerusalem to serve the High Court as their appointed instrument-maker and Astronomer Royal to the Kingdom. In fact, he had been appointed Chief Astrologer, but this was unofficial because divination by the stars was not considered respectable in a Christian state, but rather looked upon as sorcery. Everyone consulted astrologers but no one would admit it, especially Raymond III, the new Regent.

Abraham-ben-Isaac had brought beneficial poultices and herbs to alleviate the worst of the brave young King's suffering. Leprosy itself is not a painful disease, because it numbs the nerves of the body. But this leaves the limbs especially open to injury, for without the warning of pain, much damage can be done accidentally by the patient to himself. Abraham's knowledge of herbs and potions helped the dying King in his last few months of life, for which Baldwin was profoundly grateful.

So was Simon, for other reasons; now he could continue his learning under the wise Jewish philosopher's guidance. The time they spent together seemed to fly past. Dimly, but with growing clarity, Simon began to understand what the Gnosis meant, and why the Templars had used their Order to seek out its innermost secrets.

'"As above, so below",' said Abraham. 'These are the words of Mani, the great prophet Zoroaster's spiritual guide. They mean that from the infinitely small to the infinitely vast, all nature is one. You and I, Simon, and all men, women animals, fish, fowl, reptiles and even insects; *all* living things are part of the whole.

'We are all made of what we stand upon; we are part of everything that we eat and drink; we are part of the air that we breath; we are *all* a part of God. Never forget that, Simon de Saint Amand, for that, boy, is your real name. No man ever deserved it better. You were sent to me by God and by your dead father, just as *he* once came to me, to start you along the broad path of the Gnosis.

186

'There is one who will soon come into your life; my voices tell me that this is to guide you further along your course of destiny, this time into the way of love. Then yet another will come, to take your hand and guide you through the realms of Netsach, Tiphereth, Hod and Yesod, to Kether, the Crown itself. But this is in the future. You will have much to learn before this.'

Now Simon's education really started. There were long hours of study and nights of careful observation under the stars. Alchemical experiments had to be undertaken. Alembics had to be blown from white-hot crystal glass. Herbs needed to be gathered; extracts to be distilled, and, above all, the powers of the mind had to be explored, by releasing the subtle-body from Simon's physical one. This was accomplished by gazing at a flawless crystal, or into the infinite depths of a black bowl, filled with clear spring-water.

Abraham also had the power to hold the mind in abeyance; to render his pupil unconscious and to place Simon into a deep sleep. All this he taught his young disciple during the long months in Jerusalem. Belami arranged Simon's duty roster so that he could spend as much time as possible with the Jewish savant. He knew that Odo de Saint Amand would have wished it so.

Now Simon's flying dreams were controlled by his increasingly powerful will.

'Your Lord's Prayer is far older than Christianity,' said the sage. 'Use it wisely, *never* for evil. Say the words before every flight of your subtle-body. Say it when you return, to waken your physical one.

'Remember, the word 'occult' only means 'hidden'. But such things must be revealed slowly, one by one, like peeling the skin from an onion. No wise man bites into a fruit, until he knows it is neither poisonous nor contains a worm. Caution must be your watchword! Impatience can bring death, or even worse . . . madness.

'*Poli-poli* is what the African witchdoctors say. It means: slowly, slowly. Infinity cannot be taken by storm.'

Under Abraham's spiritual guidance, Simon never felt

187

fear again, though in the realm of Netsach and on other pathways of the Tree of Knowledge, he sometimes saw terrifying sights.

'Thy rod and thy staff, they comfort me,' said Abraham. 'The rod is the love of God, the staff is the knowledge God gives you, Simon. Use them only for good. Then they will never fail you.'

12
THE HOLY CITY

Abraham also knew the evil side of Jerusalem, which evolved as the natural result of unscrupulous men's scramble for temporal power.

The commercial exploitation, the plotting and conspiracies, and the availability of 'free love', both male and female, had turned the intense spirituality of the First Crusade into a glittering sham. The wise old man knew the Holy City and its history, from years of research.

'Here is a city that should be sacred to *all* men,' he told Simon. 'Instead, the men who hold it spend more time fortifying it, than in sanctifying it.'

Now that Pierre de Montjoie had returned to France to claim his inheritance Simon had more time to spend with his revered teacher. His thirst for knowledge was unquenchable, which was why Abraham loved him. There was such quality in the son of Saint Amand.

The old man, whose tall, stooped shoulders had borne many burdens of responsibility and sorrow, and who had known little joy besides his own love of learning and humanity, poured out his heart to the Norman youth.

'The greatest happiness is that of inner peace, that comes from true love of God,' he said. 'I am not telling you that, Simon, in the pontificating way of some great prince of the Christian Church, but in the spirit of a great Jew . . . Jesus of Nazareth.'

Abraham's smile was gentle.

'You Christians use the word 'gentleman'; Jesus was a gentle man, a soul as near to God as mankind can ever be. He said: "These things and greater, shall ye do." There is a statement of hope, Simon. I am proud that the Nazarene and I came from the same town.'

Simon was astonished. 'You never mentioned that before.'

'Pure coincidence, believe me.' Abraham was not attempting to claim kinship in any way. 'However,' he continued. 'I went back to Nazareth and examined its earthly lines of force. For this examination I used only my hands. The detection of these subterranean watercourses, underground springs and sources, which run through our world like the arteries and veins through our bodies, can be felt through the hands alone, without the use of twigs or pendulums.

'Our nerves carry the messages of sight, touch, hearing and emotion to the centre of our being, the brain. In the same way, in *all* religions, the priests and worshippers alike point themselves towards the four quarters of the compass before their acts of homage or their prayers. They are orientating themselves; tuning their minds to the flux of the earth's energy.

'Christian, Jew, Mohammedan, Essene, Pagan, Heathen, Infidel, even animals, sense the different currents of these powerful earth-forces that flow beneath our feet. That is why the Muslims go unshod into their mosques, to contact the ground with their bare feet. They turn towards Mecca, where their source of power and faith resides in its closely guarded sacred place.

'The *Khaaba* is a stone. Osama once told me that it had fallen from Heaven. It is a metal stone, harder than the ores from which we extract iron, stronger than steel; welded densely together by its long journey through the heavens, from whence it came. The true Muslim senses the powerful drawing force of that sacred stone, as you Christians sense the power in your True Cross.'

The old rabbi lowered his voice. 'Whether the True Cross is actually a fragment of the crucifix on which that wonderful man died or not, it is the *belief* in its authenticity that makes it true. That is the power of the Gnosis.'

To show Simon the alignments of these flows of 'subtle' telluric-forces, radiating from certain parts of Jerusalem, Abraham walked with him all over the Holy City.

They made a strange pair, the gaunt elderly man, white-bearded and stooped from long years of study, walking with the aid of a curiously carved stick, accompanied by the tall handsome sergent of the Templar Corps, engrossed in his teacher's dissertations.

Every now and again, at a fountain, a wellhead, a spring of clear water or a towering cedar tree, they would pause and hold out their hands, as though to touch something.

Most of the people scurrying by, intent on profit or pleasure, failed to notice their rapt progress around Jerusalem. Not so Belami who, on these 'field-trips' of discovery, followed them at a discreet distance, like an unseen shadow.

If anyone became too interested in what his friends were doing, he would interrupt that person's trend of thought, by asking directions or by bumping into them 'accidentally', and then profusely apologizing. It was sufficient to distract anyone who wished to pry into his friends' privacy, and his actions were never noticed by the pair of 'seekers'.

Simon would long remember Abraham's discourses on the relationships of form, weight and number. Meanwhile his own rapidly developing ability to detect these lines of telluric-force gave him a new awareness, which stayed with him for the rest of his life.

'The great radiator of energy in Jerusalem appears to be the Rock of Abraham, my namesake,' said the philosopher. 'Feel how these multiple lines of energy which flow beneath our feet are reflected just above the surface of the earth, where we are standing.'

Simon's hands involuntarily twitched as he opened his mind to the lines of force. His teacher continued: 'Just as iron-filings gather around a lodestone in definite patterns, as though they have been regimented by a flow of force, so these lines of energy flow outwards from a central point of radiation.' He stroked his fine white beard. 'Who knows? Perhaps the Rock of Abraham also fell from Heaven.

'On any night, an observer of the skies can see shooting-stars crossing the horizon, or coming from certain points in the heavens. I have seen such magnificent displays at every season but I have noted, through the years, that these showers of shooting-stars appear with great regularity on certain dates in our Jewish calendar, which is different from your Christian one. However, if we convert the one into the other, you will observe that these dates are identical.'

It seemed to Simon that the central focus of the main-lines of these earth-energies in Jerusalem, came from the area where Solomon, the Master Magician, had sited and built his great temple. When he mentioned this to Abraham, the old man nodded his white-maned head so vigorously that he nearly lost his *yamulkah*, the traditional Jewish head-covering that he always wore.

'Precisely, Simon! Solomon was a powerful exponent of the great magical art, even as Moses was. All of our great prophets have been scholars of the Gnosis, and all of them have drawn their powers from these sources of energy in our sacred land. Most of them used these forces wisely, only occasionally falling into the trap of vanity and the misuse of such power.

'Using the earth-forces contained in flint-stones taken from the river-bed, David, the young shepherd boy, killed the Philistine giant Goliath, with his sling.'

Abraham was full of such anecdotes which he used to illustrate his discourses on various manifestations of the Gnosis.

When he showed Simon how the Mount of Olives and the site of the Garden of Gethsemane generated, or radiated, these strong lines of earth-energy, he said: 'That is why a similar mount to this sacred place was chosen by Jesus as the focus for His Sermon on the Mount, by the shores of Galilee. They were words spoken by a wise prophet indeed, and think about this – they were heard by a whole multitude of people. Whence came the power to transmit the voice of the gentle carpenter of Nazareth to the ears of so many thousands of people, gathered on the slopes of the Mount by the lakeside?

'Go, Simon, to the top of the Mount of Olives and shout with all your might. Few people down at the bottom of the slopes will hear you. Yet every word that your Lord uttered on the Mount at Galilee was heard by that whole multitude.'

On another occasion, Abraham said with a chuckle: 'I have always believed that Moses, our great Prophet, was a twin. If, as our history tells us, the infant Moses was found in the bulrushes by Pharaoh's daughter, whence came Aaron, his brother?'

Simon gasped. He had never before questioned the Holy Bible.

'Remember how Moses says: "My brother Aaron shall speak for me; for I am slow of speech." Moses suffered from an impediment. He hesitated often, finding speech very difficult. It is interesting, Simon, that he never refers to Aaron as: "my younger" or "elder" brother, but only as "my brother".

'In a book as full of pedantic detail as the Holy Bible, the exact relationship of each son and daughter, father, mother, uncle and aunt, cousin, nephew and niece, is meticulously laid out; yet the exact relationship Aaron to Moses, and any indication of whence he came, is never given. In such a document, which gives the precise measurements of the Ark of the Covenant, surely that is strange?'

Simon nodded. 'Then you believe that Aaron and Moses were twins, both being found abandoned in the floating crib?'

The savant's eyes seem to glow with the power of the Gnosis. Their gaze focused far back into history.

'Twins were considered to be an unlucky omen in Egypt. They were a sign that the gods were undecided into which body to place the *Ka*, or soul. I believe that the daughter of Pharaoh concealed one of the twin boys, and declared that she had found the other in the bulrushes.'

193

'As the daughter of the tyrant Pharaoh, why didn't she have the twins killed, or at least order the death of Aaron when she decided to keep only Moses?' asked his pupil.

'Simon,' said Abraham, 'no mother would kill her *own* sons, twins or not!'

The young Norman was fascinated by his teacher's line of thought. 'Her sons?' he asked excitedly.

'The daughter of Pharaoh had fallen in love with an Israelite craftsman.' The Jewish philosopher drew himself up to his full height, his hawk-like features glowing with pride. 'We Jews are an ancient people. Israel was not a race of ordinary slaves. The Holy Book tells us that Israel was in bondage in Egypt, not in slavery. The Israelites were bonded craftsmen: some were skilled shepherds and breeders of great flocks; others were master-craftsmen in wood, stone, and metal. Moses was brought up as a Prince of the House of Pharaoh. Why?

'I believe it was because he was one of the twin sons of a Princess of the Noble House of Egypt.

'Had the Israelites been merely slaves. Pharaoh would have felt little sense of loss when they left Egypt under the leadership of Moses. Yet he pursued them, as though they were a very valuable asset to his kingdom. Simon, the Jews were his master-builders, the skilled masons and engineers who helped to construct the great temples and the other wonders of Egypt.

'You have not yet seen the mighty Pyramids, not the great palaces and temples at Karnak and Phyllae. These marvels in stone could only have been constructed by master-masons, with a deep knowledge of the Sacred Geometry, the Golden Mean of proportion.'

Abraham's eyes glowed with an inner light. 'Such a one was Moses, a master of stone, a free-mason with a great awareness of the arcane secrets of the Gnosis. So also was Aaron the Priest. Presumably he was brought up by the priests of Isis, as another adopted member of Pharaoh's household.

'Is it not logical that Pharaoh's favourite daughter, one whom he would be loth to punish, fell in love with an Israelite craftsman, a temple builder, and by him conceived twin boys? When she discovers her condition she tells her trusted handmaiden and retires on a spiritual retreat among the priestesses of Isis, until the child is born.

'To everyone's consternation, however, she bears two children, twin boys!'

Simon's eyes were riveted on Abraham's face.

'She cannot bear to kill them, so she concocts this fantasy which has become accepted by both our peoples, and has become part of our joint religions.

'Pharaoh suspected the truth, but he had no wish to see his daughter punished, perhaps by death, for bringing dishonour to the Royal House of Egypt. But there was a convenient solution to the problem . . . Moses was "discovered" in the bulrushes, presumably sent to the childless daughter of Pharaoh as a gift from Isis, the sacred Earth-Mother. Meanwhile Aaron is brought up separately by the priesthood. Protocol had been observed! Everyone was content with the outcome. The Great Secret was protected under a sacred oath of silence.'

'But how could such a secret be preserved?' asked Simon.

Abraham looked deeply into his pupil's eyes. 'Who would know that better than you, Simon de Saint Amand?' he said.

The whole of the year 1184 was a continual revelation to the young Templar sergent. He was beginning to see what Bernard de Roubaix had meant when he said: 'Only in the Holy Land will you find many of the answers to the mysteries of the Templars.'

Already, through his own experiences and the teachings of Abraham, he was beginning to see the outline of the Gnosis.

Simon realized that as a totality, it was unknowable. He saw why the Christian Church was set against lay-people investigating what had become the inner mysteries of Christianity.

'If you try to storm the walls of the Gnosis, you will destroy your mind,' warned Abraham. 'Slowly, bit by bit, you must learn to unlock the right doors of your mind, at the right time. If you open the wrong doors, unprepared, the sheer horror of what you will see beyond them could blast your sanity to pieces.'

A terrifying example of what Abraham was talking about showed what could happen if a seeker became too impatient and attempted to find out more than he could control.

One afternoon, an Arab boy hurried to the Templar headquarters. He had a message for Simon from Abraham:

Come at once. I need your assistance.

Simon got leave from Belami and, pillioning the lad on the back of his destrier, he hurried over to Abraham's house, in the Street of the Silversmiths.

The magus had already left, but his destination was given to the Templar by his servant. Shortly after Abraham, Simon arrived at a house on the north side of the Holy City, near the Gate of Flowers.

This house, of some opulence, was set back behind a walled garden. It belonged to a wealthy merchant who had recently purchased it from the mistress of a dead alchemist. The purchaser had spent a lot of money on redecorating and reconstruction which had taken nearly a year to complete, due to various delays in the work.

One of the workmen had fallen off a ladder, another had been hit by a falling roof-tile and his skull fractured. A third craftsman had become a hopeless drunk and a fourth workman had broken his back when a ceiling beam had suddenly crashed down upon him, leaving him totally paralyzed.

The builder had flatly refused to carry out more work on the building.

'This house is accursed. Things inside it move of their own accord. Bricks and roof-tiles suddenly fall or fly across the room. I want no more to do with it. Pay me for what I have done and get some other fool to finish it!'

This had been easier said than done. No respectable builder would touch the job. Word travelled fast in Jerusalem. The merchant-owner was a Muslim turned Christian, and he had paid priests of both religions to carry out their rites of exorcism.

The Armenian Christian priest had entered the court-yard with complete confidence, armed with bell, book and candle. But although he was wearing a heavy crucifix around his neck, he had been struck by a shower of stones, soaked in water from an upturned barrel, and finally flung head-over-heels into the small front garden. In addition to these indignities he had been subjected to a dreadful smell of decay and covered by a huge swarm of flies.

Eventually, the terrified priest had rushed out of the walled garden, jibbering like a maniac. Once outside, he had fled to his church and locked himself in, refusing all entreaties to leave his vestry until the bishop was sent for.

The Imam, who had become a convert to the Christian faith, also tried to subdue the evil entity manifesting in the house. He had fared even worse. His prayers had been received with mocking laughter, and a whole plaster ceiling descended on his head. He had been dragged out of the house by his assistant, and had lain unconscious for a week.

Finally, in despair, the merchant had sought the assistance of Abraham-ben-Isaac.

The elderly savant listened carefully to his story and then gave his opinion. First, however, he asked a question.

'What was the name of the dead alchemist whose mistress sold you the house?'

'Malik,' replied the agitated merchant. 'Malik-al-Raschid.'

Abraham's eyes opened wide. He gave a stifled gasp. 'The brother of Sinan-al-Raschid, the Grand Master of the *Hashashijun*? Are you sure?'

The merchant swore this was the previous owner's name. 'You knew him?' he quavered nervously.

'Yes,' said Abraham. 'He was the embodiment of evil, an alchemist who also acted as Sinan-al-Raschid's spy, one of many in Jerusalem. I believe he himself was an Assassin, and I further believe he sacrificed virgin children to Moloch and Beelzebub.'

The merchant was terrified. Abraham's advice had been

to burn down the house and raze it to the ground; to dig up the cellar beneath it; and finally to have the Patriarch carry out a full-scale exorcism over the site.

The new owner, a kindly soul who had helped many people in distress, was desolate. He had invested a lot of money in the house and now seemed doomed to lose it all. Abraham took pity on him.

'You will never be able to live in it, but I can at least make it a safer place . . . to be used for stables, perhaps. That way you will not lose everything.'

The merchant saw the wisdom behind Abraham's words and gladly offered him money.

'If I took payment for what I must do, I would fail,' said the magus. 'What I shall do, I do for the good that you yourself have done.'

'But you hardly know me!' gasped the bewildered merchant.

'I know one thing about you. You are a good man with much compassion, therefore I honour you. It was the story of Jesus' compassion that drew you to the faith of Christ, not mercantile convenience.'

'That is true,' said the merchant. 'But I must repay you in some way.'

'Give generously to the poor!' was Abraham's final word on the matter.

The elderly savant knew that he was faced with a manifestation of Beelzebub, the Lord of the Flies, one of the Princes of Hell conjured up by the insane Assassin-alchemist. Abraham needed Simon's strength to help him.

'Remember,' he warned his pupil, 'do exactly as I instruct you, no matter what you see or hear!'

'I understand,' said Simon, his heart pounding with excitement.

Abraham gave him precise instructions. 'You must be unarmed. Chain-mail will avail you nothing. Wear a clean linen robe, which I have provided for you, and first wash youself all over. The house of my friend, Lamech, is just across the square. He will let you use his *mikphah*; it is a small pool for ritual bathing purposes.

He also is a Jew; a skilled goldsmith, whose work is much valued by Raymond III of Tripoli. Therefore, like me, he is allowed to live in Jerusalem . . . *our* Holy City.'

Fifteen minutes later, Simon, now dressed in Abraham's white linen robe, returned to the haunted house. Abraham awaited him, holding a metal mirror in his hand. He handed it to Simon.

'Look only into this if some demon appears,' he said, as though giving his pupil instructions on how to take a potion. 'You are unarmed?' he continued.

'Completely!' replied Simon. 'I feel half-naked.'

Abraham smiled. 'You are, Simon, except for your faith. *En avant, mon brave!*'

Unnoticed by either of them, Belami had been observing their actions from the shadows of a nearby house. It worried him to see Simon unarmed and unprotected by his chain-mail.

When the pair of them opened the garden gate, set in the high wall surrounding the haunted house, he moved nearer. Belami totally trusted the old magus, but he was worried about this strange venture. His keen ears had picked up some of the conversation held outside this house of mystery. He had not liked what he heard. When the door closed behind them, Belami waited a minute and then climbed a large vine which covered the outside wall. At the top, he peered into the inner courtyard. The house was silent. The two friends, master and pupil, approached it. By this time it was late afternoon and the sun was about to dip behind the city walls. The shadows quickly lengthened.

Belami saw Simon cross himself and Abraham make certain cabalistic signs in the air as he stood before the door of the house.

Immediately, with a rush of air, the heavy door swung open and a dreadful, rank smell seemed to fill the courtyard, even reaching Belami's nostrils as he clutched the top of the wall. Unable to restrain himself, he vomited.

Abraham did not hesitate but entered, holding a strange, star-headed wand before him, like a sword raised to strike. Simon followed him closely. Abraham intoned some half-heard prayers in an ancient tongue.

Immediately, all hell broke loose inside the house. Heavy knocking sounded on the inner walls; a horrifying moaning sound filled the courtyard as an evil-smelling whirlwind circled the walled garden. Belami had to cling on to his vine as though perched in the rigging of a storm-tossed ship. The stench of decay became overpowering like that of a newly opened grave. The veteran prayed earnestly, crossing himself again and again.

Suddenly, the strange, fetid blast of wind stopped, as though cut off by the closing of a door. A bright green light shone through the windows of the accursed place and then abruptly went out. A high shout followed and there was the sound of cracking plaster as part of the ceiling fell in.

Then, loathsomely, from every window, doorway and hole in the walls of the house, swarm after swarm of bloated black flies rushed out, forming up into a nauseating cloud which whirled round and round in a funnel-shaped column. Through the doorway strode Abraham, his white auereole of hair blown back as though by a gale; his long white beard flowing beside it, streaming in the magical wind. Behind him, looking steadfastly into the bronze mirror, came Simon, bending forward as though walking into a gale.

Abraham cried out the exorcism in an unknown tongue, yet within their minds Belami and Simon each heard the words translated into the *languedoc* of Outremer: 'Avannt thee, Sathanus!'

The dreadful maelstrom of stinking flies rose high into the air, and swept up above the city walls.

Abraham immediately made a cabalistic sign of banishment above his head and a flock of birds, swooping from all parts of the city, attacked the swarm of blow-flies. To the fowls of the air, Beelzebub's cohorts were just food.

Suddenly a sense of peace descended on the empty house. Several birds descended into the garden, to perch on the neglected trees and shrubs.

Belami, who had been unable to move throughout the alarming proceedings, was spotted by his friends.

'You were in danger up there, my son,' said Abraham disapprovingly. 'Your sword would have availed you nothing, Belami.'

'What in the name of all that is unholy were you doing? asked Belami hoarsely, already knowing part of the answer.

'House-cleaning!' said Abraham, and laughed, a deep chuckle of relief. 'How say you, Simon?' He turned his majestic head to his pupil, who grinned back at his teacher.

'I am still shaking,' he said. 'I was holding the mirror so hard, I think I bent it.'

'Back to Abraham's place,' suggested Belami, 'and tell me everything. What I saw outside that house was bad enough. I can't imagine what it was like inside that accursed place.'

'Hell!' said Abraham shortly. Simon nodded in agreement, as Abraham continued: 'It was a gateway to the underworld. The Devil's doorway to the nether-pit.' He paused and made a last cabalistic sign in the air. 'Now it is closed. Blessed be Adonai!'

The others crossed themselves reverently.

The street and the square were still deserted. For some unexplained reason, the strange sounds coming from the haunted house and garden had seemingly passed unnoticed by everyone except the three of them.

'Listen to the birds,' said Abraham. 'They are singing inside the garden again.'

It was the first time that had happened for many years.

Back at Abraham's modest house, the sage explained what he believed to have been the sequence of events leading up to the place becoming possessed by evil, and the final culmination of that terrifying afternoon.

'Malik-al-Raschid, like his elder brother Sinan, was hungry for the power of the Gnosis. As I have explained, Simon, the Cabala, the ancient Judaic chart of the inner planes of man's mind, with its intricate pathways to different aspects of thought, is one of the ways by which a seeker may obtain control over certain powerful forces which affect his destiny. These forces can be Angelic or Demonic, according to how the practitioner of the art invokes them to manifest.

'Malik was, as I explained to you, an Assassin. A member of that evil murder-cult. 'As "like attracts like", Malik naturally filled his house with demonic forces. Their dreadful manifestation was in the personae of the retinue of Beelzebub, whom Malik worshipped. The Lord of the Flies brought his hellish foulness with him and when Malik died the place became accursed.

'That building lies over a focus of earth-energy, a deep spring that bubbles up, to end in a 'blind' dome of rock, just underneath the house. It is a generator of neutral power, raw earth-energy. It can be used either for good or evil. Malik used the force for Darkness and took human life within its walls. Therefore, the house became imbued with evil, and harm came to those unprepared to meet its onslaught.

'I can no longer combat such strong negative forces alone. Therefore, I needed you, Simon; first, for your strength and moral courage, and second, because you are still a virgin. You are also twenty one years old, three times seven years, a number which has great significance in both Numerology and Magick.

'The body of man undergoes great changes every seven years. You are near the end of the third cycle of your life. A normal life-span lasts for three score years and ten; seventy years, or ten times seven yearly cycles. Such is the belief of the Magi.

'Armed with your goodness and courage and armoured by your moral integrity, the forces of Darkness could not prevail against you. I used your strength and youthful energy to focus the power of the earth-force below our feet, and by my modest knowledge of alchemy, was able to transmute that energy into the essence of Light. Had you not been looking into the dark bronze mirror at the moment I released that force, your eyes, my dear Simon, would have been blinded for life.'

To those who have no understanding of Magick and its 'ability to bring about change in future circumstances by the exercise of Will' – *id est* the law of '*Ce que vous voudrez*' – Abraham's wise words would have sounded like the ravings of a madman.

For Belami, with his long experience of the Holy Land, and for Simon, who had just been through the ordeal of an effective exorcism, the savant's explanation was simple and understandable.

'Did you see anything besides the sudden appearance of that swarm of flies?' the veteran asked Simon.

'Only the distorted features of a dreadful face, reflected in the metal mirror. At first, the features were twisted into an expression of malevolent hatred. Then, when Abraham intoned the Prayer of Banishment, the face became filled with terror and finally dissolved, as though its features were made of wax, melting in a fire. I somehow knew that this demon was the Assassin, Malik.'

Simon looked at Abraham for confirmation. The Magus nodded, stroking his white beard.

'The house is now at peace, otherwise no birds would sing in its garden. But it will never again be fit for human habitation. One evil thought, or even a single negative attitude adopted by anyone living within its walls, would recall the monstrous, demonic forces which are still locked within the confines of the house. Animals seldom produce such negative forces, and grooms and ostlers are usually by nature placid individuals, in tune with horses. Therefore, it will be safe for our merchant friend, a man of compassion, to use the premises as a stable.

'But he must never let anyone live there. After the sun sets, and before dawn, the horses must be left alone in the stables which he can now build on the site. The house itself, however, must be razed to the ground.'

Simon at last understood why the craftsman had been killed in the cathedral at Chartres, and he recalled Bernard de Roubaix's remarks regarding his death.

The *Wouivre* had only struck because for some reason the mason had murder in his heart, and was unshriven. In other words his own evil, perhaps engendered by jealousy or some other basic human emotion, had been magnified by the presence of the 'dragon-power' being generated by the '*puits*', the well-spring, underneath the cathedral.

This had blinded him to the habitual craftsman's caution of one who works in high places on narrow scaffolding. Unable to concentrate on his task, due to the dark forces stirring within him, the craftsman had missed his footing and hurtled to his death. The *Wouivre* had claimed a sacrifice.

From these lessons and other strange experiences with his learned teacher, Simon began to understand the power of the Gnosis. The year 1184 proved to be the Year of Initiation for Simon de Saint Amand. He had seen both aspects of the Holy City, the sacred and profane.

13
DEATH OF A KING

In mid-1184, a group of Jerusalem's most import leaders set out for Europe. The purpose of this voyage at such an uncertain time was to raise the capital and the enthusiasm for a Third Crusade.

The mission was led by the Patriarch Heraclius, accompanied by the Grand Masters of both military Orders, Hospitaller and Templar.

The Emperor Frederick and King Louis received them with pomp and ceremony, and King Henry with more restrained hospitality; but Germany, France, and England had strong reservations about joining in a third attempt to sweep the heathen from the Holy Land.

In vain, the three persuasive leaders from Outremer and Outrejourdain tried to obtain a firm commitment from the three kings. Only Richard, the Prince of England and heir to the throne, felt the call to arms stir within him. This was more due to the powerful, strong-minded prince being a man of action, who loved the thrill of battle, than to his religious zeal as a Christian knight. But he was still not King of England, and therefore chafed under the restraint placed upon him.

Richard was a complex mixture of soldier and poet, a romantic who enjoyed the physical demands of war. Undoubtedly brave and a lion in action, hence his nickname 'Coeur de Leon', Richard was also in love with poetry, and the romantic mystery of the Holy Grail.

As a leader of the cult of mystical poets, the Troubadours, the English prince was familiar with the Arthurian legend of the Pendragons, from whom he claimed direct lineage. Membership of the troubadours' quasi-magical cult was confined to men, and they believed that by chanting a poetical scenario, the events described in their poems became fact rather than legend.

They also believed that these song-poems, chanted repeatedly as a form of magical invocation, besides being a romantic record of past events, could actually bring about a change in the future. Poetry is an art and so is Magick, therefore such beliefs were not unfounded. A battle-cry can rally demoralized troops; an ancient curse can affect generations to come; a slogan can gain the confidence of the people; so, they believed, a troubadour's poem could affect the future of a nation.

Prince Richard saw himself as Gawain, rather than as Percival, in the mystical hierarchy of the Dragon-King's Round Table, and he longed to be the spear of Christendom.

Heraclius knew this and played upon Prince Richard's obvious susceptibilities; but, until he became King of England, there was no hope of his commitment to the Third Crusade.

All these efforts exhausted the three emissaries from Jerusalem, and the round of lavish wining and dining they were forced to undertake took its toll on them. Neither of the Grand Masters partook of the wine but they were trenchermen, as was the Patriarch. They were also no longer young. The result was that on the voyage home, Arnold de Toroga, the Templar Grand Master, died of the colic after a short illness. The mission had been a fiasco.

In Jerusalem, the situation was tense. This was not unusual for the Christian kingdom, but the tension was aggravated by the absence of the three powerful ambassadors, in their search for support for the new Crusade, and by King Baldwin IV's approaching death.

'That he has lived so long is a miracle. His willpower is extraordinary,' said Abraham. 'I have seen him on several occasions, when I went to administer to him to ease his suffering. But although his physicians try everything, even the alchemy of a Jew, to save the brave wretch from too much agony, only the essence of the poppy and the distillation of the soporific mandragora are of any use.

The course of leprosy destroys the sensitivity of the extremities first, before finally paralyzing the vital organs. Therefore actual pain is not the problem. But the mental agony of frustration, and the King's inability to command when he knows that only *he* is holding the kingdom's reins in check from the greed of the barons, that is the real pain which ravages the tortured young monarch's mind.

'He is only twenty four years old, barely three years older than yourself, Simon. Can you imagine what that poor soul is enduring? Would to Adonai that I could do more for him.'

The philosopher had a deep knowledge of the herbs of sleep, culled from long years of study of copies of the *Herbals of the Egyptian Priests of Isis*, a rare papyrus which had escaped the Alexandrian Library fire. Abraham could decipher the hieroglyphics on these copies, the originals having long ago fallen into dust.

He had bought them from a grave-robber whom he had been treating for a wasting-disease, probably contracted from a plundered tomb. The key to the hieroglyphics had been a second copy in Greek, made by Apollonius of Tyana, the great Magus of the first century, whose religion of Light had been a close rival to Christianity.

Like Mithras, yet another rival to Christ, Apollonius had been martyred. Mithras, whose birth had also been of a virgin mother, had been crucified as well.

The Mithraic religion had been practised by many Roman legionnaires at the time of Herod, whereas Apollonius's followers had been confined to the Magi and their disciples. All had been Gnostics.

'Can many scholars read the picture-writing of the ancient Egyptians?' Simon asked his teacher.

'Their number grows less by the year; but I spent some time in that land of wonders and a priest of Isis, who still practised the old religion, taught me the little that I know. These scraps of knowledge are confined to the herbs and roots used by the Royal Physicians of Pharaoh. I also know enough about the ancient gods of Egypt to realize that the origin of their pantheon is zodiacal. Ptolemy, the great mathematician, who, as pharaoh, spent most of his life studying the stars, gave us much cause to be grateful. My own simple understanding of the heavens mainly stems from using that astronomer's methods.

Abraham's humility was as genuine as the rest of his character. He was a true scholar.

The Court notables in Jerusalem tolerated the Jewish savant and astrologer, because they all wanted to know when their King would die. Each of these power-seekers, in the absence of Guy de Lusignan at Ascalon, was manoeuvring for supremacy in the coming power-battle. If anyone moved at the wrong time, he or she could jeopardize the outcome for themselves. If they moved too early, while the tortured young King still lived, they could lose everything; conversely, if they acted too late, they would come in as one of the last contenders for the tottering kingdom.

'It is a filthy business!' said Belami. 'Like watching vultures circling above a dying lion.' Simon agreed disgustedly. By now he had no illusions about the integrity of the Frankish nobility.

'It has always been so,' remarked Abraham, 'when the leader of the pack is dying, those he led wait eagerly to pick his bones.'

As the young King lay in bed, the smell of his own decaying flesh surmounted the costliest perfumes. Fortunately for him, his nasal organs had been destroyed by the dreadful disease, so at least he was spared the stench of his own putrefaction. That fact and Abraham's soporific potions kept his sanity from tottering into the abyss.

He had confirmed Raymond of Tripoli as his Regent; but he also appointed Count Joscelyn, his uncle, as the personal guardian of his heir, still only a small boy.

At last the failed mission returned from Europe, bearing the pickled body of the dead Grand Master, Arnold of Toroga. This meant that the Grand Chapter at Jerusalem had to choose a successor.

'It will be Gerard de Ridefort,' pronounced Belami. 'He is the only senior Templar able to take over the Mace of the late Grand Master.' He was right, but he was uneasy about the future. 'De Ridefort may not be experienced enough in battle,' Belami said.

In March 1185 the young King Baldwin was finally released from his long martyrdom.

Though the sad event had been long expected, a cloud of gloom descended over Jerusalem. The royal child-heir was taken to the Church of the Holy Sepulchre, and held in the arms of Balian of Ibelin, was crowned by the returned Patriarch, Heraclius.

It was a farce, for few of his 'loyal' Court believed that the tiny boy would live long enough to wield power within the kingdom. Either his royal uncle's leprosy would claim him, or else some power-seeker would poison him. For that reason, Joscelyn had been loth to accept responsibility for the little boy's guardianship, and had been relieved when the dying Baldwin had given that perilous task to Balian of Ibelin. This knight was a brave and honest man, but in no way equal to the political wiliness of the others.

'Joscelyn is frightened that if anything happens to the heir, he will be blamed. Now he can lay that charge on Balian's head, should the worst occur.' Abraham's words proved to be prophetic.

These events kept Jerusalem on tenterhooks and increased the sense of impending disaster which hung over the Holy City. Plots and counterplots, secret alliances and conspiracies, seethed among the nobles. Saladin would have been a fool not to have taken advantage of this chaotic period in the Holy Land.

The forces of nature also seemed to be affected. Famine stalked the land when the rains failed. The situation was stark and fraught with terror.

Mercifully Saladin saw the time was ripe to renew the truce and agreed to the general terms of a non-aggression pact, when the emissaries of the anxious barons approached him.

The Saracen leader still had problems of his own. He

had to weld Islam into a stronger weapon than the one with which he had failed to destroy Kerak. He needed time, and bought it with the truce.

The Treaty was signed. Saladin released large grain supplies from the East, and Christendom was saved from certain starvation.

Belami, however, was not too optimistic: 'That clever Saracen is not doing this out of charity, compassionate though he is. This truce will give him enough time to muster the biggest army that Islam has ever seen.' Once again the veteran had seen straight to the heart of the matter.

The arrogance of the conniving barons prevented them from sensing the coming storm. After their successful relief of Reynald de Châtillon's besieged Kerak, they actually believed that they had instilled fear of Christian might into Saladin's heart. Why else would he have agreed to the truce without penal clauses? they argued. Preoccupied with their own ambitions and petty conspiracies, they failed to see the danger. They believed they had bluffed Saladin. They were mistaken.

'Can they be *so* blind?' Abraham shook his head in bewilderment. '"Those whom the gods wish to destroy, they first make mad",' he quoted.

Meanwhile, in April 1185 Saladin marched north to join Kukburi of Harram, an old ally, who had once helped him to consolidate his position as the Saracen supremo. Saladin's intention was to move against the Seldjuk rulers should they fail to join him in the *Jehad* against Christendom.

Before he could succed in this strategy, the Saracen leader fell ill. Almost dying from a savage fever, Saladin managed to seek sanctuary with Kukburi, at Harram.

His personal physician, Maimonedes, who was known to the Saracens as Abu-Imran-Musa-ibn-Maymun, saved his life. Abraham heard news of this from one of Saladin's agents in Jerusalem.

'I remember Bernard de Roubaix and Raoul de Creçy telling me about this great Jewish healer,' Simon said.

Abraham smiled. 'You have a good memory. Your

mentors were correct in their assessment of Maimonedes' capabilities. If anyone can save Saladin, it is my old friend. I met him during my travels in Egypt, when he first arrived from Spain. He is a great magus.

'If Saladin dies, the Christians in Outremer can expect little mercy or compassion from his successors.'

Simon now spent all his spare time with Abraham, absorbing the basics of the Gnosis. He learnt why Jerusalem was called the Holy City; how it had grown over 3,000 years, and yet contained itself within such a small compass.

'The Romans rebuilt Jerusalem, relaying its foundations on the true axis of the cruciform focus of its power. They were not fools,' the old man told him.

'By leaving the temple site as the great generator of power, coming from the Rock of Abraham, they insured the Holy City's continued effect on all who lived within its walls, and on those who see it from the surrounding hills. The Romans understood the power of those mounts, otherwise why did they build their own capital on its seven hills?'

There was little that escaped Abraham. Even in his late seventies, the old man's mind was as clear as rock-crystal. Simon's youthful strength was a constant source of energy for the magus, and in return he gave his pupil every scrap of knowledge that he possessed. Abraham had known from the first moment they met that Odo de Saint Amand's natural son had been sent to him for a great purpose. He never questioned why, but gave his love and his wisdom unsparingly.

He was deeply troubled by the news of Saladin's illness, and, during sleep, he left his physical body to join Maimonedes in Harram. Unseen by the Saracen leader's guards, but sensed by Saladin's Jewish physician, Abraham's subtle-body gave his healing energies to the sick man.

Simon, too, at his teacher's suggestion, allowed Abraham to place him into a deep trance and projected his alter-ego to the place where Saladin lay. As Simon's subtle-body hovered beside the Saracen's bed, Maimonedes sensed the presence of another healing ally.

During this strange dream, a blue light seemed to bathe the stricken man's fevered body. The azure glow of the healing energies surrounding Saladin shimmered violently.

Simon knew that the slight figure of the attending physician must be that of Maimonedes. The Jewish magus was wearing a white *gallabieh* and turban, and even as Simon watched, the physician became aware of his spirit presence. Maimonedes smiled.

On the other side of the sick-bed, Abraham's shadow-self materialized into the subtle-body of Simon's mentor. Again, it was evident that Maimonedes recognized this other presence for what it was.

Saladin's physician smiled and nodded his head, in acknowledgment of the manifestation of these two helpers.

The Saracen leader's eyes fluttered open with returning consciousness. Before this, Simon had noticed that the vision of Saladin had seemed to double . . . as though the images of *two* Saracens were superimposed, one slightly above the other.

As Saladin regained consciousness, the second shadow-image merged back into his body. For an instant, Simon felt that the Saracen leader had seen both Abraham and himself beside his bed. Then the whole dream vision faded and Simon felt his own subtle-body rushing backwards through space, to re-awaken in Abraham's bedchamber. Beside him, his teacher was seated in a large, Arabian cane-chair, which he used for meditation. He also was awake.

The philosopher smiled. 'Well, Simon, what did you dream?'

His pupil told him. Arbaham nodded. 'I too had the same vision. Maimonedes was aware of both our presences.'

Had this experience of trance-projection been related to Simon two years before, he would not have believed it. Now, he accepted the experience as part of his normal life-pattern. He also knew that one day he would meet Maimonedes, and would see recognition dawn on the physician's face.

Discussing the strange experience with Belami later,

Simon said: 'There was no sense of illogicality in the dream. I could describe in detail the whole interior of Saladin's sick-room. What was extraordinary, was the feeling that Maimonedes was totally aware of our presence there, and welcomed our help. I still don't know how *I* helped the sick Saracen but presumably Abraham was able to harness my health and strength.

'I am also certain that we arrived in Kukburi's palace in Harram at the moment of crisis. The sense of mighty forces in operation was overwhelming. I still feel disorientated by the whole experience. Abraham tells me that this will soon pass. He wanted me to profit by this joint projection of our subtle-bodies, for the specific purposes of healing. It certainly has given me a new perspective on my attitude towards physical death. I see what Abraham has been trying to tell me.

'The difference between an experience out of the physical body and death itself is merely one of degree. At the moment of phsycial death, the subtle-persona has no further need of the physical body, which it has inhabited during its earthly life. This extraordinary revelation is experienced every time we dream, but we do not recognize it for what it really is: a foretaste of death.

'We are not normally frightened by a dream experience; why then do we dread death? I am grateful to Abraham for this knowledge which of course my teacher himself has long possessed and enjoyed.'

Belami agreed with Simon, in principle, but remarked in his practical way: 'A healthy fear of death is part of man's survival mechanism. If it was too easy, we might not struggle so hard to stay alive. That would be the end of the human race. My mother once told me that when I was born, she felt herself leave her body and watch the whole process of my birth. I was her fourth child and her only son. She had experienced nothing like that before.'

Whilst Saladin recuperated in Harram, and later in his beloved Damascus, the Frankish barons struggled for power and the Kingdom of Jerusalem tottered on the brink of disaster.

A king had died, another was near the end of his short life, and the Saracen Sultan stood at the crossroads of destiny.

During Saladin's convalescence, a plot against his Sultanate failed when an old enemy, Nasr-ed-Din, died after celebrating the 'Feast of Victims'. Poison was suspected, but never proven.

Still weak from his close brush with death, Saladin spared the traitor's young son when the boy quoted an appropriate verse from the Koran about the despoiling of orphans. The Saracen leader also returned all the possessions which had been confiscated from the child's father by the Emirs. He could afford to be compassionate, for Saladin was now the undisputed supreme ruler of all Islam.

Fortune was not so kind to the Christian kingdom. The boy King died at Acre, in August 1186 and once more the Kingdom of Jerusalem was plunged into mourning and political chaos.

The first ploy was on Count Joscelyn's part. He suggested that he should take the dead child-King's body back to Jerusalem for burial, while Raymond III of Tripoli united the barons against the patriarch, Heraclius, his followers, and their sympathizers.

Raymond accepted the suggestion in good faith and left immediately. No sooner had he gone than Joscelyn moved against Tyre and Beirut, proclaiming Sibylla as Queen. He sent the little King's body back to Jerusalem with the Templars.

Belami and Simon were part of the escort that met the funeral-party half-way, to ensure their safe passage to the Holy City.

Meanwhile, Joscelyn had made an alliance with Guy de Lusignan and urged Reynald de Châtillon to join him. They all converged on Jerusalem. Joscelyn, de Lusignan and de Châtillon were each accompanied by strong forces of picked men.

Raymond realized that he had been tricked, but it was too late to retaliate.

The new Grand Master of the Templars, Gerard de

Ridefort, supported Sibylla against Heraclius, who had once been her lover. In an unprecedented move, de Ridefort massed his Templars together and closed Jerusalem, his black-clad sergents guarding every gate into the Holy City.

The Patriarch was forced to proceed with the coronation and crowned Sibylla Queen of the Kingdom of Jerusalem. She promptly summoned her husband Guy de Lusignan to her side and herself placed a second crown on her consort's head.

It was all neatly and swiftly done, long before the dissenting factions led by Raymond of Tripoli could intervene. The assembled citizens of Jerusalem duly acknowledged the validity of the coronation, and accepted it as a *fait accompli*.

'I told you there was a woman behind it all,' said Belami to a bewildered Simon, who was confused by the speed of events.

'So now we have an indecisive commander at the head of the Frankish forces, and we Templar and Hospitaller sergents will have to try to pick up the pieces. Saladin must be laughing his head off. One good push from his well-disciplined forces and this whole pack of tarot cards will collapse.'

The new truce, barely a year old, was once again shattered by Reynald de Châtillon's treachery. The Kingdom, which under the treaty had enjoyed renewed prosperity, had reason to curse de Châtillon's impetuosity.

In a copy-book repetition of his attack on Sitt-es-Sham's caravan to Mecca, which had nearly cost Saladin the life of his beloved sister, de Châtillon fell upon a rich Saracen caravan passing peacefully northwards from Cairo.

The Christian raiding-party cut the Egyptian escort to pieces and ransacked the supplies, slaughtering and raping indiscriminately. Finally, they dragged the merchants and their terrified families, with all their possessions, to Kerak de Moab. This time there were no Templar sergents and a flying column to intervene.

When he heard the news, Saladin swore revenge. But

his emissaries, were refused entry into Jerusalem and his righteous demands for compensation ignored. It was as though de Châtillon had a death wish.

The Muslim world was appalled by the dreadful episode. Saladin seized his opportunity and declared a second *Jehad*.

'We are not going to win *this* Holy War,' declared Belami gloomily. 'Let us at least die honourably!' Simon had never seen the veteran so depressed.

14
THE HORNS OF HITTIN

The reason for the old sergent's despair would have been obvious to anyone who could have seen the full array of Saladin's united Islamic force. Seldjuks, Fatimids, Sudanese, Scythians, Turks, Kurds, Egyptians and Mameluks, led by the Ayyubid hierarchy, had joined Saladin and his Saracen heavy-cavalry to make up an army never before assembled under one banner. The crescent flag waved everywhere over the long columns of Muslim troops as they made their way westward towards Damascus.

To meet this powerful force of angry Muslims, burning for revenge and the extermination of de Châtillon's raiding party, the Frankish forces could muster 1,000 knights, 600 Templar and Hospitaller lances, taken from every garrison that could spare them, and a further 5,000 turcopoles. Including infantry and archers, their total force came to barely 20,000 men.

Untrained in Belami's Roman tactics of combined cavalry and infantry, these Frankish forces could only move at the pace of marching men. This meant that their strongest tactic, the grand charge of the armoured lances, knights, sergents and turcopoles, would have to leave their vital infantry, crossbowmen and spearmen out of the reckoning. The balance of power lay with the Saracen army, and courage alone, no matter how reckless, was no match for well-trained Muslim lances, backed up by hordes of Scythian horse-archers and skirmishers.

Though the Turkish and Scythian arrows were light when shot, *en masse* they could bring down many of the Frankish chargers which, apart from their heavy saddlecloths, were not at this period in the Crusades adequately armoured. An unhorsed knight is as static as an infantry spearman or swordsman. He cannot stand up to the weight of even a light-cavalry charge.

Saladin's new tactics were to shoot at the horses of the Frankish knights and then to overwhelm them on the ground.

Arnold of Toroga, the late Grand Master of the Templars, had fully appreciated the vulnerability of unsupported cavalry and always waited for infantry back-up, especially from his crossbowmen. Gerard de Ridefort, his successor, had not the same long experience of patrol skirmishes and battle *en masse* that de Toroga had gained when he had ridden beside Odo de Saint Amand.

Simon's father had fallen victim to a reckless mistake when he had attacked a far superior force of Saracens, and been taken prisoner, to die in Damascus. Only Belami, badly wounded and barely conscious, had cut his way out of that trap and led a few battered turcopoles to safety. He would have preferred to have died beside his Grand Master, but his horse, maddened by many arrow wounds, had bolted with him and he had been too weak from loss of blood to stop it. The few survivors of the massacre had followed Belami in his flight.

'I fear that de Ridefort has not got enough battle experience to lead our whole Templar force. You and I, Simon, must try to keep our trained lances together. Would that young de Mountjoie was still with us. But we'll do our best. God, he knows, we can't do more!'

The old soldier managed to sort out a small number of his old flying column and they mustered to his pennon. The turcopoles knew that their best chance of survival lay with the battle-wise sergent and his junior troop-commander.

In all, Belami managed to gather 70 turcopoles who had fought beside him before, and 40 crossbowmen who could not only ride pillion but could also shoot at least one volley of their deadly crossbow bolts, before they had to jump down to reload. It was not the most satisfactory arrangement, but it was better than leaving the infantry behind.

De Ridefort knew about the veteran's battle prowess and sent him on a scouting mission. Belami took Simon, old d'Arlan, the veteran from Acre, who had joined him, and 20 lances with accompanying crossbowmen. The object of their mission was to ascertain the size of Saladin's force.

Riding by starlight, on a few moonless nights, and laying up during the heat of the day, concealed in an out of the way wadi, Belami avoided detection by Saracen scouting parties. By sheer daring and years of experience, the two veteran sergeants managed to position themselves in concealment on rocky high-ground near to Saladin's line of march.

What they saw appalled them. Squadron after squadron of cavalry, both heavy and light, passed below their hiding-place. Hundreds of horse-archers, accompanied by marching columns of Turkish bowmen, equipped with new and more powerful weapons, light steel crossbows as well as their ordinary long-range composite bows, filed past their rocky outpost. The procession seemed endless.

'Jesu save us, Belami!' whispered d'Arlan. 'There are thousands of them. All Islam is on the march.'

Unlike their usual practice of proceeding to the sound of drums and cymbals, the Saracen army advanced in an eerie silence, only broken by the occasional snorting and neighing of their horses and the clanking of harness, while the ground shook with the tramp of marching men.

Like some great juggernaut, the grim-faced determined Saracens force-marched across the arid desert towards the southern end of the Sea of Galilee.

'He's making for Tiberias,' muttered Belami. 'Then he will divide his great army and lay siege to the town and the castle with a holding force while he swings up towards Hittin with the rest of his army. I can feel it in my bones. We must get back and warn de Ridefort, before it is too late. Saladin knows this country like the streets of Damascus. If he catches de Lusignan unprepared, he can cut him off, with half the Frankish army divided.'

The two old soldiers had to wait until Saladin's last columns had filed past into the distance before they could mount up and make their way back to the small wadi where Simon was waiting anxiously for them. He had nearly disobeyed Belami's strict orders to stay concealed at any cost, and ridden out with his small force when his friends became overdue. Simon was on the point of leaving when Belami and d'Arlan galloped into the end of the wadi. Without a word, the young Norman followed their urgent signals and the flying column rode hell-for-leather towards de Ridefort's encampment.

What neither veteran knew was that although they had reconnoitred Saladin's main army, they had missed an advance scouting force, under the command of the redoubtable Kukburi; he had also taken advantage of the moonless nights to position his force around the Springs of Cresson, or as the Saracen called the oasis, Saffuriya.

As luck would have it, a short skirmish between one of de Ridefort's scouting parties and a few of Kukburi's skirmishers ended in a brief Frankish victory. The Christians galloped back to de Ridefort's encampment and raised the alarm. The new Templar Grand Master was too impetuous and thought he had sufficient lances with him to massacre what he believed to be a small Saracen reconnaissance force.

Leaving his infantry behind, de Ridefort led his Marshal and 80 Templar brethren forward, gathering another 140 knights from Qaqun and Faba on the way. With him went Roger des Moulins, the Master of the Hospitallers. The new Grand Master was heading straight into a trap.

Kukburi was watering his horses before rejoining the main Saracen army, when a cloud of dust announced de Ridefort's approach. Without waiting to ascertain the size of the combined Seldjuk force, de Ridefort charged the dismounted Saracens.

The trap had been sprung by the Grand Master's own recklessness. In a moment, scores of Saracens and Seldjuks were back in their saddles.

Suddenly, the Frankish charge found itself facing 5,000 yelling Muslims. Storms of arrows from the horse-archers poured in to smother the Crusaders' headlong rush. Knight after knight, Templars, Hospitallers and Franks, crashed to the ground. Half-stunned, with their chargers dead from the arrow storm, or with the poor animals staggering in screaming circles, their entrails ripped open by Saracen spears, the unhorsed Crusaders tried to stem the flood of battle-hardened Muslim cavalry.

There was no lack of courage, but it was to no avail. The Saracen and Seldjuk horde swept over them like a flash-flood.

De Ridefort panicked and, with a couple of other Templar knights, rode for his life, closely pursued by his jubilant victors. The battle became a massacre. Among the dead were Roger des Moulins and 97 Templars and Hospitallers. Eventually Kukburi called a halt to the killing and rode off to rejoin Saladin, taking 40 Frankish knights captive with him.

Belami and d'Arlan topped the ridge overlooking the Springs in time to see the results of this disaster. The desert around the oasis was covered with the dead and hundreds of expended arrows stuck up from the ground like a scattered crop of wheat stalks. There was nothing they could do. Simon joined them as they slowly cantered down to count the slain and help the dying.

'Damn de Ridefort to Hell!' swore Belami. 'He has lost good men, and God, he knows we need every one of them. At least our gallant Grand Master could have died with them. Des Moulins did.' Belami saluted the dead Hospitaller commander.

'Bury them before the vultures dishonour these brave men's bones,' he said.

Raymond III of Tripoli was appalled by the massacre and hastily made up his quarrel with Guy de Lusignan, the new King of Jerusalem. They mustered the largest force that they could gather at Acre, and were joined on the march from the seaport by Reynald de Châtillon and his whole force from Kerak.

Meanwhile, Tiberias came under siege from Saladin's troops. The scene was being set for a major confrontation by the Crusader army with the Saracen leader and his huge combined Muslim horde.

Neither side knew the exact size of the opposing force, but de Lusignan believed that he had a good chance of beating Saladin with his newly assembled army. The King had under his command close to 1,000 knights, 1,200 mercenary lances, 4,000 turcopoles and an infantry force of some 15,000 mercenaries, Armenians and some belligerent pilgrims armed with spears. In crossbowmen alone, de Lusignan and his new allies mustered about 2,000 archers. Guy de Lusignan's confidence rose when he realized that he had around 22,000 knights, lances and infantry under his combined command. His vanity soared to new heights.

'We will sweep the accursed Saladin from the Holy Land,' he cried.

Belami winced as though he had been struck.

'Oh, Abraham!' he groaned. 'My wise old friend, how right you are. The gods have made the new King mad.'

Saladin's army, a total force of at least 40,000 men, was encamped at Kafar Sebt, seven miles south of Count Raymond's stronghold of Tiberias. The Saracen leader held the main road to both Tiberias and Sennabra. The castle was stoutly garrisoned, its seneschal being Count Raymond's wife, the redoubtable Princess Eschiva.

By fast messengers, who barely escaped with their lives as they rode hell-bent through Saladin's outposts, she sent urgent appeals for help to King Guy de Lusignan. The moment of decision had arrived.

Bernard de Roubaix had once explained to Simon how vital water was to the Templars. For *all* the Crusaders, the lack of this strategic necessity would be the most sinister factor in the horror that was to come.

The Frankish forces had mustered at the Springs of Cresson, the place called Saffuriya by the Saracens, and the site of Gerard de Ridefort's recent humiliating defeat.

'At least we have water,' said Belami.

Simon's mood alternated between elation at the prospect of the coming confrontation, to natural apprehension caused by waiting for the battle to begin. In soldiers' parlance he 'sweated-out' the hours before the attack. Like all young warriors, Simon felt that he was immortal. He did not fear death, especially since Abraham-ben-Isaac's demonstration of voluntary mind-projection. But the young Templar sergent was even now, in 1187, only twenty-four years old and he feared being badly wounded far more than dying. Most young men dread the sort of wound that had robbed Raoul de Creçy of his manhood. Simon had already been wounded at the battle of the bridge near Orange. He knew what pain was. But the thought of dying did not trouble him. Only the nagging doubt that in some way he might not measure up to Belami's and his guardian's expectations haunted him.

Belami had no such doubts. He knew that Simon would acquit himself well. The veteran had come too close to death on numerous occasions to fear it, and his tough tanned body bore the scars of many honourable wounds; but, as an old soldier, he suffered the 'sweating-out' of tension before any battle, and especially before the coming one.

When Simon admitted his fears, Belami told him: 'Only a fool is not afraid before the action starts. If he is afraid after the battle has commenced . . . *then* he is a coward.

'Don't fret, Simon. You are no poltroon like de Ridefort, our By-Our-Lady Grand Master proved himself to be here at this very place. Otherwise, I would not have you by my side. You will do well, my young friend. I will see you dubbed Knight yet.'

The Saracens had paraded the severed heads of several of the dead Frankish knights from de Ridefort's defeated force, before the gates of Tiberias. It was not Saladin's idea. More probably the order had come from Kukburi, or from one of the Seljuk Emirs.

The Saracen leader was now engaged in the seige of Tiberias. The whole town burned, as Saracen torches set it alight. Still the Princess Escheva held out in the castle above the town. Her husband, the stoic Raymond, realized that to move against Tiberias to relieve it would only be to Saladin's advantage. Choking down his natural desire to rescue his wife and all his possessions from the castle, he nobly advised Guy de Lusignan against any attempt to lift the siege.

'There's a man!' said Belami, when he heard of Raymond's self-sacrifice. 'That was a hard decision to take. I salute him.'

To the north of the little town of Saffuriya, which stood on low hills north-west of Nazareth, the Frankish army now occupied the Springs of Cresson, with its all-important fresh water.

Ample food could be obtained from the surrounding villages, and the defensive position was sufficiently strong to make Saladin think again before attacking it. The Saracen camp lay ten miles east of King Guy's position, near the village of Hattin, or Hittin as the Arabs called it.

There was an abundance of water in the valleys beneath the village, and plenty of olive groves and fruit trees for the army to browse among contentedly. Between the two encampments, Christian and Saracen, lay the forbidding waterless plateau, stark and baking-hot in the noon-day sun. To relieve Tiberias, King Guy must march his army across the arid desert in punishing heat. It looked like stalemate.

Admittedly, the Saracens had their backs to the Sea of Galilee and it made a tempting picture in the King's mind, to visualize his heavy-cavalry driving Saladin's army over the steep slopes and into the great lake, where Jesus of Nazareth had once walked on the waters. Perhaps it was that mirage in King Guy's mind that moved him to listen to Gerard de Ridefort's impassioned pleas: to attack Saladin *before* he moved against Saffuriya.

In vain, Raymond of Tripoli warned the King of the danger and folly of such a move, even though it might mean the death of his own family in the razed ruins of Tiberias.

It could be that King Guy wanted a great victory to

justify his position as the new monarch of Jerusalem; a title which he had only been granted by the neat trickery of his wife, Queen Sibylla. Whatever the reason, Guy de Lusignan listened to the false counsel of Gerard de Ridefort, who must have seen himself as an inspired prophet of the Templar cause.

Unlike some of the other past Grand Masters of the Order, especially among the founding Chapters, which had been full of remarkable men of great vision and foresight, de Ridefort was a stop-gap figurehead rather than an experienced and worthy successor to the late Arnold de Toroga.

His only gift seems to have been that of a persuasive tongue. Ignoring Raymond's warnings of the perils of an advance across the indefensible Plain of Hittin, the King of Jerusalem ordered his army forward.

Belami groaned when the news came through.

'Take every goatskin water-bottle you can find, lads,' he ordered his small command. 'Simon, we are in for a hot day's ride. Fill every container you can lay your hands on to the brim with water. We will need every drop we can get.'

Crossing himself, the veteran clashed down to his knees and, together with old d'Arlan and Simon, led his flying column in a soldier's prayer:

'Blessed Mother; Blessed Son of God; grant us the courage to endure pain and fear, and the ability to do our duty to the end. Be with us, whatever the outcome. *Non nobis, Domine, sed in tui nomine debe gloriam*. Not for us, oh Lord, but in Thy name, give the glory. Thy will be done. Amen.'

They crossed themselves once more and remounted their horses.

Each turcopole carried a spare water-skin and some citrus fruits in a small forage bag. Belami reckoned he could keep his small command alive and also help others, who would all too soon be in dire distress. Already the pitiless sun beat down upon them. On the march, it would be far worse.

The camp at Saffuriya was bustling with activity as the

Crusaders assembled their troops, and rode and marched out towards Tiberias. As many as could find suitable containers took as much water as possible with them, but it was not nearly enough unless the army was to be uninterrupted in its advance across the arid plain. The only vegetation was the dry salt-bush that straggled across the desert plateau.

Facing them was an army of double the number of Crusaders and their auxilaries. Reinforced by Kukburi's scouting parties, Saladin now had nearly 50,000 angry and determined Muslims under his combined command. They were well-fed, their forces well-foraged, and all were amply supplied with water. It was this last vital commodity which would decide the final outcome of the day.

The Frankish forces made a brave showing, as column after column streamed out from the Springs of Cresson. Battle banners hung limply in the near-windless early morning, but there was just enough breeze to flutter the guidons, pennants and bannerets of the Crusader knights. As yet, the Gonfanonier of the Templar force had not unfurled the Beauseant. That would come only when battle was joined.

Praying, cursing, grumbling or silent, the army of King Guy de Lusignan slowly paced out of the green oasis and tramped across the dusty plain, their ponderous progress raising a cloud of finely powdered sand into the still morning air.

On high ground, overlooking the plateau, Saracen scouts could not believe their eyes. Whooping joyfully, they rode their fast skirmishing mounts to tell Saladin the incredible news.

'Allah has delivered the infidel into our hands!' cried the Saracen commander, when the dust-covered scouts rode in with the unexpected message.

It was Friday, 3 July 1187, a Muslim Holy Day.

'Sound the alarm!' commanded Saladin and strode from his tent, to mount the pure white palfrey he had chosen for the fray. Beside him rode his young son, the sixteen-year-old El-Afdal. It was to be his first battle.

'Allahu Akbar!' shouted his father, and a thunderous

yell of fanatical acknowledgment of the 'Greatness of God' swelled out from his huge army.

Saladin rode rapidly around his large force of skirmishers, personally seeing that the horse-archers carried extra quivers, filled with arrows. Seventy camels loaded with spare shafts went with the Saracen flying columns. Besides these replenishments for the archers, 400 more wagonloads of arrows were ready for them to reload their quivers on the march.

With their water-skins bulging with the precious fluid, the Saracen army moved out, leaving behind only a token-force strong enough to hold Tiberias besieged. The hour of reckoning was at hand.

Inexorably, the two armies moved nearer to each other. Above them, the Palestinian sun beat down. The fate of Islam was in God's hands, and the circling vultures seemed to sense the coming massacre.

Two miles south-west of Hittin the battle was joined. Wave after wave of skirmishers swept round the flanks of the Crusaders. The arrow-storm was unremitting, seeming to blot out the sun, as clouds of shafts whirred down on to the Christian soldiers. Horse after horse screamed in agony as the feathered darts found vulnerable points in their lightly protected bodies. Knight after knight, sometimes with a dozen or more Saracen arrows sticking out from his armour, was unhorsed and, wounded or not, forced to join the long infantry columns.

They too suffered grievously; many infantrymen, being less well protected, received serious wounds from the deadly arrow-storm. The increasing need for water added to their pain.

The Christian crossbowmen returned the Saracen fire and emptied many of the skirmishers' saddles, but the preponderance of casualties was on the Crusader's side.

'May de Lusignan and de Ridefort roast in Hell!' muttered Belami huskily. 'God, he knows, their army is roasting already.'

The two veteran sergents, leading their turcopoles, broke out from the long column and, with Simon, counter-attacked the skirmishers, cutting down more than their own numbers. But the clouds of Saracen arrows were undiminished and the swarms of skirmishers seemed to be endless.

'They are like By-Our-Lady locusts,' shouted Belami. 'Come on, *mes braves*, rally and charge again!'

Still the Crusader column tramped grimly onwards, their throats drying ever more painfully in the dense dust clouds raised by the attacking Saracens.

Saladin was everywhere, encouraging his men, urging them on to harass the slowly tramping Christians now almost at a standstill on the arid plain. Seeing his opportunity, the Saracen leader ordered a charge of heavy-cavalry, while his horse-archers hurried back to the camels to replenish their supply of arrows.

It was a hand-to-hand struggle as the Mamelukes' heavy-cavalry crashed into the Frankish knights'. In the dense dust clouds it was hard to distinguish friend from foe. The Christians fought like men possessed, but they were no less determined in the Saracen ranks. It was a desperate battle . . . bloody and merciless. The red frenzy had seized both Christian and Muslim alike.

Simon fired his yew-bow from the saddle until all his cloth-yard shafts were expended. After that killing-spree, which took the life of a Saracen with each arrow, the young sergent had no means of replenishing his empty quiver. Drawing his sword, Simon de Saint Amand laid about him, oblivious of his own wounds, cutting man after man from his saddle. Belami and d'Arlan, armed respectively with battle-axe and mace, smashed their way through beside him; they were like three of the Four Horsemen of the Apocalypse. The battle madness was on all of them.

At last, d'Arlan fell, a Saracen spear transfixing his chest. With his dying gasp he decapitated the Mameluke who had killed him.

The dusty ground soaked up Christian and Saracen blood with equal thirst. For generations to come, the Plain of Hittin would reek of death. Any sensitive traveller would sense the horror and hurry past that terrible place, just as Belami, Simon and Pierre had done on their first desert patrol years before.

Attack followed attack and still the stricken Crusader army staggered on. Mercifully, the sudden darkness following the setting of the blood-red sun, brought a temporary respite.

King Guy was appalled by what he had done and turned north off the road, towards the wells of the Wadi Harram. Saladin let him commit his army to the manoeuvre and then cut him off, driving him away from the desperately needed water.

Night had come; a moonless wall of darkness blessedly eased the heat of the day. The exhausted Crusaders encamped, or rather collapsed where they stood. Only half the Christian army would rise again the following dawn.

Belami and Simon moved among the wounded, giving them a few gulps of water apiece from their spare goat-skins. There was little else they could do. Both of them were near exhaustion and weak from their own wounds. Still they kept watch and ward until sleep claimed even these iron men.

'Tomorrow will be a long day,' was all that Belami said as he drifted off into a healing sleep.

When dawn crept over the ridge, a pitiful remnant of the once-proud army found themselves with no choice but to make a last stand on one of the Horns of Hittin.

Grimly they waited for the final massed charge of the Saracen army, which had refreshed itself during the long hours of the night. They did not have to wait long.

A red tent had been pitched on the low hill of Hittin to shelter the few wounded knights who were left out of all that gallant host. Thirst was a raging torment. All their reserves of water had gone. Even Belami's small command, now reduced to a score of wounded turcopoles, had only a gulp of water apiece left.

'By-Our-Blessed-Lady,' croaked Belami, 'we fought well!'

Simon nodded briefly, his mind numb with fatigue. Like Belami, he had suffered several arrow wounds, none serious but all severely depleting with the loss of blood they entailed. Simon's left arm, however, was useless, a

Saracen sword-cut having sliced deeply into his forearm. Belami, ignoring his own serious leg-wound, bound up the cut with linen torn from his spare *jupon*.

'I'll not need a clean under-shirt this day,' he muttered hoarsely when Simon protested.

Saladin, ever mindful of unnecessary casualties to his own army, waited till the heat of the rising sun had weakened the Crusaders even more.

'Fire the brush!' he ordered.

Galloping skirmishers set alight to the dry salt-bush. The wind had risen and its hot breath spread the fire like a summer storm. The agony of thirst was now increased by the torture of the choking smoke.

'Finish it!' shouted Belami hoarsely. 'Come on, you heathen sons of whores. My axe is still thirsty for blood.'

As though in answer to that last defiant shout from the veteran's cracked lips, the Saracens swept in from every side. The Crusaders still fought, their swords often falling from hands too weak to hold them.

'Father!' cried Saladin's young son, 'they fight bravely, but surely we have won.'

Shading his eyes from the glare of the desert sun, Saladin gazed sadly at the tattered remnants of de Lusignan's army

'Only when the red tent falls will Allah have given us the victory, my son,' he replied.

As he spoke the words, de Lusignan's red tent collapsed under the weight of the Saracens' charge.

'*Allahu Akbar*!' shouted Saladin. 'It is over! Stop the killing. I want de Châtillon alive! He is mine alone to kill.'

The last charge of his heavy-cavalry swept over the few Crusaders who were still standing like a wave scouring a rock. When it had passed, only the wounded still moved feebly on the blood-soaked Horn of Hittin.

'It is finished!' were Belami's last words before he slumped forward over Simon's unconscious body.

15

DESTINY TAKES A HAND

The battle-frenzy slowly left the yelling Saracen troops who held the blood-soaked hill. Saladin rode forward, his mind occupied by his promise to his sister, Sitt-es-Sham. If he could find the three sergents who had saved her life he would succour them as his honoured guests.

'Belami, de Creçy and de Montjoie,' he told two of his scouts who had been survivors of de Châtillon's treacherous attack on his sister's caravan to Mecca, and therefore would recognize the Templar sergents. 'I want them afforded every aid and courtesy, if it be Allah's will to have spared them. My personal physician, Abu-Imram-Musa-ibn-Maymun will attend them.'

Allah was compassionate, for it took only minutes to find the two badly-wounded sergents, the body of the older still shielding the younger as they lay unconscious together. Naturally, they found no sign of Pierre de Montjoie.

When his scouts led the Saracen commander to them, he dismounted and wetted their unconscious lips from his own water-bottle.

'With Allah's help and my physician's skill, they will live,' he said. Maimonedes had accompanied Saladin's forces into battle and now hurried forward to arrange their transport by litter to Tiberias, which had fallen to the Saracen forces. But first their wounds must be dressed.

231

'They must be given every care and courtesy,' instructed his master.

Maimonedes nodded, stroking his short grey beard, a habit he had picked up from Saladin. 'Their wounds are serious, Sire, but provided the fever does not kill them, they will live. *Allahu Akbar*!' said the Jewish physician.

'*Inshallah*!' cried Saladin, and, turning towards Mecca, bowed his head to the ground and led his victorious troops in a prayer of gratitude.

His treatment of the other prisoners was stern, but merciful. He only desired the death of one man, de Châtillon, and that must be by his own hand.

However, some extremist Muslim Sufis had already killed most of the wounded Templars and Hospitallers. Saladin halted the slaughter and had the survivors led to his tent. This had been erected on the battle-field, away from the slaughtered mass of the Christian army. There, Saladin formally received his noble prisoners. Raymond had fled the field after an abortive charge against Taki-ed-Din, Saladin's nephew, and Balian of Ibelin and Reynald of Sidon had cut their way free. They were the only ones to escape the massacre. Their men lay at Hittin.

The Bishop of Acre was dead and the True Cross had fallen into Saracen hands. Only a pathetic handful of exhausted survivors were led to the Supreme Sultan's tent.

Saladin received King Guy de Lusignan and his brother Almaric, Reynald de Châtillon and his stepson, Homfroi de Toron, Gerard de Ridefort, the Templar Grand Master, and the elderly Marquis of Montferrat. Apart from the Lord of Jebail and the Lord of Botrun, only a few lesser barons and knights had survived.

They made a sorry spectacle as they stood uncertainly before their conqueror. He was courtesy personified, handing King Guy and the others goblets of chilled rose-water, iced with snow from Mount Hebron. The King drank some of the refreshing liquid and then handed the goblet to Reynald de Châtillon.

Saladin immediately cried out: 'King Guy, *you* gave de Châtillon the goblet, *not I*.'

This was to prevent the treacherous Reynald from

pleading immunity, which he could have done had he received the goblet from Saladin's own hands. According to the protocol of Muslim hospitality, such an act as the offering of food or drink by a host to his prisoner, or guest, immediately entitled the recipient to immunity from harm, while he remained within his host's domains. By denying de Châtillon the right to claim his life and safety, Saladin had shown everyone his intentions towards the forsworn knight. Saladin cursed him for his crimes. His words were bitter.

'You have disgraced your knighthood, slaughtered innocent women and children, broken the Sacred Truce between us and abjured your own word of honour to me.'

In the tense silence that greeted Saladin's words, de Châtillon tried to reach a dagger concealed in his surcoat. With a flash of steel, Saladin drew his razor-sharp scimitar and with one blow, lopped off de Châtillon's head.

As his decapitated trunk crashed to the rich carpeting of Saladin's tent, the bearded head rolled on to the silk cushions upon which the other royal prisoners were seated.

While this drama was being played out in Saladin's tent, Maimonedes and two Arab physicians were fighting to save Belami's and Simon's wounded limbs from amputation. In both the sergents' cases, the severity of their wounds had not been immediately apparent. On closer examination, the deep gash in Balami's right thigh, and the near severance of Simon's left forearm, had given the physicians cause for serious concern.

Cold compresses of iced rose-water and vinegar had been applied, and heavy doses of opium had been trickled down the patients' throats. Both were unconscious from severe loss of blood, but their iron constitutions would see them through. Lastly their wounds were cauterized with red-hot irons.

This silent battle took place in Maimonedes' tent, which was prepared as an operating theatre, complete with a well-scrubbed wooden table and a large chest of instruments, medicines, drugs, potions, salves, ointments and plenty of clean linen.

Water was also boiling over a charcoal fire outside, and Maimonedes carefully cleaned his scalpels and all his other surgical instruments in the steaming hot liquid before using them.

The wise philosopher, physician and surgeon knew that infection and suppurating wounds were either caused, or enhanced, by dirt and flies. The first danger he reduced by using clean instruments and other materials, and the second he avoided by employing assistants to brush flies away from his patients' wounds while he operated upon them.

He wore a tight clean turban while operating, and avoided breathing directly into his patients' faces or wounds. Maimonedes had learnt many of these secret techniques from copies of the papyri of the Ancient Egyptians.

The Arab physicians who were part of his battle-field medical staff assisted in applying a succession of hot and ice-cold poultices, to draw out any poison from the wounds. All the while, Belami and Simon were heavily sedated, but cooled and refreshed by the icy rose-water being dripped into their mouths through a narrow porcelain funnel.

Within an hour, both patients had their wounds sewn up, with clean silken thread and bronze needles, and their limbs dressed with clean linen soaked in astringent distillations. Once again, as with Brother Ambrose's medical procedures, the *Aquae Hammamelis* of the Romans figured prominently among these healing liquids. Maimonedes now prescribed rest and sleep, and left the tent to report to Saladin.

'They have an excellent chance of surviving. Only Allah knows whether their limbs will be saved.'

Touching his brow, lips and heart in obeisance and respect, Maimonedes withdrew from Saladin's presence, to spend the rest of the night seated beside his patients in silent meditation.

At midnight, he fell into a deep sleep, and soon became aware of two presences standing beside the cots on which his patients lay. One figure he immediately recognized as that of his old friend, Abraham-ben-Isaac. The other, he sensed, was a close relative of the young sergent who lay deep in his drugged sleep.

The name 'Saint Amand' flashed into his mind. Abraham's voice seemed to say: 'The boy's father!'

Maimonedes smiled in his sleep. He now knew where he had seen the face of the young Templar before; it was in a previous dream, when he had spent an anxious night during the crisis of Saladin's severe illness at Harram.

In the morning, the whole of Saladin's army moved away from the corpse-littered battle-field. Flies had appeared everywhere and the danger of contagion from rotting bodies was becoming pressing. The Saracens left the dead, including their own, to the vultures who were already at work, picking at their grisly feast.

The two wounded Templar sergents were gently lifted into their litters and carried, still semi-comatose under Maimonedes' drugs, to Tiberias, where his assistants had ridden earlier that morning to prepare temporary quarters for Saladin's honoured guests. From there, they would be taken to Damascus for a lengthy convalescence.

Maimonedes felt that too long a journey, too soon, would further endanger their wounded limbs. He preferred them to have a week's rest and healing in Tiberias, before being carried by horse-litter to Damascus.

Saladin, having settled his bile by killing de Châtillon, was in a generous mood and allowed Princess Eschiva to leave with all her possessions. He greatly admired her staunch defence of the castle, and sent her under escort back to her husband, Raymond III of Tripoli.

The rest of his prisoners the Saracen ransomed and they swore a solemn oath not to continue the fight against him. Once safely back in their various provinces, however, they all abjured their words of honour. Their freedom, in some cases, was to be short-lived.

In Tiberias, now under Muslim domination, Belami and Simon regained fleeting consciousness. Though they were both in pain, Maimonedes' potions and soporifics kept their suffering to a bearable level.

During Simon's long periods of drugged sleep, his subtle-body left his physical form lying in Tiberias, and wandered among dream landscapes.

Because his will was temporarily suborned by the strong opiates, he was not able fully to control his dream journeys as Abraham had taught him to do. Simon's unconscious needs drove him to distant lands and he found himself hovering over de Creçy Manor.

He seemed to melt through the walls, and entered the great hall. A roaring log-fire burned in the large stone hearth. Seated on either side of it were Raoul de Creçy and Bernard de Roubaix, both of them dozing. At their feet lay two great hounds which soon became aware of Simon's 'presence' in the hall. The animals started up and growled, their ears laid back.

Raoul de Creçy woke and glanced around him, to see what had caused his hounds' disturbance. Seeing nothing unusual, he reached out and stroked his big hunting-dog. Reluctantly, it calmed down. The other hound started to bark, waking de Roubaix. He also looked round him, even reaching for his sword which hung in its scabbard from his carved-oak chair. Both old knights were puzzled by their hounds' behaviour; but when the animals relaxed, they soon drifted off again into the doze that elderly people enjoy. It is one of the few pleasures of old age.

Simon's alter-ego returned swiftly to his waking, pain-wracked body in Outremer.

On another occasion, he found himself flying over Chartres cathedral. Dropping down, he passed through the great vault to the nave to hover just above the mysterious maze inset among the flagstones of the cathedral floor.

The whole church was filled with golden light, but seemed to be empty of people. Suddenly a dim figure appeared, gliding down the long nave. It was hooded in the cowled white robe of a Templar knight. Just as the ghostly presence reached the maze, its right hand drew back the cowl to reveal a strong, iron-grey bearded face with classical features and piercing blue eyes. The generous mouth broke into a smile.

236

A deep voice spoke: 'This is my son, in whom I am well pleased!'

The light around the figure of the phantom Templar became unbearably bright; then the whole vision receded at great speed, as Simon returned to his badly wounded body in Tiberias.

One vision recurred in his dreams, sleeping or waking. It was that of a veiled woman. Simon sensed her gentleness, and he knew that his visitor was there to heal him.

Sometimes she reached out to stroke his wounded arm, or to run her soft hands over the many other injuries which covered his body. Immediately, he sensed the warmth coming from her fingers, radiating deep inside his wounds, soothing the severed flesh and broken bones. The feeling of peace that this woman brought with her was past his understanding. It was something holy.

Sometimes, there seemed to be two women, one on each side of the bed. Simon sensed that one of them was older and smaller than the other. Both were veiled. He was certain that he knew them both.

It was several weeks before his emaciated body woke to a day free from pain. Maimonedes' potions had kept the worst agony under control, but even bearable pain, if continuous, is exhausting, and when Simon was free of it at last he felt as weak as a premature baby. His eyesight had been affected and he had difficulty focusing. That morning, his blurred vision finally resolved itself into a clear picture of his sickroom.

It was a high-ceilinged chamber, painted creamy white, with a waist-high panelling of intricately patterned tiles lining the walls. A large arched window was open to a cooling breeze. Through its Arabian arch he could see waving palm-trees and blossoming bushes set out in extensive gardens.

The sound of fountains and the trilling of birds wafted into his sickroom, while a zephyr carried the music of tinkling wind-chimes to his ears.

'Paradise!' Simon murmured contentedly. 'This must be Paradise.'

There was someone there whose face he seemed to

237

recognize, yet could not name. It was a beautiful face, full of compassion.

'An Angel,' he thought. 'Verily an Angel!'

The lovely face was smiling, bright violet eyes alight with joy.

Suddenly Simon knew who she was. 'Sitt-es-Sham,' he whispered. But then who was the older woman? he wondered.

Immediately, Saladin's sister drew the veil across her face. She turned and spoke to someone else in her low-pitched vibrant voice.

'He is awake, Maymun. Praise be to Allah!'

Another figure joined her. It was a man, grey-beared, lean-featured and smiling.

'God is great, Your Highness,' he said. 'The young man is well again.'

He bent over Simon's cot.

'Can you understand me, my son?'

His patient's voice, rusty with disuse, croaked a faint: 'Yes!'

The man, who was in his late middle-age, wore a white *gallabieh* and a tight turban without ornament. Simon recognized him.

'Maimonedes!' he murmured the words, just loud enough to hear.

The Jewish physician nodded. 'Our dreams have served us well, Sergent de Creçy,' he said in lisping Arabic. 'I recognized you on the battle-field. You are a pupil of my old friend, Abraham-ben-Isaac; the favourite disciple he wrote about, when he sent me a letter after the Battle of Hittin.'

Simon looked troubled, his gaunt face filled with dread.

'Belami?' he asked hoarsely. 'Is he alive?'

'And well!' Maimonedes reassured him. 'He is in the next room. He also will recover the use of his wounded limb. You are both most fortunate.'

'Amen,' muttered Simon. 'But we lost the battle.'

'A battle is not everything. Little scathe has come to the few survivors. They have been returned to their homes. Saladin sweeps across Outremer and Outrejourdain like

238

the desert wind. He only kills those who have to die. The rest, and their women and children, are safe. Saladin is a compassionate man.'

'Indeed, we know that and we thank him.' Abruptly, the young Norman's face was tense with anxiety. He gasped out: 'We lost the True Cross. I saw it fall into Saracen hands. The Archbishop was dead, and the holy symbol was captured. I could do nothing to stop it.'

'Do not concern yourself, my son. Saladin is a devout Muslim. The True Cross, as you call the holy object, is in reverent care. Our leader does not spit upon sacred symbols.'

Maimonedes now laid a soothing hand on Simon's brow.

'Sleep, my son!' he murmured in a low insistent tone. 'Your eyes are becoming tired – so tired. Let them rest; you feel drowsy; allow yourself to relax and drift out of your body. Sleep, my son, sleep.'

Simon's last thought before he dozed off, was that Maimonedes used the same techniques as Abraham to release his patient's subtle-body from his physical form. He completely trusted the Jewish savant. No man with such compassion in his eyes could be anything but good.

'*Allahu Akbar*!' murmured the physician.

When next Simon woke, it was early morning. A familiar face was grinning at him.

'Belami!' he said, his voice still hoarse, but stronger.

The scarred veteran, his head heavily bandaged, grasped his pupil's hand in his iron grip.

He was sitting in a high-backed cane chair, his legs supported by a pouffe. One limb was also bandaged while the other was shod comfortably in a pointed red slipper.

'You did well,' said the old soldier, his voice gruff with emotion. 'But you are guilty of rank insubordination.'

Simon looked surprised. Belami smiled his usual broad grin.

'You scared Hell out of me! I thought you were dead. That is wrong in my drill book. I, Belami, as senior sergent, am supposed to scare Hell out of *you*, Junior Sergent de Crecy!'

Simon chuckled weakly. 'By the Blessed Virgin, we are lucky we both survived. I am so relieved I didn't fail you, Belami, or my father, or my guardians or comrades.'

They were both too tired to talk for long, and soon dozed off. When they woke, it was late afternoon and they were given their first solid meal. Fruit and milk, a strong meat-broth and unleavened Arab bread, washed down with copious draughts of ice-cold rose-water.

Belami's appetite was better than Simon's, but they found their intake was much lower than normal. Lack of exercise had taken a heavy toll of their bodies and both sergents were well below their fighting-weight. Building up their wasted muscles was going to take longer than either of them suspected. In fact it was another month before the battle-fatigue had left their battered bodies.

Maimonedes came every morning and evening and helped them to exercise their wounded limbs, which at last were free from pain.

Long periods in the steam-baths in which Saracens loved to relax, accompanied by skilled massage from two of Maimonedes' assistants, finally gave back the two wounded men the full use of their bodies.

It was an exciting day when Simon and Belami made their first circuit of the extensive palace gardens. They felt like cheering.

Considering the extent of their battle injuries their full recovery was a minor miracle, due not least to Maimonedes' skill as a physician, and the Lady of Syria's loving care. It was she who planned their diet and often, unseen, watched over them at night.

This attention from Saladin's sister was directed especially at Simon. Neither of her two patients knew that this remarkable woman devoted so much of her time to their welfare. Even when they exercised in the palace grounds, Sitt-es-Sham watched discreetly from a screened window, her eyes following every move that Simon made.

It was a week later that Simon saw the Lady of Syria again. Her slim veiled presence entered his bedchamber just as the sun was setting. The Saracen princess was accompanied by her lady-in-waiting whom she quietly dismissed. Her companion left discreetly, with a conspiratorial giggle. Simon's senses were even more acute than usual since his close brush with death and he could now hear, see, feel and sense things more quickly and at greater distances.

In this case, the young Norman had sensed the presence of Sitt-es-Sham even before she had turned the corner of the corridor outside his room. It was quite uncanny.

When they were alone, Simon became acutely shy. Sitt-es-Sham sensed his extreme self-consciousness and spoke first.

'Sergent de Creçy,' she said in the low-pitched lisping tone that sent a cold ripple down Simon's spine. 'I have much for which to thank both you and your gallant companion.'

The young Norman stammered: 'For what, Your Highness?' He was genuinely puzzled.

The Lady of Syria smiled. She was still veiled, but her lovely features were just discernible below her light silk *yashmak*.

'For my life. You and Sergent Belami and your other companion.'

'Sergent de Montjoie. Pierre de Montjoie was with us at that time, Your Highness.'

'Of course!' Saladin's sister gave a light laugh.

Like a summer breeze, thought Simon.

'The three of you saved me from death at the hands of the *Hashashiyun*.'

'It was our duty, Your Highness. Belami immediately realized tht the Frankish knight attacking you was really an Assassin.'

'I remember well,' the lady replied. 'I can never repay my debt to you. . . .' She paused momentarily. 'To *all* of you. I have thought about what you did for me, many times.' Her slim figure moved closer to Simon. 'I am deeply in your debt.'

'Nay, Your Highness. It is I – that is to say, Belami and I – who owe *you* so much. We thank you in all humility and deep gratitude, for your great kindness and compassion.' He paused as his newly heightened senses caught the subtle bouquet of her perfume, redolent of wild-flowers and the scent of orchids.

Despite his reserve, Simon gasped. Immediately, Saladin's sister let drop her veil, and once again the Norman's senses reeled as he looked into her startling violet eyes. The Princess's moist lips were parted in a warm smile of invitation.

Simon hung on to his dwindling self-control. Sitt-es-Sham was very close.

'Your Highness,' he stuttered. 'who was the other lady who stood beside my bed when you came to visit me?'

The question spilled out of him involuntarily. Sitt-es-Sham was startled.

'I came alone,' she said, 'only Maimonedes was here with me.'

'But, Your Highness, I saw this woman clearly, even though I was in some pain. She was smaller and rather older than yourself. I clearly remember that she was unveiled and that she was smiling. In a strange way the lady resembled you, as though she were a close relative.' Simon was genuinely curious to find out the identity of his other visitor. Sitt-es-Sham was disconcerted.

'By your description, you could be referring to an aunt of mine, on my mother's side of the family. The "Lady of Tiberias", she was called. I remember her from when I was a small child. I could hardly forget her, for she had the most unusual eyes. They were a bright blue . . . like a peacock's breast.' Her voice trailed off into a whisper. 'Like yours Sergent de Creçy.'

There was a short silence, then Simon spoke. 'May I ask what happened to her, Your Highness?'

'I believe she died, in Tiberias, but that must be at least twenty five years ago.'

'How did she die, My Lady?' Simon's voice was urgent, insistent.

'In child-birth,' whispered Saladin's sister. 'There is some mystery about her death. Her child, my cousin, was never found. Apparently, the baby was kidnapped. It is believed by Sinan-al-Raschid's men. Why do you ask?'

'I don't know exactly,' answered Simon, now acutely

embarrassed. 'I thought the lady I saw beside you, those nights, was real. She certainly seemed to be. It must all have been a dream.'

To cover his confusion, Simon had leant back against the wall. His face was red with embarrassment, and he felt faint.

'Have you a fever?' Sitt-es-Sham was concerned for him.

'No, Your Highness. It is just that the lady I thought I saw, fitted another description as well. I have just remembered that Belami told me that my mother died in Tiberias.' His voice lowered. 'That too would be about twenty five years ago.'

Before either of them could continue, there was a discreet knock at the door. Sitt-es-Sham immediately replaced her veil.

'Enter!' she said softly.

It was her lady-in-waiting. For a moment they conferred quietly in Arabic, then Saladin's sister turned to Simon.

'We will speak again of this strange coincidence. I must leave now.'

Simon felt her soft fingers brush his arm and then she was gone.

Damascus was Saladin's favourite city. It was also one of the architectural jewels of Islam. Here was the university where the Saracen leader had spent his youth at the feet of his teachers.

The beautiful city was laid out according to the proportions of the Sacred Geometry. Its shapely, yellow clay buildings and tall white minarets dreamed in the warmth of lazy afternoons. It was the scholarly home of the arts and, like Isphahan, its rival university city, Damascus encapsulated all that was sacred and worthwhile in the Mohammedan way of life.

When Simon and Belami were strong enough to walk among the ubiquitous roses and palms of the city's fountain-sprinkled squares and gardens, the young Norman fell in love with it. Once again, he experienced the strange certainty that he knew the city from dreams in which he had flown over it, admiring its mosques, minarets, palaces and spacious buildings, so perfectly set out below him.

All its pleasing sense of space and purpose flooded back into Simon's memory as soon as he set foot outside the Sultan's palace. This new acuity of his senses also gave him a deep insight into the proportions of things.

Flanked by Belami on one side, and Maimonedes on the other, those first short excursions into the rose-bedecked city stayed in Simon's mind for the rest of his life. Later on, when the Templars could ride once more, these tours of Damascus were eagerly looked forward to by both of them. Belami, for all his practicality, had long before become deeply interested in the Muslim way of life, learning to appreciate the soaring beauty of Arabian architecture, even though he did not possess such a facility with mathematics and geometry as did Simon.

Maimonedes' reaction to his friend's favourite pupil was as enthusiastic as Abraham-ben-Isaac's had been. Any true scholar, who is not by nature vain-glorious, appreciates a dedicated pupil and both these Jewish savants sensed that quality in the young Norman's genuine humility and inquiring mind. His teachers gave him of their best.

Maimonedes told Simon: 'Everything that I have learned so far has come from the Mediterranean civilizations, including the Middle East, and most of it at some time must have been recorded and stored in the lost libraries of Alexandria and Byzantium.

'My small knowledge of medicine and healing owes much to the work of Galen and Abu-ibn-Sinah, the physicians who looked so deeply into the causes of disease and the ills which plague the human body.

'Much wisdom in the use of herbs and simples has come from the Muslim, Greek and Latin worlds. In Cathay also there are those who have made a painstaking study of a system within our bodies which, they believe, conveys the results of all our senses, and processes them in an orderly fashion within our brains.

'I have had many patients who had suffered sword-cu
and other traumatic blows to the head. Their brains wer
often affected and sometimes their limbs became paralyzed, even though apparently their arms and legs had
received no wounds. By careful massage, which is an
Arabian invention, and by manipulation of the limbs, I
have observed that some if not all, mobility can often be
restored to the affected foot, hand, arm, or leg.

'It follows that there must be a communication system
in the body which we call the nerves. These act as carriers
of the signals from the brain to the various organs and
extremities of the body and back again. Moreover, pressure applied to certain specific areas of the body, such as
one of the main arteries in the neck, called the carotid, can
cause unconsciousness almost immediately.

'Conversely, I believe that the stimulus of massage and
the 'healing-flux', which certain very energetic people can
demonstrably pass on to an injured person, benefit
patients who have been severely weakened. By a mixture
of these techniques and a regular diet of nutritious foods,
my colleagues and I have, with Allah's help, restored both
of you to a reasonable level of health.'

'For which we are forever in your debt.' said Simon,
while Belami nodded his vigorous agreement.

'Yet, without your own desire to live and get well, all
our efforts would have been to no avail. In the end, it
seems to be up to the patient whether he lives or dies!
That and, of course, the Will of Allah.' Maimonedes was a
devout Deist.

Within the palace there was an excellent library, and
built into the landscape of its gardens was an astronomical
observatory, equipped with a tall stone flight of stairs,
angled steeply upwards towards the sky, providing an
excellent observation post for determining the relative
position of the stars. There was also a circular pool of
pure white marble surrounded by several tiers of stone
benches, in whose crystal-clear waters a perfect image of
the night-sky was reflected.

A circular tower, ascended on the inside by a long
spiral of broad flat steps, afforded yet another excellent

245

observatory for positional astronomy by means of the windows cut into its walls with exact mathematical precision.

The Arabian astronomers had an extensive knowledge of the stars, many of which, like Aldebaran, Mizar, Altair and Niobe, had been named by them.

Apart from the use of astronomy in the art of navigation, a full understanding of the seasonal divisions of the solar year and the effect of the lunar phases on crops, animal-mating and birth-cycles was of prime importance to this part of the world, where famine and drought could strike to such terrible effect.

Simon was fascinated by the extent of the Muslim knowledge of astronomy and by the intricacy of their instrumentation. His joy was complete when one morning a beaming Maimonedes brought him an unexpected visitor.

It was Abraham-ben-Isaac.

Master and pupil embraced silently, too overcome with emotion to speak. At last, Simon found his voice.

'What on earth are you doing here in Damascus?'

'Destiny, as usual, has led my steps to this beautiful city . . . or, to be more accurate, fortune led me to *ride* a camel to Damascus.' The old scholar rubbed his buttocks. 'I was not designed for that form of transport, and my days of riding horses are long gone. Lacking a suitable litter and four stout Nubians to carry me, a camel seemed to be my sole choice.'

'What has happened to Christendom? We have been so out of touch. But for the great kindness, skill and compassion of these good people, both Belami and I would be dead, these many weeks.'

Simon was hungry for news of the *Jehad*. It had only just dawned on him how completely cut off they had been during their healing and long convalescence. He realized with a stab of guilt that because of all the wonders of Damascus, he had failed to enquire what had been happening outside the city and the immediate orbit of his recovery.

Abraham smiled. 'So much has happened, it is hard to

choose form which point to commence. After the disaster at Hittin, nothing could stop Saladin. Only Tyre and Acre are still firmly in Christian hands, though some isolated castles, such as Krak des Chevaliers, still hold out. Even Jerusalem itself has fallen, after only a short siege.'

Belami interrupted: 'The walls were strong enough. Which side did Saladin attack?'

'From the east,' replied Abraham. 'His sappers mined a breach and part of the wall collapsed. There seems to have been little spirit of resistance.'

Belami grunted his disgust.

'Did many die?' asked Simon anxiously.

'Comparatively few. The garrison at Jerusalem had been previously denuded by King Guy and Duke Raymond. It fell without grievous slaughter. Saladin was extremely compassionate and let most of the citizens leave the Holy City on payment of a token ransom, amounting only to a few besants. Many of the elderly, or impecunious, he let go free without even the payment of this small sum.

'Saladin is more interested in cleansing and reconsecrating the many Muslim holy places which the Christians inexcusably defiled, than in exacting the last gold piece from the citizens of Jerusalem. He truly is a great man. Had their roles been reversed and de Lusignan, Raymond or Heraclius been the conqueror, all the Muslim prisoners would have been put to the sword. Saladin has given Christendom a great lesson in mercy and generosity. Sadly, I cannot call to mind anyone among the Christian nobles who will profit by that great lesson.

'Heraclius, the Patriarch, was more concerned with robbing Jerusalem of the huge store of treasures that he had amassed over the years, than with thanking Saladin for sparing his life and possessions.

'It was sickening to see the Holy City being plundered not by the Saracens, who have treated it with remarkable respect, but by the greedy Christian notables who have robbed its shrines and holy places of any objects of value that they could lay their hands on.'

247

Belami's bellow of cyncial mirth counter-pointed
Abraham's disgust. 'That By-Our-Lady Patriarch must
be a devil-worshipper. He has Satan's own luck when it
comes to looking after his own despicable hide. What
about Raymond of Tripoli and the Princess Eschiva? The
last I saw of Duke Raymond, he was galloping westwards
from Hittin, on a fast horse.'

'The rumour is that he has died at Acre of grief and
chagrin, even though Saladin allowed his wife to join him
with all their possessions. De Châtillon also is dead, slain
by Saladin's own hand.'

'That makes me believe in Divine Justice!' snorted
Belami. 'What of de Lusignan?'

'Ransomed, on the undertaking of a Sacred Oath -
from which, of course, Heraclius has absolved him. King
Guy is now holding out at Tyre.'

'And our gallant Grand Master?' Belami's tone was full
of scorn.'

'Gerard de Ridefort is plotting to recoup his territorial
losses. Tyre holds out largely because of Conrad de
Montferrat's resourcefulness. He sailed in from Byzantium with a determined force of Frankish knights and
took command of Tyre just before Saladin's forces broke
through its defences. It is a vital position, protecting the
narrow neck of rock joining the port of Tyre to Outremer's mainland. After months of siege, it still remains
uninvested.

'De Montferrat is a born leader. Saladin has made a
serious mistake in withdrawing from there. It has lost him
the impetus he gained after the massacre at Hittin. Until
Tyre, the Saracens swept across Outremer almost unop-
posed.'

'How did you escape from Jerusalem and cross the
Saracen lines?' asked Simon.

Maimonedes interjected: 'I sent for Abraham and
obtained a *laissez-passer* from Saladin. Raymond was
dead, therefore he had no benefactor. Such a scholar as
my good friend is more usefully employed in making
instruments for our observatory at Damascus, than in
looking for another Christian sponsor.'

With all the excitement of Abraham's arrival and the lessons from Maimonedes on the principles of anatomy, medicine, and the basics of physics and herbalism, Simon's mind had little time to ponder on the lovely Lady of Syria; but at night, his dreams were filled with her image. He was deeply disturbed.

A similar situation faced Sitt-es-Sham. She loved Simon, but she was confused as how best to present herself to him. Here was no ordinary infidel who would have been overjoyed to take advantage of her gratitude at his having saved her life. Simon was a man of honour, obviously shy and inexperienced in the ways of love.

His principles and scruples would be a difficult obstacle to overcome, if the Lady of Syria was to offer herself. Besides all this, there was the possibility that, in fact, Simon de Creçy's mother and her own had been sisters. It was a situation that required considerable thought and some sound advice from a trusted friend. That, she decided, would be Maimonedes.

The Jewish physician advised not only Saladin on medical matters, but his whole family as well. Sitt-es-Sham sought his advice, requested ostensibly 'on behalf of a close relative.' This, of course, was pure invention. Maimonedes had a shrewd idea of the gravity of the situation in which the Lady of Syria found herself. He pondered deeply and then told her: 'Saladin has a great sense of honour, and his gratitude is already manifest. I know that he deeply respects the two Templar sergents, whereas the Order of the Temple has been the object of his wrath up to now. He told me that he wishes to discuss the sergents new tactics with cavalry and infantry. He understands that young Simon de Creçy is an excellent scholar and, in return for the saving of Your Highness's life, he intends to ask both of these brave men what best would gratify their desires. He already knows that Sergent Belami is a man who enjoys beauty and the love of women, so doubtless, Saladin will arrange for the Court *houris* to satisfy the older sergent's needs in that direction.'

'However, I cannot see our Great Leader taking too kindly to the thought of one of his own family becoming involved with a young infidel except by way of marriage which would mean his conversion to the Faith of Islam. You did say, Your Highness, did you not, that your relative who finds herself in this difficult situation is a cousin of yours?'

Sitt-es-Sham inclined her head in agreement.

'However,' continued Maimonedes, 'I can hardly see your brother objecting to a close friendship, providing of course that *a priori*, this did not lead to complications.

'Therefore I would advise your relative, Highness, to be exceedingly discreet. I, myself, will of course instantly dismiss the whole matter from my mind.'

It was sound advice and Sitt-es-Sham acted accordingly.

As yet, Saladin had not returned from the siege of Tyre, so time was not entirely the deciding factor. As for the place and the opportunity, that proved to be the observatory, where Abraham and Simon spent long hours observing the stars.

Naturally, it would require the Jewish astronomer's full co-operation. That was another matter for Maimonedes to insure.

One warm, flower-scented night, in the dark of the moon, Simon had arranged with Abraham to share some hours of his watch observing the planet Jupiter, which was then in the ascendant.

He was standing inside the secluded observatory tower, waiting for his teacher, when he heard a soft rustle of silk. Simon moved back into the shadows, for the sound was an unfamiliar one in the observatory precincts.

Before he could challenge the intruder, a natural reaction from a trained Templar sergeant, Sitt-es-Sham's soft fingers were on his lips.

Without a word being spoken, she led him to a couch set against the observatory wall and sat, drawing Simon down beside her.

Her veil slipped from her face and she swayed towards him. Her scent was subtly provocative and her natural body perfume added to its effect on Simon's reeling senses.

He gathered her into his arms. Their lips melted into a long ecstatic kiss; both giving and neither taking. Sitt-es-Sham's tongue slipped between Simon's lips and their passion mounted.

Both the Templars had adopted Arab costume since their arrival in Damascus. In Maria de Nofrenoy's case there had been Simon's chain-mail to hinder her eager hands. Saladin's sister's caresses found no such obstacle. Simon was lost in ecstasy as her slim fingers explored his eager body. When she found his manhood, they both gasped at the depth of their longing.

On the cushioned couch, draped with the Lady of Syria's cloak, Simon de Creçy and the Princess Sitt-es-Sham became lovers.

Simon felt the *Wouivre* stir in its sleep as his ecstasy reached its climax.

The urgency of his royal mistress's sighs told him that she also felt that soaring moment when her yearning loins released her spirit. They reached the pinnacle of love together.

16
THE GNOSIS

Saladin returned to Damascus in triumph. Now his empire stretched from Egypt to Northern Palestine. Only a few isolated strongpoints held out against the all-conquering Ayyubid leader. The Holy City had been won back in a short, almost bloodless, campaign. The Dome of the Rock, the Al-Aqsa mosque and all the Muslim sacred places in Jerusalem were being cleaned out and reconsecrated by the Imams.

To Saladin's horror, he heard that many Muslim sanctuaries had been desecrated by use as latrines and, of course, the Al-Aqsa mosque had suffered from Templar abuse. They had used it as their headquarters and their stables. The Hospitallers did not appear to have been involved in this sort of wanton desecration, which resulted from the degree of fanaticism that a number of Templar Grand Masters had displayed. Odo de Saint Amand, a choleric and determined man notwithstanding, had not been guilty of this kind of vandalism. But others, like Gerard de Ridefort, had encouraged these base attitudes towards 'heathen idolatry'.

Saladin had been back in Damascus for only a few days when he sent word to his Christian guests to join him at a private *diwan*. This general term was used to describe any meeting of notables, but in this case the only people present were Saladin, Maimonedes and Abraham, as the new Court Astrologer, Saladin's personal bodyguard and his honoured guests, Simon and Belami.

First of all he embraced them, then formally thanked them for their gallant rescue of the Lady of Syria. The official part of the *diwan* being accomplished, Saladin cast aside his role as the Supreme Sultan of the Saracens and became what he best enjoyed being: a sincere and considerate host of honoured guests.

He told the Templars: 'I saw you in battle. You are brave men. Maimonedes tells me that you are now fully recovered. I honour you. We are enemies by the force of Destiny; that is, so far as a meeting on the battlefield is concerned. I hope that here in my realm, these differences of religious opinion will not interfere with our relationship as host and honoured guests, and I hope you will become my friends as well. Forget that you are Templars and tell me how I can serve you best. You, Sergent Belami, I know to be a famous warrior in your Order. One of our cavalry commanders, Taki-ed-Din, my nephew, was most impressed by your use of cavalry and infantry in a unique combination. I too saw your column in action. It was a delight to behold. Was this new manoeuvre your own idea?'

Belami grinned, his stocky one-armed figure dressed in a white *gallabieh* and *burnous* contrasting with the taller, leaner, hawk-featured Saracen leader who stood beside him.

'No, Sire, the manoeuvre goes back to the Romans. It is said that Caesar Augustus invented it.'

'Nevertheless,' replied the smiling Saracen, 'you use it well. I admire you for your honesty. And you, young sir' – Saladin turned to Simon – 'I saw you use a weapon unfamiliar to me: a great bow that shot long arrows with deadly marksmanship. How is it called?'

'The longbow, sir. It is made of a springy wood, called "yew". The Welsh people have turned it into their most dreaded weapon.'

'Have you such a bow with you?' asked Saladin.

'Alas, no, sir! I lost it at the Horns of Hittin, along with my horse, Pegase.'

'It is sad to lose a good destrier. Please feel free to choose a worthy mount from my own stables. Our Arab horses are not as heavy in the bone as your great Frankish war-horses; but we are proud of them, and they are swift as the wind.'

The conversation had become so relaxed that an observer would have taken the *diwan* to be a meeting between friends rather than a face-to-face encounter between sworn enemies; but these were exceptional men.

Dinner was, as is the custom in Arabia, a cheerfully informal event, in which many communal dishes were served from which both host and guests helped themselves. The fingers of the right hand only were used to convey the spicy food and its rice accompaniment, from the great brass trays warming over charcoal braziers, to the mouths of the diners.

Often, Saladin himself would spy a choice morsel and, scooping it up, would offer it to one of his guests. Throughout the long meal, copious draughts of iced rose-water and small cups of mint-tea were drunk, and Simon learnt to belch appreciatively at the end of each course.

'I congratulate you both on your excellent Arabic,' said their host. His smile became mischievous. 'I understand, Sergent Belami, that your vocabulary of Arabic curses is extensive. Abu-Maymum, with reverent awe, heard you utter several choice phrases while you were suffering from your grievous wounds.'

A gruff bellow of laughter from Belami greeted Saladin's remark.

'Sire,' he said, 'I would be honoured if you would teach me some new ones. I find Arabic a fine language for poetry, love-making, and cursing.'

Saladin laughed. It was as honest an expression of good-humour as Belami's. It was altogether a splendid evening.

During their conversation, Abraham and Maimonedes both praised Simon's scholarship and Saladin's physician asked permission to take his young patient to meet Osama. Saladin's eyes twinkled.

'Now there is a great teacher. He is nearly ninety years old, yet his mind still soars like a mountain eagle. What subjects do you wish to discuss with him?' Saladin looked at Simon quizzically.

'Rather than discussion, which implies equality of scholarship, I wish to learn from him. I would be honoured just to listen.'

Saladin grinned. 'Well said, Sergent Simon. There are too many braying jackasses who wish to impress Osama with their book-learning. He calls it: "Giving him the benefit of their ignorance".'

They both laughed.

'But what knowledge do you particularly seek?' enquired the Saracen leader.

Simon took the plunge. 'The Gnosis, Sire.'

Saladin's eyes held a far-away look.

'That is what we all seek, my young friend. Sergent or sultan, rich or poor, the Gnosis is the diadem in the Crown of Knowledge.' His eyes returned to their piercing normality.

'Magick is the ability to turn will-power into action, to bring about a change in future circumstances, by the exercise of the human ability to concentrate the totality of its thoughts and turn that into *effect*.' His eyes seemed to bore into Simon's.

'Some men seek to misuse this knowledge to gain power. What reason have you, Simon de Creçy, to seek the Gnosis?'

Simon's reply was clear and concise. 'To help me to obey the Will of God, Sire.'

Saladin's face lit up with joy. Basically a simple and devout Muslim, the Saracen leader was deeply moved by this answer.

'That is why you must meet Osama. I salute your scholarship, my honoured, infidel friend.'

What none knew was that throughout that memorable evening, the Lady Sitt-es-Sham had heard every word spoken by her brother and his guests. She had impressed upon Simon that what had passed between them was the Will of Allah, a secret wonder, not to be shared by

255

anyone other than the two of them. What he had experienced was the pinnacle of human love, and he now knew it to be a holy thing. He honestly felt no betrayal of his host's protocol, because Simon held a growing conviction that he himself was half-Arabian and a cousin of the Saracen princess. Simon de Saint Amand felt that, through his love for Sitt-es-Sham, he had made contact with his long-dead mother, the Lady of Tiberias.

When he asked Belami point-blank if that had been his mother's name, the veteran told him: 'I am breaking no sacred oath by agreeing with you, Simon. Indeed, that was your mother's name. She was a wonderful person and your father adored her. I am glad that at last you know her for what she was. Had she lived, you would have enjoyed the wonder of a mother's tender love. I know that your father was ready to recant Christianity and join your mother in marriage as a Muslim when she died. How did you find this out?'

'By a miracle, Belami.' Simon explained what had happened.

'*Inshallah*!' said the astonished veteran. 'De Roubaix was right, when he said that all would be revealed to you in the Holy Land.'

Simon's meeting with Osama was forever stamped on his memory. The venerable sage lived in his own quarters at the university. There, he was looked after by a number of his devoted disciples. The only discomfort that the elderly philosopher suffered was a tendency to feel the cold. Even in the heat of the afternoon, charcoal braziers were placed near him.

When sleep eluded him, which was often, Osama would discuss obscure points of theology and philosophy with a small group of 'late-watchers' who preferred to study with him at night.

His reasoning was impeccable and his knowledge profound. Light in build with a pronounced stoop, partly due to his great age and partly to his long years of study, Osama's most arresting features were his eyes. Hooded by heavy eyelids and shaded by his shaggy white eyebrows, their dark-brown depths seemed to glow with inner light.

Simon had only seen that peculiar chatoyance before in Brother Ambrose's strange stone and in the Lady Elvira's gold-flecked eyes. In Osama's case the effect was doubly compelling because his eyes shone from a face that radiated wisdom. From his wide forehead, rising into his simple white turban, to the long silver-grey prophet's beard, Osama's ascetic features compelled respect and inspired devotion. Simon felt a sense of awe as soon as he met the sage, and it increased with each session that they spent together. When Osama spoke, his gentle voice was vibrant with a surprising energy.

'Saladin, our Great Leader and my erstwhile pupil, has requested that you, Simon de Creçy, be given special treatment as a single scholar, rather than as part of a group of my students. So be it. May I ask what it is you wish me to teach you, if I can?'

A faint smile hovered around the sage's lips.

'Honourable sir, I am an inept student who has only grasped a few basic essentials of learning, but I know that you can clarify many points and close many of the gaps in my knowledge.'

'I will certainly try. I like your honest humility. It reminds me of a Grand Master of your Order whom I met here in Damascus. His name was Odo de Saint Amand, and Saladin also honoured him for he had refused to be ransomed, or to take an oath not to continue to fight against Islam.

'He was indeed a remarkable man. Maimonedes and I both attended him when he contracted a severe fever, but, alas, he died. Ah, yes! It is your eyes which remind me of him. Strange are the ways of Destiny for your eyes remind me also of another, the Lady of Tiberias who died in child-birth these many years past. Is it possible that you are related to Saint Amand?'

'He was my father, sir.' Simon felt that he was not breaking his sacred oath, as he sensed that Osama already knew his lineage, perhaps by reading his thoughts or through possible conversations with Maimonedes and

Abraham, both of whom were the philosopher's close friends.

Osama continued without further comment on Simon's parentage: 'It is most unusual for an infidel to become a pupil of mine, but Odo de Saint Amand also came to me highly recommended by Saladin. He proved to be an apt pupil. I still mourn his loss.'

Simon's mind was whirling with these extraordinary coincidences. Above all, the fact that both his parents had similar colouring to their eyes fascinated him, especially as he might have expected his mother, a Saracen, to have had brown eyes. This was a simple example of the strange workings of Destiny.

'May I ask you, sir, if you can assist me to understand something of the Gnosis? Both Abraham-ben-Isaac and Maimonedes have given me a basic idea of its structure.'

'I know little more than they do,' said the sage modestly. 'But I can try to explain what I believe to be the truth, so far as I have been enlightened by Allah!

'Know then, Simon, that there are two opposing forces at work within you and all mankind, as a microcosmic reflection of *all* things. When we say: "As above, so below", and conversely: "As below, so above", we are trying to encapsulate the *unknowable*, within the finite boundaries of our limited thoughts.

'We Gnostics call these forces, which are positive and negative, Ormudz and Ahriman, or, as they named them in Cathay, the Yin and the Yang. Yang is of the Light and Yin is of the Darkness. The one intrudes equally upon the other like male and female. To visualize this, you should imagine a circle containing equal black and white areas; *not* bisected, but with the *same area* of each colour.'

Osami drew a diagram in the white sand which filled a large flat bronze bowl before him.

The philosopher continued: 'This then is the plan of your soul, the actual *you*. Part light, part darkness; part positive, part negative; half good, half bad. The way of Gnosticism is called the Great Work, for it is the path of the alchemist. He must learn to distil this equal mixture, until he has refined all the dross into pure gold. This

258

principle I am sure you have already learnt from Abraham and Abu-ibn-Maymun, as we know him.'

Simon nodded.

Osama paused, then went on: 'The Gnosis is the sum total of all knowledge. By its very nature, it is unknowable except to God, Allah, Adonai, Ainsoph, or whatever name your religion gives to the origin of all things.

'However, by careful study of the mechanism of change which controls all matter and all energy, a dedicated scholar may gain sufficient knowledge, within the range of his mental compass, to bring about certain effects within his environment. Do you follow me?'

Simon nodded silently.

'You will already have been warned as to how you should apply such knowledge, and what your guiding motive should be?'

Again, Simon nodded.

'Good! Then we shall begin to learn these techniques. The Jews call these pathways the Sephiroth, the Tree of Knowledge, and they give names to each Sephira, or stage of experience – or, as we Gnostics say, each plane of existence – in other words, each realm of knowledge and awareness.

'Both the Persians and the Jews, who learnt this concept from the Ancient Egyptians, have settled for a minimum number of seven planes of thought, this being the number of such planets as we know exist. There may well be more.

'From what Abraham tells me, you can reach the

creative realm of Netsach at will, in the form of a dream experience in which, he also tells me, you can now effectively control your actions and observations. That in itself is quite a journey along the wide highway of the Gnosis.'

'I found that I had no control,' said Simon, 'when I dreamed under the pain-killing influence of Maimonedes' drugs.'

Osama's eyes glinted with interest.

'That is a common error, but in your case an involuntary one into which many searchers after truth fall disastrously. They believe that by drugging the mind with the root mandragora, or by eating the sacred mushroom, they release the essence of their being to wander freely at will; whereas, of course, as you know from experience, their wills actually become suborned by the power of the drugs and they are cast, without volition, anywhere within the different planes of experience. That way lies madness.

'I will teach you definitive techniques; by meditation, by contemplation of sacred symbols, and by learning to recognize the symbolic sign-posts on each pathway. That will tell you whether you are being deluded, or are indeed in complete control of your mental journey. That is what your Templar knights attempt to do in the chapter-houses of your Order. There, they exercise group ritual-magick.'

Simon was astonished. It had never occurred to him that Templars were magicians.

Osama made his point more forcibly.

'Their mistake lies in their motives for so doing. In the early days of your Order when poverty and celibacy were the guiding principles, those iron disciplines forged the first founding Templars into men of great will-power. Their motives were impeccable and they earnestly sought and found the Gnosis, here in the Orient. Some say that Hugues de Payen and Godefroi de Saint Omer, with others, found the lost Ark of the Covenant, hidden in the ruins of Solomon's Temple at Jerusalem. That may be so. But undeniably the Holy City is as sacred to us, the Muslim people, as it is to the Christians and the Jews.

Therefore we respected what the early Templars were trying to do.

'The Rock of Abraham is the place where your religion commenced as a social entity, and where our religion also was founded. Jesus is believed to have said to Peter, the Fisherman of Galilee: "You are the Rock upon which I shall build my Church."

'Your Lord's original Jewish religion was also founded on a Rock, the Rock of *Abraham*. The same Rock where Mohammed, the founder of our Faith, was taken by angels in a dream in order to found, or change into reality if your prefer, the Faith of Islam.

'In each case, Abraham's, Jesus' or Mohammed's, their motives were immaculate, impeccable, and selfless. They were enacting, as they believed, the Will of God. But, in the case of the Chapters of the Templars, the original motive of unselfish dedication to God's Will has now given way before the darker side of their religion: the pursuit of temporal power and political advantage. Their great fleet roams the seas seeking gain and profit; their intricate system of protective strongpoints along the routes of pilgrimage guard the transfer of great wealth as well as keeping vulnerable pilgrims from harm.

'The Templars' motives are no longer impeccable, even though they well know how to use the basic magical powers given to them by their studies of the Gnosis.'

Osama's voice rose in pitch: 'I tell you, my son, that one day not too far distant, when the Crusades are no longer fought for the Faith, but solely for gain, the Templars will be destroyed by the greed of others, their temples razed to the ground, and their names and reputations reviled.'

Simon was badly shaken.

'But it was my father's wish that I should become a Templar knight. I am intended to follow the path of the Quest for the Holy Grail.'

His voice conveyed his deep distress. Osama's eyes glowed with compassion.

'And so you shall, Simon.'

261

Each day in Osama's company was a time of self-revelation. Simon learned more about his own faults and strengths from the sage's guidance than ever before, even with the help of Abraham or Maimonedes. It was a time of wonder; an interlude of magick, as it should be understood and practised; above all, it was a time of Cosmos, the total order of thought, aligned with the love of God.

Once again, along with the essence of philosophy of the Gnostics, Simon practised the application of all the principles of Cosmos. Mathematics, astronomy, architecture and the basic principles of medicine, all took on a new meaning in the light of the Gnosis.

The young Norman now knew that he would never follow the present Templar path. Of course he would continue to protect the routes of pilgrimage, for on that subject he had sworn his oath as a sergent of the Order. Simon would never forswear his faith as a Christian, therefore he must continue to fight the heathen, much as he now deeply respected them. He would still strive to win back Jerusalem and the True Cross, but he would be much more compassionate to the heathen; just as Saladin and his wise teachers had been to him.

Simon had truly grown into the full flower of his chivalrous manhood. Above all, he had known the love of a great lady. The time was near for his return to the Crusade.

It was a year and more since the horrors of Hittin. In late 1188, Simon told Belami, who had been waiting patiently for his decision, that he wished to rejoin the Templar forces at Acre.

Together, they immediately sought an audience with Saladin. The Sultan already had a shrewd idea of what his guests were going to say. He greeted them warmly.

'What can I do to please you, my friends?'

Simon, as agreed between them, acted as spokesman. 'Sire, we have enjoyed your splendid hospitality for well over a year. It has been a time of great pleasure and we have been shown many wonders. We truly thank you.'

Saladin looked at them quizzically, a slight smile crinkling the corners of his mouth.

'I am delighted that my humble hospitality has pleased you,' he said without irony. He glanced at Belami. 'I trust you found enjoyment in the beauties of Damascus, Sergent?'

The veteran grinned, knowing what Saladin implied.

'I have never seen such loveliness before, Sire, nor felt better because of it.'

The Sultan's laugh came straight from his belly.

'So my Captain of the Guard has told me. You are indeed, Sergent Belami, extremely popular with the ladies.'

Belami's grin was broader than ever. Saladin turned to Simon.

'Osama thinks highly of you, Sergent Simon. He tells me your aptitude for learning reminds him of me, as his student, many years ago. I am flattered, my young infidel friend.' He leant forward. 'I would like you to spend a few evenings with me, discussing the finer points of the Gnosis, and telling me of your attitudes to what has been revealed to you.'

Simon stammered his thanks. Saladin was honouring him greatly. Belami was proud and delighted.

'Now tell me,' said the Sultan, 'why have you asked for this meeting?'

Simon spoke without hesitation.

'We both feel that we should return to our duty.'

Saladin nodded thoughtfully.

'I understand your feelings, my friends. You must also understand mine. To return two such effective warriors, to fight against me, would be a foolish thing to do. You are not my prisoners, but my honoured guests; nevertheless, you are sworn to restore your Christian kingdom to Jerusalem and to regain possession of your holy symbol, the True Cross.

'Therefore, you must inevitably become, once again, my sworn adversaries. That will mean that many of my people may die upon your battle-axe, sword, or lance. I also well recall the effectiveness of your use of the longbow, Sergent Simon. Therefore, I must put a proposition to you.'

The Templars waited expectantly while Saladin carefully considered his next words.

'I offer you both the Faith of Islam.'

This was an honour afforded to few. The two sergents gasped. The Sultan looked directly as Simon, his eyes searching deeply into his mind.

'I have reason to believe that you, Sergent Simon, would gladly stay among our savants for the rest of your life. I know that you, Sergent Belami, are completely loyal to your oath to protect your junior sergent with your life.'

They both nodded.

'My oath was to guard Simon, no matter what happened,' said Belami.

Saladin's mouth relaxed into a broad smile. 'Then, Simon de Creçy – or should I say Simon de Saint Amand? son of a man for whom I too had great respect and honour – if *you* decide to stay, whether you become a Muslim or not, Sergeant Belami will do the same.'

Again the veteran nodded.

Saladin approached Simon and grasped his broad shoulders.

'My young warrior friend, should you wish to join the faith of Islam, I would see no obstacle to your marriage to a Muslim lady.' He paused significantly. 'Even to a member of my own family.'

Simon blushed. Saladin embraced him.

'It is up to you, then, to choose between your love of learning and the love of a lady, or your duty to become once again my sworn enemy.'

Simon's mind was in a turmoil. The Sultan sensed his confusion.

'Naturally, you do not have to make such a choice immediately. Come to me tonight, alone or together, as you wish. To show you how much I trust and honour you, you may come armed and sleep in the next room to mine.'

The Templars looked at each other, saluted and made formal obeisance to Saladin, and marched out.

Back in their rooms, Belami said: 'There is the most

remarkable man I have ever met. Comparing him with our Grand Master, Gerard de By-Our-Lady Ridefort, makes me doubt the validity of my Templar oath. However, once given, such an oath cannot be gainsaid without a formal release from the Grand Master himself, whoever he may be.

'But, Simon, I also swore a sacred oath to protect you, my beloved godson, and if you decide to stay, I must honour that sacred oath above all else – for I gave my word of honour on that matter to my revered Grand Master, Odo de Saint Amand.'

'Poor Belami!' said Simon. 'You seem to lose both ways.'

'Rather say, Simon, that I win both ways. So long as my conscience is clear, I am content. It's up to you, my dear godson.'

'I love Sitt-es-Sham, and I know she loves me. I now know that should I become a Muslim, Saladin would accept me as his brother-in-law.

'I also love learning, and here in the Holy Land of Islam is the focus of the Gnosis, the Fountain of Knowledge.'

Belami leant forward, his face full of compassion. He knew the struggle going on inside his godson's mind.

'However,' Simon continued, 'my father wanted me to become a Templar knight and, as a Templar sergent, I have taken an oath of allegiance to the Order. Therefore, I have no choice but to return to the Order's headquarters at Acre.'

Belami relaxed.

'I knew you would say that, Simon. You are indeed your father's son.' The veteran clapped him on the shoulder. 'Go and join Saladin in learned discussion. It is best that I do not accompany you.' The old soldier's grin broadened. 'Besides, if we are to return to Acre, I must enjoy the beauties of Damascus for as long as I can.'

Belami returned to the delights of his *houris* and, that night, Simon presented himself at Saladin's royal apartments.

The Sultan was in fine form. They discussed their

attitudes towards the Gnosis until well after midnight. Both of them being natural scholars, even though they were warriors, their opinions were presented and received with honest humility and equal respect. There was little disagreement between them, for each followed the same broad highway. The only difference was in their personal approach to the Gnosis. Saladin used the Koran as the word of God – Simon, the Holy Bible.

Both the prophets whom they followed had interpreted the Gnosis in his own way; yet their basic principles were identical.

Truth, compassion, mercy, and love of God were paramount requirements for the great work of Divine Alchemy.

A genuine affection had sprung up between the two men, Muslim and Infidel. Their mutual respect bridged the years between them. Saladin was on the brink of fifty years of life. Study and hard fighting had been his everyday lot. Tough though he was, the Saracen leader's body had taken the punishment of fever and stress. He was no longer as resilient as he once had been.

During their time with him, when Saladin had not been actively engaged in the Second *Jehad*, he had taught both Templars to play polo or, as the Saracens called it, *mall*. This was his favourite sport and he was a master player. The Saracen supremo looked upon the game as a form of fast-moving chess.

The great board-game itself often occupied the few hours that Saladin had free. During their week of discussion on philosophy, Simon enjoyed matching wits with his host, who played a fine strategic game of chess.

The one-armed veteran sergent had also mastered polo, but he had played the game before. It was a joy to see Belami's powerful right arm whacking the ball between the goal-posts, with the speed of a sling-stone shot from a ballista. However, the master sergent did not enjoy playing chess.

'I am one for immediate action,' he said ruefully. 'Chess has too much plotting and counter-plotting in it for Belami.'

Simon immensely enjoyed his time with Saladin. On the last night of their time together, after a stimulating discussion on the merits and demerits of different breeds of horses, Simon reluctantly retired to his couch in the adjoining room.

Saladin had to rise before dawn, to set out once more on a campaign against Krak des Chevaliers. Hence his retiring early. They both slept lightly, their weapons ready to hand.

Outside the respective bedchambers, the duty-guards were keeping watch. Just after one o'clock, in the lost hours of darkness, when the body restores the energies which it has expended during the day and decision-making is unwise, Simon woke. He was instantly alert.

With this newly acquired extra-sensitivity, the result of his close encounter with death, his mind could scan the area around him even when asleep. Simon sensed his dead father's presence, warning him of danger.

Something, or someone, was moving stealthily in the shadows of the curtained archway, separating his bed-room from that of Saladin's.

Simon moved quickly and silently, his unsheathed dagger poised for throwing. He was certain that this was an Assassin, moving in for the kill on Saladin.

In three giant strides he was across the room and sweeping aside the dividing curtain.

Standing over the Sultan's bed, a dark, skeletally thin figure was savouring the murderous moment. A thin, claw-like hand raised a ritual dagger and poised it ready to strike the unsuspecting Saracen leader.

Simon's right arm flew back and forward, in a blur of movement.

The sound of this slight movement turned the Assassin away from his target for a fraction of time. Simon's dagger took him full in the throat. Belami had taught him well.

The thin figure of the Assassin jerked upwards, his feet leaving the floor with the force of the blow. His body crashed backwards to the mozaic tiled floor. Only a strangled cry had issued from his lips.

Saladin had leapt to his feet as his would-be murderer fell. The Sultan took it all in with one burning glance and shouted: 'Alarm!'

Immediately, sword in hand, Saladin faced the possibility of a second attack from the Assassin's habitual two-man murder team.

He could see what Simon had done. Saladin's face shone with gratitude as he saluted the Norman.

'I owe you my life, Simon de Saint Amand,' he said, throwing an arm round his young protector's shoulders. 'First my sister, and now me. The Ayyubids are ever in your debt.'

By this time the Sultan's guard had rushed into their leader's bedroom. When they saw how close Saladin had come to death, they wept with chagrin. They also expected death as the least punishment for their laxity.

Saladin was compassionate. 'These Assassins are sorcerers. They move unseen, invisible, like wraiths. Where is the other killer? These murderers always work in pairs.'

Simon's voice interrupted him urgently.

'Before you, Sire!' he cried, and hurled himself upon a tall, red-bearded guard with a black patch over one eye whose drawn sword was inching imperceptibly upwards. He had immediately recognized him as the second Assassin, one of the team involved in the attempt on Robert de Barres' life in Acre.

The surprised guard was caught off-balance. Simon's fingers grasped his sword hand in an iron grip. Simultaneously, the Templar's left hand cut viciously sideways across the bridge of the one-eyed guard's nose.

Without a word, the Assassin dropped in his tracks as Saladin's scimitar passed through his belly.

'I recognized him, Sire.' said Simon. 'He once tried to kill our commander.'

Saladin dropped his sword and embraced his infidel guest, his eyes filled with tears.

'What woke you?' he asked simply. Simon looked at the Sultan, his eyes gazing deeply into Saladin's.

'I believe it was my father, Sire,' he said.

17
RETURN TO DUTY

Saladin was in a quandary. By saving his life twice within minutes, Simon yet again had put the Sultan deeply in his debt. The Saracen leader already owed Sitt-es-Sham's life to both Templar sergents and now had no honourable recourse but to let them go free if they so wished.

He made one last appeal to his friends to embrace Islam.

'I can only reimburse you with the full honours that I owe you by your remaining with me. I will gladly make you both Emirs. I also swear that you will not be asked to fight Christians. I have many enemies besides the Crusaders.'

The Templars courteously declined his fulsome offer. They knew that riches and great honours would be their lot if they embraced Islam, but neither of them were men who could, or would, break their oath of allegiance to their own people.

'Very well,' said Saladin, sadly. 'I fully understand your decision.' He looked meaningfully at Simon. 'I know that there is one whose heart will be heavy at the prospect of your leaving. But I also know that you are both men of honour. Therefore, I applaud your decision. If there is anything I can give you as some small recompense for all the services that you have rendered me, you have but to ask.'

Belami spoke: 'We would be grateful for the loan of

horses for our journey. As for the rest, we take with us far more than riches . . . the memories of your great compassion and kindness. You saved our lives, Sire.'

Simon impulsively grasped Saladin's hand, and he and Belami found themselves being warmly embraced. It was an emotional leave-taking. After they had gone Saladin wept, so strongly had he been affected by their comradeship. For him, it bore out the old saying: 'Comrades in battle, friends for ever.'

The Sultan felt that it had never been truer. Simon and he had fought the Assassins side by side and, for that reason alone, the Saracen would never forget him. As for Belami, Saladin's respect for his bravery and his admiration for the veteran's skill in battle was unstinting.

Neither of the Templars had ever presumed on their host's magnanimity, and between all three a close personal bond had been forged, during their many months in Damascus.

Simon paid his affectionate respects to Maimonedes, Osama, and especially to Abraham, who now looked upon him as a son. Once again among these remarkable men, tears were not shameful. They all wept at Simon's leaving Damascus. Osama, now ninety years old, had also been drawn deeply into the Norman's aura of unselfish charm.

'You remind me so much of your late father,' he said, as he sat shivering over the charcoal brazier, warming his old bones. 'And Salah-ed-Din as well. You were all three such ardent scholars, yet you were also men of action. Your experiences in battle seem to have forged you into even finer metal, so that you all attract knowledge like lodestones. I have not had the same pleasure in teaching others. I shall never forget you, Simon de Saint Amand.'

The gentle sage's eyes were brimming when Simon reverently kissed his hand.

'*Allahu Akbar!* God is great,' he murmured in farewell.

Abraham also wept when Simon left.

'These are foolish tears from an old man who should know better. After all, your physical presence is not an essential requirement for us to meet. We will do so in our dreams. God bless you, dear friend. You have a fine mind and you will go far, Simon, my son. I shall follow your career with great interest. Here is a parting gift . . . a translation on vellum of the Ancient Egyptian *Treatise on Herbs*.'

Maimonedes was equally practical, giving Simon two of his works on medicine and a set of surgical instruments made of the finest Damascus steel.

'Adonai protect you, Simon,' he said. 'Your destiny is a splendid one.'

Simon's last meeting with the Lady of Syria was heart-rending. They both felt that they would never see each other again.

There love had been unselfish. Sitt-es-Sham had wanted passionately to repay the debt of her life and honour by giving herself to her handsome infidel lover. That she had fallen deeply in love with Simon while so doing, was an added pain to her when the time came to say goodbye.

Sitt-es-Sham was a young widow. She had lost her first husband, Omar Lahim, who had died of fever two years before she had met Simon. Their marriage had been arranged and Saladin's sister had been a dutiful wife, but the first man she had truly loved was the young infidel. She was now nearly thirty years old and, in the full flower of her beauty. She had shown Simon what the love of a woman could mean.

'My wonderful Infidel,' she murmured, as they became one for the last time.

Their love-making was leisurely and ecstatically sensuous, their earlier passion supplanted by an unselfish enjoyment of each other's delight.

Their final night together had been so fulfilling that it had allowed them to part without the awful wrench that frustrated lovers feel when they leave unsatisfied.

Simon would never forget her beauty, her gentleness, and her loving kindness. She would always be his beloved Lady of Syria.

All her life, Sitt-es-Sham would love her handsome Templar, but, being an exceptional woman, she also felt about Simon the same way that a mother feels when she grieves for the loss of her son.

She had been all things to him. She had awakened him to love and had taught him the subtleties of its beauty. She had nursed him and healed his wounds and, above all, she had fulfilled Simon in every way.

Despite his womanless childhood and his enforced chastity as a youth, Sitt-es-Sham had brought him into close contact with their blessed Earth-Mother and, by so doing, she had made him a complete person. She had been mistress, nurse and mother to her beloved infidel and he would always have her love.

While these tearful farewells were being made, Belami also had kissed goodbye to the three delicious *houris* who had delighted him during his long months in Damascus.

Each of them was convinced that she was the only woman he had ever loved. It was yet another remarkable gift that Belami possessed.

The next day, the Templars rode out of Damascus, accompanied by all the honours given to only the most favoured of Saladin's guests. Trumpets, drums, and cymbals sounded their departure as, mounted on magnificent white Arab horses and with an escort of forty Mamelukes, they cantered out of the city gates and headed west towards Acre.

Saladin stood alone on the highest tower of the city and waved them goodbye, his eyes full of tears.

They encamped that night at Hunin whose castle, Neuf Château, was now in Saracen hands. At dawn, they changed into their black surcoats and rode on with the sun at their backs. Once again they were Templars.

To see them safely through the many Saracen patrols that criss-crossed the land, they were escorted to within sight of the walls of Acre. There, the Mamelukes reined in, saluted them and, wheeling round, spurred their horses homewards to Damascus.

Simon and Belami had already passed unhindered through the Saracen lines and now cantered slowly across the desert scrub separating the two armies towards Guy de Lusignan's encampment.

The Crusaders' army was entrenched round the east side of Acre, with 'saps' and zig-zag trenches dug right across to the shores of the bay on the south side. This meant that the Saracen garrison of Acre could effectively only be supplied by sea.

Saladin's army, under Taki-ed-Din, was centred round the high ground at Kahn-el-Ayadich, to the east of the Crusaders' army.

When Saladin had taken Acre in July 1187, four days after the Battle of Hittin, he had left a strong garrison in charge of the city. He had then gone on to conquer Jerusalem and Ascalon and had only failed to take Tyre, the other main port of disembarkation for Crusader reinforcements, when Conrad de Montferrat arrived by sea with his small army and took over the port's defence. That had been a bad set-back for the Saracens, who, like their predecessors under Saladin's command, had decided to abandon the campaign and return home for the winter. Despite the Sultan's warnings and protests, half his huge army had virtually vanished overnight. He was suddenly rendered powerless.

Meanwhile, King Guy de Lusignan had gathered together an army and was further reinforced by a Sicilian fleet, which had moved in to relieve the pressures being brought against the Crusaders by the Sultan's all-conquering Saracens.

He had then been joined by the Pisans from Tyre and an unexpected bonus of fifty ships, manned by Danes and Frisians, carrying 10,000 more Crusaders, of whom a small proportion were knights.

This gave de Lusignan some 20,000 men all told, a motley collection of lances, mercenaries, auxiliaries and armed pilgrims, as well as some 700 knights. Among these latter were such seasoned warriors as Sir James of Aves-nes, the lusty Bishop of Beauvais, and the mysterious 'Green Knight', a Spanish nobleman who remained anonymous during his entire time in the Holy Land, dressed all in green and fighting like ten men.

Simon and Belami rode into this encampment, to be greeted by incredulous cries of recognition from those who knew them. After all, it had been nearly two years since they had been reported missing following the Battle of Hittin.

TheTemplar sergents immediately reported to their Grand Master who, to Belami's disgust, was still Gerard de Ridefort. However, adversity had somewhat changed this arrogant man and, surprisingly, he greeted them with enthusiasm.

'How did you survive?' was naturally his first question.

'With God's help,' replied Belami, 'and by virtue of the great kindness and compassion of the Sultan Saladin.'

'His sister, Sitt-es-Sham, and his personal physician Maimonedes, saved our lives by nursing us back to health.' Simon explained the situation as briefly as possible.

'Did you take an oath of fealty or of non-aggression to Saladin?' asked de Ridefort. 'If so, I absolve you: Saladin is a heathen.'

Both sergents looked at him coldly.

'We took no such oath. The Sultan did not require one from us. He freely allowed us to return to our own people, knowing full well that we would continue to fight against him,' said Belami, flatly.

'Because we had saved his sister's life from de Châtill-on's men, the Sultan felt he owed us our freedom. He is an honourable man,' added Simon.

De Ridefort glossed over the implied rejection of his offer to absolve them.

'Two years is a long time,' he said ruminatively. 'You were his prisoners then?'

'No!' said Belami. 'We were his honoured guests and we were treated as such. Only after Sergent de Creçy saved the Sultan from an Assassin's attempt to murder him, did Saladin finally agree to let us rejoin our Order, without taking an oath of fealty or of non-aggression to him.'

The Grand Master's face was suffused with blood.

'Sergent de Creçy, why in Heaven's name did you stop Saladin's murderers from accomplishing what we have been trying to do for years?'

Simon looked straight at de Ridefort.

'Because it was one of Sinan-al-Raschid's Assassins who was about to kill the Sultan,' he said coldly. 'And the Grand Master of the Assassins is as much *our* enemy as he is Saladin's. It could only have been to the murderous cult's advantage to kill the Saracen leader, who would gladly ally himself with Christendom to stamp out Sinan-al-Raschid's monstrous regime. Instinctively, I took Saladin's side in the matter.'

Obviously, Simon was giving an honest explanation of the affair. De Ridefort reluctantly accepted their story, because he knew it was true. These two Templars, young and old, were honourable men who had fought bravely at Hittin, and he had left them for dead on its blood-soaked ground when he made his escape. Their report was concise and unembroidered. It bore the stamp of authenticity.

De Ridefort was intelligent enough to realize that he was a fortunate Grand Master to have such men as these two Templar sergents who had now rejoined him. He badly needed experienced cavalrymen, and both Belami and Simon were splendid troop commanders. Faced with no other choice, de Ridefort saluted and formally embraced them. He then took them to see King Guy de Lusignan, to whom they repeated their extraordinary story.

'We are dealing with a remarkable man,' said the King thoughtfully. 'Saladin is both determined and skilled in battle; the Horns of Hittin taught us that dreadful lesson. Yet the Sultan is a compassionate man. You, Gerard, and I both owe him our lives. I honour him for his great compassion.'

He turned to the Templar sergents.

'Will you now continue to fight the Saracen paladin?' he asked.

'We are bound by our oaths to our Order, Sire,' said Belami. 'I know I speak for Sergent de Creçy when I say: we fight for Christendom!'

Both Templars drew their swords and saluted the King. In token of acknowledgement Guy de Lusignan returned the gesture.

Later, when they were alone, Belami said: 'Were it not

275

for our Sacred Oath, I wonder at whose side we would prefer to fight?'

Simon nodded grimly.

Their new quarters were in a leaky tent, set up behind earth-works as part of the extensive trench network thrown up on the landward side of Acre.

The Crusaders had laboriously sapped their way forward with these earth banks, until they were within crossbow-shot of the walls of the city. This kept them just out of range of anything except the light arrows of the garrison archers, which usually failed to penetrate chain-mail or a steel helmet. Conversely, their own heavier crossbow bolts could pick off the Saracen garrison on the battlements of the city walls.

The siege had developed into an affair of sniping, sallies and small mêlées, and hunger was now the Crusaders' biggest enemy.

Meanwhile, Saladin's men had waited for reinforcements from troops returning after their winter leave.

The Saracen leader, during his campaign against Jersualem, Tyre, Ascalon, Belvoir and other Crusader strongpoints, had returned to Damascus a number of times. Those were the occasions when he met Simon and Belami. Now, once again, they found themselves facing Saladin, back in command of his relieving force, on the high ground to the east of Acre. It was a strange feeling. Simon prayed that he would never have to face Saladin in battle, because he knew that now he could not kill him. Belami felt exactly the same.

'We owe him our lives,' he said. 'Better to die than to dishonour that debt.' Simon agreed whole-heartedly.

Starvation was only averted when Crusader ships ran the Saracen blockade after a fierce fleet-action against Admiral Lulu. They brought provisions, remounts, and military supplies to the besieged army which had by then reached the end of its endurance. It had even been reduced to eating its own war-horses.

This welcome reinforcement raised de Lusignan's hopes and as soon as he could restore his small army's fighting strength he planned an attack against Saladin's field army.

This time, at least, he did listen to more experienced voices than de Ridefort's.

De Châtillon was dead and Raymond III of Tripoli had died of grief after the Battle of Hittin. De Lusignan had learnt caution, if not battle wisdom.

De Ridefort too was much subdued, and listened to the tactical advice of his experienced sergents. He had learnt the hard lesson that at a tactical level, as well as at strategic command level, there is no substitute for experience. The Templar sergents, battlewise and tactically skilled, must be heard. Belami was chosen to speak for them all.

'Worshipful Grand Master,' he said. 'Saladin is a master cavalry tactician. The ponderous charges of our knights are now out-dated. When directed against the Saracen crescent formation, as we saw at Hittin, the Crusader charge expends its energy on thin air. Then, when our spearhead of attack has gone through the gap which they open in their ranks, their skirmishers wheel round and attack us from all sides.

'If you must attack in the old way, at least use waves, each one made up of a compact group of lances, say 60 to 100 knights at a time. Each wave should be separated by 200 yards, so that, as the Saracens open their formation to let the first wave through, the second wave hits them on one flank, and the third wave strikes them on the other, and so on, wave following wave.

'That way gives time for each charge to re-form, wheel round, and attack the Saracens from the rear.

'Of our 700 knights, supported by another 1,000 turcopole lances, you can keep a strong reserve ready to repeat the manoeuvre as often as you need to.

'At the same time, if you pillion some of your cross-bowmen on the backs of the horses of each wave, you can shoot a volley of crossbow bolts against the Muslim heavy cavalry.

'Aim for their horses, as they do with us. If you bring *them* down, the Saracen cavalry become infantry, just as we did at the Horns of Hittin.'

For once, the Crusaders' commanders listened and some agreed to try out the new tactics, but to Belami's chagrin the rest were too impetuous and launched their attacks before they had fully mastered the technique of the use of flying columns. Even then, they had more success than they had before.

Their main adversary was Taki-ed-Din.

Belami commanded 100 turcopoles and Simon 50 more. The Norman had not been able to replace his deadly longbow, because no yew wood was available in Outremer, but he found a reasonable substitute in lemonwood. It was not as powerful as his old longbow, but it still made a formidable weapon. He had six dozen new cloth-yard shafts made by a Danish fletcher and bowmaker who had arrived with the reinforcements. So when de Lusignan finally moved against the Saracens, Simon had two quiversful of arrows. One was on his back and the other was attached to the saddle of his new Arab war-horse. This was one of the two white stallions presented to him personally by Saladin. Simon called his mounts Castor and Pollux, after the twin stars.

The redoubtable Conrad de Montferrat had come down from Tyre with his forces to join de Lusignan and de Ridefort. This made the Frankish army in excess of 20,000 men, including 1,000 knights and some 2,000 lances, sergents, turcopoles and other auxiliaries.

Facing them was Taki-ed-Din who had ridden out with 6,000 cavalrymen on a probing raid. Behind him was the bulk of Saladin's relieving force, more than 30,000 men, ready to intervene if needed.

At Belami's entreaty, de Ridefort had persuaded the King to leave a holding-force behind, so that, if Saladin should prevail, the Crusaders' encampment would be solidly held.

At least de Lusignan had tried out the Templar's suggestion of waves of attacking knights, and the Crusaders advanced in four separate divisions. Had the King sub-divided each division into smaller spearheads, of 100 knights each, he would have won the battle. In fact the conflict came closer to defeat than to a victory, but at least it wasn't a total disaster.

There had been insufficient time to train all the troops

in Belami's manoeuvre, but the two sergents were able to drill another 100 crossbowmen to work with their own turcopole lances.

When the time came to advance against Taki-ed-Din's probing cavalry columns, the Frankish force advanced behind their infantry and slowly approached their chosen killing-ground.

The cunning Conrad de Montferrat, who had now decided to fight alongside King Guy, if not under his command, pushed forward with a compact fighting-force which contained 200 Genoese crossbowmen, the best in the world.

'We've got a chance,' muttered Belami. 'But it's still in God's hands whether we can break right through to Saladin's main force without losing too many lances on the way.'

The veteran sensed the moment when de Montferrat quickened his pace into the charge. To his dismay, it was much too early.

'Judas Iscariot!' Belami snarled. 'He's hitting them too soon, with *all* his cavalry! Why don't these whoresome imbeciles listen to us?'

'After all, Belami,' said Simon sardonically, 'We are only sergents. Please God, this isn't going to be another Hittin! Now *we've* got to back up de Montferrat. So let's get on with it.'

The Norman couched his lance and shouted to his flying column to charge. Belami cursed and followed suit.

The Frankish knights had swept through the lines of their own infantry, who had hurriedly opened up a path to let them through. The Crusaders thundered forward. he formed a massive wedge of knights, charging so closely together that their mailed limbs often rasped against those of their comrades riding on either side.

Taki-ed-Din waited till the unwieldly attack was fully committed, and then opened his centre ranks. The mass Crusader charge, wrapped in its own blinding dust-loud, pounded through to spend its terrific weight on he open plain beyond. It spread out like a fan, breaking

279

up into disorganized groups. The well-trained Saracens immediately wheeled round and rushed after them. A hail of skirmishers' arrows whistled around de Montferrat's men. Many of their chargers fell, throwing riders to the ground where they lay half-stunned, easy prey for the Saracen horse-archers.

A second wave of Frankish cavalry smashed into the Saracens, unseating many of Taki-ed-Din's lances. But once again, the Saracens opened their ranks and the main impact of the Crusaders' second charge also spent itself on empty space.

This time, the scattered group of Christian knights continued up the valley with de Ridefort leading them. They were rapidly becoming a disorganized rabble.

The third and fourth divisions of heavy cavalry lanced a path through the Saracen crescent, meeting enough resistance to scatter the heathens' heavy cavalry.

Belami and Simon led their flying columns straight through the demoralized Saracens, while their pillion-riding archers poured a heavy fire into the startled Muslim skirmishers. Many of these fell shrieking to their death, mangled beneath the Frankish war-horses.

The crossbowmen jumped off to reload and, as infantry, fired a second deadly volley. This emptied more Saracen saddles.

The Crusader force swept on up the plain towards Saladin's position on the high ground, where the main Saracen army was bivouacked. The Sultan had just enough time to organize a counter-attack. Saracen horsemen appeared from among the tents and rushed down on to the milling ranks of Christian knights. A pitched battle ensued.

The fighting quickly disintegrated into a series of mêlées with small groups of opposing horsemen hacking at each other with sword, battle-axe, scimitar and mace. The thud of axes on shields, the clash of blades and the dull crunch of splintering bones, as maces found their targets, were counterpointed by the battle-cries of Christians and Heathens and the death-shrieks of gallant men. Lopped-off limbs, hands, and decapitated heads, strewed the rocky ground like the debris from some dreadful slaughterhouse.

The frenzied neighing of the horses, and their high-pitched screams as they were disembowelled by opposing lances, or ham-strung by the swords of fallen Christians and Saracens, seeking to unseat their rivals, rose in a dreadful chorus of animal agony to add to the appalling human holocaust. It was a hecatomb, an inferno of suffering and terror, all in the name of God.

Belami and Simon raced their columns to the aid of small groups of these beleaguered knights, bringing them instant relief as they smashed their way through the surrounding mass of Saracen skirmishers and horse-archers.

All the time, de Lusignan won back yard after yard of ground in an orderly retreat to his encampment outside Acre. The attack had now become a defensive rear-guard action.

However, unlike the Battle of Hittin, this time the Crusaders were well supplied with water and therefore their strength was not disastrously sapped by thirst. Even then, some 5,000 Christians fell before Saladin's counter-attacks, or were captured by his skirmishers. The Sultan's forces lost about half that number, including 150 Royal Mamelukes and two senior Emirs. These were the equivalent of top Christian commanders.

Nevertheless it was not a decisive victory for either side. De Ridefort, the Templar Grand Master, died in the midst of the battle. Some said by Saladin's own hand, in return for the betrayal of his word of honour which he had given the Sultan, and which had freed him from his previous capture by the Saracens.

'God rest his soul!' said Belami. 'He has paid for his part in the massacre of Hittin.'

The Templar sergents had fought until they were forced to follow King Guy's retreating army; even then, they continued to carry out cavalry sweeps to keep the Saracen horse-archers from picking off the Crusaders' rear-guard.

When the battered Christian army finally regained its

entrenchments it was exhausted, but the strong force left behind by King Guy surged out to beat off the Saracens, who had expended their last arrows on harrying the retreating Crusaders.

'It wasn't a resounding success,' muttered Belami sarcastically, lowering his bruised and aching body on to his blankets. 'But we gave the Saracens a bloody nose. At least it was better than sitting outside the walls of Acre, twiddling our thumbs and starving to death. Eh, Simon?'

His junior sergent did not reply. He was already fast asleep.

A week later, a Templar marshal called Robert de Sablé was installed as the new Grand Master. Belami thoroughly approved of the choice.

'Here at last is another Arnold de Toroga. This knight, Simon, is one of your father's men. He is intelligent and will have a profound effect on all our fortunes from now on.'

'Have you served under him, Belami?' Simon was curious.

'Not directly, but old d'Arlan swore by him. He had been out on patrol with him many times, and had also served under him at Krak des Chevaliers. He's a tough determined commander, but, thank God, he's not reckless. I am interested to know what he will do with us.'

Belami did not have long to wait. Soon afterwards, he and Simon were sent for by the new Grand Master. Robert de Sablé was a stocky knight, with a broad chest and sturdy body. Deeply grooved and powerful, his face said everything about him. From his clear brown eyes to the firm slash of his tight-lipped mouth, he was the picture of a tough fighting man. Yet there were signs of humour and compassion in his strong features, and around his eyes radiated the lines of one who often smiles. It was essentially the face of a good-humoured man.

Here was a Templar Grand Master worth following, if need be into the mouth of Hell itself. When his sergents saluted, de Sablé cheerfully acknowledged their respect. This was no traditional grim-faced Grand Master of the Temple, arrogantly sure of his Divine Right to lead the

Order into battle. This fighting-monk was a soldier's soldier. It did not surprise Simon to find out later that de Sablé had himself once been a sergeant in the Order. A battlefield knighthood conferred by Odo de Saint Amand had raised him from the ranks.

'He took the Templar oath of poverty and celibacy from the Grand Chapter in Jerusalem, shortly before your father was captured by Saladin,' Belami told Simon.

However, the veteran was sure that de Sablé knew nothing of Simon's parentage. The reason their new commander had sent for them soon became apparent.

'I congratulate you on your tactics, Sergeant Belami,' he said. 'Sergeant d'Arlan, God rest his soul, told me about his exploits with you under de Saint Amand's command. I understand that you were recovering from severe wounds when I joined Odo de Saint Amand. So, the fortunes of war have dictated that so far we have not served together. Tell me everything you know about Saladin. You are both valuable sources of information on that subject.'

The Templars gave their new Grand Master every scrap of information they possessed. Neither of them felt that they were betraying Saladin's trust, because they had taken no oath of non-aggression or fealty to the Supreme Sultan. Therefore they held nothing back.

At the end of two hours of detailed reporting, Robert de Sablé, who up till then had remained silent apart from putting the odd pertinent question, saluted them.

'You certainly have had extraordinary adventures.' he said.'I honour you both, Brethren.'

The Grand Master used a term seldom employed by Templar knights when addressing their Order's sergeants. He also grinned broadly, making a welcome change from their previous Grand Master's attitude towards them.

'I intend to send you on a delicate mission,' he said. 'You must remain close-mouthed about it, because there is already far too much intrigue going on in this Godless camp.'

His sergeants nodded in agreement. The Templar commander continued: 'King Richard of England and a considerable force of troops have been persuaded to join

283

up with Louis, the Margrave of Thuringia, and Henry, Count of Champagne, to form a Third Crusade against Saladin.'

Involuntarily the sergents gasped. De Sablé smiled.

'Furthermore, Frederick Barbarossa, the Holy Roman Emperor, has gathered an army of over 200,000 troops, and intends to march on Outremer from the north.'

Belami interrupted respectfully. 'But, Worshipful Grand Master, the great "Red-beard" is now an old man. He must be nearly eighty years old.'

De Sablé grinned at the veteran's description of the Holy Roman Emperor.

'That is undoubtedly true but, God willing, he will make the pilgrimage. He is still a redoubtable fighting Emperor, worthy to carry the Sacred Lance of Charlemagne.'

They all three crossed themselves, for it was believed that like the True Cross, the Spear of Charlemagne, the first Holy Roman Emperor, was a sacred relic. It was said to be the actual spear that had pierced the side of Jesus on the Cross.

De Sablé continued: 'Such a large army will have many problems. King Richard is expected to reach Sicily at any time now. First, he had a number of minor squabbles to resolve in France, but King Louis is now his ally and intends to "take the Cross" as well.'

He paused to let the information sink in.

'I want you to take ship from here and meet King Richard in Cyprus where, apparently, he intends to make his Mediterranean base, with or without the resident tyrant, Isaac Ducas Comnenus's permission.'

'But we are only sergents, sir,' pointed out Belami.

'You are far more than that, Brethren. You have been among our most successful weapons on the battlefields of Outremer. Moreover, you both know Saladin and have a shrewd idea of how his mind works in battle.'

Belami nodded and de Sablé resumed: 'King Richard appreciates good fighting-men. Especially tacticians such as yourselves, skilled in cavalry warfare and the sort of fast-moving battles that the English king loves to command. So I am sending you on ahead, as a token of my respect, to act as a personal bodyguard against attacks by anyone, foe or so-called friend. But especially, in view of your personal experiences, to guard Couer de Leon against the Assassins of Sinan-al-Raschid!'

Simon was confused.

'But why, Worshipful Grand Master, would the Assassins seek Richard's life?'

His new commanding officer looked shrewdly at him.

'Because the *Hashashiyun* can be bought, and it is possible that Conrad de Montferrat has his heart set upon the crown of Jerusalem. Our Queen Sibylla, and both her children, are gravely ill. Her physician tells me that she is not expected to live and neither are they, poor mites. They all have Arnaldia fever. This could mean that de Montferrat will seek to marry Isabella, the last of Baldwin's line, and then seize the crown of Jerusalem.'

'But surely she is already Homfroi de Toron's wife?' interjected Simon.

'True!' replied de Sablé. 'But for how long? Remember! This is Outremer, the Holy Land, where all things unholy can happen.'

He hesitated, then, his mind made up, continued: 'I am entrusting you both with an exceptionally difficult mission. Your purpose will be to protect the English king at *all* costs, your own lives included. Do you understand?'

They both nodded grimly.

'Doubtless, we will be engaged in more battles against Saladin. At least it will keep the Crusaders' minds off their empty bellies. But I want you both to stay out of these affairs, until I send for you to carry out this mission. I realize it is a strange order, a Grand Master commanding his sergents *not* to fight, but I know a great deal about you both and I have decided that you are the best men for this mission. So stay out of trouble. That is an order!'

The Grand Master stepped forward and embraced them both warmly. Then they all three knelt and prayed for the successful outcome of the task they faced.

When they left, Simon said, 'Belami, you once told me that only a dubbed knight could become a Templar brother. Yet now you tell me that our new Grand Master was a Templar sergent, like ourselves.'

Belami chuckled.

'De Sablé was the younger son of a feudal family, as penniless as we once thought Pierre de Montjoie to be. But your father found out that de Sablé was in line for the title if his elder brother died, and he used that fact as an argument with the Grand Chapter of the Temple at Jerusalem. Your father had great respect for the young sergent's abilities and persuaded King Almaric to dub him Knight on the battlefield. It is a very rare honour indeed, but for such an accolade to be awarded by our Order, the full family background of the one to be so honoured must first be known. In your case that is impossible, within the Order.

'However, many a young Frankish squire, whose background was also shrouded in mystery, has been dubbed Knight outside the order, and then later become either a Templar knight, or a *Donat*.'

Simon sighed and Belami grinned.

'Mayhap King Richard the Lionheart will be the one to raise you to the Knightly Order of Chivalry. Who knows?'

But they still had many weary, bone-chilling months to wait for Simon's next date with destiny.

The long winter of 1190 crawled past without further news of King Richard and the great new Crusade. Rumours flew around the Frankish camp, but little else happened to ease the dull ache of hunger and the lack of firewood to fight the chilling damp of the night.

Once again the Crusaders were reduced to eating their hounds and their horses, even fighting over the bones like starving dogs. At last, a small convoy fought its way through the Turkish blockade and, for the first time in months, the Crusaders ate a decent meal which made most of them violently sick.

The extreme cold and the lack of food had affected them all. Arnaldia, the dreaded fever of Outremer, stalked through the shivering underfed troops. Many died, including Queen Sibylla and her children, leaving King Guy a widower.

That was all that Conrad de Montferrat needed to make

his move. He first declared Isabella's marriage to Homfroi de Toron invalid, then forced the Archbishop, and the Patriarch Heraclius, to agree and married Isabella as soon as he could.

It was blatant treachery, a conspiracy of the worst kind. Poor Isabella, still barely eighteen years old whereas de Montferrat was middle-aged, loathed her coarse demanding new husband, who virtually raped her on their wedding night.

Gone were the happy days with the undemanding gentleness of Homfroi de Toron. De Montferrat wanted a royal heir and he spared no effort to ensure himself of getting one. The unfortunate Isabella wept unheard by the soulless men around her, who backed de Montferrat as the next King of Jerusalem if Guy de Lusignan should die.

De Sablé's suspicions were all too well-founded. Already, plots were being hatched by the de Montferrat faction to ensure that their rival, King Guy, should suffer a convenient death in the next battle.

The year was well into 1191 when the Templar Grand Master finally sent for his two sergents.

'You leave at the end of this week. King Richard has set sail from Messina, and a storm has blown his ships into the harbour at Limassol, on the island of Cyprus. This news has just come in with the relief convoy.'

He outlined some of the difficulties facing them.

'Richard has many so-called allies who would be glad to see him dead. He is a popular leader among the English who will follow him to Hell itself, but such a powerful determined soldier easily makes enemies. You will have to keep your eyes open, not only for Assassins but for treachery among his allied commanders.

'This strange young English king is as handy with a pen as he is with a sword or the twin-bladed Danish battle-axe, which like you, Belami, he favours. Among the Troubadors and Minnensingers, he rates high. In fact, he is considered to be a prince among poets.

'If he likes you, as I am sure he will, he makes a loyal friend. If, on the other hand, you incur his displeasure, you will probably both die.

'He's always in the forefront of the battle, where the action is hottest. I honestly believe he does not know the meaning of the word fear. He is a worthy opponent to match against Saladin. The Sultan is probably the cleverer of the two, but in courage there is nothing to choose between them. They are both lion-hearted. God be with you both. *Vive les sergents!*'

They saluted and embraced.

Six days later Simon and Belami set sail for Cyprus.

18
THE LION KING

The Templar galley *Saint Bernard*, which carried Simon
and Belami to Cyprus, was in sharp contrast to the
broad-beamed Hospitaller transport which had originally
brought them to the Holy Land.

Sleek and fast, the single-banked oars of this slim galley
were rowed by twenty strong men on either side. Her
speed under oars alone was over four knots, and with a
following wind filling her lateen sails she could even raise
it to seven knots, while her oarsmen could keep up the
pace.

Her Viking ancestry was evident in the lap-straked
planking of rot-proof cedarwood laid over her staunch
ribs, adzed from the same timber and fastened with tree-
nails, which were tough dowels of oak. Overall she was
an excellent seaboat. The Templars had brought their
white Arab horses with them, and these were stabled
below decks in well-padded stalls, specially built for the
voyage. Normally, this fast courier-vessel only carried
passengers and vital supplies, so the stalls had to be added.

The fresh, off-shore wind bowled the *Saint Bernard*
along, assuring a speedy passage to Cyprus. Although the
island was only a day and a night's voyage from Tyre,
they had been forced to detour around the Turkish fleet
patrols and then to sail westward, before turning north
for Cyprus. They eventually made landfall three days
after leaving Acre. On their arrival in the Bay of Limassol,

sheltered from the westerly gales by Cape Gata, they were met by an English patrol boat of King Richard's large fleet, which lay anchored in the lee of the jutting foreland.

These English troop transports had been severely damaged by savage storms, which had nearly wrecked the royal ship carrying King Richard's bride-to-be, the Princess Berengaria, and his younger sister, Queen Joanna, the widow of King William II of Sicily.

The English vessels were busily engaged in repairs before setting out for the Holy Land. The Templar galley was easily recognizable because of its large Beauseant flag flying from the foremast. This ensured them a warm welcome and they were soon efficiently berthed alongside a stone jetty, built out from the rocky shore.

Within minutes of tying-up to large iron rings let into the stone wharf, Simon and Belami led their white Arab chargers down the narrow gangplank on to the stone-paved jetty.

Their welcome by Sir Roger of Sherborne, the King's harbour-master, was cordial and efficient. Formalities were kept to a minimum.

As usual, Belami's speech was a model of brevity. After introducing himself and Simon, he said: 'We bring greetings to His Majesty King Richard from our Grand Master, Robert de Sablé. My orders are to present the King with these Letters of Credence and this document, which guarantees support for His Majesty's Crusade in the sum of 30,000 gold besants.'

The smile on Sir Roger's face broadened perceptibly. And on their short walk along the harbour mole, the harbour-master told the new arrivals something of the present situation in Cyprus.

'Isaac Ducas Comnenus, the self-styled Emperor of Cyprus, is at present skulking in the hills, as well he might. King Richard is enraged at the barbarous reception given to his Princess Berengaria and his royal sister, Queen Joanna, when Isaac Comnenus refused them supplies and water after they had been driven into Limassol by the storm that nearly sank our entire fleet.' The experienced old English knight grinned sardonically.

'The tyrant Comnenus has made a bad mistake incurring King Richard the Lionheart's wrath. My monarch will make him pay dearly for his savage discourtesy.' There was a bluff honesty about Sir Roger of Sherborne that immediately earned him the Templars' respect.

'Have you visited the Holy Land yourself, sir knight?' asked Balami.

'Indeed, I have,' the harbour-master waxed enthusiastic. 'I also have reason to remember my second Crusade.'

He tapped his left leg, which was perceptibly shorter than his right limb, causing him to limp heavily.

'A Saracen lance bit deeply into me at the Battle of Harim, when I served under Bohemond of Antioch and Joscelyn of Edessa. That was twenty seven years ago. I was a callow young knight of twenty five years at the time, and it has left me with a nautical-roll, on land as well as at sea.' The old campaigner chuckled wryly at his severe handicap.

'I am looking forward this time to evening the score!'

The Templars warmed to the veteran's cheerful personality. As they reached the end of the stone mole and turned on to the sandy strip of the foreshore, the elderly harbour-master pointed towards a strange building that guarded it.

'There are the King's headquarters,' he said. 'That is the Castle Mategriffon. Our ingenious monarch likes to invent new weapons of war. It is, as you can see, a sturdy and compact castle, including a mobile siege tower, made out of wood. This is easily transportable by ship in its component parts and simple to erect or disassemble. King Richard prefers it to a large tent and it is, of course, defensible, being strongly built. It even boasts a great hall and an audience-chamber, and has several other adjoining rooms. Within its walls, it can accommodate pavilions for guests. Mategriffon may not be the complete answer to foreign campaigning, but it is an improvement on sleeping under canvas, or under the stars.'

'Surely, being wood, it must be vulnerable to Greek-fire?' Belami interjected.

Sir Roger laughed. 'For that reason, the walls have been clad with untanned hides soaked in vinegar. In time you may even get used to the smell! Here, beside the shore, it is less noticeable than it would be were the castle sited inland. We usually sleep under canvas when we are pursuing the enemy. King Richard enjoys his campaigns. Were I a younger man, I would probably feel the same.'

Sir Roger led the Templar sergents past the grim-faced English archers guarding the gates to Mategriffon, and left them in an ante-room while he limped away to inform the King of their arrival. Five minutes later he reappeared and motioned them to follow him.

Their first sight of King Richard the Lionheart was that of a near-giant who rose from his throne to greet them. His broad forehead was crowned by thick golden-red hair and girt with the fillet of his crown. His face was that of a king, strong, ruggedly handsome and self-assured, without the petulant arrogance that the Templars had come to expect from visiting Crusader nobles. For once, the Templars felt that rumour had not disappointed them. This warrior King was every inch the 'Lionheart' of legend. Richard I of England was truly a magnificent animal.

The Templar sergents saluted and then knelt in obeisance. Immediately, Coeur de Leon signed to them to rise.

'Templars have no need to bow the knee to a brother Crusader. After all, we have all 'taken the Cross'. By your battle scars, I can see that you have fought hard and well for the Holy Land. Richard of England welcomes you to join him in this the Third Crusade.'

This was no glib speech spoken for effect. The King's smiling face gave full weight to his words. Advancing to meet them, King Richard grasped their right hands with an impressively strong grip and, to their surprise, embraced them both. Richard Plantagenet's impulsive informality was in keeping with his mercurial nature.

'We have great admiration for the deeds of our Templar brothers-in-arms,' he said, accepting the letter proffered to him by Belami. As he quickly read the contents, he chuckled.

'Your Grand Master writes of you both as if you were

292

his favourite sons. That is unusual, coming from a Templar. But I hear that Robert de Sablé is a fine soldier, and one who admires good fighting-men. He offers you to me as experienced guides to the ways of our worthy heathen adversaries. He also suggests that you should become part of my bodyguard. So be it. I have a fancy to have Templars fight beside me, so I gladly accept your Grand Master's generous offer. How say you, *mes braves*?'

His startling use of Belami's favourite term made the veteran grin, his rumbling diapaison answering the King.

'May we both serve Your Majesty well. My battle-axe and my companion's sword are yours to command, Sire.'

King Richard's eyes lit up.

'I see,' he said eagerly. 'You favour the weapon I carry in battle. Let us see how well you can use it, Sergent.' He turned to his squire, a good-looking, merry-eyed youth whose lute was slung over his shoulder. Without a word, the young man handed the King a broad double-headed Danish battle-axe.

Richard hefted it expertly and selecting as his target a large wooden shield hanging on the far wall of his audience chamber, he effortlessly flung the heavy battle-axe. It flashed across the wide room and thudded up to its socket in the middle of the shield, bringing it crashing to the ground. The King looked quizzically at Belami.

The veteran growled his respect for the Lionheart's skill and said: 'With your permission, Sire?'

Richard nodded.

Belami adroitly unhooked his own battle-axe from its clip on his belt and paused for an instant as he selected his target. The shield had landed flat on the floor, with the long wooden haft of the King's axe sticking upright.

Belami took careful aim and with an expert swing sped his own axe across the room in a blur of steel.

The razor-sharp weapon struck the handle of the King's battle-axe, splitting it neatly in two. A spontaneous burst of applause and admiring cries greeted the Templar's feat.

Coeur de Leon smiled broadly, his fine teeth gleaming

in the light of the flambeaux. He clapped a hand on Belami's shoulder.

'If I didn't know you as a Templar, *mon brave sergent*,' he laughed, 'I would take you for a sorcerer. *Bien fait*, Sergent Belami!'

Richard turned to Simon, openly admiring the good-looking young Norman.

'Your Grand Master writes to me that you, Sergent de Creçy, are a master bowman. Let us see what you can do with the English longbow.' He signed to his page, who took the weapon and a quiver of arrows from one of his archer-guards.

Simon habitually wore an archer's leather bracer-guard on his left wrist, and his right hand was already gloved. He quickly inspected the long yew-bow and nodded approvingly. The eyes of the Court were upon him.

'As your Majesty pleases,' he said, selecting two arrows from the archer's quiver. Holding one arrow parallel with the belly of the longbow in his left hand, he knocked the other cloth-yard shaft to the bowstring.

'Shoot at the white buckler hanging at the end of the room,' said Richard, pointing to a small round shield, set high up on the ceiling-beam.

Simon nodded and sped his first shaft. It whirred through the air to skewer the wooden buckler, knocking it from the beam. Even as it fell, Simon had bent the longbow a second time and loosed it, in one fluid movement.

Before the small white shield had reached the floor, Simon's second shaft transfixed it in mid-air.

Once again, cries of approbation rang out from the Court. The King's face beamed with pleasure. He loved to witness skill at arms.

'I thank Robert de Sablé for his offer, and welcome you both to my personal bodyguard. Now go, refresh yourselves, for tonight you will dine with us.'

The Templars bowed, saluted and withdrew. As they marched out of the King's audience-chamber, Belami said quietly, 'There's a man we can follow gladly. This is going to be a royal Crusade.'

It certainly proved to be a splendid dinner. Escorted by Sir Roger of Sherborne, the Templar sergents were the only members of their Order present at the banquet. To their surprise they were seated in places of honour, on either side of the English king.

The Lionheart presided over the banquet with good-natured banter, interspersed with moments of due solemnity when he toasted the successful outcome of the Third Crusade.

'Tomorrow or the next day, according to the vagaries of wind and tide, we expect to welcome a full delegation from the Holy Land. King Guy de Lusignan will be there with his brother, Geoffrey, Count de Lusignan, and Bohemond of Antioch is also coming. Homfroi de Toron and the Grand Master of the Templars, Robert de Sablé are also to be our honoured guests. It was the Grand Master who sent me my two brave Templar sergents to give me the benefit of their long experience in the Holy Land. And so, my dear friends, the royal toast is 'Our guests', coupled with the name of the Poor Knights of Christ of the Temple at Jerusalem.'

All his guests, except the Templars, Princess Berengaria, Richard's bride-to-be, Queen Joanna, and their respective ladies-in-waiting, stood for the toast. When the Court was reseated, Berengaria was joined by yet another lady-in-waiting. She was a small slim blonde, with elfin features and large merry eyes. Simon couldn't take his eyes off her. She also stole covert glances in his direction. Their eyes met and the lovely girl smiled; then to his astonishment, she waved to him.

'Who is she, Belami?' he asked excitedly.

'My sister Berenice, you big oaf,' laughed a familiar voice behind him, and Simon found himself being half-strangled by his old friend Pierre de Montjoie's bear-hug. Simon was overjoyed.

The King turned to this tableau of happy reunion.

'You have fought beside Sergent de Creçy, Count de Montjoie?' he asked, more as a statement than as a question.

The irrepressible Pierre de Montjoie bowed in token contrition.

'Your pardon, Sire, but Simon, Belami and I fought in the Holy Land for a number of years. Forgive my lack of courtesy in not first paying you, Sire, my respects.'

The Lionheart was in an expansive mood.

'There is nothing like a reunion of old friends, especially when they have been comrades-in-arms. You must tell me of your encounters with the Saracens, *mes braves sergents*. And I charge you, Count de Montjoie, to do the same.'

It was characteristic of this big impulsive man, that though he was an incurable romantic and a poet, he preferred the company of fighting-men to that of women, no matter how beautiful or intelligent they might be.

Princess Berengaria was both of these things, but quiet and reserved due to her strict upbringing. She was also nervous of her coming alliance with the King of England, and, truth to tell, so was Richard, who was actually acutely shy with the opposite sex.

Dominated by his formidable mother, Queen Eleanor, and brought up by his father, Henry II, to use the sword and battle-axe to devasting effect in battle, Richard Plantaganet, now thirty two years old, was ill-equipped for his coming role of husband.

Even Berengaria's blonde beauty and tranquil intellect failed to allay his secret fears of inadequacy, when put to the test of the marriage-bed. King Richard the Lionheart was the king of beasts in battle, but an inept lover in bed, and he knew it. He found conversation with his betrothed strained and made up for it by talking to his sister, while Berengaria dutifully remained silent or answered the guests who came to pay her their respects.

'The young woman has fine, child-bearing hips if King Richard ever gets round to siring her child,' murmured Pierre de Montjoie irreverently.

Simon was still Templar enough to be shocked by his friend's remark.

'Surely that shyness will disappear when they are married,' he said.

Pierre chuckled. 'You are still a simple soul, Simon. Belami tells me that recently you have been instructed in the art of love by a splendid lady. Being discreet, he refused to give me her name, knowing that I gossip like a cackling cock. But you still have a lot to learn about women—' He paused, looking at the King who was sharing a jest with some of his handsome squires. 'And men!' he said cryptically.

The English king caught Belami's attention and signed to him to join him. They exchanged a few words and the veteran returned with a message.

'We are to attend His Majesty after the ladies retire,' he said. 'The Lionheart wants to know a lot more about Saladin.'

The banquet slowly wound down, from the spectacular pies and pasties, through the fine *loups-du-mer* and *lenguados* from the land-girt sea, to the boar's heads, truffled geese stuffed with ham and livers, and, in the last stages of the feast, the fruits and cheese brought from Sicily.

Somehow, the royal cooks had foraged for most of these fine foods in and around Limassol, and the Templars were overwhelmed by the banquet's richness and variety. They were only able to eat a token amount of the dishes presented to them, because their stomachs had still not recovered from the long deprivation during the siege of Acre.

In fact, the banquet would have been an ordeal for them both had it not been for the sparkling presence of Pierre de Montjoie and, for Simon especially, the delight of meeting Pierre's younger sister.

When at last they were introduced, Simon, for all his newly acquired experience of love, found himself just as tongue-tied as he had always been with women. He blushed furiously.

Berenice de Montjoie was equally impressed by her elder brother's handsome friend, about whom she had heard so many tall tales. Now he towered over her small self, with his fine features surprisingly flushed, like a schoolboy's.

Berenice, at twenty two years of age, had very little experience of men; her ventures into 'puppy-love' had been confined to a few unskilled kisses with some of her father's squires and pages.

Queen Eleanor, who intensely disliked male domination and abhorred lechery, having rescued her from betrothal to Count de Valois, had instilled into Berenice de Montjoie a healthy respect for the value of her virginity.

Normally, such a prize as this half-Spanish beauty would long ago have been taken in matrimony or by seduction, but Pierre had set his heart on matching his younger sister with his Templar friend, Simon de Créçy. He had therefore seized the opportunity to bring the two of them together when Queen Eleanor had brought Berengaria and her young lady-in-waiting to Sicily, with the object of their joining Richard on the Third Crusade.

Pierre was a dedicated romantic and his plan was working. He could plainly see the mutual attraction of these two fine young people.

Belami also saw it and heartily approved. There remained only the problem of Simon's present situation as a Templar sergent. Pierre and Belami agreed that the most urgent matter was to bring about Simon's inclusion into the ranks of chivalry.

'Damn all protocol!' said Belami. 'Were Simon the bastard of some Frankish noble, there would be no problem. He just happens to be the natural son of—' he suddenly paused, as Pierre looked at him quizzically '—of someone whose name I am sworn to keep secret,' he finished lamely.

Pierre was intrigued.

'I knew it!' he said. 'I never probed, because you were both unforthcoming about Simon's parentage. So that's the reason behind it all! Simon is the bastard of some important noble.'

'Something like that, Pierre – now, *mon ami*, drop it!' Belami's tone was chilling.

Pierre, for all his merry prattling, was no fool, and a loyal friend.

'Don't fret, Belami, my mouth is sealed. But – ' again he hesitated – 'we will have to work hard on the Lionheart. He is obviously taken with Simon, and surely he is one who could solve our problem, by knighting our fine young Templar?'

Belami's broad grin lit up his seamed, walnut-brown face.

'Pierre, Count de Montjoie, you are definitely not as simple as you look!'

Later, when the Princess Berengaria, Queen Joanna and their retinue had retired, King Richard rose from the table and signing to Belami and the others to join him, strolled out of his wooden castle for a midnight ride along the seashore. It was an action typical of the Lionheart. The King loved to ride, feeling the power of his great charger throbbing between his thighs as he galloped over the sandy strip where it met the near-tideless sea. Together, the small party of horsemen pounded along the beach, their horses' hooves throwing the creamy sea-foam high into the air.

Richard enjoyed winning and hated losing but in this impromptu midnight race, he was hardly able to keep up with the Templars' magnificent Arab steeds.

However, the Lionheart was also an ardent admirer of thoroughbred horses and those skilled in riding them, and his appreciation of Saladin's white stallions and the Templars' horsemanship quickly overcame his momentary pique at not leading the field.

Belami sensed that flash of antagonism on the King's part and deliberately reined in his white destrier. With a discreet shake of his head, he indicated to Simon to do likewise. His companion quick-wittedly grasped the veteran's reason for slackening his pace, and the English king forged ahead.

As soon as he had established himself as their leader, the impulsive monarch reined in his powerful charger. The rest of his companions immediately did likewise.

'Your stallions ride like the wind, my Templar friends. They are Arab steeds, are they not?'

'You have a keen eye for fine horseflesh, Your

299

Majesty,' said Belami tactfully. 'Our mounts were a welcome gift from the Saracen Sultan. We rendered his family some small service by rescuing his sister, Sitt-es-Sham, from an Assassin's blade. Saladin is a great man, Sire, worthy of your steel, and he does not forget a favour, nor easily forgive an injury. He is an exceptional man, Sire, and shows great compassion to those who are his enemies. But, if they should break their word of honour to him, he kills swiftly, without mercy.'

King Richard's eyes sparkled.

'I like such a man. Mayhap, with the fortunes of war, we may yet meet.'

'I would like to see that, Sire,' said Belami.

They slowly walked their horses back to Mategriffon, with Simon and Belami now riding alongside the English king, who was eager to hear the full story of their encounters with the Saracen leader.

Their readiness to praise Saladin, and their evident sincerity when they did so, impressed the Lionheart more than all the tall tales he had heard before about the great Saracen Ayyubid.

'Then you both believe that Saladin is open to parley, for a treaty?' he asked.

'Such is my belief, and Sergent de Creçy has even more reason to concur with this.'

'How so?' The King looked surprised.

Simon explained. 'Due to circumstance Sire, I was able to save the Sultan from an Assassin's dagger.'

'According to your Grand Master's letter, you both seem to have had numerous close encounters with these murderers,' remarked the King.

'Pure accident, I assure you, Sire,' said Belami. 'But ever since Odo de Saint Amand, one of our most gallant Grand Masters, tried to annihilate that evil murder-cult of satanic sorcerers, Templars have often been singled out as targets for Sinan-al-Raschid's killers.'

'Sultan Saladin, as well,' added Simon. 'He too would be pleased to see the end of the Old-Man-of-the-Mountain and his murderers. Three times, Assassins have tried to kill Saladin and, by chance, I was able to forestall their last attempt.'

Coeur de Leon looked thoughtful.

'This could be the reason for an alliance,' he mused. 'Surely, with the united strength of the Christian and Muslim armies, we could sweep this mad-man and his Assassins from the earth. He seems to be a blight upon the land of Outremer. However, first we must retake Acre, and then prove by force-of-arms that we are indeed worthy opponents of the Sultan Saladin.

'After that, we may honourably treat for peace and, mayhap, if God wills it, we can join forces and destroy the satanic forces of these murderous Assassins.'

They cantered their horses the last mile to Mategriffon and, retiring to their quarters, monarch, nobles, and the two Templar sergents slept until dawn.

In the deep sleep of a clear conscience, Simon once again found himself hovering above his physical body, and his unconscious needs drew him towards his beloved guardian's home, at de Creçy Manor in Normandy.

Simon's subtle-body entered the familiar surroundings of his childhood home, to find his surrogate family asleep in one bedchamber.

He was instantly aware that all was not well. His Uncle Raoul lay beneath a heavy fur bed-covering, his white mane of hair lank with the sweat which also covered his unaccustomedly emaciated face, gaunt with fever.

Simon knew immediately that his guardian was dying. Back in Mategriffon, his physical body wept uncontrollably. This was no nightmare but grievous fact.

Beside the dying knight's sick-bed, Bernard de Roubaix sat silently, half dozing, keeping the long night's lonely vigil.

Suddenly, the dying knight's eyes lit up with an inner glow. Raoul de Creçy was aware that Simon was in the room. His gasp of joy as he raised himself in the bed, alerted his watching companion, who leant forward to support his dying friend and to sponge his sweat-beaded forehead.

301

Raoul de Creçy's eyes were blazing with love as he saw Simon standing beside his bed.

'My son!' he said. 'My dear son!'

His gentle smile abruptly changed into the rictus of death, and the gallant old men fell back into his devoted friend's supporting arms as his brave spirit left his body.

Simon's soul gave a great sob of love and grief and, involuntarily, swept back into his physical body, lying half a world away in Cyprus.

He woke, gasping with the pain of his sorrow and weeping uncontrollably. Belami, who had been alerted by the loud sobs coming from Simon's bed, was kneeling beside his friend and holding him in his arms.

When Simon could speak, he said brokenly: 'I saw Uncle Raoul die, and I could do nothing to help him, or Uncle Bernard. Yet I know that Raoul saw me just before he died. His face was bright with joy. He spoke, and then died in Bernard de Roubaix's arms.'

'What did he say, Simon?' asked Belami gently.

'"My son. My dear son!" That's all.' Once again Simon wept uncontrollably.

'For all those years that you were with him, Simon, he was your father, mother, teacher and friend. What man, even your own father, had a better right to say those words?' Belami too was weeping.

When dawn came, the sails of King Guy de Lusignan's small fleet shone in the morning blaze of orange light as they entered the bay of Limassol and dropped anchor beside the English fleet.

The eagles were gathering! The arrival of the Crusaders from Tyre and Acre coincided with King Richard's wedding to Princess Berengaria. This ceremony took place in the Romanesque church at Limassol.

It was marked by an austere pomp occasioned by the presence of the many Knights of the Cross. The marriage ritual was performed by the Bishop of Evreux, whom both Simon and Belami knew from visits that he had paid to the Templar church at Gisors.

The Bishop was a mystic who had often stayed en route

with Simon's Uncle Raoul at de Creçy Manor. A truly holy man, with a deep commitment to the new Crusade, he was an inspiring presence at the royal marriage.

Belami was not one for exotic ritual, and he found the proceedings over-long. This was the natural outcome of the presiding priest's sense of royal occasion, for it is not often that a bishop conduct's a king's marriage service. That is usually the province of an archbishop.

Simon remembered nothing of the royal occasion. The Templar only had eyes for Princess Berengaria's brides-maid. In fact, Berenice de Montjoie made a profound impression on every susceptible male in the packed church.

Queen Berengaria, as she automatically became when King Richard's wedding ring was placed on her finger, was a bride of outstanding grace. But Berenice's small, honey-blonde, changeling beauty filled Simon's eyes with the wonder of dawning love.

With Maria de Nofrenoy his youthful desires had been aroused to frustrated ecstasy. With the Lady Sitt-es-Sham, Simon had known the fulfilment of physical love, in response to the Saracen beauty's unselfish affection.

But with Lady Berenice de Montjoie the young Nor-man's whole being thrilled to the syrinx pipes of the great god Pan.

Limassol Church had been built over a previous pagan site, a sacred grove dedicated to the horned god and Simon's heart leapt within him as the blessed Earth-Mother smiled upon her two beautiful children, while the local *Wouivre* stirred contentedly in its long sleep.

Belami noted Simon's rapt attention to Berenice de Montjoie's every move and grinned happily.

'Things are going to work out splendidly,' he mused, then added to himself cautiously, 'with God's blessing, of course, and if it be the wish of Our Blessed Virgin.' He crossed himself.

After the ceremony came the lavish wedding-feast, which once again presented a considerable problem to the under-nourished Crusaders, whose winter campaign had left them half-starved and unable to cope with the endless courses of rich food.

Out of courtesy to the English monarch, who was himself a sturdy trencherman, King Guy de Lusignan, Geoffrey, his brother, Bohemond of Antioch and his son Raymond, Homfroi de Toron and Robert de Sablé struggled manfully to taste each exotic dish. All of them ended up outside Mategriffon, trying to vomit discreetly.

Queen Berengaria, overtired by the endless loyal toasts and dreading her duties as Richard's new bride, left early to prepare for the marriage-bed, but her bridegroom kept up his energetic hosting of the wedding-feast until protocol finally forced him to withdraw to the royal marriage-chamber.

Despite the usual lewd hints and knowing glances at the lusty handsomeness of the giant English king, the wedding-night was an anticlimax, if not a fiasco.

The two Templar sergents were designated by the King himself to guard the royal bedchamber and they stood on either side of the double doors, permitting no-one to approach until the King and Queen should command their wedding-breakfast.

By the sounds of deep male snoring soon after the royal couple had retired, and the gentle weeping of the young Queen, Belami judged the occasion had not been a resounding success.

This was confirmed by the King's sudden appearance just after sunrise, when his whole Court and his distinguished guests were still sleeping off the effects of the lavish wedding-feast.

He ordered Belami to let no-one enter the bridal suite, save the Lady Berenice de Montjoie, and then commanded Simon to accompany him.

Unarmoured, and dressed solely in a light robe, Richard Plantagenet raced through the wooden halls of Castle Mategriffon. Simon found himself hard put to it to keep up with him as, crossing the beach in a swirl of sand, the King hurled himself into the dawn-chilled waters of the Mediterranean.

Whilst Simon stood guard, the English monarch ducked and plunged, grinning like a truant schoolboy. It was a bizarre start to a royal honeymoon.

As the sun climbed higher in the heavens, the sails of the rest of the storm-delayed English fleet finally hove into sight, rounding the headland of Cape Gata.

Within forty eight hours of their arrival, King Richard left his new bride. Boarding his ship, he divided his fleet into two and sending them in opposite directions round the island of Cyprus, set sail to crush the self-appointed Emperor, Isaac Ducas Comnenus between the jaws of his two fleets.

For the Lionheart, the honeymoon could wait. First, he must show the visiting Crusaders what an English king was made of.

19

THE THIRD CRUSADE

The four days since May 8, when King Richard's fleet had sailed into Limassol harbour had changed the whole situation in Cyprus.

For over a decade, Isaac Comnenus had held sway over the island. But since Berengaria's storm-tossed arrival, his days had been numbered.

The tyrant relied heavily on his system of static defences, and his four powerful castles controlling northern Cyprus. These were sited at Kantara, St Hilarion, Kyrenia and Buffavento, where they offered Comnenus the illusion of security. At Kyrenia, his massively-walled stronghold had been built to resist an army, and he installed his wife and child there, believing it to be impregnable.

It might well have held out against a long siege, had the self-styled 'Emperor' commanded it himself, but his army was split up into small groups to try to cope with the numerous attacks being launched from the sea against his strongholds. These came from Richard's fleets, sailing round opposite sides of the island, as well as from the King's land-forces which seemed to be attacking everywhere.

The Lionheart fought a rapidly moving series of actions, in the same way that he led his hunting parties. There was no hesitation once the quarry was sighted. Away would go the King, hallooing his men as though they were in pursuit of a royal stag, which in a way is what Isaac Comnenus proved to be.

He was certainly quick off the mark when it came to flight, hardly waiting for the first clash of arms before taking to his heels, to hole up in one or other of his fortresses until he was once again winkled out into the open.

After his initial attempt to best the English king's field army at the short, sharply fought battle at Trimethus, Isaac kept on retreating from one mountain refuge to another. He was completely demoralized, especially when King Guy de Lusignan took command of the Lionheart's army and stormed Castle Kyrenia, while King Richard was temporarily stricken with fever.

The Crusader met with little resistance from the garrison, who deserted *en masse*, and he captured the so-called Empress and her child. King Guy then went on to blockade St Hilarion and Buffavento.

Simon and Belami fought alongside the English king at Trimethus, finding it hard to keep up with Coeur de Leon, whose battle-frenzy carried him wherever the fighting was the thickest.

Laying about him with his two-headed Danish battle-axe, King Richard smashed a gory path through Isaac Comnenus' stoutest warriors. He seemed oblivious to any need to defend himself, relying solely on the speed and strength of his deadly axe as he met every onslaught of the enemy head-on. With the skill of a master-gardener, the Lionheart lopped off the limbs from a score of the Emperor's personal bodyguard as though he was pruning trees. Beside him, the Templars hacked their way to the enemies' battle-flag. It was King Richard's own hand that seized it, as one of Simon's cloth-yard shafts unhorsed the Emperor's standard-bearer.

In an instant the mêlée was over, as the remnants of Isaac Comnenus' army saw their standard in the English king's left hand. They turned and fled, each screaming horseman trampling over his own infantry in the wild frenzy to escape.

As for the tyrant, he was heading north as fast as his steaming war-horse could gallop.

The rest of the campaign was equally inglorious for the Emperor. None of the islanders cared whether he lived or died and it was only a few days later, at the end of May, that Isaac Comnenus unconditionally surrendered.

At a whim of the English king, the tyrant was loaded with silver chains and forced to take an oath of fealty to the Lionheart, while at the same time, he 'took the Cross'.

Thus, at one stroke, King Richard captured Cyprus and gained valuable reinforcements for his Third Crusade. More than that, he also financed the whole costly venture out of the vast booty that Isaac Comnenus had amassed during his long reign of tyranny over the island.

Latin and Frankish garrisons were put in charge of every castle and strongpoint on Cyprus. The island became the Mediterranean base for the Third Crusade. Two English knights, Richard of Canville and Robert of Turnham, were placed in command, to act as a temporary judiciary whilst King Richard decided what to do with the island and its apprehensive Greek population.

This left the Lionheart free to turn his full attention to the invasion of the Holy Land. The Crusade was off to a fine start. At Famagusta, the reunited English fleet was packed with English and Frankish soldiers who, as a result of their victorious campaign in Cyprus, were all fired with the resolve to win back Outremer. Furthermore, King Richard now had all the funds he might need to pay for the whole expensive operation.

The taking of Cyprus had been accomplished in just over two weeks of intensive campaigning. The fighting had been minimal, with very few casualties among the Crusaders, all because the divided English fleet had been able to roll-up the exposed flanks of Isaac Comnenus' untried bully boys.

The Greek islanders, who had been delighted to see the back of their tyrannical Emperor, now began to feel the weight of the English king's hand. Many of the basic rights which they had been able to retain under the tyrant's regime, were usurped by King Richard's designated commanders.

This meant more and heavier taxes than they had been forced to pay under Comnenus' tyranny. Indeed, things looked grim for the Greeks, who seemed to have changed one tyrant for another.

Those of military age saw that their best alternative lay in 'taking the Cross' and joining the Third Crusade. They reasoned that if the English king could smash Isaac Comnenus in a few days, he might well win back the Holy Land, with all its loot, within six months. If they joined him, it seemed logical they would be allowed a share of the booty.

Simon barely had the time or opportunity to say a hurried goodbye to Berenice de Montjoie before he was whisked away to Outremer. It was a tearful farewell, for Pierre's sister had fallen as much under the bronzed Norman's spell as he had been entranced by her innocent beauty. It had been literally a case of love at first sight on his part, though for Berenice, Simon de Creçy had long been her image of a peerless paladin, due to her brother's many tall tales of the three Templars' exploits in the Holy Land.

Berenice loved Pierre, and he loved Simon, so it had been a natural progression for his sister to see in her brother's best friend all the virtues that Pierre had applauded in his erstwhile comrade-in-arms. Fortunately, Simon really was as fine a character as he seemed to be, and so too was Berenice de Montjoie. Pierre complacently congratulated himself on his successful matchmaking, and Belami heaved a sigh of relief that his junior sergent had found his future wife. The only obstacle to their marriage that remained was Simon's present rank of Templar Sergent. A countess couldn't marry a commoner.

'I'm more certain than ever that our best bet for Simon is the Lionheart,' said Belami. 'Thanks to Robert de Sablé, we are now acting as the King's bodyguard and I tell you, Pierre, this English king is the one to give

Simon the accolade. If we live long enough for that to happen,' he added, with a wry grin.

'Coeur de Leon is the most battle-happy warrior I have ever seen in action. I truly believe he only completely becomes alive, when he is face to face with the Angel of Death. I swear to you, Pierre, that at one moment when the three of us were cut off by some forty of Comnenus' bodyguards, the Lionheart was actually singing as he swung his battle-axe like the Dark Angel's scythe. He loves fighting and he loves fighting-men. If anyone is going to hand Simon his Golden Spurs, it has to be King Richard. But our Norman paladin is going to have a hard time earning them.'

Though Simon was quite oblivious to his friends' subtle planning, he stayed close to the English king, partly because that was his appointed task, and partly because the strange impulsive soldier-poet had such a strong effect on those who were close to him. If there was poetry in a man's soul then Richard became his friend. If there was bravery in a man's heart, Richard became his comrade-in-arms. But if there were both these rare qualities in a man, then the Lionheart became his brother. So it was with Simon.

At last, with high hopes and stern resolve, the Crusaders turned their faces towards Outremer, to win back the Holy City and to retrieve the True Cross. King Richard sang of the Holy Relic:

> *Lignum crucis*
> *Signum ducis*
> *Sequitur exercitus*
> *Quod non cessit*
> *Sed praecessit*
> *In vi Sancti Spiritus*

The words were by Berter of Orleans, but the music of the chant was by Richard Plantaganet, the Troubadour. Roughly translated it means:

> Cross of wood
> Our Leader's sign

The army follows
That which yields not
But leads it
Into the life of the Holy Spirit

King Philip of France had already landed in Outremer, to a joyous welcome from the besiegers of Acre. Frederick Barbarossa was on the march through Germany and the Balkans with nearly 200,000 troops. Finally, there was Richard Coeur de Leon, setting sail from Famagusta with his original 25 ships now reinforced by the other half of his fleet, making 60 ships in all.

Together with the Templars and King Guy's men, the Crusaders mustered some 10,000 tough, seasoned warriors.

As far as force-of-arms was concerned, the Third Crusade was blessed. The only obstacle to a swift victory was a political one. There was no way that Conrad de Montferrat, with his newly acquired bride Isabella, was going to relinquish command of his considerable army from Tyre, to fight under King Guy or King Richard's banner.

The impulsive English king was hot to confront de Montferrat, and to make a working agreement with him before tackling Sultan Saladin head-on.

The key seemed to lie in taking Acre.

To that end the Crusader fleet bent on all sail and with their galleys pulled by sweating oarsmen, Richard's taskforce made straight for the beleaguered city.

On board the English king's galley, Simon and Belami had been joined by their Grand Master, Robert de Sablé. The mutual respect and attraction between the tough, celibate monkish knight and the hard-drinking Lionheart had been evident at their first meeting. Their ethics might be different, but their trade was war, and both fightingmen recognized each other for what they were.

King Guy de Lusignan kept to his own galley with Bohemond of Antioch and Joscelyn of Edessa, as befitted their rank and station as Frankish overlords of Outremer. They intended to stay out of the way until after King

Richard had landed the spearhead of his army. The Lionheart wanted his foot to be the first to be placed on the Holy Land in this Third Crusade. The shrewd Frankish nobles allowed him to fulfil this ambition.

As the battlements of Margat Castle hove into view, followed by those of Tortosa, Tripoli, Nephyn, Botron and almost immediately afterwards the Tower of Gibeleth, the Crusaders became fired with religious fervour. At long last the Holy Land was within sight.

Sailing fast between the English fleet and the rapidly approaching coast of Palestine was a large vessel, three-masted, with all sails set to take full advantage of the fresh off-shore wind. Her high-sided, broad-beamed construction was covered with green and yellow hides.

Peter de Barres, King Richard's galley-master, shrewdly assessed her.

'She's Turkish, Sire,' he said. 'She looks like a fast transport. I'll wager she carries supplies to the garrison at Acre.'

'Then after her, Master Ship-man!' cried King Richard, his eyes alight with the chase.

Somehow, the straining backs of the galley's oarsmen put extra energy into pulling the long sweeps and the King's ship crept up on the large Turkish vessel.

Simon's only previous experience of fighting at sea had been when the Hospitaller ship, the *Saint Lazarus*, bearing him to the Holy Land, had been attacked by Barbary Coast corsairs. That now seemed half a lifetime ago. Yet the pattern of this encounter with the Turkish supply ship was almost identical.

First came the exchange of large rocks, catapulted from both sides, followed by the hurling of Greek-fire at each other. In this exercise, the Turkish vessel outranged the Crusaders' by virtue of the greater size of its mangonels and trebuchets. The bigger the ship, the larger the weaponry carried, and the enemy vessel was at least twice the size of any ship in Richard's fleet.

'Close the range!' commanded the English king, and the galley's oarsmen pulled harder than ever, slowly closing the gap to bring the enemy vessel within range of the English archers. Most of these were armed with longbows, some were even using the Welsh yew-bow that Simon shot so expertly.

The return-fire came from Turkish crossbowmen, armed with their new version of captured Genoese weapons. The hiss and thud of their deadly bolts and quarrels heralded the end of a number of the pursuing Crusaders.

King Richard's reply was to order the raising of wooden mantlets on the bow of his galley, behind which shelter he himself kept up a brisk fire with a hunting crossbow. At his invitation, Simon joined him, exchanging a dead archer's Welsh yew-bow for the weapon made for him during the siege of Acre. The two of them, monarch and Templar sergent, soon found the range, forcing the Turks to raise mantlets themselves. Simon made things so hot for the Turkish mangonel crew that their fire slackened as he feathered shaft after shaft into them, or their massive, wooden-beamed weapon.

As the Crusaders' galley drew nearer, they could see that the Turkish transport ship was carrying several large siege-engines, presumably intended for the garrison at Acre.

These were far too valuable a prize to be allowed to reach Saracen hands.

With the beleaguered city almost within hailing distance, something had to be done quickly to stop the Turkish supply-ship. Soon she would be safe under the protection of Acre's own catapults, mounted on the high towers.

'Somehow we must slow her down,' cried King Richard.

'If you could keep close ahead of her, Sire, for a few moments, perhaps I could swim over to her stern and jam the rudder with rope,' Simon suggested.

'But if you fail to catch hold of her,' answered the King, 'you could be swept out to sea. We can't stop for you, and it's a long swim to the shore.'

'Not if I have a light line attached to me, Sire,' answered Simon. 'If I miss the Turkish ship, Belami and the others can haul me back. Unless we slow them down, Acre is going to get those vital supplies. The ship must be packed with food and siege weapons.'

The Lionheart reluctantly nodded his acceptance of the plan, and took Simon's hand before the Norman stripped off his armour.

'Good luck, young Templar. It's worth a try.'

With a supreme effort, the exhausted English galley oarsmen pulled like madmen. The royal ship slowly forged ahead to lead the Turkish transport by a cable's length.

The arrow-storm intensified from both sides. Crossbow bolts and cloth-yard shafts whirred and whistled through the air in a deadly hail. Casualties rapidly mounted on either vessel.

Simon carefully judged his moment and slipped unseen over the stern of the royal galley.

The sea, other than where the water was disturbed by the galley's long sweeps or the ship's wake, was calm enough for swimming and, watched by the anxious eyes of Belami and Pierre the young Norman swam strongly across the narrow gap. The light rope which was floating behind him, attaching him to the galley, looked like a hempen umbilical cord, Belami thought.

Luckily unseen by the Turkish archers, who could easily have picked him off in the water, Simon was now swept into the seaward side of the wake of the bluff-bowed Turkish ship.

For a moment, he disappeared and Belami groaned in anguish.

'There he is!' shouted Pierre, his voice shrill with relief, as Simon's head bobbed up beside the enemy ship's great rudder-blade.

In an instant, his strong right hand grabbed the lower rudder-pintle, a massive bronze hinge. Two turns of the spare rope round it gave Simon a firm hold on the metal pintle and he was able to put several more turns over the rudder-hinge itself, effectively jamming it in the pintle-socket.

At that moment the Turkish commander ordered the

314

helm of his ship to be put hard over, to head for the shore, now only a few cable lengths away.

Immediately the rudder jammed tight, and the Turkish transport swung off her course into a tight circle from which she could not free herself.

With cries of consternation, several of the Turkish crew tried to wrestle the steering-arm free, but Simon's rope jammed ever tighter as they struggled with the locked rudder-blade.

Simon let himself go and swam under water to clear the wake, until he felt his light safety rope tighten.

His head bobbed up once again and Belami gave a heartfelt cry of joy as he and Pierre hauled Simon in towards the galley.

'Slacken speed!' commanded King Richard. 'Hold your oars! I want that young Templar alive, not drowned.'

The galley oarsmen collapsed across their sweeps, gasping for air, their sweat-beaded chests heaving. The maximum effort had exhausted them.

The galley's speed fell off immediately. Simon was now safe from drowning.

The English king seized his Ship-master's speaking-trumpet, a wide-mouthed brass cone, and shouted his commands to three of his other galleys which were following close behind.

'We've got her now. She's helpless driving round in circles. Ram her!' commanded the King.

The other galley captains waved their arms to signal their understanding and, raising the beat of their oars, turned in towards the circling enemy ship.

At full speed, some six knots, the bronze-clad beaks of the three English galleys smashed through the thick planking of the Turkish transport.

Nothing could resist the combined ramming attack, and the whole starboard side of the transport ship splintered under the impact and stove in.

The weight of her cargo was so great that the big ship filled within minutes, despite every effort by the Turkish crew to close the gaping holes in her side.

In helpless fury, the city's defenders turned their

315

catapults on to the English fleet but they were barely within range, and though the most powerful mangonels and trebuchets splashed their big rocks almost alongside their English targets, there were no hits scored on the ships themselves.

Richard watched grimly as the Turkish transport rapidly settled lower in the water. The final plunge was only moments away. Simon at last was hauled back aboard. He barely had the strength to clamber over the galley's side, and the King himself helped Belami and Pierre to lever the Templar's big frame over the high stern-rail.

Simon collapsed on the deck, gasping for air and vomiting water.

'Stand back, Sire!' cried Belami, kneeling astride the half-drowned Norman's back. The veteran applied pressure to Simon's rib cage with a rythmic swing of his arms, alternately bearing down and releasing his weight assisting Simon's lungs to clear themselves.

'What witchcraft is this?' asked the astonished English king.

'It's a useful trick that Simon taught me, Sire. He saved my life with it when I nearly drowned in the River Seine.'

'It's a trick worth knowing, Sergent Belami. You must teach it to my crews,' said the Lionheart.

'With pleasure, Sire,' grinned the veteran as Simon vomited up the final dregs of the Mediterranean.

Pale with effort and shivering with cold, despite the warmth of the sea, Simon was quickly wrapped in the Ship-master's sea cloak.

King Richard bent over him, grasping his hands.

'That was as fine a deed as I have ever seen, my young Templar. I'll not forget it!' he said.

The giant Englishman meant every word. Richard Coeur de Leon was no braggart, and he never forgot a favour, nor failed to reward a valiant deed of arms.

Pierre winked at Belami, who curtly nodded his head in understanding.

They could have lost Simon, but both of them felt that his supreme effort in jamming the Turkish ship's rudder had been well worthwhile.

Robert de Sablé had been in charge of the English bowmen on board the galley, and was now able to rejoin them on the poop-deck.

The King told him of Simon's gallantry, and the Grand Master added his own congratulations to those of the admiring knights who thronged around the young hero.

For Simon de Creçy, it was to be a day of destiny.

As the daylight quickly faded into the west, the English fleet lay just off the Holy Land. The Lionheart had no intention of trying to enter the Bay of Acre before first light.

On board the English ships the crews, and especially the galley oarsmen, slept like dead men, exhausted by the long stern-chase and the sea-fight against the Turkish transport.

Her valuable cargo of supplies and siege-engines lay at the bottom of the Mediterranean almost within bowshot of the walls of Acre.

The blow of seeing their relief ship, with its badly needed reinforcements and vital supplies of raw materials, sunk so near to its destination, had its demoralizing effect on Acre's gallant defenders.

With first light, another blow struck them. The English fleet, 60 strong and carrying some 10,000 eager Crusaders, sailed into the bay and dropped anchor, just outside the range of the garrison's catapults.

'At last!' breathed King Richard, and clashed to his knees to give thanks to God for their safe arrival in the Holy Land.

'Bless this, our Third Crusade, O Lord, in humble thanks for our deliverance from the storms of the sea and treachery of men.

'In token of our faith and gratitude, accept the sinking of this heathen vessel and all its cargo of war against this thy Holy Crusade, as a small sacrifice to thy glory. *Non nobis Domine, sed in tui nomine debe gloriam.*'

Simon gave a start of surprise as Coeur de Leon used the Templars' invocation to end his prayer of thanksgiving.

Belami, however, was fully aware of King Richard's

close alliance with the Poor Knights of Christ of the Temple at Jerusalem.

The Cult of the Troubadours and the Templar Magicians of the Cross had common interests. Both ritual organizations were dedicated to influencing the future by the power of their group-wills.

The Military Order carried out its own master plan, under cover of its dedication to the Crusades, to win back the Holy City and the True Cross. King Richard and the Troubadours used the cloak of their reputation as poet/singers of romantic history to cover their real magical nature. And in Europe, the Minnensingers, another chivalrous ritual-cult, was rapidly coming into powerful being with similar intentions.

In Richard the Lionheart's case, his initiation into Magick had been through his mother, Queen Eleanor, whose methods of power-manipulation had been deeply rooted in a religion far older than Christianity. Eleanor, who had been instrumental in the initiation of the founding of the ritual Order of the Garter, by Henry Plantaganet, wielded enormous influence in her time, and even in her present old age had chosen her son Richard's wife, Berengaria, and had personally brought her out to Sicily to ensure this important union.

Queen Berengaria, whose tranquil beauty stoically masked the difficulties of marriage to the impulsive Richard Plantaganet, was not just the tool of a political alliance. She was in her own right a knowledgeable practitioner of the ancient Earth-Magick. She also followed the true path of the blessed Virgin in her aspect as the Great Isis, the Earth-Mother, as had her mentor, Eleanor.

Years later, Queen Berengaria would devote her widowed life to the foundation of various Orders of Vestal Virgins, under the guise of being strict sisters of contemplative nunneries. Above all, she understood the power of the human will when expressed in group-prayer. The Vestal Virgins of Isis, or Astarte, and the Brides of Christ were all one to Queen Berengaria, High-Priestess of the ancient religion. For her the

Earth-Mother, by any other name, was still the same prime-mover in the Earth-Magick of our world.

Belami, through his faithful service to Odo de Saint Amand, Grand Master of the Templars, and his long experience in the Holy Land, had acquired more than a surface knowledge of what went on in the strict secrecy of the Chapter-houses of the Order.

Some of what Simon was assimilating through one pathway of the Gnosis, Belami had come to understand through his years of experience among the Gnostics. The veteran possessed the knowledge of an initiate.

Now at last, Richard of England stepped ashore in the Holy Land, to be greeted by hordes of cheering well-wishers who came flooding out of the besiegers' camp.

All this must have struck terror and despondency into the hearts of the besieged, as they gazed impotently on the triumphant scenes below them, so close, yet out of range of even their most powerful weapons.

King Philip of France and Duke Louis of Thuringia accompanied King Guy de Lusignan, each vying with the other to welcome the Lionheart to the Holy Land.

But amid all the rejoicing, one horrific piece of news had been confirmed. The Emperor Frederick the First, Barbarossa, was dead, drowned in the swift-flowing waters of the icy River Calycadnus, near the Armenian port of Seleucia. He had led his huge army all the way from Germany, only to lose his life on the way down the coastal road of Asia Minor.

Apart from the blow to the morale of the Christans, the loss of the leadership of the great Redbeard had dispersed his army. Three-quarters of his Crusaders took his death, at the age of 73, as an ill-omen and returned home. Others half-heartedly struggled on, but without the stern resolve with which they had set out. Only a remnant of Barbarossa's original 200,000 Crusaders reached the Holy Land.

They brought with them his corpse, pickled in a barrel of vinegar, but the embalming mixture was insufficiently strong to withstand the heat of the Holy Land, and the Royal remains had to be hastily buried in the cathedral at Antioch.

Such was the unnerving news with which the Crusaders were greeted at Acre. King Richard had actually heard rumours in Cyprus of the German Emperor's death, but had discounted them as false. He realized that the Third Crusade was now on less than equal terms with Sultan Saladin's Saracen armies.

The presence of the Great Barbarossa and his huge force would have turned the scales toward an instant peace treaty.

'Now we shall have to fight harder than ever,' Belami summed up with his usual perception.

No sooner had King Richard landed and supervised the offloading of all the vital cargo and supplies, than he called a council-of-war with the other leaders. All of them conceded the necessity for unifying the High Command of the Third Crusade, except Conrad de Montferrat who was conspicuous by his absence.

The Lionheart had been right to listen to Robert de Sablé who, as Grand Master of the Templars, had seemed the most trustworthy member of King Guy de Lusignan's welcoming mission to Cyprus. De Sablé had not painted a rosy picture of the political scene in the Holy Land and had shrewdly summed up de Montferrat's character.

'Arrogant, self-willed, and an intriguer, this adventurer is unscrupulous; his handling of the de Toron divorce was scandalous. He literally forced Queen Isabella to give up her husband, whom she dearly loved, to take his own hand in a forced marriage. If he will play such havoc with Christian ethics, he will stop at nothing to win the Holy Land for himself. I tell you, Sire, that Conrad de Montferrat is set on a personal crusade to rule Outremer, and he does not care whom he destroys to gain his ends. He is a very dangerous man, Your Majesty. He is not only a danger to you, as the obvious choice for Supreme Commander, with all your experience of war, but he is also perilous to the Third Crusade itself. Would that the Blessed Virgin would take a hand in this matter and stay Conrad de Montferrat with Her own hand.'

The Grand Master's words were to be strangely prophetic.

Meanwhile, Richard Coeur de Leon addressed the assembled Crusaders. His words were simple and to the point.

'Your Majesties, and my noble lords, I have come here with but one idea. To win back the Holy Land and to regain the True Cross. I will be blunt.' There was a nervous rustle through the group of nobles. 'There has been too much internecine war between various factions in recent years in Outremer and Outrejourdain, leading up to the near-loss of the Holy Land itself. Only by the providence of our Blessed Lady have you held on to what you still control in Outremer. The man we face is a worthy adversary to our steel. Sultan Saladin is as devout a Muslim as we are devout Christians. He can only be beaten by Crusaders who are as united and resolved as the Saracens are themselves.

'Therefore, unless each member of this Crusade, noble or commoner, is determined to win back the Holy City and the True Cross, we will fail. Do you agree?'

Amid various cries and shouts of assent, some enthusiastic and others reluctant, Richard had carried his first point: unity of purpose.

'As for command,' he continued, 'I am the most experienced amongst you in the modern techniques of warfare. . . .' He paused for effect. A murmur greeted this statement, which was in fact true, the Lionheart having won most of his battles involving siege-warfare in Europe.

'Therefore, I am putting myself forward as a candidate to lead the Third Crusade,' he went on, making each word count for its full weight. 'That means that I shall take full responsibility for its success . . . or failure.'

There was an almost audible sigh of relief at this last statement. Simon and Belami, who as his appointed Templar guards were standing on either side of the Lionheart, watching every face for signs of a hostile move, duly noted this. Although they felt the relaxation of tension at the King's last remark, their hands stayed ready to draw instantly both sword and dagger in his defence.

321

King Richard made his final point a political one.

'Of course, you will *all* share equally in the glory. If we lose, however, I shall take full responsibility for failure and for what may happen afterwards. Do you agree to this?'

As honour had been satisfied, because Richard had acknowledged that each noble and his following should have full credit for the success of the Third Crusade, and that any blame, if there should be failure, would be borne by the English king alone, the assembled nobles and knights enthusiastically agreed to the Lionheart's assumption of general command.

They drew their swords with a loud rasp of steel and shouted in assent: 'Long live King Richard of England! *Vive le Coeur de Leon!*'

The Third Crusade had begun.

The Castle Mategriffon with its mobile siege tower had been landed and assembled. The Lionheart was installed in his rightful place as leader of the Third Crusade. His first priority was to take Acre as quickly as possible. Then he could march directly against Sultan Saladin.

Everything looked set for an early victory, but then Destiny took a hand in the proceedings. King Richard was struck down with arnaldia, the endemic fever of Outremer. He lay near death in his wooden castle, outside the walls of Acre.

Two things saved his life. One was his magnificent constitution. The other was Simon's gift from Maimonedes of the ancient Egyptian treatise on herbs and simples. Even the King's physician, a smooth-talking quack, part-barber, part-astrologer and part-alchemist, had heard of the great Maimonedes. He gratefully accepted the herbal distillations which the Jewish physician had given Simon. Preparations of opium and kaolin stopped the king's diarrhoea, and essence of mandragora root eased the pain and delirium. As for the fever, Simon dealt with this as Maimonedes had instructed him, with a special preparation of belladonna and tannus leaves, mixed with a distillation of boiled willow bark.

The ancient papyrus also prescribed copious draughts of pure boiled spring-water with sea-salt added, flavoured with rose-petals.

The effect on the Lionheart was magical. Within two days he had come out of his delirium and was able to eat nourishing soups. Two more days and he had himself carried down in a litter to the front battle-line where, shielded behind wooden mantlets, he and Simon sniped at the garrison of Turkish archers who were shooting at the English sappers mining the walls of Acre.

Simon used his new yew-bow and the Lionheart fired a hunting crossbow with great accuracy. Together, they accounted for a dozen over-bold Turkish archers and kept the rest of Acre's garrison's heads down. By this time the relationship between the King and the Norman Templar had developed into a warm friendship, and when Richard found out that Simon's scholarship was more extensive than his own, his interest in his young body-guard became even more pronounced.

The strange pairing of Belami, the hard-bitten veteran, and the young Norman Templar scholar further intrigued the King, but Robert de Sablé could not answer the royal enquiries about Simon's background and neither of his Templar bodyguards vouchsafed further information on their individual origins.

'There is something deeply mystical about young de Creçy,' King Richard told the Bishop of Evreux. 'Yet he is neither a fully fledged Templar Knight nor a Trouba-dour. De Creçy is not a poet and he does not use the power of the chant to bring about a change in the future, yet I feel that he is an initiate.

'His knowledge is deep and he tells me he has had several great masters of philosophy as his mentors. Withal, he is modest and has genuine humility. I would to God that at my Court we had more like him. My rede is that he is the bastard son of some noble house. Why he is a Templar sergent defeats me – and that wily old soldier, Belami, whose battle-axe is as deadly as mine, treats him like a son. Always watching over him, he is ever-present

323

in times of danger. There's more to this than de Sablé has told me. See what you can find out.'

But the churchman got no further than had the King. Every time he started to probe deeply, either the Grand Master or Sergent Belami politely evaded his queries. He had to report back to the King that he had made no progress whatsoever.

The final stages of the siege of Acre, which had languished miserably before the arrival of both King Philip of France and Richard of England put new heart into the besiegers, at last got under way. Both monarchs were now free of their crippling arnaldia fever and the assault commenced.

Besides Mategriffon, the Lionheart had brought other ingenious siege-engines with him, all designed by himself and built by his team of master weapon-makers.

'Kill-Greek', as it was called, was the high mobile tower which was moved by levers, operated from inside. Belami, who preferred fast-moving cavalry actions to protracted sieges, poured scorn upon it.

'A waste of time! Look at that ponderous turret. It is too slow and too big a target. Give me plenty of scaling ladders, rushed up under cover of darkness and planted in as many places as possible beneath a barrage of arrows. That's the way to take the walls of Acre.'

Philip of France also had brought some siege-engines with him and the two kings vied with each other to prove the superiority of each monarch's ingenious equipment for siege-warfare.

The French weapon was called 'the bad neighbour'. It often exchanged rocks with its Turkish counterpart within the walls, called 'the bad kinsman'.

The Turkish operators were more experienced than were their French counterparts, and jagged stones from the huge swinging beam, with its spoon-shaped rock-holder, smashed into 'the bad neighbour', knocking it to pieces.

The surviving French engineers loudly cursed their jubilant Turkish opposite numbers and promptly set about rebuilding their monstrous stone-hurler, meanwhile keeping it well out of range of the Turkish catapults and mangonels.

'They're like wilful children,' grumbled Belami. 'Why don't they listen to us old ones? Scaling ladders are much cheaper and far more effective!'

Simon laughed at the veteran's chorus of grumbling oaths.

'It seems to me, *mon brave ami*, that both kings enjoy playing this siege game. It makes a change from what Saladin called "the fast-moving chess-game of cavalry warfare".'

So it went on, while Saladin waited for the Crusaders to move against him *en masse*. Meanwhile, at night, he managed to sneak in a few reinforcements, under cover of patrols between the Saracen positions on the high ground of El-Ayyadiya, and the Crusaders' entrenchments, which grew more extensive by the hour.

'We're like a lot of By-Our-Lady moles, Simon,' complained Belami. 'Just look at our engineers!' He pointed to yet another sap entrenchment, being dug under cover provided by Genoese crossbowmen who shot at everything moving on the battlements.

'Whack!' went a huge stone against the crumbling face of a particularly strong part of the wall, called the 'Accursed Tower'.

'That big sling of ours really hits hard!' For once Belami's voice sounded proud of this particular siege-engine's effectiveness. 'You can tell that this one was built by Templars and Hospitallers. When it comes to siege-engines, we old Crusaders have got these newcomers beat.'

It seemed that every leader of each contingent of Crusaders had brought his favourite siege-engine. The Count of Flanders was particularly proud of his stone-sling and until his death from a chill caught during a skirmish, had spent hours happily bombarding the walls of Acre. After he died, King Richard added the gallant Count's slinger to his own extensive battery and kept up a day-and-night assault on the massive walls, hitting them hard with giant flint sea-rocks, which he had brought specially with him from Messina in Sicily.

These jagged missiles cut deeply into the thick walls, pulverizing the softer local stone of which the defences of Acre were built. When the great flints overshot the walls and landed in the town itself, they took a heavy toll from among the unfortunate inhabitants. More and more, the Turkish garrison kept under cover. Periodically, however, they had to leave this comparative safety, to man the walls or to make a sally, should the defences be breached. Life in Acre was becoming perilous.

The Turkish version of Greek-fire was fired from a bronze pipe, equipped with a reservoir of inflammable naphtha and pitch, and propelled from the metal nozzle by huge bellows. Trundled up at night to the top of a tower, this weapon twice set one of King Richard's siege towers alight as it attempted to approach the walls.

Belami got angrier than ever at these games of pitch-and-toss.

'Just give me the By-Our-Lady scaling ladders and we'll be in the town within an hour of midnight!' he raged impotently.

The English and French kings replied to this attempt at arson by hanging wet hides soaked in the usual vinegar solution around their siege-towers. They succeeded in getting within yards of the wall before the Turkish stone-slings got in a few shrewd blows and knocked them both to pieces.

Down they came in a shower of broken beams, shattered planks and screaming men. Hoarse with cursing, all Belami could do was to shake his head in despair.

The Templar sergents were forced to be present at these various fiascos, because their main task was to guard the Lionheart from assassination. They both felt frustrated that their assignment precluded their taking a more active part in the proceedings. Only when a breach was made in the walls and the King rushed forward to exploit his engineers' efforts, did the fighting become personal rather than just the usual faceless struggle of long-range combat.

Then it was a matter of man-to-man, the clang of sword

on steel, the crunch of battle-axes biting through helmets and skulls, and the slither of sharp daggers between chinks in chain-mail. The air was full of the screams of the dying, and the shrieks of the wounded, as the steel bit deep. Limbs were sent flying from bodies and gape-mouthed heads were chopped from the shoulders of brave men.

It was a bloody, fevered, frenzied struggle to carry or defend the breach, ending in stalemate and the piles of reeking corpses which filled the gap on either side.

The whole affair was too close-quartered for archers to shoot without hitting their own men. It was essentially a battle of man against man. It was hack and hew and thrust and parry, as long as arms had the strength to wield the blades.

'Keeping Coeur de Leon alive is an exhausting busi-ness!' remarked Belami after one such mêlée, throwing himself down on to his camp-bed of horse-blankets laid over a straw-filled mattress made of forage sacks.

Simon was so tired by his own exchange of blows with the Turks, defending the breach, that he merely nodded before drifting off into a warrior's deep sleep.

In his dream, he soared away from his sleeping body and his will took him immediately to Cyprus, where his love lay sleeping.

Queen Berengaria and Queen Joanna, and their ladies-in-waiting, Berenice de Montjoie and Lady Rebecca of Kent, were quartered comfortably in Castle Kyrenia, waiting for King Richard to send for them.

Berenice lay restlessly tossing in her bed, her dreams concerned with the safety of her brother Pierre and her adored Templar sergent.

As Simon hovered over her, his love was so intense that it communicated itself to the uneasy spirit of the sleeping girl. Immediately, her sleeping form relaxed beneath the fur coverlet, while her subtle-body released itself.

Suddenly, the astral counterpart of his sleeping sweet-heart floated up to join Simon as he hovered above her bed. Her small oval face was radiant, her eyes alight with love.

Wordlessly, for there was no need for speech, they embraced, their spirit bodies seeming to melt into each other as they became one complete soul. It was an ecstatic experience. For Simon, the rapture was as real as if they had been physical lovers; for Berenice, who was normally unconscious of this other world, their spirit meeting was just a beautiful dream.

The whole experience was a wonderful release from the sordid realities of war.

All this time, Sultan Saladin had not been idle, constantly sending out patrols to probe and harass the Crusader entrenchments round the beleaguered city. The more extensive these earthworks grew, the more aggressive the Saracen patrols became.

Meanwhile, Richard had decided the time was ripe to put into operation his plan to breach the walls in several places, simultaneously.

He called a special emergency council-of-war.

'Your Majesty, my lords,' he said. 'I present for your approval my plan which I call "The Walls of Jericho". Recall for a moment how Joshua, the son of Nun, breached the defences of the Canaanite city. He marched his army of Israelites seven times round the walls, all of them shouting and blowing their trumpets. After the seventh tour of the city, his priests sounded their shofars, the rams' horns used to assemble the Israelites for prayer. Then and there, down tumbled the walls of Jericho.'

There was an excited buzz of puzzled agreement among the nobles, as King Richard continued: 'We will do a similar thing, to distract the Turkish garrison. We will all march back and forth just out of range of their catapults, as though we were performing some complicated preparatory manoeuvre, while ceasing for a time to ply our siege artillery. This will confuse the enemy. All the time we will make much play with our trumpets, drums and cymbals. All this ordered confusion will distract the Turks and cover up the sound of our engineers, who will be busily sapping their mines forward, digging under cover of their earthworks, which are now within yards of several towers in the city walls.

'The Turks will be far too busy trying to reach our manoeuvring troops and cavalry with their stone-throwers and bowmen, to notice the muffled sound of tunnelling going on below their feet.

'On the seventh day,' the King continued, 'just as was Joshua, we will be ready for our final move. Our mines will have been dug under the towers and walls, filled with straw and propped up with thin tree-trunks soaked in naphtha and lamp-oil.'

The King paused for dramatic effect. 'At the sound of the rams' horns, which we have already obtained from local shepherds, the trains of oil-soaked straw rope will be lit and the mines will catch fire, burning through the mineshafts' wooden supports. And down will fall "The Walls of Jericho" – *id est*, Acre!'

Coeur de Leon finished with a dazzling smile at his council-of-war, and was answered with a thunderous burst of spontaneous applause. The plan seemed to be a good one.

The mining was mainly directed at the Tower of Saint Nicolas, the Tower of the Bridge, the Tower of the Patriarch and, lastly, the Accursed Tower.

Sultan Saladin watched all the loudly accompanied manoeuvring of the Crusaders from his position at El-Kharruba, the Hill of the Carob Tree. This was a piece of high ground just off the road between Acre and Saffuriya.

'This is getting perilously like the Greek story of the Siege of Troy,' he murmured sagely, stroking his beard. 'All it lacks is the wooden horse. Mayhap, all this parading, shouting and martial music is Coeur de Leon's version of that famous strategem.'

Communication with the Saracen garrison was now confined to the besieged sending carrier-pigeons to Saladin's headquarters. The tone of these messages became daily more desperate.

Saladin, accompanied by his brother Seyf-ed-Din, or as he was known Saphardin, had brought two pet lions with him, as a symbol of his respect for the Lionheart, but also as a sign that there was more than *one* lion on Saladin's side.

The walls of the city were fully manned day and night. Still, the Crusaders kept up their noisy manoeuvres, feigning attack after attack, only to wheel round at the last moment and retreat, just before coming into bow-shot.

In vain, the defenders cast their stones and poured down a hail of Greek-fire on to the besiegers, only to find them always tantalizingly just out of range. It was a war of nerves, and the Turks were becoming further demoralized by sheer lack of sleep.

The Crusaders took turns at mounting these fake attacks; under cover of darkness especially only a small token force would be deployed, more than making up for its size with the sheer volume of noise produced. Meanwhile the attackers scheduled to carry on the charade the next day slept with cotton in their ears to deaden the racket.

The garrison of Acre could afford no such luxury. They had no idea when the real attack would come. Therefore, they had to remain awake with all their senses alert.

Saladin knew that to attack the Crusaders' encampment, with all its strong points and maze of trenches, would court disaster and possibly lose him the Holy Land as well. He was forced to wait while Richard counted the hours to the final move.

'How I hate this game of hide-and-seek,' grumbled Belami. 'The Turks must have heard the digging of our sappers by now.'

But hunger and taut-stretched nerves had induced a torpor among the sleep-deprived garrison, and any dull thumping that the Turks heard, they put down to the blood pounding in their heads at the incessant, deafening manoeuvring of the Crusaders.

At last, the mines were finished, their shafts filled with supporting pit-props and surrounded by naphtha-soaked straw.

The chief English engineer, Gilbert of Nottingham, reported to the Lionheart.

'All is ready, Sire. Attack when ye may, Your Majesty.'

King Richard, who had been dozing just before dawn, came out of Mategriffon and sprang on to his war-horse, shouting: 'God be with us. May the True Cross deliver us from the heathen. Sound the rams' horns!'

The shofars were sounded and a hundred ready-fired flambeaux were thrown deep into the straw-filled mines. They blazed up like tinder lighting bonfires at a witches' sabbat.

At the same time the Lionheart gave the command for the siege artillery to recommence firing. The signal was a fire-arrow shot in a high arc from Simon's yew-bow.

As the blazing cloth-yard shaft crossed the dawn sky, every catapult, mangonel, trebuchet and ballista hurled its load of rocks and iron darts against the towers of Acre.

At that precise moment, the arrow-storm burst forth from five hundred English archers and Genoese cross-bowmen, sweeping the battlements clean of every living creature.

Belami's advice had been heeded and, under cover of the smoke, thudding rock-barrage and hail of deadly shafts, the infantry ran forward, carrying a hundred scaling ladders between them. These were mounted immediately they were placed against the walls.

Only a few Turkish bowmen showed themselves momentarily among the crenellations of the battlements in order to shoot down upon the advance party.

One by one the great towers rocked and trembled as the pit-props beneath them burnt through. Their quivering walls resounded to the constant crashing shock of the great stones hurled against them.

Then suddenly a tower collapsed. It fell in a tumbling avalanche of rock and rubble, the choking dust and smoke from the mine beneath cutting off the cries of its descending defenders. Another tower rumbled down into dusty ruin. The attackers screamed with joy, while the defenders shrieked in despair.

At last the walls of Acre were breached. At this point there was nothing that Saladin and Saphardin could do but watch in distant horror as the Crusaders swarmed out of their entrenchments and attacked Acre, wave upon wave.

Amid the smoke and dust, the clamour of battle rose to

new heights of cacophony, the yells of triumph and screams of agony vying to drown out the clash of arms.

Set against the fiery dawn it was a holocaust. In the hecatomb of blood, the scaling ladders rose to the battlements, swarming with climbing men who either reached the top or fell to their deaths among the arrow-slain at the foot of the towers of Acre.

In the thick of it, the Lionheart dismounted and led the main attack against the breaches in the walls, charging the gaps which had been left, like drawn giant's teeth, by the fall of the great towers.

Everywhere, Simon and Belami, now joined by Pierre de Montjoie, guarded the English king, their axes and swords running red to the hilt. So close was the fighting that crossbow bolts sank up to the fletching, even in armoured bodies, and cloth-yard shafts pierced clean through shields and chain-mail.

Only the exhausted grunts of supreme effort, the groans of the dying, and the stifled shrieks of the gravely wounded sounded now. The drums were still, the trumpets unblown, the cymbals silent. A chorus of death and agony was heard above the clash of steel.

The crenellated walls swarmed with Crusaders, forcing the defenders back, as more and more Christian soldiers scaled the remaining ladders.

Saladin groaned. '*Allahu Akbar*!' he prayed. 'God be praised. They Will be Done! My brothers are dying in Accra. Receive their gallant souls, O Allah the Merciful, the Compassionate, this day in Paradise.'

Saphardin, overcome with grief, mounted his white charger and galloped despairingly towards Acre, waving his scimitar above his head like a flail.

'God is Great!' he shouted in his despair.

Before he could reach the Crusaders' front line, Saladin had sent a troop of fast-mounted Mamelukes to head his brother off from what was virtually suicide.

Throwing himself from his foaming horse, Saphardin flung his body to the rocky ground and, turning towards Mecca, cried to Allah for mercy for the defenders of Acre.

Suddenly, the Crescent flag surmounting the Tower of

Saint Nicolas fell, and the standard of the Lion of England rose, fluttering bravely in the morning breeze.

'We have won!' shouted Pierre de Montjoie, his face alight with joy. Then his voice abruptly changed to a shriek of agony as a Turkish shaft thudded home through the gap left in his chain-mail armour by his raised arm. Only its feathers showed in the gout of blood that shot out from his severed axillary artery.

Pierre swayed and fell back into Simon's arms as the young Templar groaned in horror. The sound alerted Belami, who rushed to assist, but both of them were too late to do more than catch Pierre's last words, as his gallant spirit fled. Faintly, they heard: 'Marry Berenice! I love thee, Simon,' before he died.

Acre had fallen. But for Simon and Belami, the price was too high.

20

THE SWORD AND THE CROSS

Simon kept his word to Pierre. He searched for the now unmarked grave of Phillipe de Mauray, which he and Belami had dug with Pierre's help eleven years before.

By using the divining methods taught him by Abraham-ben-Isaac, Simon quickly located the spot outside the walls of Acre, and he and the veteran soon uncovered the water-barrel in which Phillipe's body had been interred. It was in an unchanged condition. The Holy Land had preserved its honoured dead.

The Templars dug another grave beside Phillipe's and, wrapping Pierre's body in a Templar sergent's black tunic, they laid their friend, fully armoured as befitted a Crusader, reverently to rest, his head towards the walls of the retaken city and his crossed feet pointing homewards to the West.

No pomp marked this simple burial. No priest was present to intone a ritual for Count Pierre de Montjoie's passing. Simon prayed silently as tears ran down his bronzed cheeks and Belami, his voice hoarse with restrained sobs, spoke a simple soldier's plea.

'Blessed Mother, take this, Thy faithful son, Count Pierre de Montjoie, into Thy loving care, to cherish him as he has protected Thy Blessed Name.

'Gallant soldier, loyal comrade and beloved friend' – the veteran's voice faltered – 'his love for You was always foremost in his heart.'

As the two Templars murmured 'Amen', a third voice joined in. It was the deep bass of the Lionheart. Unseen and unheard, he had knelt beside the grave, his mailed fingers resting on the hilt of his sword, set point-down in the sand, Crusader-fashion.

His handsome face was streaked with dust and tears. Belami and Simon started to rise from their knees, but King Richard restrained them with a gesture.

'Let us pray in remembrance of a fine soul, who I was honoured to call my friend. Pierre had a loving merry heart and a golden tongue. He was also a fine Troubadour.' Coeur de Leon's gentleness surprised them.

The sun slowly dislimned into its final blaze of shimmering glory as it dipped below the western horizon of the land-locked sea. All three of them sensed the hiss as the Day-Star quenched its alchemical flames in the warm waters of the Mediterranean.

Just as the Templars had done all those years before, the English king spoke the same words: 'This is a blessed spot for a soldier to lie. I loved that boy very much.' The Lionheart's voice choked on a suppressed sob. 'May this honoured grave be a peaceful one. With the walls of Acre at his head and the sea at his feet, this is a fitting tomb for a knight to rest until Judgement Day. *Non nobis, Domine, sed in tui nomine debe gloriam!*'

All three Crusaders joined in the final Templar invocation. They stood up, the fine sand dribbling from their chain-mail, and saluted their fallen comrade-in-arms.

'*Vivat! Vivat! Vivat!*'

Their imperative cry for the resurrection of Pierre's soul echoed across the waters of the Bay of Acre.

Each thinking his own sad thoughts, they strode with a clashing of mail up the sandy beach, mounted their patient chargers and rode silently into the recaptured city.

Within the walls the killing was still going on. Isolated pockets of stubborn resistance were being met with savage subjugation, sometimes at the sword's point, sometimes by a flight of the fatal cloth-yard shafts, and sometimes with the fiery blast of the Turkish flame-thrower, now in Christian hands.

This was the first successful outcome to the siege of a major city that Simon had witnessed. His stomach turned at the scenes of unnecessary slaughter that were being enacted before him, and he prayed that this would be the last time that he would be present at such a massacre. The killing-fields of battle were one thing, but this was quite different. The Crusaders seemed to relish their immolation of the Turkish garrison.

On the high ground to the east of the city, Saladin stood surrounded by his commanders, all of them gazing in mute horror at the smoke still rising inside the walls of Acre. Even at that distance the faint screams and high-pitched keening of the dying and the bereft carried clearly across the desert, borne inland on the evening sea-breeze.

'I swear that for each Saracen, ten Infidels shall die!' Saphardin's bitter words rang out.

'Nay, my brother!' said Saladin, laying a comforting hand on his kinsman's shoulder. 'We kill in battle, as Allah wills it. We do not stoop to slaughter helpless women and children or badly-wounded men. That is the Devil's work. I will have no part in it and neither will my family, while I am there to stop them.'

Saphardin hung his head in shame. He knew that for a devout Muslim the slaughter of the helpless was a sin in the eyes of Allah.

'So be it, brother,' he said. 'I spoke in anger.'

But his frustration proved too much for him to bear and once again he gave way to the blind fury inside him. Flinging himself into the saddle, Saphardin galloped madly towards Acre, screaming curses upon the heads of the merciless Crusaders. He only reined in when he got within bowshot of the besiegers' camp and crossbow bolts started to whirr past him.

At last the massacre died out. The surviving defenders were herded into the cells of the old Hospitaller barracks and kept under guard without food or water, until King Richard heard of it.

'We do not torture prisoners of war,' he cried. 'Give refreshment immediately! Especially to the women and children.'

The impulsive monarch had again undergone a sudden change of heart.

'At last his chivalry is showing,' muttered Belami cynically. 'But for how long?'

The massacre of the Muslim defenders had hardly taken the Templars by surprise. They had seen many such spontaneous slaughters of the wounded and unresisting, notably by Kukburi's men after the Battle of Hittin. It was the sheer scale of the killing, and King Richard's tardy halting of the slaying, that had shocked them. It was another side to the English monarch's unpredictable nature.

Robert de Sablé had been wounded during the last attack on the breach in the walls and had lain semi-conscious for some hours. However, as soon as he had sufficiently recovered his wits to see what was going on, he had hurried to persuade the Lionheart to stop the massacre.

'It is as though the King is possessed by some demon at times. It is not like him. In battle he is as brave as the king of beasts, from whence comes his name. He is exhilarated and seems to be filled with the ecstasy of fighting; carried away by the red tide of battle.'

The Grand Master was puzzled.

'Yet I saw him show mercy to at least three badly wounded men who had fought him gallantly. But this tolerance of mass murder, mainly by camp-followers who took no part in the forefront of the fighting at the breaches, is something quite different in the nature of the King.' Like Simon, the Grand Master had been deeply shaken by the Lionheart's conduct.

The victorious Crusaders gathered for another council-of-war. King Guy de Lusignan, Bohemond of Antioch, Joscelyn of Edessa, Homfroi de Toron and others, still without Conrad de Montferrat, joined the English king and the Duke of Burgundy to formalize a master-plan, now that Acre was once more in Christian hands.

The Lionheart was hot to pursue Saladin's army as soon as possible. He realized the enormous moral victory he had scored over them by taking the city before their eyes, leaving them helpless to intervene. Now, he reasoned, was the time to strike, while the memory of that defeat burned brightly within them.

The two Grand Masters, both Templar and Hospitaller, were in absolute agreement with him, but King Guy's vacillating nature hung back from too hasty a decision. He counselled caution and several of the other nobles of Outremer agreed with him. In view of the weight of numbers that the Frankish king commanded, Richard had to compromise; something that his fiery nature found hard to accept.

Robert de Sablé saw a possible solution to the Lionheart's obvious quandary.

'Might I suggest, Sire, that you send an envoy, not to Saladin but to his brother, Saphardin, thereby distancing yourself from the Sultan himself while testing out the ground for a possible treaty, in view of the greatness of your victory at Acre.'

King Guy eagerly seized the opportunity to buy himself more time, before having to make a final commitment to attack Saladin so soon after the taking of Acre. He knew of the English king's fondness for Homfroi de Toron, whose charming disposition helped somewhat to fill the gap left by the death of Richard's close friend, Pierre de Montjoie, who had been a boon companion of the English monarch. King Guy put his name forward as a suitable royal envoy.

It was a clever move on the Frankish leader's part, for rumours of Richard's intent to ally his sister, Queen Joanna, to Saladin's brother were already circulating among the Frankish court. With all the spies in Outremer, this information was hardly surprising.

Richard reluctantly agreed, realizing that the time gained by this manoeuvre could be usefully employed in reconnoitring the coastal region to the south of Acre, along which he had already planned to drive his main thrust towards Jaffa.

Seeing that the time was ripe to make a further important point, the Templar Grand Master again spoke up.

'There is another matter, Sire, which is becoming pressing. In the unusually hot season that we are passing through the dead can rapidly become pestilential. Beelzebub's legions of flies have already covered the stinking corpses, and I believe that we are in real danger of plague if we do not bury the dead as soon as possible.'

The English king immediately saw the wisdom of de Sablé's remarks.

'We must bury them at sea. Load the bodies into sacks and weight them with rocks. We don't want any involuntary resurrections.'

It was certainly an ingenious solution. Gangs of masked infantry loaded the rapidly bloating corpses on to the transport vessels of the fleet, which hurried out into deep water and hastily disposed of the dead. Meanwhile the cleaning up of the recaptured city proceeded.

The reconsecration of the Christian holy places, which despite Saladin's orders had been deliberately defiled in revenge for the Crusaders' desecration of the Muslim mosques in Jerusalem, took over three weeks to complete, with full services being held by the Bishop of Evreux and other church dignitaries at each holy site.

Only after these rites had been carried out, and all danger of the plague in Acre had been eradicated, would King Richard agree to the campaign being renewed and sent for his wife, Queen Berengaria, his sister and their retinues.

While the royal galley raced for Acre, bearing its precious burden, Simon and Belami accompanied the Lionheart and his force commanders on a reconnaissance of the land south of Acre.

'The coastal road to Jaffa would seem to offer us the quickest and safest route to our turning point, from which we can make our final thrust through to Jerusalem,' said Coeur de Leon reflectively. 'Sergent Belami, you have patrolled these parts of Outremer for years: how say you?'

The veteran combed his fingers through his short beard, a habit he had when thinking deeply, and replied gruffly, without mincing his words.

339

'No one likes to march with his flank too close to the sea, Sire, and there are marshes on our other, eastern flank for the first part of the coastal road to Jaffa.

'Saladin cannot attack us while the marsh stands between him and us. But the ground becomes firm about a third of the way along the route. Then, from the tree-covered high ground, the Sultan can launch continuous attacks by his excellent Scythian skirmishers and his mounted Turkish horse-archers, who can play havoc with our columns.'

As he spoke the veteran bent down and scraped a rough diagram in the soft sand with a pointed stick.

'But before Saladin can launch any full-scale charges against your eastern flank, Sire, he must cover the open ground beyond the trees. If you station your English archers on your inland side and use the technique of the Roman flying columns, as Sergeant de Creçy and I have done many times before, pillioning selected archers on the back of our chargers, you can inflict heavy casualties on his lances before his own horse-archers' light arrows can penetrate our armour. We may begin to look like porcupines, but I trow we will escape serious hurt.'

The Lionheart nodded curtly. Encouraged by this, Belami continued.

'If I might suggest a device that my sergents have found effective?' Again the English king signified assent.

'Heavy quilted or double-folded blanket material, like the Saracen alquôton under-jackets, which many old Crusaders wear in the heat of summer in preference to chain-mail, will stop the Turkish light, long-range shafts, particularly if we also drape our horses. We will, of course, suffer the penalty of the heat of noon, but if we avoid the fatal error of the Battle of Hittin, and carry sufficient water and salt with us to ease the torture of thirst and cramp, we can survive their arrow-storms.'

As usual, Belami's reporting was a model of brevity and condensed experience. The Lionheart grinned that surprisingly boyish smile, which held the key to his charm.

'So be it. The commanders will see to these things. Let everyone, noble, knight or soldier, carry a spare goatskin water-bottle and wear it on the side away from the Turkish arrow-storms. The baggage-train, loaded with barrels of fresh water, will keep to the seaward side of our line of march. Furthermore, I order the fleet commanders to sail a parallel course, close inshore, to give us the protection of their mangonels and trebuchets. I want each ship to carry a minimum of twenty archers, to provide a barrage of arrows over our heads and cover our retreat, should we need to reboard our vessels. Is that understood?'

The sea-captains nodded their assent and the commanders of the Crusader columns dispersed to carry out the King's orders.

Robert de Sablé smiled secretly to himself. He had never seen the King of Jerusalem, nor any of the princes and lords of Outremer and Outrejourdain, listen so readily to a veteran sergent of the Templars.

'That may well be the reason that we failed before, with such heavy losses. The voice of experience is still the only yardstick by which to judge the situation,' he remarked to the Grand Master of the Hospitallers.

'But then Richard Coeur de Leon is not like other kings!' said the leader of the rival Order of monkish knights.

Throughout the reconnaissance of the route to Jaffa, Conrad de Montferrat remained aloof, ignoring the English monarch's envoys. His plan seemed to be to wait for King Richard to offer advantageous terms for the use of his army, with all its battle experience against Saladin. These troops amounted to over 6,000 men, including infantry, giving de Montferrat a flexible force for attack or defence. He could muster scores of heavy cavalry lances and a large number of Genoese crossbowmen and mercenary archers, armed with longbows.

However, the Lionheart would sooner command a small and enthusiastic force than wield a larger mercenary army who owed their allegiance to another, and who were only in the fight for the loot that they hoped to gain from a massive defeat of the Saracens.

This was typical of the sort of petty power-politics

which had plagued the Crusades right from the start, for de Montferrat was banking on the loss of Barbarossa's dispersed army to sway Richard towards his way of thinking. But the Lionheart was resolved to go up against Saladin with those troops he already had. Unless de Montferrat came willingly and placed his army under Coeur de Leon's supreme command, the Englishman preferred to carry on without Isabella's new husband.

The Duke of Burgundy, a lusty bull of a man with plenty of stomach for the fight against the heathen, presented another problem. He was reluctant to command the rear-guard, preferring to fight at Richard's side in the forefront of the battle. The Lionheart handled this situation with all the tact and charm he could muster. Finally, Burgundy was persuaded by the king's honeyed words.

He growled a mirthless laugh.

'That son of a whore de Montferrat only fights for gold, Richard. I trow that Conrad would side with the Devil, or Saladin, if the terms were right.' The burly Duke hefted his great iron mace. 'Scatter-brains here is eager for his skull. You have but to say the word, Sire, and we will march together against Tyre.'

At that moment a messenger arrived from the harbour-master to inform the Lionheart that his Queen's ship was in sight. He dismissed the council, and in leisurely fashion made his way down to the stone mole to greet his consort. Simon, on the other hand, was impatient to welcome his beloved Berenice.

The Norman's mind was harrowed by the thought that the death of his friend Pierre was, in some way, due to his own negligence in not noticing the Turkish archer whose bow had fired the fatal shot. With his eagerness to see Berenice clouded by this irrational fear, he could hardly refrain from preceding the Lionheart, instead of pacing slightly to the rear of the English king, keeping a watchful eye out for an Assassin attack or other treachery.

Although a welcome had not been planned by Richard, who was too intent on battle-plans to think about his new bride, his Earl Marshal, the Duke of Norfolk, had already alerted the Court to the Queen's arrival. The royal galley was greeted by scores of cheering courtiers and a fanfare of trumpets. This happened before the Lionheart had left Mategriffon, which as yet had not been dismantled and towed aboard the King's galley ready for the next move.

The Earl Marshal's plan was to house the two queens and their retinues within the palace at Acre, now cleansed of its grisly reminders of the long siege, and once more attractively decked-out with welcoming flags and banerets, as befitted the arrival of English royalty.

The Queen's galley finally rounded the Tower of Flies and berthed against the stone jetty that jutted out into the harbour. All that Simon saw, with the eyes of love, was his dear Berenice, becomingly dressed in mourning black, obviously already the recipient of the tragic news of her brother's death.

The Templar's heart beat faster at the thought of holding his beloved once more in his arms. He turned to Belami.

'What if Berenice blames me for Pierre's death?' His voice was anguished.

Belami shrugged his shoulders as he replied, 'I shall strenuously deny that you were responsible in any way. At the breach we were all taking the same chances, while we protected the King. This is folly, Simon. In no wise can you be blamed for that tragedy. Take my advice and try to forget it. We will always hold the memory of Pierre in our hearts. Remember our friend's last words. He wanted you to marry his sister. Don't let him down.'

'But I am still undubbed a Knight,' protested Simon.

'It will do you and Berenice precious little good if you become a Knight Templar! I know that Robert de Sablé has a strong inclination to present that idea to the Grand Chapter at their next meeting. You can hardly refuse if that honour is offered to you, as I believe will be the case. Remember that such a knighthood was awarded to our present Grand Master, and that rare honour could well be repeated in your case. Then, with your oath of celibacy, it will be goodbye to any idea of marriage to the Countess Berenice de Montjoie, as your lady now has become.'

Queen Berengaria greeted her royal husband with chaste kiss and the Lionheart escorted her along the ston mole, to the resounding cheers of the assembled Cru saders. King Guy de Lusignan offerred his arm to Queen Joanna, and the royal party entered the City of Acre, to the sound of flourishes of trumpets.

Simon, as bodyguard to the royal couple, was unable to greet Berenice with the warmth and tenderness that he longed to show her, but later, kindly Berengaria, who knew the anguish her lady-in-waiting and dearest friend was enduring, made certain that the two young lovers had the opportunity to meet in her private apartments.

It was at the same time a tenderly loving and sad reunion for them. Berenice was desolate at the loss of her brothe and Simon was equally bereft by the death of such a close friend.

Although the strict protocol of the time forbade Ber enice the enjoyment of physical love during her period of mourning, at least Simon was able to provide her with all the tenderness she so desperately needed. The young Norman also had been strictly brought up to respect the mourning of the dead, so no thought of taking advantage of Berenice's vulnerability even entered his head.

Queen Berengaria, whose own unhappy marriage only accentuated her desire to see her friend comforted by the man she so obviously adored, now set about trying to make the path easier for these two star-crossed lovers. I would not be difficult for the new queen to suggest that an English accolade should be given to the young Templar and to this end Berengaria sent for Sergent Belami, from whom whom she hoped to learn all about Berenice' choice.

'Your Majesty, I wish I could give you more informa tion beyond the fact that Simon de Creçy is the ex-ward of the late Sir Raoul de Creçy, who held de Creçy Manor near the village of Forges-les-Eaux in Normandy. That regrettably, is as much I can tell you, as I am under a sacred oath to reveal no more.'

The Queen tried the Lionheart with equal lack of suc cess. Her king could tell her no more than he himself knew

'I have only the barest details about Simon de Creçy. The Bishop of Evreux tried to gain more information on my behalf and also came up against a wall of silence. I am certain that there is nothing evil in this apparent conspiracy to keep our young Templar's parentage a mystery, but I confess the whole thing puzzles me. His past record is one of total commitment to the Templar cause. He inspires absolute loyalty in his companions, and his Grand Master has nothing but praise for the young man. He fought bravely beside me with no thought for his own safety and, I tell you, Berengaria, I would sooner have those two Templars at my side than any men I know. Robert de Sablé is fortunate to have such lances under his command.'

Such a mystery only served to fire the intelligent Queen with even greater curiosity and she resolved to try every source of information on the subject of Simon de Creçy's parentage.

Meanwhile, another nagging doubt had plagued the Norman. Like many men before him whose trade was war, there had come a time when the thought of further killing sickened his soul. It had nothing to do with cowardice. Many hunters also have suffered the same revulsion after many years of killing game, either for the pot or for sport. Suddenly the whole spirit revolts against the idea of taking life. This is the most dangerous moment in a soldier's career, for without the instantaneous reactions of the trained killer, the distracted warrior becomes vulnerable and a danger, not only to himself but also to others whose safety lies in his hands.

It is hard to pinpoint the exact moment when Simon's soul turned from the dedication of his entire upbringing to the career of the sword, in the name of justice and the Order of the Temple; but it was most likely to have been engendered by the pointless slaying of the gallant defenders of Acre. Simon's admiration for their tenacious resistance to the long hard siege had been that of a born soldier. His instincts had all cried out against the Crusaders' merciless massacre of the disarmed prisoners, their wives and even their children.

In his agony of mind, doubly painful because of the loss of Pierre, Simon turned to Belami for the benefit of his wise rede and the solace of his warm friendship.

The veteran listened silently to everything that Simon said, curtly nodding his head as all his friend's doubts and fears poured out. At the end of this catalogue of woe, Belami put his right arm around his favourite pupil's shoulder.

'Tell no one else of your fears, Simon. They might mistake your present doubts for something else. You are no coward, *mon brave*, or Belami would not have you to fight beside him. This sudden revolt against killing for the sake of killing is from your mother's side of your parentage, though I saw your father go through a similar agony of doubt shortly before he was captured.

'I believe that he deliberately refused to be ransomed by Saladin because he felt that in some way he had betrayed the Templars. The thought of Odo de Saint Amand failing to live up to his oath to defend the Templar cause is too ridiculous to countenance; and so it is in your case, *mon ami*. Simon, you have fought like a lion in this land to uphold the good name of the Poor Knights of Christ of the Temple at Jerusalem.'

Belami realized how alike father and son were in their characters. Both were stubborn men who were hard to argue out of a fixed idea, once it had implanted itself in their minds.

'Furthermore,' the veteran continued patiently, 'you were badly wounded at the Battle of Hittin, carrying out Templar orders.

'At the behest of our Grand Master you have bravely defended the Lionheart, and we both know how difficult a job that can be! So don't blame yourself. These same doubts have assailed many men before you, and I'm certain you won't be the last man to turn away from war to the gentler arts of peace.

'Take my advice, *mon brave*, and hang on a little longer. I'd bet my own head that you will not fail in battle. But, as you value your life, Simon, tell nobody else what you have confessed to me, not even Berenice de Montjoie.'

Despite Belami's encouraging words he was deeply concerned by Simon's sudden change of heart. Even though the veteran fully understood the situation, he had to have time to think how best to help his friend resolve his difficulties. Belami had no doubt that Simon's overwhelming love for Berenice and his unreasonable guilt over her brother's death had started the destructive train of doubt in the young Norman's mind.

The old soldier was certain of one thing. He sensed that Simon de Creçy's career as a fighting Templar was over.

At this point, an attempt on King Richard's life was made, apparently by Assassins. It was so badly bungled, and the two would-be murderers were so unskilled that Belami and Simon had their doubts that Sinan-al-Raschid's men were involved in the attempted assassination. By the time the Templars had arrived on the scene, the relief-bodyguard sergents, Arnold Compiègne and Henri Malmont, had dispatched the pair of inept would-be killers.

This foiled attempt determined Richard to use the trustworthy corps of Templar sergents as a troop, to act as the flanking protection of his main spearhead of attack, and he quickly adopted Belami's original suggestion of the flying column of combined archers and crossbowmen mounted pillion on the Templar and turcopoles' horses. This was to have a significant effect on his march to the south.

Throughout this short period of reorganization and regrouping of the Frankish forces, Saladin also had not been idle. His main force now advanced to take over the heights of Carmel, to await Richard's expected move south towards Jaffa.

Since the fall of Acre, Saladin's respect for the Lionheart's tactical fighting ability had increased so much that the Sultan now considered King Richard to be the greatest threat to the Muslim world since the Crusades began. Saladin discounted the massacre at Acre as the work of the Frankish Crusaders' bitter frustration at the length of the siege.

He was sure in his own mind that a monarch as

chivalrous as Coeur de Leon would not have been the crazed instigator of such a senseless slaughter. However, this was by no means the general consensus of opinion among his contemporaries in the Muslim world. Many of them blamed the Lionheart directly for the massacre, and as a result hated the English king.

The Sultan considered this to be a fatal mistake as hatred in any form tends to cloud the judgement, and the unpredictable English monarch, with his impulsive, mercurial nature, needed more consideration than the easily predictable plodding efforts of a de Lusignan or a Bohemond, whose tactics were seemingly the same clumsy use of massed cavalry that they had always been.

Saladin saw Richard the Lionheart as a fellow chess-player. He carefully considered what the King's gambit would be. It could be either a direct thrust across from Acre towards the city of Tiberias, as Guy de Lusignan had attempted and which had resulted in the disaster at Hittin, or Richard would drive down the coast southwards to take Jaffa.

After long deliberation, Saladin chose the latter as the most likely route for the English commander. After all, the King had his large fleet in undisputed control of the sea and this could guard his western flank. Had the Sultan been in the King's place, this was the move he would have made.

If he was wrong and Richard chose the other route to Jerusalem, Saladin would be caught at a disadvantage, with his troops too far south to intercept the Lionheart before he attacked Tiberias. But the Sultan was certain that Richard would play for safety and move his much smaller force, as far as he could, under the flanking protection of the English fleet.

While the opposing leaders were making their preliminary moves, Simon was spending as much time as possible with Berenice. This was more in the role of a comforting brother than as the ardent lover that they both wanted him to be, but protocol was all important in the Court circles of chivalry and the lover had no other choice but to obey its dictates.

Once again, under the stress of circumstance, Simon's subtle-body left his sleeping form and seemed to speed across space and time to his childhood home in Normandy. This time there was no sense of tragedy awaiting him at de Creçy Manor.

His astral-body passed through the sturdy walls and entered Bernard de Roubaix's bedchamber, hovering beside the sleeping knight. Simon noted how the years had aged his beloved guardian, and gazed fondly at the lined features of the old Crusader, snoring contentedly in the deep sleep of the elderly. At the foot of the knight's bed lay his boar-hound, also in the twilight years of its life. Once again, as had happened during a previous dream-visit to his childhood home, the old dog stirred in its slumber as it became aware of Simon's subtle presence, but age had dulled its responses and it barely acknowledged its role of watch-dog before drifting back to sleep. Simon smiled and then became alert as another presence entered the bedchamber.

It was the figure of the tall cowled monk whom Simon had encountered when an earlier dream had taken him to Chartres Cathedral, and which he knew was the spirit of his father.

Instantly, the scene changed from that of the old knight's bedroom at the manor house to the lofty nave of the cathedral. The tall monk threw back his cowl and once again Simon looked at the stern features of the late Grand Master, who had died in Damascus. This time the rugged face was smiling and Simon felt a surge of love pass to him from his father, bringing a new warmth to this strange relationship. He responded with a sob of joy, as he sensed the strong bond that existed between them.

Inside his mind, Simon 'heard' his father's voice.

'You have done all that I ever expected of my son, and more.' The feeling of love was intense. 'Do not worry, Simon. Soon, your path of Destiny will lead you from war to peace. You have learned much from the wisest men in the East. It was never by chance that your paths crossed. Everything that has happened to you has been for a purpose, and a part of the Great Work. You have a strong faith in your Destiny. Do not lose it now. You will take part in a last battle for the Holy Land and then your task there will be complete. Your life's work lies here, at Chartres. Your lady will be by your side. Have no fear. I love you, my son.'

With those words the whole scene dissolved and Simon felt himself rushing back through time and space, to wake once more in his bed in Outremer. He knew that he had reached the most important crossroads in his life.

21

THE ADVANCE ON JERUSALEM

On Thursday, 22 August, in the year of Our Lord 1191, King Richard led the combined armies of the Third Crusade out of Acre. The walls of the city were thronged with well-wishers waving flags and bannerets in a show of enthusiasm which had not been seen since the start of the previous Crusade. Evidently, the Lionheart had the full support of the people of Outremer.

The only Crusaders missing were those who followed Conrad de Montferrat. They remained in Tyre, while the English king headed down the coastal strip southwards towards Jaffa. Richard was left with a total of some 7,000 men, including his own English knights, both Military Orders, de Lusignan's knights, the combined lances of Bohemond, Joscelyn and Homfroi de Toron, as well as the forces under the command of the Duke of Burgundy. They faced a Saracen force of more than 30,000 men and a large proportion of these were mounted.

The sole tactical advantage that the Lionheart possessed was the English fleet, which hovered off-shore, paralleling his line of march down the coastal road to Jaffa. Riding at the head of this column of heavy cavalry, intermixed with trudging infantry, King Richard was flanked by Templars and his rearguard was safe in the hands of a picked troop of Hospitallers, placed there to stiffen the resistance of the Burgundian forces. Behind the King, Simon and Belami rode on either side of their

Grand Master, keeping their position as royal bodyguards while still serving the needs of their Templar commander. All the time the veteran sergent kept an eye on the rising ground leading eastwards from the coast road to the line of trees that would, in his opinion, inevitably contain Saladin's forces.

'The Sultan is waiting for our columns to clear the marshy land lying between him and us. Then he will send in his skirmishers and horse-archers, I am sure of it,' he told Robert de Sablé.

The Grand Master nodded his agreement.

'It is only a question of time. I trow that Saladin is waiting for the sun to climb higher before attacking. He is hoping for another disaster, like Hittin. This time thirst won't be his biggest ally. We have more than enough water to last us for five days.'

Simon's thoughts were a strange mixture. His vivid dream experience had convinced him that this was to be his last battle as a Templar. This filled his mind with anxiety. He knew that the visions he had while sleeping always presaged events which were soon to take place. Only if he intervened deliberately in the course of events would the dream predictions be unfulfilled. This was what Abraham-ben-Isaac and Osama had taught him.

He had not confided the whole content of his dream journey to the veteran; only his doubts and fears at his own inadequacy as a Templar. Even though Simon felt that Belami was his closest friend, mentor and surrogate uncle as well as his godfather, he still could not bring himself to share the strange communion that seemed to exist between his dead father and himself. This made him feel guilty, because no one living had ever been closer to him than Jean Belami. Time and again Simon had owed his life to this dedicated man who had faithfully followed his late Grand Master's instructions regarding his natural son.

It was the first time that the young Norman had held anything back from Belami. As he rode beside him, Simon felt remorsefully that somehow he was going to let down his best friend. Belami was also deeply troubled because he sensed that Simon was not telling him everything and was holding back something important. He shrugged away these demons of doubt and concentrated on watching the approaching forests to the east of their line of march. From time to time he glanced at King Richard who had lapsed into silence, in contrast to his usual commentary on the progress they were making.

The English king was unusually anguished by his present relationship with his wife. 'Beautiful and dutiful,' Pierre de Montjoie had mischievously described her, ignoring the fact that Queen Berengaria had an intelligent mind, probably equal if not superior to the Lionheart's.

Richard's failure in bed with her had stemmed from the latent fear of women instilled in him by the domineering attitude of his mother, Queen Eleanor, of whom he was still afraid. This was not just the attitude of a dutiful son to an overbearing parent, but was also due to the Queen Mother's undoubted powers as the High-Priestess of the old religion, which he practised at the same time as his Christianity. In his capacity as Master-Troubadour, Richard Coeur de Leon was as much a practitioner of Wicca, the ancient Earth-Magick, as Abraham-ben-Isaac.

While he walked Roland, his great Cyprian war-horse, at the head of his formidable army, the Lionheart was thinking more of his sadness at the loss of his handsome witty companion, Pierre de Montjoie, than of his beautiful blonde wife, whose body he had so far miserably failed to penetrate. Richard longed for battle, hand-to-hand with the Saracen hordes, as a lover longs to be in the arms of his mistress. Only in the swirl, action and danger of the fight did this strange king feel the ecstasy that rightfully should have been his as a virile man in bed.

Beside him rode Guy de Lusignan, pondering an offer of the rulership of Cyprus. It had been made to him following the English king's proposed handover of control of the recently captured island to the Knights Templar, in exchange for the sum of 150,000 gold besants.

At the same time, Robert de Sablé was coming to the conclusion that Cyprus would make an ideal safe base for all the Templar operations in the eastern Mediterranean, to supply their forces in the Holy Land.

Each Crusader, noble, knight or commoner, rode with his mind full of thoughts as to what this Third Holy War would bring him in the way of honour, wealth or religious fulfilment, as his character dictated. Yet all the time, the experienced veterans of Outremer kept alert to the expected sudden onslaught of the massed Saracen skirmishers who, now that they were clear of the marshes, could rush down upon them from the long line of tress to the east.

In column of route, the Christian army slowly wound its way, like a great desert snake, along the coastal road south towards Jaffa. Occasionally, they were harried by small groups of Turkish horse-archers, but suffered only a few superficial wounds from these nuisance-raiders. Meanwhile, hidden inside the forest covering the high ground, just as Belami had predicted, Saladin's scouts watched and counted the steadily advancing Crusader force.

'The English king has arranged his army in five battalions. Tell Saladin that the Lionheart has twelve divisions of knights, flanked on the landward side by his archers, and to seaward by his baggage train. Hugging the shoreline beside them are the ships of the English fleet. De Montferrat, apparently, is not with Richard. None of his banners are present. I estimate that we outnumber the Infidels three to one. Allah is great! He has delivered them into our hands!'

These words, spoken to his messenger by Saphardin, were delivered to his brother the Sultan within minutes of their utterance. Saladin turned to Taki-ed-Din, his favourite nephew.

'If Richard has not learned wisdom from the past experience of de Lusignan's disasters, we could have another Hittin. But I fear that Saphardin is being too optimistic. The Lionheart fights like seven *djinns* and his lances are deadly. His English archers, armed with their longbows, like the one my young Templar friend shoots so well, are fatal even at long range. Their shafts go through chain-mail as if it were goat's cheese. Our own Scythian skirmishers and Turkish horse-archers will have to close the range to pierce the Crusaders' armour. Tell them so! Launch the main attack now, while the sun is in their eyes.'

At the point where the forest came down to within three miles of the coast, the Battle of Arsouf commenced.

First came the Turkish horse-archers. In a swirling cloud of fine sand, yelling their battle-cries, a great wave of these fanatical warriors thundered out of the trees.

'There must be 10,000 of them,' gasped Simon, startled by their numbers.

'Near enough, *mon brave*!' assented Belami, coolly turning to his accompanying Templar lances. 'Keep your shields up high, *mes amis*. Here comes the arrow-storm!'

His warning coincided with the swishing of thousands of light Turkish shafts as they hissed through the clear morning air to descend around the ranks of Crusaders, huddled expectantly behind their shields. Only a dozen shafts feathered into incautiously exposed flesh, seriously wounding several lances. The rest either stuck into the soft sand, or failed to penetrate the double thickness of quilted cotton under-jackets, now worn by most of the Crusaders beneath their chain-mail. The result, as Belami had predicted, was to give the impression of a mass of mounted porcupines as the Crusaders slowly advanced through the hail of Turkish arrows with many of the reed shafts sticking in their armour.

Behind the horse-archers, who had swept round to the right and left, clearing the way for the following infantry, came wave after wave of Egyptian foot-soldiers and dismounted Bedawis, fierce desert-bred warriors eager to join in the fight. From their bows a second storm of arrows swept towards the trudging columns of Crusaders. Again, the slowly moving troops crouched down in their saddles behind their long shields, or huddled beneath the smaller bucklers of the Christian infantrymen. Once more, only a small proportion of the incoming shafts feathered dangerously into the exposed portions of their targets.

At this point, King Richard raised his sword high in the air, giving the pre-arranged signal to his English and Genoese bowmen.

Immediately, the Christian shield-wall was opened to let the archers give full play to their arms and, from 500 longbows and about half that number of crossbows, a murderous barrage streaked out towards the advancing enemy infantry. The Saracen armour, of light chain-mail and alquôton under-jackets, though quite adequate as protection against their own light shafts, proved to be no barrier against the deadly cloth-yard arrows of the English archers, or the equally murderous crossbow bolts of the Genoese.

Within seconds, the ground was littered with the screaming wounded, or the huddled shapes of the arrow-riddled dead. Watching from the high ground, on the fringe of the trees, Saladin ordered a second wave of cavalry to advance and a large body of Mameluke horse-men broke into the trot preceding their final thundering charge. At the same time a second body of horsemen, made up of Scythian skirmishers, swept round in a half-circle to attack the Hospitaller troops acting as the rear-guard of the Crusader column.

The Lionheart saw the danger of the two-pronged attack and ordered all ranks to close up, at the same time holding his own impatient cavalry in check. The battle-wise English king knew that this move of the Sultan's was a deliberate attempt to draw out the Crusader cavalry on to the open plain, where they could be surrounded and cut to pieces by the Saracen lances, outnumbering them three to one.

Both King Richard and Sultan Saladin realized that the temptation to break out from their close columns, in which formation the Crusaders were forced to absorb the continuing Saracen arrow storms, was almost overwhelming. But to do so could end in only one result: the total annihilation of the Christian army.

'This waiting game is the worst part, Belami,' confided Simon to the stone-faced veteran, who also was itching to lead out his flying column against the attacking Saracen hordes.

'The King is right,' growled the old soldier. 'We wasted half our men at Hittin, trying to contain Saladin's cavalry charges. We've got no alternative, except to keep on south and take whatever punishment the Saracens mete out to us on the way. Then, when their energy is spent and our own archers have whittled down their numbers to manageable proportions, we can move out and smash through them, right up to Saladin's tent. Till then, we must sit tight and soldier on south.'

Although Simon had suffered the usual tightening of his guts before each action in which he had been engaged, now, for the first time, he felt the cold wind of fear. This did not mean that he was becoming a coward; only that, at last, battle-fatigue was beginning to claim him as a victim. It was the waiting that was doing it, while wave upon wave of Saracen troops charged out of the thickening pall of dust, or rode yelling to challenge the Crusaders' plodding advance.

Simon began to pray for the King's signal to ride out against their tormentors; anything to break the tension of being on the receiving end of the endless assault. Belami could sense this happening in the taut features of his friend and he was deeply concerned by what he saw.

The seasoned campaigner knew that Simon was near the end of his tether. He was sure that only the young Norman's dedicated sense of duty was keeping him from wheeling his war-horse towards the enemy and charging suicidally into the thick of them, to find peace on the end of a Saracen lance. The veteran had seen it happen many times before, to many brave men. He dreaded it happening to Simon. Belami prayed that King Richard would soon give his long-awaited order to close the enemy and fight it out hand-to-hand. None of them could wait much longer. They were all near to breaking.

Meanwhile, at the rear of the Crusader column, the skirmishers were giving the Hospitallers no rest. Already, Christian casualties were mounting among the rearward-facing ranks of Hospitaller sergents and their auxiliary lances, as they fought off the harrying troops of Scythian skirmishers who constantly assailed them. The added difficulty of advancing forward to the south, while facing to the rear to repel their attackers, made their situation intolerable.

For a time, it looked as though the battle would be as big a disaster as Hittin. Only their plentiful supplies of water kept them from the added suffering of thirst, the factor that had finally decided the outcome of the previous battle. At this point in the slow advance, the Crusaders found the coastal road so near to the shore, that their baggage-train had barely enough room to pass between them and the sea.

Richard also noticed that his ships now were able to sail much closer to the shore-line. He immediately sent a messenger to relay his signal to the nearest vessels, to commence firing on the skirmishers attacking the rear-guard. Within a few minutes large rocks and darts, fired from the ship's mangonels and trebuchets, started to crash around the teeming hordes of Scythians, bringing many horses and riders to the ground.

It was a welcome relief for the Hospitallers, who cheered wildly at the fleet's intervention. At the same time the ship-borne archers poured in a hail of cloth-yard shafts, which further emptied enemy saddles. At least it helped to release some of the pent-up fury which was sapping the Crusaders' morale. Saladin, who had ridden down from the forest with his headquarters staff, now commanded a closer view of the battle. He sensed that soon the King would make his move. He therefore redoubled his efforts to break the stubborn line of defence, as the Crusaders ponderously advanced along the coastal road. Still Richard refused to be drawn into a head-on clash, even with the decimated ranks of the Saracen cavalry.

The Sultan began to see any chance of another Hittin rapidly receding. Richard's rear-guard was still holding out against the repeated blows of the Turkish and Scythian cavalry and the Saracen troops were becoming exhausted. Saladin had to commit the remainder of his army. He did not hesitate.

Led by Taki-ed-Din, the Saracen heavy cavalry poured

down from the high ground and hurled itself against the stubborn wall of Crusaders. At the same time, with a supreme effort, the skirmishers spent their last strength on the battered rear-guard. It was the last straw for the Christians. They broke out of their close formation, raging with long pent-up frustration and striking out like madmen at their attackers. By a miracle, their battle-frenzy coincided exactly with the moment the Lionheart had chosen to make his move. The King wheeled his charger round and gave a great shout: 'God and the Holy Sepulchre be with us!'

With those words ringing in the Crusaders' ears, the giant English king rode straight at the charging Saracens. The move was so sudden and unexpected that the Sultan's crack cavalry broke. Like a dam bursting, the flood of Crusader lances followed the Lionheart straight through the scattered Mamelukes.

Richard dropped his broken lance and grasped his two-bladed Danish battle-axe, striking out on either side with invincible fury. This was Richard the killing-machine at his deadliest. With each crushing blow a Saracen skull was shattered, or an armoured breast beaten in. Nothing could withstand the power and skill behind the Lionheart's battle-axe. The double-headed weapon sheered through steel helmets and reinforced chain-mail with equal ease.

The Mamelukes lay in heaps, their Emirs among them. Even Taki-ed-Din, the near invincible young kinsman of the Sultan, panicked and fled the battle-field with the scattered remnants of his heavy cavalry.

Like Hittin it was a disaster, but this time a Saracen one.

Relentlessly, Richard pushed on through the demoralized Mamelukes until his charge, still compact and deadly, thundered across the rising ground towards the Saracen commander's headquarters. Close behind him, riding either side of the Templar Grand Master, Simon and Belami protected the King's back.

In the mêlée it had been cut and thrust, blow for blow, as fast as the eye could follow the action. Already the battle-fury had left Simon, and that same unreasoning wave of fear was creeping back into his heart. Belami, always alert to his dedicated task of protecting Simon, felt that all was not well. He rode closer to give better cover to his godson. King Richard was quite capable of looking after himself. It was Simon who was the veteran's main concern.

Like a wave rushing towards the shore, the Lionheart led his lances against Saladin's position on the hillock overlooking the Plain of Arsouf. Already the gardens and trees of the small town were on the horizon. Beyond them rose the distant battlements of Jaffa.

Coeur de Leon had timed his move perfectly, even though his lances had broken out just before he gave the order to wheel round and charge the Saracens. Following close behind King Richard, his knights and the Templar lances, came Homfroi de Toron, King Guy de Lusignan, Duke Bohemond and Count Joscelyn, with the Duke of Burgundy and the surviving Hospitallers galloping hard to catch up with the leaders. Everywhere the plain was covered with scattered heaps of slaughtered Mamelukes and the broken bodies of Saladin's skirmishers and horse-archers.

Belami's flying columns, with their pillioned English archers, were able to keep up a running fire of cloth-yard shafts at the fleeing Saracens, bringing many more to the ground. It was turning into a bloody rout for Saladin's army. Only the Sultan's personal guard now stood between him and the charging Crusaders.

But the impetus was being lost as the Christian lances swept up the hill. Now, if ever, the counter-attack must go in. Saladin, wise general that he was, sensed the moment and, mounting his white stallion despite all protests from his staff, led the final charge. It was a moment of Destiny, such as that on which hangs the fate of an empire. For Simon, too, the turning-point had come.

The Saracen horde swept down from the hillock, led by a huge wedge of lances, grouped tightly together. The sheer weight of the charge matched anything that the

Crusaders had launched against Saladin. Richard immediately saw the danger and wheeled round to face the new threat. Screaming and yelling like demons, the Syrians, Fatimids and Seljuks, who formed the hard-core of Saladin's heavy cavalry, pounded across the rock-hard, dusty plain towards the Frankish knights, sergents, and turcopoles, who had turned hurriedly towards them.

The shock as the two opposing forces met threw many of the lighter-mounted Saracens to the ground, their smaller Arab stallions overwhelmed by the massive destriers of the Crusaders. The shrieks of the dying, trampled under the iron-shod hooves of the Frankish war-horses, rose in an eldritch chorus above the clash of steel and frenzied battle-cries of the living. This final mêlée, amid the swirling clouds of choking dust, was a holocaust. Severed heads littered the plain, like an obscene crop of melons. Bodies with lopped-off limbs syphoned their life's-blood into the thirsty sand. Screaming horses, entangled in their own entrails, struggled to rise on broken legs. The stench of blood and excreta, human and animal, choked the combatants, who retched as they fought.

Where is the glory? thought Simon, his surcoat stained with blood and vomit, as he thrust, cut and parried his way beside the berserker English king, who demonstrably revelled in the apocalyptic slaughter. Sickened by the mindless massacre, only his innate sense of duty kept Simon fighting.

Behind the King, guarding his back, Belami still kept a watchful eye on his godson, noting with concern Simon's increasing deterioration as a fighting-man.

'Holy Mother of God, protect Thy son,' prayed the veteran, in silent anguish, as he traded blows with the surrounding Seljuks. The old soldier knew that it was only a matter of minutes before his ward, whom he had sworn to protect with his life, would finally break, drop his guard and invite the peace of death.

That moment came when the Lionheart broke out of the encircling ring of Saracen steel and spurred his charger towards a second group of Ayyubids who were bearing down on him, led by Saladin.

The King's heart leapt and his battle-cry again rang out: 'God and the Holy Sepulchre protect us!'

Simon and Belami, closely followed by the Grand Master of the Temple, pounded alongside the charging English giant as he rushed towards his valiant opponent. Who knows what the outcome would have been had these two great warriors met in battle, face to face?

It was not to be. In that fateful instant, a Scythian skirmisher, lying beside his dead horse, swung his scimitar at the King's destrier which was leaping over him and hamstrung the massive Cyprian charger.

With a high-pitched neighing scream, Roland crashed to the ground, half-pinning his royal rider beneath his heavy body. Belami, riding close behind, had no time to avoid the fallen war-horse and crashed into the writhing animal, bringing his own Arab steed to its knees and the veteran sergent down with it.

Simon rushed past to one side, wheeling his white stallion to protect his two half-stunned comrades. Saladin had already recognized the English king as the Lionheart broke out of the dust-shrouded mêlée, and he now charged towards him with a loud cry of: 'Allahu Akbar!'

The Sultan set spurs to his white stallion, laid his lance to rest, and bore down on Coeur de Leon, now rising groggily to his feet. Only Simon stood between them.

In that fateful moment, the Templar's future was decided. Wheeling to face Saladin, the young Norman leant down to pick up a fallen lance and urged his mount into a charge, his mind racked by anguish.

The promptings of duty said: 'Kill Saladin, to protect Richard!' Yet his heart, full of love and respect for the onrushing Sultan, forbade him to strike. All he could do was interpose himself between the two leaders, until the King was protected by his closely following Crusaders.

Saladin saw Simon as just another black-tunicked sergent standing in his way. Suddenly, with only yards separating them, the Templar inexplicably lowered his lance. At the same instant, Belami shouted desperately: 'Saladin, its Simon! Spare him! He can kill no more!'

In that split-second, the Saracen leader recognized his

young friend. But even the Sultan's serpent-fast reactions could do no more than slightly divert the levelled lance from streaking straight towards the Templar's heart. The Lionheart gave a gasp of surprise when he saw Saladin, at the last moment, suddenly twist the steel-tipped bamboo spear to one side.

All four participants in this strange drama cried out as the Sultan's lance tore into the Templar's side: Saladin in horror, Simon in agony, Richard in amazement, and Belami in despair. It was a nightmare, directed by Destiny.

Belami, in his grief and horror, had instinctively whirled his deadly battle-axe, ready to hurl it at Saladin. But he, too, had seen the Sultan's moment of horrified recognition and his lightning attempt to avoid spearing Simon. Dropping the weapon to his side, Belami, weeping like a child, rushed to catch his wounded comrade as he slid from the saddle.

Saladin, aghast at the thought of having killed his friend, reined in and leapt to the ground, kneeling beside the badly injured Templar. His eyes were filled with tears as he rocked from side to side in his grief.

This extraordinary tableau had halted both sides in mid-charge, their horses sliding to a halt in clouds of fine sand. The squadrons of gasping men and panting steeds waited for a signal from their leaders, to break off or renew the action. Both commanders held up their hands to prevent any hasty moves. It was a magical moment.

'I would to Allah, He had stayed my hand!'

Saladin's deep voice rose on a wail of despair. Belami comforted him, while he supported Simon with his strong right arm.

'It was not your fault, Sire. In the dust-clouds of battle it is hard to tell friend from foe, especially when that friend wears the tunic of the enemy. I saw you swing your lance to one side when you recognized who opposed you. Simon could never have killed you, Sire. He told me so, just before the battle.'

'I sensed that too, Belami,' replied the Sultan, wiping his eyes. Abruptly, the Saracen leader was in full control of himself.

'With your leader's permission, I will have Simon de Créçy cared for by Maimonedes. I believe that only my personal physician's skill can, once again, save my young friend's life.'

The Sultan looked expectantly at the English king, who had managed to free himself from his dying destrier, which he had mercifully dispatched with one blow. He now stood behind Belami, patiently waiting for his translation from Saladin's Arabic.

An eerie stillness descended on the battle-ground, while Belami swiftly explained the unusual situation. All the time the veteran tried to stem the flow of blood pumping from Simon's riven side. At last, with the help of the Sultan's scarf, he succeeded. Once he understood the content of Saladin's request, the Lionheart smiled and saluted his valiant opponent.

'If this great physician is as good as you say, Sergent, Simon de Créçy must be placed immediately under his care. I gladly grant Sultan Saladin's request.'

By the expression on the English king's face the Sultan knew that all was well. He gave the Lionheart a royal salaam and turning towards his staff, drawn up fifty yards behind him, he shouted a command that immediately brought six horsemen of his bodyguard forward, bearing a horse-litter.

After a short pause, while the litter was slung between two horses, they were joined by Abu-Imram-Musa-ibn-Maymun, better known as Maimonedes. With a curt, friendly nod to Belami and a formal bow to the English king, the physician quickly examined the unconscious Simon. As he straightened up, he looked grave.

'If Allah wills it, he will live. But I must attend to his wound as soon as possible. With your permission, Sire?'

Maimonedes' last words were spoken in French and addressed to King Richard. The Lionheart smiled tautly and nodded his agreement. Simon's limp form was gently picked up by four Mamelukes and under Maimonedes' instructions, carefully placed in the horse-litter and covered with a blanket.

Belami saluted the two great leaders and conversed

shortly with Saladin, who nodded. Then, turning to King Richard, the veteran asked bluntly: 'Your permission, Sire, to accompany Sergent de Creçy and the physician Maimonedes?'

The English king's romantic soul was captivated by the chivalrous behaviour of his opponent. Perhaps, in this brief meeting, face to face, Richard's poetic nature recognized the same magical quality in Saladin. Whatever the reason, it is certain that Richard Coeur de Leon would gladly have granted any request pertaining to this dramatic situation. He also realized that time was all-important to the badly wounded Templar.

'Your request is granted, Sergent Belami. Stay with de Creçy for as long as is needful, and keep me informed of his progress.' The King paused thoughtfully. 'The Sultan must have a high opinion of our young friend. He affords him great honour.'

Belami saluted the Lionheart with his sword and hastily remounted his white Arab stallion, which was none the worse for its fall. Followed by him, the Mamelukes slowly returned to their own lines, carrying Simon, secure in his litter, between them.

Without another word, King Richard and Saladin saluted each other, with sword and scimitar. Resheathing their weapons as a sign of temporary truce, they were about to part when Saladin paused, smiled, and shouted a few words over his shoulder to his waiting staff. Immediately, an Emir rode forward, leading a superb white Arab charger.

The Lionheart needed no interpreter to translate Saladin's magnificent gesture. Smiling broadly, with his distinctive boyish grin, Richard sprang into the silver-mounted saddle. His royal appreciation of the Sultan's thoroughbred was equally obvious to Saladin.

It was a magical moment, long to be lovingly savoured in their memories by all those who wonderingly witnessed that entrancing scene. It was truly a meeting of Troubadours.

Wordless, the Lionheart wheeled his new charger and galloped back to his waiting lances, watched admiringly by Saladin who had remounted his own snow-white stallion. Silhouetted against the mass of his great crescent of cavalry, the Sultan, dressed in the sacred green ephod and turban of the Prophet, made a memorable picture.

With a shout of: '*Allahu Akbar*! Praise be to Allah, The Lord of Creation!' Saladin curvetted his steed and trotted leisurely back to rejoin the Saracen army.

At that moment, the sun, which was setting, dipped below the western horizon, its shimmering image blood-red and distorted by the sea-haze. Taking their cue from the vanishing Day-Star, both commanders led their battle-weary armies from the killing-ground, Saladin withdrawing to his forest encampment and Richard taking his Crusaders to bivouac beneath the shelter of the walls of Jaffa.

The Battle of Arsouf was over.

22
DESTINY

At dawn the next morning, Saladin returned to the attack, to find Richard solidly encamped outside the walls of Jaffa. It was obvious that it would be a costly business to dislodge the Crusaders from that position, especially as the English fleet had sailed in close to the shore and resupplied the Lionheart with weaponry, food and forage for his horses.

Wisely, Saladin withdrew. At Arsouf, he had lost over 7,000 of his men, including a number of Emirs. He could not afford additional heavy losses so soon. King Richard's smaller army had suffered scarcely 700 casualties. Altogether, it had been an overwhelming victory for the Crusaders.

However, it had not brought them much closer to the Holy City. The advance on Jerusalem would mean that first Richard must make a strong base at Jaffa, and only then swing east to advance straight up the old Roman road which led directly to the spiritual capital of Christendom. The Third Crusade had still got a long way to go.

The Lionheart was busy strengthening the fortifications of the small sea-port, setting up Mategriffon and making an encampment for his army, protected by substantial earthworks. But he still found time to be concerned about the fate of his Templar friends.

It may seem strange that the English king should be so strongly involved with two members of the Corps of

Sergents. Nevertheless this was the case, due to the close link that had been forged in battle, when the three of them had fought side by side. For Richard Coeur de Leon this bond was a mystical one, binding comrades in arms closer than brothers.

Furthermore, the King found the handsome young Norman even more attractive than Pierre de Montjoie, who had been such a beloved companion ever since he had joined the Lionheart at Messina in Sicily. Pierre's merry irreverence had delighted Richard, but Simon de Creçy's intellect and surprising knowledge of the Mysteries had more than captured his interest. In fact, after the siege of Acre, a feeling akin to love for the young Norman had crept into Richard's heart.

The English king felt the loss of Simon's close companionship as poignantly as he had mourned for the death of Pierre de Montjoie. He impatiently awaited news of his progress at the hands of Saladin's physician.

The Lionheart had already sent news of Simon's wound and treatment by Saladin's physician to Acre, making the best of this information to spare Berenice de Montjoie as much anxiety as possible. Although Richard felt so strongly drawn to Simon de Creçy, he suffered no pangs of jealously.

When the King arrived at Acre, he went straight to the Queen's apartments. His eagerness to be with his wife was not that of a lustful husband returning to her loving arms, for their strange relationship had formalized into a marriage of convenience, without physical love on either side.

Richard was anxious to see her for another reason.

Because of Simon's grave wound, the King needed Berengaria's undoubted talents as a healer; the miraculous gift that this beautiful and spiritual woman possessed, for healing at a distance, by prayer, was part of her power as an accomplished practitioner of the Art of Wicca.

The Queen, however, sensed her husband's request before he made it: 'I have prayed, day and night, for the young Templar's recovery. I know what Simon de Creçy means to you, Richard.'

The lovely High-Priestess's melodious voice was full of compassion, with no hint of irony in her last remark.

'That was good of you, Berengaria.' The anxiety in Richard's voice was apparent. 'He will recover . . . won't he?'

His wife smiled gently.

'I feel sure he will. I sense that he is in good hands.'

The Lionheart heaved an audible sigh of relief.

'I hope that Berenice de Montjoie is not too distressed.'

Richard's voice was genuinely concerned, for, with his close friends, he was capable of much kindness.

'She has been with me constantly, and has joined me every day in our prayers for Simon's recovery,' his beautiful Queen reassured him. 'She loves him even more than you do, my husband.'

Again, there was no hint of irony in her voice as she spoke.

Richard knew that Berengaria was well aware of his growing feelings for the handsome sergent, and felt embarrassed that his preference for men should be so obvious to his wife.

'As you know, my dear,' he continued, 'young de Creçy is in the skilled hands of Sultan Saladin's private physician, the one they call Maimonedes. Evidently, the Saracen leader has the same affection and respect for Simon that we feel.'

Berengaria wondered whether her husband was using the royal 'we' to include her own and her lady-in waiting's feelings towards the wounded Templar.

She felt no twinge of jealousy, for her husband's sexual proclivities were so alien to her own spirituality that, for her, they did not exist.

Her temporary chagrin over the fiasco of her wedding night had long since ceased to trouble her. The ingenuousness of her next remark proved this.

'When Simon de Creçy recovers, we will have a wedding on our hands. My little Berenice is quite determined to marry her handsome young sergent. There is, however, the problem of his rank. Although we know nothing of his background, de Creçy's integrity, charm and courage are unquestionable.'

'I understand also that the Grand Master thinks most highly of him, Richard added. 'Should he become a Templar knight, this marriage, of course, would be impossible because of Simon de Creçy's consequent Oath of Celibacy. Yet the young man must be knighted, at least, before I can allow my royal ward to marry him.'

Berengaria's beautiful features showed no hint of slyness or intrigue, as she asked: 'Therefore, can you not ennoble him, my liege?'

The Lionheart, his sun-bronzed face glowing with pleasure at this new train of thought, considered the request for no more than a moment before replying, 'That is a splendid thought, my dear! After all, they are perfectly suited. Simon's long-standing friendship with Berenice's brother, my dear and sadly-missed friend, has already drawn them closely together. Berengaria, you are such a clever woman!'

The King laughed with delight. Furthermore, his tone of voice clearly conveyed his genuine respect for his wife's intellect, for Coeur de Leon was well aware of his beautiful consort's magical powers and predictive ability.

'Of course, I will knight Simon as soon as he returns to us, hale and well.'

In his joy at the thought that, as Countess Berenice de Montjoie's husband, his much-loved friend soon would be constantly at his side at Court, Richard Plantagenet had no doubts whatsoever that Simon would be victorious in his battle for life.

This struggle was taking place at Saladin's new headquarters, which the Sultan had set up at Ramla, a few miles east of Jaffa. It was a close-fought battle, with Maimonedes once again matching his skill against the onslaught of the Angel of Death.

Saladin's lance had torn a grievous wound in Simon's side, shattering several ribs, ripping the chest muscles apart on his right side, and slicing into the base of his right lung. Only the Sultan's split-second reaction had diverted the spearhead from tearing straight into his heart.

Simon had lost a lot of blood before Belami had finally succeeded in staunching the flow with the Sultan's sacred green scarf that he wore as the leader of the *Jehad*. It was an astonishing measure of the love and respect that Saladin felt for Simon that the Sultan had, without hesitation, given his sacred scarf to Belami, to stop the young Templar bleeding to death.

Devout Muslim though he was, Saladin's affection and concern for the friend he had so lucklessly wounded transcended his religious feelings, no matter how deeply implanted. Before everything, Saladin was the soul of compassion to the ones he loved. Though we was an implacable enemy to the unrighteous, the Sultan was a prince among friends.

Belami spent two days and nights of hell while he sat tensely beside his gravely wounded godson, watching Maimonedes' healing hands as the great Jewish doctor used every skill he had acquired, through many long years of study and practice of his art, to keep death at bay.

Meanwhile, Simon's subtle-body had soared out of his pain-wracked physical form and momentarily hovered over the scene of dedicated activity at his bedside, in the Sultan's own tent at Ramla.

Maimonedes had chosen it as being more suitable for the radical chest-surgery required to repair the damage wrought by Saladin's lance, than an uncleaned room in the small town of Ramla.

The alert physician was aware that his patient had temporarily left his body, and sighed with relief that consequently he would not have to administer stronger doses of soporifics and analgesics to lower the pain level in Simon's mangled chest.

From long experience Maimonedes knew that these drugs, while beneficial in relieving pain, presented a problem in their tendency to weaken the patient's will to live. In fact, he had seen many seriously wounded patients die due to their overwhelming need for the pain-killing drugs.

Therefore, Maimonedes welcomed Simon's ability to leave his body, so that he could operate on the traumatized tissue without having to race against the time when Simon should wake to consciousness, as the effect of the soporifics wore off.

This way, Maimonedes knew, he had at least an even chance of repairing most of the damage without further weakening Simon's resistance. He set to work to clean up the shattered bone and torn muscles that formed a jagged mass of injured tissue surrounding the wide gash in his patient's side.

Meanwhile the astral-body that contained the soul of Simon de Creçy soared through time and space to Damascus, where it sped quickly to the Sultan's palace. In a fraction of earth-time, Simon's spirit-form had found and entered the garden observatory where Abraham-ben-Isaac was studying the heavens. Above the elderly magus's head the Constellation of Orion the Hunter had wheeled into position, dominating the zenith.

Immediately, Abraham became aware of Simon's presence and, for a moment, the chill of fear swept over him that this manifestation might signal the physical death of his much loved pupil. Simon's expression quickly dispelled that anxiety, yet the wise old man sensed instantly that his young friend's body must be lying somewhere not too far distant, gravely injured.

He sensed that Simon, once again, was in the care of Maimonedes. Instantly, Abraham relaxed and sat down on the bench next to the observatory wall. He knew that he must help the efforts of the great Jewish healer by mentally linking up with him.

As he did so, Abraham felt a wave of love and gratitude pass from Simon to himself. Then the presence of his former pupil faded from the observatory, leaving his teacher praying silently and gently weeping with joy that the contact had been made.

Simon's next dream journey was a short one, to the apartments of Osama, his other elderly mentor.

Here he found the ninety-year-old Gnostic dozing beside the warmth of two charcoal braziers. He too was immediately aware of the presence of Simon's spirit. Osama stirred and smiled in his sleep and then abruptly sensed the danger that faced his beloved disciple. Just as

Abraham had done, the master-magician let his healing powers channel themselves across the gulf of space and time, to aid Maimonedes in his fight for Simon's life.

From Damascus, Simon's subtle-body now bore his soul over the broad sea and continent separating the Holy Land from de Creçy Manor in Normandy.

Here the young Norman's spirit sought Bernard de Roubaix's bedchamber, where his old guardian lay slumbering away his own last few hours on earth. Beside the knight's sick-bed, Brother Ambrose sat watching the dying man.

For a moment, the old monk sensed Simon's unearthly presence and shivered, though the night was oppressively warm under the stifling blanket of a summer storm. Yet there was something reassuring in the atmosphere of the room, as though a wave of love had entered it. Which is exactly what had happened.

Hearing an unexpected cry of joy issuing from the dying knight's lips, Brother Ambrose hurried forward to put his comforting arms around the shoulders of the old man, now struggling to sit upright in the bed.

Bernard de Roubaix's face was radiant as he saw the shining form of his ward standing at the foot of his sick-bed. His voice was vibrant with the strength of his love when, for the last time on this earth, he spoke his name: 'Simon. At last! It is Destiny! *Inshallah*!'

With that last word, the Dark Angel gently enfolded him in his great wings and Bernard de Roubaix, Knight Templar, passed through the doorway of death to the shining light beyond.

Simon had kept faith with both his beloved guardians and visited them at their final hour. It was the bond of pure love between them that had made this possible.

Abruptly his spirit felt drawn back in the rushing journey to meld with his ravaged physical body, lying on Maimonedes' operating table in Saladin's tent at Ramla. The physician noted that his patient had returned and that he was weeping. He immediately called Belami's attention to the fact that Simon was regaining conciousness.

The veteran, who had spent the past two days assisting

the Jewish physician in his long battle for Simon's life, gently grasped his friend's hand as the long-lashed, peacock-blue eyes fluttered open.

Mistily, through a haze of drug-controlled pain, Simon could see his two friends leaning over him. A faint smile hovered on his lips. He was not yet capable of audible speech, but his lips formed a name which Belami instantly recognized.

The old soldier was weeping with gratitude for Simon's return from the long corridor of death, but he sensed his godson's distress. Putting the whispered name 'Bernard' together with Simon's tears, Belami knew that the old Templar had died. Furthermore, he sensed that Simon had been at his guardian's side when he had passed through the dark portals into the light beyond.

'God, he knows, the old warrior deserved the glory!' he gently whispered into Simon's ear, and saw his friend's pain-racked face break into a faint smile as the wounded Templar slipped back into a deep healing sleep.

Maimonedes heaved a long sigh of relief.

'With God's help, if Allah so wishes, Simon will recover, but I doubt that he will ever be fit enough to fight again.'

Belami shook his head and shrugged resignedly.

'So be it, Maimonedes. The boy had come to the end of the road as far as taking up the sword in the cause of Christianity was concerned. He had already fought his last battle before the Sultan's spear hit him. His destiny, if he is to be spared, lies in another direction.'

The physician, exhausted by his long struggle with the Dark Angel, nodded his leonine head.

'Now we must sleep, Belami. There is one coming who will watch over him.'

The veteran sensed the presence of Sitt-es-Sham before she entered the tent.

'My lady,' he said, making obeisance to Saladin's sister.

The Saracen princess smiled behind her veil as she acknowledged the Templar's greeting.

'Saladin sent word to me that Simon had been wounded. He is deeply distressed that it was by his hand. How did it happen?'

Belami briefly explained what had occurred and the reason behind it.

'I am glad that he will no longer fight our Muslim world. His mind is too fine to be wasted in battle. Simon is a builder of dreams. It is the will of Allah that this shall be so. I know this in my heart.'

The old soldier felt distressed by what he knew he must say.

'My lady, Simon has fallen in love.' The statement was blunt, but spoken gently.

Sitt-es-Sham nodded her head, understanding.

'This too I know. First, I sensed it, and second, my brother has many spies. They keep a close watch on all that happens in Outremer. I understand that her name is Countess Berenice de Montjoie, the sister of your late friend, Pierre.

'I still owe him a debt, for having participated in my rescue from Reynald de Châtillon's raiders, all those years ago. Now perhaps I can, in some small fashion, repay my debt of honour to that brave young man.

'I never hoped to see my beloved Simon once more, but Destiny had decreed otherwise. *Inshallah*!'

Belami showed his respect for the Princess by taking her hand and raising it reverently to his lips.

'Neither he nor I can ever repay our great debt to you, Your Highness!' he said simply.

'Go now and sleep. I will keep close watch on Simon. If there is any change, I will let you both know immediately.'

Maimonedes and the old Templar retired to another apartment within Saladin's tent and, easing themselves down on to the piles of cushions, were soon asleep. Throughout the night, until dawn, the Lady of Syria sat beside Simon's unconscious body, gently holding his hand and letting herself be used as a willing channel for the healing forces that flowed into his wounded flesh. It was an act of love typical of this remarkable woman.

In Acre, a distraught Berenice de Montjoie waited for news of her beloved Templar. She had sensed the seriousness of the situation even before news from the King had been brought by fast-riding messengers. No matter how encouraging his words had been, Berenice knew that Simon's life hung by a thread. She prayed constantly. Throughout her long vigil, Queen Berengaria joined her in begging the Blessed Virgin-Mother to restore Simon to health.

King Richard remained in Jaffa, further reinforcing the already adequate fortifications, turning the small sea-port into a strong-point from which he could launch his final assault on Jerusalem.

One more thing concerned him. Now that it had become safe to travel the coast road between Acre and Jaffa, the army was being plagued by the attentions of numerous camp-followers.

Most of these were women, whores from Acre, who sensed easy pickings among the knights, sergents and soldiers relaxing victoriously from the toils of battle. It was rapidly becoming a serious problem, for many of the Crusaders were willingly returning with these women to enjoy the flesh-pots of Acre. It began to look like wholesale desertion, just at the time when the Third Crusade had started so well and needed every man it could get for the coming advance on the Holy City.

Robert de Sablé summed it up best.

'Sire, unless you return to Acre and stop this venal tide of destruction, you will soon have no Crusade. These women have been sent by the Evil One to destroy us. I beg you, Your Majesty, to ride there with all dispatch.'

The King had deep respect for the Templar Grand Master's judgement, especially since his sympathetic attitude in agreeing to Belami's accompanying his wounded comrade into Saracen hands. De Sablé had not been present when the veteran Templar had made his unusual request to the Lionheart. His temporary absence from the King's side in battle had been occasioned solely by the Grand Master's horse having been killed during the final charge. This was why Balami had appealed directly to the King.

When de Sablé had heard about the incident, however, he had given his full approval. This action had further endeared him to Coeur de Leon. The English king felt that he could ride to Acre, knowing that Jaffa would be safe in the Hands of the Templar Grand Master. He set out forthwith to round up his deserters.

It was typical of the Lionheart's romantic nature that although he did not condone the action of so many of his Crusaders, he fully understood the reason for his men, after such a resounding victory, seeking reward in the arms of the women of Acre. Richard the warrior was essentially a man's man, and he understood a soldier's needs.

'A strong sword, a good general, a fast horse, a full belly and a victor's spoils.'

This was the maxim, in King Richard the soldier's opinion, that best fitted these military circumstances. Therefore the Lionheart rode swiftly to Acre, not in the role of the Avenger, ready to mete out death to the deserters, but rather as the voice of conscience, pleading for their swift return to regain the True Cross and free the Holy City.

It was this mixture of stern discipline in battle and his relaxed attitude to his army's venality, once victory was assured, that made the Lionheart such a popular commander.

However, it didn't best serve the needs of the Third Crusade. In fact it held up the all-important requirement of pushing on towards Jerusalem, as soon as possible, before Saladin could fully regroup his badly mauled army.

Because of this quirk in the Lionheart's character, the Sultan was able to remuster a formidable array to face King Richard's drive to Jerusalem. It also marked the turning-point of the Saracen fortunes in the Third Crusade.

It was while the English king was rounding up his drunken, womanizing men in Acre, that another unexpected element entered the equation of war. Conrad de Montferrat was suddenly obliterated from the Lionheart's calculations, by assassination.

This complication had several repercussions.

First, although de Montferrat's elimination was immediately seen as Sinan-al-Raschid's handiwork, nevertheless, there were circles in Outremer who strongly suspected that King Richard had somehow instigated the assassination, through a secret treaty with the Old Man of the Mountain.

Second, there was the subsequent upheaval in the whole political scene, when many unscrupulous nobles plotted to succeed to the dead adventurer's position as the ruler of Tyre, and become the husband of the unwilling Isabella. This complicated the situation at a time when this was least needed.

While the various factions in Outremer were engaged in the new struggle for power in the Holy Land, the Crusade had to wait for the outcome which further delayed the attack on Jerusalem.

The main protagonists in the new power-struggle were Guy de Lusignan, who wanted to marry Isabella, de Montferrat's widow, and Homfroi de Toron, who still earnestly desired to regain the lost bride whom Conrad had snatched from him.

Apart from these two suitors for Isabella's hand, there were numerous other nobles, who all saw their opportunity in de Montferrat's sudden death.

Actually, Richard was totally innocent of any involvement in de Montferrat's murder. The tyrant's assassination had been brought about entirely by his own previous unprovoked attack on one of Sinan-al-Raschid's ships and the leader of the Assassins had sworn revenge. The Grand Master of the murder-cult had no ulterior motive in disposing of Conrad, because his own interests would scarcely be affected by whichever side won in the religious war in the Holy Land.

Whether it was a Christian or a Muslim victory hardly concerned the Old Man of the Mountain. Either way, his insane cult of Assassins would remain aloof until the final outcome was decided.

Prior to Conrad's demise, King Richard had entertained some hope that, eventually, the tyrant's conscience would prick him into voluntarily joining the Lionheart in the final assault on Jerusalem. Now the Tyrian army was in pawn, until Isabella's new husband had been chosen for her. It never entered King Richard's or anyone else's head to ask the still beautiful young widow whom she would prefer to marry.

Meanwhile, Queen Berengaria was reunited with her husband, and eager for news of Simon de Creçy's progress in Saracen hands. This was, of course, because of her close bond of friendship with her favourite lady-in-waiting. Berengaria was also the gentlest of women and fully appreciated the anguish that Berenice was suffering.

Unhappily, Richard had no further news to give her. On this subject information had dried up. The Lionheart correctly guessed that the battle for Simon's life was still being fought.

In Ramla, amid all Saladin's preparations for regrouping his army to meet King Richard's expected attack, the Sultan had still found time to visit Simon's sick-bed, which had been moved into specially prepared quarters in the small fortified town.

It was, of course, Saladin who had sent for Sitt-es-Sham in the first place, knowing that her loving and healing presence could well turn the tide in Simon's favour. Maimonedes was now more optimistic about his patient's progress, but he made it plain to the Sultan that there was no possibility of the young Templar's ever being fit enough to take any further part in the war for the Holy Land.

Saladin left Simon's sick-quarters with a lighter heart, knowing that everything possible was being done for his friend, who now seemed to have an excellent chance of pulling through the crisis. Belami's gratitude for all these efforts was plain to all, especially in his words to Saladin.

'Our debt to you, Sire, is beyond recompense,' he said in a voice hoarse with emotion. 'Were it not for my sworn oath to follow the Beauseant banner of the Templars, I would gladly serve you against all your enemies, save my erstwhile comrades in arms. With that proviso, my sword is ever at your service.'

Those words, coming from such a dedicated sergent of

the Corps of the Poor Knights of Christ, touched Saladin deeply.

'Rest assured, Belami, you will both be returned to your Christian friends as soon as Simon is fit enough to travel.'

Now that Sitt-es-Sham's presence was no longer the vital factor in Simon's recovery, she once more bade a tearful farewell to her sleeping ex-lover.

'Take good care of him, Belami,' she said, her eyes brimming. 'You know how much he means to me. By helping a little to save his life, I feel that I have repaid the debt I owed to Pierre de Montjoie. Simon's happiness is everything to me and I know that Berenice de Montjoie will make him a fine wife. I envy her very much.' Her melodious voice choked into a sob and, further words failing her, the Lady of Syria left, weeping.

'There goes a saint. Muslim or Christian, that remarkable woman is without peer,' said Belami to Maimonedes, who had discreetly rejoined him.

'Indeed, the Princess is one of the richest jewels of Islam,' Maimonedes agreed, with a sad sigh at her evident distress.

Ten weeks after Simond de Creçy had been borne from the battle-field at Arsouf, the young sergent, gaunt with his past suffering but now nearly fully recovered, returned to Acre, accompanied by a beaming Belami and escorted by a royal bodyguard of Saladin's Mamelukes.

With them, the returning Templars brought rich gifts from Saladin for King Richard and Queen Berengaria, and a magnificent wedding present for Berenice from Sitt-es-Sham.

Even though this beautiful necklace of gold and sapphires delighted Simon's intended bride, the gift of her beloved's renewed health and safe return was even more appreciated.

Of course, Berenice had no idea of the real reason behind Sitt-es-Sham's generous gesture, apart from Belami's explanation that it was a repayment of her debt to Pierre de Montjoie, for helping to save her life and honour.

Simon, though still in considerable pain, found his

convalescence a joyful experience, due entirely to Berenice's gentle, loving care.

As for the lovely little Countess de Montjoie, she soon lost her shyness and nursed her injured warrior with all the ardour of Queen Guinevere for the wounded Lancelot.

His love for her, at first, had been sparked off by her striking resemblance to her brother, whom Simon dearly loved. Similarly, her love for Simon had grown from the roots of her adored brother's devotion to the handsome young Templar sergent, long before Berenice had met him.

It certainly seemed that they had been fated to meet and fall in love. Their love had blossomed into total devotion. Yet, so far, they had only exchanged kisses and gentle fondling, and both of them longed soon to fulfil their dreams of bliss.

'I cannot believe that I am alive and in the arms of my love,' Simon murmured as he lay luxuriously on a day-bed, set out on a secluded part of the battlements overlooking the sea.

Berenice sighed deliciously and cuddled him closer.

'Even when I was a little girl,' she murmured, ' I dreamt that in a far-off land, I would meet a gallant and gentle knight who one day would become my husband.'

Simon chuckled.

'I am scarcely the knight of your dreams, my dearest. I am just a humble sergent of our Order.'

His smile faded abruptly.

'You must realize that if I am knighted within the Order of the Templars, we could never marry, because I must then take the Oath of Celibacy.'

Berenice shivered in his arms, as the thought momentarily marred her happiness. But, with the resilience of youth, the clouds of doubt quickly passed and the next words came bubbling from her eager lips.

'The Queen has spoken already to King Richard about this very subject, and the noble Coeur de Leon has given his word that he will dub you knight of his own Order of Chivalry.'

Simon gasped his surprise, for even though he had discussed with Belami the vague possibility of knighthood outside the Order of the Templars, this sudden, wonderful revelation overwhelmed him. He flung his arms wide with joy.

The agonizing stab of pain from his broken ribs quickly reminded him that his days as a fighting man were over; and, furthermore, that his chances of gaining a high position in King Richard's Court had gone with them. The Lionheart loved stout-hearted warriors and loaded them with honours and wealth. Simon knew that he would fight no more. What use would he be to the English king?

He groaned, as much from chagrin as from the pain of his healing wound.

Berenice was stricken with concern and remorse that she had girlishly kept the news of Simon's impending accolade from him, as a special surprise.

'I know what you are thinking, my darling. You are worried because you have no wealth to offer me as your bride. But I have my dowry, as the Countess de Montjoie, and I am the sole heiress to all our estates, which passed to me on Pierre's death.' Here Berenice stifled a sob, but continued 'This has made me a very wealthy woman, yet I have neither skill nor sufficient knowledge to run these extensive lands. You have much experience of these things, from helping to run the de Creçy estate in Normandy; the Grand Master has told us so. He thinks very highly of you, dearest Simon, as we all do.

'Believe me, my darling, there is no problem except that you get well, as soon as possible, so that King Richard can knight you and we can be married!'

For all her apparent ingenuousness, the lovely little Countess was no fool and, furthermore, she knew exactly what she wanted. It had been her suggestion to her close friend, Queen Berengaria, that had ensured Simon's coming accolade.

While Simon convalesced at Acre, surrounded by loving care and comforted by the arms of his intended bride, King Richard, after giving the young Templar a genuinely loving greeting, was forced by pressing circumstance to move on to Ascalon.

However, before he did so, he knighted Simon with the full honours of a royal accolade.

The only formality was the touching of Simon's shoulder with Richard's sword, and the words spoken by the King.

'I dub thee, Simon de Creçy, a Knight of the Order of Chivalry. Rise, Sir Simon, and may God defend the right.'

This ensured that any further barrier to the Templar's marriage to the Countess Berenice de Montjoie was now removed.

Apart from the need to reconstruct and fortify this key position in the west of the Holy Land, nothing further was stopping the Lionheart from pursuing the Third Crusade towards Jerusalem.

Strangely, with all the preparation and excitement being generated by the coming assault on the Holy City, an unaccountable lethargy seemed to grip the Lionheart.

'It is the arnaldia fever,' Belami told Simon. 'I have seen this loss of drive affect many victims of the sickness of Outremer. I have always believed that this fever has done more to mould the events in the Holy Land than anything else.'

'But King Richard has an inflexible will,' replied a surprised Simon. 'Surely mere fever will not deter the Lionheart from pressing on to Jerusalem!'

Simon was appalled by the thought that he could no longer fight at the English king's side, but his wound had left him with some difficulty in breathing due to his injured lung. In the dust of the battle, the injured Templar would be at a grave disadvantage; more a hindrance than a help. His days as a fighting Crusader were over.

However, his destiny as a knight of King Richard's Court, and the soon-to-be husband of a wealthy French countess, was about to be fulfilled. The Bishop of Evreux had promised to marry the young couple and Queen Berengaria had suggested that an appropriate setting for the wedding could be the church at Limassol in Cyprus, where she and King Richard had been married.

The ladies of the Court were all a-twitter with the preparations for the wedding.

'There's more enthusiasm being put into your forthcoming marriage than into the whole Third Crusade!' grumbled Belami to an amused Simon, who shrugged his broad shoulders in wonder at his inclusion in this unfamiliar new world of giggling women.

Meanwhile, another marriage was being arranged. Young Queen Isabella's fate still hung in the balance, with King Richard now having a powerful voice in the matter, favouring Guy de Lusignan as her next husband. But Fate had decided to take a hand.

This delicate matter was brought to a head by the unexpected action of Henry of Champagne, the Count of Troyes, who had fallen madly in love with the lovely little widow. He hurried from Acre to Tyre, where Isabella had shut herself up behind the stout defences of the castle.

The Count's impulsive and romantic gesture in offering his hand in marriage appealed to the frightened young Queen, and Isabella opened her gates and her arms to the gallant Henry. For once in her life, the choice of a husband had fallen to the lot of the royal bride.

With this important alliance settled, King Richard decided that he had temporized long enough, and, overcoming the lassitude of the arnaldia fever, he started to round up his army.

Saladin's spies, who were everywhere, soon got to hear of this latest development and immediately sent word by carrier-pigeon to the Sultan.

Saladin, like Richard, was heartily sick of hearing his advisers' many schemes for bloodlessly settling the present struggle in the Holy Land by various unusual alliances. He had listened to enough wild ideas, such as that of Saphardin, his brother, marrying Queen Joanna, a plan that both parties rejected out of hand.

Now he decided to make his move and marched on Jaffa. The sudden attack took the small garrison by surprise, but they managed to hold out.

When their couriers failed to penetrate the Saracen lines, the defenders of Jaffa sent a fast ship to Acre, with an urgent call for help.

King Richard shook himself out of his fever-induced lethargy and, gathering together as many lances and archers as he could find who were willing and sober, he rushed south to the rescue.

Belami comforted Simon who was bitterly disappointed that he could not join them, but as he was still walking with the aid of a stick this was impossible.

'The Lionheart will be happier back in action than he has been for a long time,' the veteran said. 'All this waiting around, has sapped his energy, as much as has the fever. I'll keep a close eye on your royal friend, Simon. I don't intend to lose the king who gave you the accolade.'

'Don't forget to look after yourself, *mon brave*. I need you more than ever, now that I can't fight for myself,' Simon shouted after Belami as he cantered away to join the Crusader column.

Ten days later Belami returned, having been sent back by the English king as his most trustworthy courier. In his usual efficient way the veteran Templar succinctly reported the progress of the Lionheart's final battle in Outremer.

'We won a splendid victory at Caesarea. It was only a few miles from Jaffa that Saladin hit us at dawn with a surprise attack. We had marched until dark the night before, at a killing pace which had made us sleep soundly, with even the guards dozing at their posts.

'Had it not been for a Genoese crossbowman who had woken up to relieve himself, we would have been dead meat before the alarm was given.

'As it was, the battle was a close-run thing; a bloody affair of steel on steel and *corps à corps*. The dagger was used as much as the sword. Only when the fighting opened up, as Saladin's heavy cavalry swept in for the kill, did the Lionheart and his lances mount up and charge out to meet the Saracen cavalry.

'King Richard fought like ten men that day, a real

Viking berserker in the grip of the battle frenzy. Saracens fell, headless or limbless, at every blow.

'Finally, the King's own charger was brought down by a barrage of Turkish arrows fired at point-blank range. But that didn't stop the Lionheart. He fought even more fiercely on foot, while we Templars kept the worst of the Saracen charges at bay.

'At this point, Coeur de Leon ordered our own archers to open fire and the whole Saracen line just disintegrated under the shower of cloth-yard shafts and Genoese crossbow bolts.

'Saladin, in that typically chivalrous way of his, once again sent the Lionheart a pure white stallion so that the King could fight as a chevalier should, and from then on the issue was in no doubt. I tell you, sirs it was a victory that rolled the Saracens right back up the Roman road.'

Simon chafed at his luxurious idleness, but he knew in his heart that he would never fight again. It wasn't just his aversion to killing. Now he had his wound to contend with also.

Berenice was radiantly happy. She had her adored fiancé at her side, and she loved looking after him and seeing to his every need. The beautiful girl could hardly wait for her wedding day, and her loving attentions soon proved to Simon that his wound had in no way affected his manhood.

The clever little Countess knew that as soon as she got Simon back to Normandy, she could absorb his interest in running her extensive estates. That would keep his mind off war.

However, Simon still felt frustrated, for his whole life so far had been dedicated by others to fulfilling the ambitions that his father, Odo de Saint Amand, had entertained for him. These were inevitably connected with participation in Templar activities, and it looked now as though this sort of life would be barred to him for ever.

Furthermore, as Sir Simon de Creçy, newly knighted by the English king who had conferred on him the lands and feudal fiefs of the Somerset town of Templecombe, a

Templar stronghold in England, Simon was in no position to become a *Donat*. He could hardly give away his bride-to-be's inheritance, and he certainly could not rejoin the Templar military presence in the Holy Land, even if Berenice allowed him to do so.

Aware that the dilemma was making Simon unhappy, Robert de Sablé comforted his favourite ex-sergent.

'Be of good heart, Sir Simon,' the Grand Master said, grinning as he emphasized his new title. 'I promise you that, knowing your interest in the Mysteries, and with your unique tuition by such great magi as Osama and the Jewish Essenic scholar, Abraham-ben-Isaac, there is still plenty for you to do for the Templar cause, besides fighting in the Holy Land.

'I fully intended that you should have had a battle-field knighthood conferred on you by the Grand Chapter of our Order, but King Richard forestalled me. Still, I am glad in one way, for this has made it possible for you to marry the Countess de Montjoie, and, Our Blessed Virgin being willing, to beget sons to serve the Templar cause in the future.'

The old soldier smiled his surprisingly cheerful grin, so out of keeping with the usual sombre image of a Templar Grand Master.

'Furthermore,' he went on,' I am sending Belami back with you. First, to act as your personal bodyguard, until you are fully fit to defend yourself, and second, because the old dog is getting past this sort of fighting and I have no wish to lay his bones alongside those of your erstwhile companions, Phillipe and Pierre who, I understand, lie buried in a seaward-facing grave outside the walls of Acre.'

Belami, who until then had been listening with approval to Robert de Sablé's comforting words, started to protest, but the Grand Master silenced him.

'You have told me before that your prime task in life was to guard and protect Simon, in accordance with the sacred oath that you gave to —' de Sablé paused significantly— 'a certain person who shall be nameless.'

Both Simon and Belami looked startled that yet another

387

man, this time no less a person than the Grand Master himself, had guessed the secret behind Simon's birth.

'Therefore,' continued de Sablé, in his most official manner, 'I am releasing you from all duties in the Holy Land, and ordering you, Sergent Jean Belami, my most gallant and respected member of the Corps of Sergents, to continue to act in your sworn capacity as the guardian and protector of the person of your former junior sergent, Simon de Creçy, now known as Sir Simon de Creçy of Templecombe, in the county of Somerset.'

At that point, in a most ungrand-masterly fashion, the scarred old Templar knight, one-time Sergent of the Corps, burst into a resounding bellow of laughter while the room filled with the warmth of their comradeship.

Abruptly, and in contrast to his cheerful mood, the Grand Master's eyes seemed to generate a misty glow as this extraordinary man felt the gift of prophecy descend upon him.

'Simon,' he said, in a lowered tone, 'I see something wonderful. It is a pattern of your destiny. What the magi call the "Akashic record".'

'I sense that you will, in your own special way, continue to serve the Templar cause, according to the wish of Our Blessed Virgin.

'You are going to build a great Temple in Her name. You have been given the skills of the Sacred Geometry in order to do this.'

Both of his listeners were taken completely by surprise at this unexpected pronouncement. Simon, particularly, was fascinated to see the sudden change which had come over the Grand Master. This had now passed, leaving Robert de Sablé almost as surprised as his comrades-in-arms. It was an experience that none of them would ever forget.

De Sablé summed up what he had said, and added: 'This conversation must remain our secret. What I have seen and told you about is not for the profane to discuss. Suffice it that it is to be. This is Destiny. *Inshallah*!'

It was now becoming evident that the impetus of the Third Crusade was lost. Jerusalem still remained out of reach of the Lionheart. Moreover, Richard seemed to sense that he would never enter the Holy City as its conqueror and liberator.

Impulsive as ever, he suddenly broke off his advance up the old Roman road, wheeled the army round and marched his Crusaders back to Jaffa. Leaving a token garrison to man the walls, he then hurried back to Acre.

The only possible explanation of this abrupt *volte-face*, at the time when he had won yet another victory over Saladin, is that Richard had received disturbing news from England. John, his brother, who was Regent, had been causing havoc in King Richard's realm.

He had imposed heavy new taxes, ostensibly to support the Lionheart's Holy Crusade, but actually these monies were being paid straight into John's treasury, causing great unrest. If this was the reason for Richard's sudden retreat, he would have had no alternative.

Back in Acre, he confronted a surprised court with a series of proposals for an immediate peace treaty with Saladin. It was as though, suddenly, King Richard had given up the whole idea of the Third Crusade. The astonished nobles of Outremer and the whole crusading army had no recourse but to comply.

The Third Crusade was at an end.

EPILOGUE

The terms of the Treaty were presented to Saphardin by Homfroi de Toron, whom both Saladin and Richard trusted. The conditions were not onerous on either side, for the Sultan was as weary of the endless war as were the Crusaders. This was a chance for a breathing spell, before some fanatical lunatic started the whole dreadful business again.

The change in King Richard's plans necessitated adjustments all round. It meant that Queen Berengaria and Queen Joanna would have to leave the Holy Land at the same time as the Lionheart left for England.

His plan was complex, involving a Templar bodyguard, which Robert de Sablé provided, and the king himself being disguised in Templar uniform.

The idea behind this bizarre scheme was for Richard to pass through Europe incognito. However, his great height, at a time when most people in the Western world were relatively small, marked him out. In fact, the Lionheart had about as much chance of making the overland part of the journey unremarked, as he would have had disguised as a woman. His consort tried to dissuade him, but to no avail. Once he had made up his mind about anything, Queen Berengaria knew that nothing would divert him from his chosen path. It was with foreboding that she prepared his personal baggage for the return home.

The change of plan also precluded Simon and Berenice from being married in the church at Limassol. Instead, the bishop performed the impressive ceremony at Acre.

It was a sumptuous affair, for the Countess de Montjoie was a much admired figure among the Court dignitaries and her choice of the ennobled Templar sergent was a popular one, in view of the young man's gallantry in the Templar cause. Both the Grand Masters were present at the wedding, and a guard of honour, made up of Templar and Hospitaller sergents, formed an archway of swords under which the radiant couple left the church, to resounding cheers.

King Richard's presence ensured that the church was packed with all the nobles of Outremer and Outrejourdain, but the young couple's popularity made this a particularly pleasant occasion, rather than just another tiresome Court duty.

Regrettably, there was not enough time for a honeymoon in the Holy Land. Instead, the newly wed Count and Countess accompanied the two queens when they boarded their royal transport, a large heavily armed and well-protected galley, and set sail for Sicily on the first stage of their long voyage home.

As Pierre de Montjoie had been the only son of the French branch of the old feudal family, the title and estates had passed to his sister, Berenice. As a courtesy, the French king had conferred the title of Count on Simon, so that Berenice should not marry beneath her station. The de Creçy estates, which had been passed on to Simon on the death of Raoul de Creçy, were now released from their *Donation* to the Knights Templar. This gave the young Norman a considerable fortune which, when more than matched by Berenice's dowry, made them a very wealthy couple.

If material success in life had been what Odo de Saint Amand desired for his natural son, then the young Norman had more than fulfilled his father's dreams. However, both Simon and Belami knew that this had been only part of the vision that the late Grand Master had dreamed so prophetically.

The Grand Chapter of the Order, which apparently had always known about Simon's origins, was only too happy to bury the past in the new Count's glittering future. This meant that Simon was now one of the richest nobles in France, and, more important, he had the knowledge and experience to use his new-found wealth to the best advantage, especially for the Templar cause.

The young couple's honeymoon aboard the luxurious royal galley was consummated in a small cabin nestling between two other larger ones, used by Berengaria and Joanna.

'A blissful occasion, I'm sure,' said Belami irreverently. 'But cramped, withal!'

The veteran was too busy looking to the efficient defence of the royal galley as she sailed through pirate-plagued waters to feel bored, which he had feared he would after his long career of fighting in the Holy Land. This relieved the old sergent's conscience, as he had been most reluctant to leave his Grand Master, just as he was about to take over the new Templar headquarters in Cyprus, without 'Belami's Bodyguard' to protect him.

It had been a clash of loyalties which had tried the old soldier's conscience sorely. However, being personal bodyguard to such a happy pair of lovers appealed to Belami's carefully concealed romantic soul, and, on this matter, he also had the blessing of his Grand Master. It virtually meant that the veteran would spend the rest of his life in the service of the Count and Countess de Montjoie et Creçy; a prospect that pleased him more with every day that passed.

Two weeks after the royal galley arrived in Sicily, word of the disappearance of King Richard's Templar galley reached them.

It was a bitter blow, yet all the royal party sensed that the Lionheart was not dead. This optimistic view of the disaster was confirmed when a second Templar messenger arrived with the news that King Richard had transferred himself and his Templar bodyguard to another vessel, after his galley had nearly foundered in a sudden storm, off Cyprus.

What made the news puzzling was that the vessel he had boarded was a pirate-galley, and that the King had persuaded the corsairs to land him on the Dalmation coast. They had been forced to do this by yet another storm, which wrecked the pirate vessel when it was thrown on to the rocky shore.

Fortunately, this had occurred without injury to the royal party and they were even now proceeding through Carinthia and Austria, with the intention of reaching Richard's cousin Henry, at the royal castle in Saxony. The Queen's sense of relief was followed by dismay when further Templar messengers brought more baleful news.

The Lionheart had been recognized by Austrian spies and the King and his Templar bodyguard had been captured after bloody resistance at an inn. The King was presently being held hostage by the Emperor Henry VI of Austria, to whom Duke Leopold had handed over his royal captive. The only possible recourse for Queen Berengaria was to hurry to England, to ensure that Richard's brother raised the ransom.

This was accomplished with all dispatch, taking the new Count and Countess along with the royal party. However, Queen Joanna stayed for some time in Sicily, raising as much money as she could to meet the Austrian Emperor's demands. She then took ship and joined her sister-in-law, to await the outcome of the negotiations.

For Queen Berengaria the year 1192 passed in an atmosphere of tension and doubt. For Simon and Berenice it was a year of love and fulfilment. King John, whose greed and perfidy had caused the dissension in England, had greeted his new sister-in-law and her royal party as affably as if they were his favourite relations. Simon and his bride were afforded every courtesy and, from their joint estates, were able to contribute handsomely to the royal ransom fund.

Belami, as usual, saw straight to the heart of the matter. 'I don't trust Prince John,' he growled. 'He reminds me too much of Conrad de Montferrat, without that scoundrel's courage. There is so little of Richard the Lionheart in him, I wonder if the brothers had the same father.

'Mark my words, Simon, the Queen will have to make him account for every penny of the ransom. One hundred and fifty thousand gold marks would be a temptation for any man, but for Prince John they are the Devil's invitation to treachery.'

The Troubadour Blondin, who was King Richard's closest friend among that distinguished cult of musical magicians, had already departed for Europe, to find out where the Emperor was holding his royal master. It was largely due to his talents as a spy, and his reputation as a fellow magician among the Minnensingers of Germany and Austria, that he was finally able to make contact with the despairing Lionheart, and bring him the joyful news that his ransom was being gathered.

King Richard was so popular that even after Prince John's savage depredations, the English exchequer was rapidly swelling, with a large part of the money coming in small sums, donated by the poorest in the land. Fortunately, Simon had contacts among the Jewish community in York. These had been given to him by Abraham-ben-Isaac some years previously, as part of the general information which the elderly magus had imparted to Simon, illustrating the widespread financial network of the twelfth-century Jews.

Perhaps the wise old man had sensed that this knowledge would one day be of mutual benefit to his pupil and to the Jewish community. If so, that remarkable seer had been right in his assumption. For Simon, bearing a letter giving Queen Berengaria's assurance that the King would afford advantageous concessions to the much persecuted Jewish community, was able to meet a cousin of Abraham's, Isaac of York, who promptly raised a large contribution from his people. Considering the previous violence shown to the Jews by King Richard's administration, this was a measure of the confidence that Isaac of York placed in his cousin's assessment of Simon de Creçy's character and ability.

For Simon, it was yet another demonstration of his wise mentor's powers of divination, and an outstanding example of the workings of Destiny.

Moreover, in his new capacity as the Count of Montjoie and Creçy, Simon was able to contact the Grand Chapter in Paris and obtain from Templar sources more gold for the King's ransom, ensuring a speedy conclusion to the raising of the huge sum. Already, it was becoming evident to Belami that his godson was more than fulfilling the ambitious dreams of his father.

The year 1193 found Berenice happily pregnant and, in the autumn, she was safely delivered of a son whom both parents unanimously named Jean, after Belami. The old soldier was delighted and devoted much of his time to playing nursemaid to the little boy, on whom he lavished as much love as he had on his godson.

These years were sunlit by their happy family life, first in England, at the royal Court and the Templar manor of Templecombe, in Somerset, as well as their family estates near Forges-les-Eaux and Evreux. But for Simon and Belami there was something missing from their lives. Both of them sensed that the true path of Simon's destiny was yet to be revealed.

'It's as though we are waiting for some indication of what that path will be,' said Belami, putting this strange feeling into words.

The pattern of the future started to emerge when certain events occurred, two of them almost simultaneously.

First, they heard the sad news of Saladin's death, in March 1193, due to a sudden fever brought on while he was out hunting. This struck Simon and Belami like a physical blow, for both of them had conceived a great love for this remarkable man.

When the Lionheart returned to England, in March 1194, he joined them in their sorrow at the loss of his late adversary.

A letter from Maimonedes, delivered by a Jewish merchant, gave Simon details of the Sultan's death.

'We have lost a great leader and a loving friend,' he wrote. 'I shall never again meet his like on this earth. Islam mourns the passing into Paradise of its finest son. He loved you, Simon, as a brother, and he felt a great kinship with Belami as well.

'I shall live out my years here in Damascus, and will always remember you both with the same affection. All your friends send their love and greetings.'

The philosopher signed the letter: 'Maimonedes, some-time physician to the great Sultan Saladin.'

But it was the third event, shortly after King Richard's return, that showed what the future had in store for Simon.

This was the catastrophic fire that destroyed Chartres Cathedral. Simon instantly sensed the path he must take. This was to be his destiny.

Returning to Paris, he sought an immediate audience with the Grand Chapter. As it happened, Robert de Sablé was on a visit from the Holy Land and officiated at the meeting. After a warm exchange of greetings, Simon came straight to the point.

'The disaster at Chartres has prompted me to offer my services as an overseer for the immediate rebuilding of the cathedral. I am not being immodest when I say that I have been fortunate in acquiring the necessary qualifications in the practice of the Sacred Geometry, from my mentors in the Holy Land. I know that our Grand Master will speak for me in these matters.

'What I propose is that I should provide, gratis, my personal services and those of my retinue for the recon-struction of the cathedral, in the earnest hope that the Order will see fit to finance the actual rebuilding and pay the wages of the necessary free-masons from the various guilds of craftsmen concerned.

'From my late guardian, Bernard de Roubaix, I learnt the power of the *Wouivre* and I intend to respect the earlier pagan religion once practised on this sacred site. I believe that my experience in the Holy Land has given me an insight into the requirements dictated by the precise tenets of the Sacred Geometry, and that, with the help of Our Blessed Virgin, our sacred Earth-Mother, I may be given the opportunity to restore Her Temple to its former glory.'

It was a moving declaration of Simon's faith in his destiny and, as one man, the brother Knights of the Order rose to their feet and thundered forth their unanimous approval of his proposal.

Afterwards, Simon told Belami: 'I suppose I should have been nervous, but as soon as I entered the Chapter-house, I knew that this is what my father wanted me to do. From then on, I have only the haziest recollection of what happened, apart from many Templars, few of whom I knew, fervently agreeing with me that we must rebuild the House of Our Blessed Lady as soon as possible.'

Belami was indispensable to the business of finding and organizing the labour required for the huge project. For Simon, this was a perfect example of what the Great Work was all about.

The reconstruction of such an enormous building, in strict accordance with the Divine Proportion of the Sacred Geometry, required a large number of skilled and dedicated craftsmen, none of whom were easy to find.

This task could be carried out only by enlisting the whole Templar network of skilled labour throughout France, Spain and England, as well as by procuring Templar craftsmen from the Holy Land itself.

In a miraculously short time, the master-craftsmen came flocking into Chartres, where Belami quickly set up billets for them among the many surrounding farms and houses. This in itself was a daunting task, but the veteran sergent had performed similar duties many times before.

Once the craftsmen were assembled and had divided themselves into their various guilds, the work com-menced. As before, no conventional plans were used to formalize the work, but once the outer dimensions had been laid out on the sacred site, plaster was poured into a huge shallow mould. When it dried, the shapes of the Gothic arches, with their sharply-pointed ogives, were carefully scribed upon its surface, using long flexible reed withes as the guides to obtain the natural sweeping curves in which lay the secret of the building's beautiful propor-tions.

The cathedral's dimensions were meticulously worked out by Simon and the Master-Mason. They were:

Length: 130 metres*
Width: 32–46 metres, allowing for the cruciform shape
Height: 36.5 metres

These precise measurements formed a larger-scale version of the original cathedral, of which only the front and rear façades remained standing.

The same methods of construction as Bernard de Roubaix had once described to Simon were used, only this time enormous amounts of Templar money financed the reconstruction. This ensured that the master-craftsmen were provided with every facility they needed. The best quality stone for the ashlars was used throughout and only the most skilful and dedicated craftsmen carried out the cutting and assembly.

The great nave soon started to form, as the walls and the supporting colonnades rose with remarkable speed. The broad flagstones of the floor were laid and locked into position, Simon taking care that the original maze pattern of the previous pagan religion was laid out in exactly its former position, in accordance with the new dimensions required by the Sacred Geometry.

At the same time the huge rose windows were installed and their intricate coloured-glass matrices in lead 'cames' were prepared, so that when fitted into their stone frames the light would fall on to the floor of the nave in precisely the same way that the original 'Mystery of the Light' had dictated.

The two tall towers, massive and yet delicately proportioned, framed the new front portico and behind them rose the soaring vault of the great nave, while the cruciform shape of the new cathedral grew out of the sacred ground within which the sleeping *Wouivre* Dragon had its lair.

Never once did Simon depart from the tenets of the Sacred Geometry, nor did he ever fail to heed the strict requirements of the older religion, to keep in balance all the earth-forces which controlled the power of the sacred site.

*The measure used was the French "royal perch" (eight metres).

This meticulous observance of the magical requirements of the *Wouivre*, and Simon's strict interpretation of the wishes of the Blessed Earth-Mother, Our Lady of Chartres, protected all those among the builders who worked with honest craftsman's pride.

Only those few workers who, for some reason, had evil in their hearts, were hurled from the high scaffolding or crushed by a falling ashlar, just as many years before the unfortunate craftsman had crashed to his death in front of Simon and Bernard de Roubaix.

During the course of the twenty-six years that the reconstruction of the great framework of the cathedral took, many of its workers died of natural causes, due to old age or disease. Among these was Jean Belami, former senior sergent of the Order of the Poor Knights of Christ, of the Temple, at Jerusalem.

His last words to a heart-broken Simon were typical of him: 'Odo de Saint Amand is proud of you. But not more so than I am of my godson . . . *mon brave Simon*!'

Then, with a long sigh, his smile stiffened into the rictus of death while his gallant soul soared upwards from his body to rejoin his many comrades-in-arms who had preceded him into glory.

When Simon told the Lionheart of Belami's passing, the King wept.

'He was the finest sergent of them all. It is difficult to find the right words to describe this great soldier. But the name of a new rank has just sprung into my mind. It is that of "Sergeant-Major". Somehow it fits Belami perfectly.'

By 1199, Richard the Lionheart was dead, killed by a rusty crossbow bolt fired from a castle wall. The King, impulsive to the last, chivalrously forgave the French archer who had shot him. Once again, Simon mourned for a lost comrade.

Throughout those twenty-six years spent supervising the rebuilding of Chartres Cathedral, Simon lost many of his friends. But his sadness was tempered by the knowledge that the parting was only a temporary one. All the time, the love and companionship of Berenice and their family of two sons and a daughter filled his life with love, joy and laughter.

When his beloved wife died, Simon found solace in the completion of the fabric of Notre Dame de Chartres. He looked upon it as a monument to all those whom he had loved.

The last task that Simon undertook was to test the colonnades of the nave for the 'Mystery of the Sound'.

With the pommel of his dagger, just as Bernard de Roubaix had done all those years before, Simon lightly tapped each of the great columns in turn. Immediately, their different bell-like tones rose to the lofty ceiling of the great vault, like a choir of angels.

The Norman knight, now in his late middle age, listened with a joyous leap of his heart as his great cathedral sang.

At last came the day when his children, Jean, Pierre and Marie-Thérèse, laid their father to rest, beside their mother, in the crypt of the new cathedral. There Simon and Berenice lie to this day, next to the body of their friend, Belami.

While their souls joyously roam through all space and time, back on Earth, beneath that beautiful cathedral, the *Wouivre* stirs in its dragon-sleep, as it guards their mortal remains for ever.

Inshallah!